THE *Lighthouse*

McCarthy ROAD

By Katharine E. Hamilton

ISBN-13: 978-1-7358125-3-3

McCarthy Road

www.katharinehamilton.com

Cover Design by Kerry Prater.

To my readers.
Thank you for your unending support and encouragement.

Acknowledgments

There's always a plethora of people to thank when it comes to writing. My cover designer, my editor, my beta team, my family, and my readers. But my biggest thanks for this book goes to my crew at ACFW. (American Christian Fiction Writers)

I attended my first ACFW Conference in September 2019 and immediately felt as if I'd met an extended family. I reveled in being surrounded by fellow authors, traditional and indie, and others from the writing world.

I wrote this book in 2018, and due to other books I launched that year, and into 2019, I delayed its release.

At the ACFW Conference, I was able to pitch and discuss this manuscript with agents, mentors, editors, and marketing gurus in the industry and I loved every second of it. However, that tied up the manuscript for another six months or so, missing my window of November 2019 yet again. So, to say I'm excited and thrilled that it is finally in your hands, is an understatement. I hope you enjoy it.

And to the ACFW family, thank you. I'd never felt so at peace and confident about my path as a writer until I left that conference fully charged and rejuvenated. Thank you.

«CHAPTER ONE»

It was freezing. That was Kennedy Donovan's first thought as she walked towards the small counter for rental car services at the Ted Stevens International Airport in Anchorage, Alaska. The vast windows showcased stunning views of mountains and mounds of sparkling white snow. Not the type of snow she saw in Manhattan; the brown and white sludge that coated city sidewalks and streets could not compare to the type of snow that created the picturesque scenes and, no doubt, dangerous traveling conditions that awaited her here. She felt a small tremor of trepidation as she thought about the 300-mile excursion that awaited her. Thankfully, she'd arrived in Anchorage early, giving her plenty of time to make what looked to be a seven-hour trip to McCarthy, according to her phone's map app. She'd never been to McCarthy, or Alaska in general, but the map promised a long, yet smooth-sailing trip.

She stepped forward in line, the elderly woman behind the counter giving her a warm smile.

"Reservation?"

"Yes, Kennedy Donovan." She patiently waited while the woman typed in her computer, awaiting the proper printouts. "I will need to see your driver's license and a credit card," the woman stated.

Kennedy fished the two pieces of plastic from her wallet and handed them over. "Okay, perfect." The woman continued reaching under the counter and grabbed a set of keys. "Just sign here." She pointed to a line on the bottom of the paperwork. "And the very back page as well." Kennedy complied. "Alright, you are all set." She handed Kennedy the keys and her receipt. "The rental lot is straight out those sliding glass doors and to your left. You can't miss it."

"Thank you. Umm—" Kennedy did not want to take up more of the woman's time, but she hoped she knew whether or not the road would be passable. "Do you know if any reports have come in about traveling conditions for McCarthy Road?"

"Heavens, you're going all that way?" The woman shook her head in pity. "I haven't heard anything about it, but we're supposed to be in for some nasty snowstorms. When you reach Glennallen, top off your gas tank before heading to Chitina. Either of those places would be the best time to inquire about passage across the road. They would know more, and they would have a place for you to stay should you not be able to continue on into McCarthy."

"Glennallen and Chitina." Kennedy made the mental note. "Thank you."

"And honey, if you plan on driving down McCarthy Road, you best pack some snacks and extra gasoline. You never know what that road will be like. So just remember to throw rocks off the bridge just in case," the woman reported.

"I'm sorry, rocks?" Kennedy asked, confused.

The woman chuckled. "It's a tradition. Three rocks for three wishes of safe travel across the bridge. You throw three before, and you throw three once you have crossed."

Not one for superstitions, but thankful for the insight into her journey, Kennedy smiled warmly and grabbed the keys. "I see. Well thank you for the information." She reached for her luggage cart and started making her way towards the freezing temperatures outside. She was used to cold winters, but she had never experienced *this* type of cold. Her eyelashes immediately felt frozen to her face and she attempted to lick her lips but feared her tongue might freeze to them. The wind tore through her bones and set her teeth to chattering. She held up a quivering hand to press the key fob and saw the lights of a small SUV flicker and beckon her forward. She squeezed her bags into the limited space of the trunk and shut the door. She then hopped inside, cranked the engine, and blasted the heater to its highest setting while keying in her uncle's address into the GPS. "Okay, here we go, Ken. You can do this," she whispered to herself as she pulled out of the parking lot and set out on the treacherous roads.

∞

She had been driving for hours. The roads, slick with ice and snow, winded through cliffs and steep drop offs, such that she feared driving the full speed limit would send her careening off the side of a mountain. Thankfully, no one drove behind her impatiently. She heard the swish of her windshield wipers and watched as a light snow continued to fall. *How long did it snow in Alaska?* she wondered. *And how did Uncle Neal live here?* She shook her head in disbelief of it all as she thought about the uncle she barely knew. Kennedy had met him a handful of times and remembered a jolly man with a full grey beard. He resembled Santa Claus, if she were being honest, but she had never told him so. The fact that he was quite absent in her life made her wish at one point that he *was* secretly Santa and that is why he remained so scarce through her early years; he was busy making toys with his elves. Her lips tilted into a faint smile at her childhood memory. Her father never explained to her why he did not care for her uncle, just that he was not welcome anymore. Kennedy grew up and had quite honestly forgotten about him until recently, when the small envelope came in the mail. An envelope containing the results of his Last Will and Testament and probate. He had died. And with his death, he left Kennedy, his only niece, all his belongings, land, and business in McCarthy, Alaska.

She had never travelled to Alaska before, but driving through the stark countryside, taking in the quiet wilderness, she understood why some might find it quite relaxing. Granted, she was not here to relax. She was here to see what was left to her and slowly sell it to the highest bidder so that she could return to Manhattan as soon as possible. She slowed the car as she reached what the GPS reported as Glennallen. She took the rental car woman's advice and stopped for gas. She also bought several granola bars and a bottle of water. The woman did say to pack snacks, and Kennedy, though still ill-equipped, felt better knowing she had a little something to take along.

As she slid behind the wheel once more, her route proceeded to Chitina. An hour and a half later, she spotted a small sign welcoming her to the town, but buildings were scarce. She saw a van pulled to the side of the road, its lights shining as snow continued to fall in soft blankets. The driver stepped out as Kennedy did and exchanged a nod of greeting. He was a burly man and wore a heavy coat of brown corduroy and rough-worn boots over the largest sized feet Kennedy had ever seen. "Where you headed, Miss?" he asked.

"McCarthy," she replied, pulling her wool peacoat tight around her. She tucked her exposed hands into the crooks of her elbows as she crossed her arms.

"Same here. Need to see if the road's passable." He pointed to a small log cabin a short walk from where they were standing. Smoke billowed from the chimney and drew Kennedy like a moth to a flame. "This here's the Wrangell-St. Elias-Chitina District office." She didn't know what that exactly meant, but followed the man anyway since he seemed to know where he was going and what he was doing. They walked inside and an elderly man glanced up from a worn desk covered in outdated magazines and newspapers.

"What can I do for you folks?" he asked.

"McCarthy Road," the man stated in a voice that sounded like he chewed gravel for breakfast. "Still open?"

The old man nodded as he pulled his bifocals off his face. "It is. Probably got a good day or so before it's blocked off. What's your business in McCarthy?"

"Delivery," the man said, and then pointed to Kennedy for her to report her reply.

"I'm to visit... family," she finished, though technically her family no longer lived, but that was too complicated a story to tell a complete stranger.

"That there your car, Miss?" the man asked.

"Yes sir. Well, it's a rental."

Both men smirked.

"You ever drive down McCarthy Road before?" the old man asked.

"No sir. This will be my first time."

"I reckon it will be your last, too, in that little root scoot. You got an extra tire or two?"

"I have a spare, yes."

"Good." The man looked to the burly stranger next to her. "You?"

"I'm prepared," the man replied.

"Alright then. Well, safe travels to the both of you."

Daunted by the inquisitive nature into her preparedness, Kennedy walked back outside and cringed as the cold infiltrated her body once more. "Have you driven this road before?" she asked the man.

He nodded. "Multiple times. I make trips frequently throughout the year to trade and sell furs. This is my last run before the winter season officially kicks in."

"That man made it sound dangerous." Kennedy's nerves betrayed her as the man studied her thin coat and pointy heels.

"It is."

"What makes it so bad?"

"Several things. The road itself is gravel and dirt, so you need to drive slower than you would on a highway. Add snow, sleet, and ice and it can get a bit hairy." He rubbed a hand over his beard as if to illustrate the point.

"I see. Well, I guess I will just drive slow."

"Right." He harrumphed as he walked towards his van and climbed inside.

Kennedy hurried towards her car so as to follow him. If McCarthy Road was as treacherous as the two men described it, then she was going to make sure she had someone in sight at all times. Surely the man would help her if she had a flat tire or something.

∞

Clearly, the two men had not been exaggerating. The van in front of her drove at a snail's pace, and Kennedy still found herself scared of hydroplaning or sliding off the side of the road. That was, if her wheels didn't bounce out from under her. And when she'd encountered the single-lane bridge, the Kuskulana Bridge, as the sign reported, her heart slammed in her throat as another car headed straight towards her. Thankfully, she still had time to reverse and let the other vehicle pass before an accident happened. Unfortunately, when she'd finally crossed, the gravel ended, and the dirt began, and she could no longer see the van's lights ahead of her anymore. Her phone had long since lost service and her map app showed her location in Chitina. She remembered the directions though. This road was only sixty miles and then she'd be there. She unclenched her fingers from the steering wheel a moment to prevent them from cramping, and gasped as she hit a large pothole, resulting in a death grip on the wheel once more. "Only sixty miles, Ken. Sixty miles. Hang in there."

The Wrangell Mountains towered over her as she rounded the base and continued down the rugged road. When she allowed her gaze to wander from the road in front of her, she could see evidence of old mining structures and railroad tracks. When she survived the trip, she made a mental note to research the area. She hadn't taken the time to do so in Manhattan before she came. She was on a short time leash from her work and set out as soon as she could to take care of her unexpected inheritance. No more than two weeks her boss had told her, and she cringed at the idea that it would even take that long. Already, she could not imagine making this trek a second time, so her best bet was to gauge the value of her uncle's home and belongings, sell them, and then wash her hands of McCarthy, Alaska.

She spotted a small public lot and obeyed the signs that said to park. Curious, but willing to see why the lot was necessary, she looked to see the van of the stranger she'd encountered earlier parked two spots over. If he had stopped here, then so would she. She walked towards the cabin next to the lot and opened the door to warmth and several bystanders.

"You need passage to the footbridge?" a man asked.

"No sir. I need to reach McCarthy," Kennedy explained.

He laughed, and she heard several others chuckle around her.

"The footbridge it is then," the man stated. "I've got the shuttle here now. Best grab what you want to take with you." He walked past her and out the door and Kennedy hurried after him, her heels sinking into the thick snow. "I don't understand," she called after him. "Can I not take my own car?"

"No ma'am. This is the only way in for non-residents."

"Oh." She followed behind him and noticed the footbridge he'd just described. On the other side, a shuttle van awaited. "I need to grab my luggage." She darted to her car and made quick work of unloading her belongings, but quickly kicked herself for packing so much. The large suitcases sank into the snow and her body, weighted down by her two carry-on bags, sank even lower. She trudged her way towards the awaiting van. She looked to the older van he stood beside, and he opened the door. He waved towards her. "Well, hop in."

"My luggage," she told him.

His eyes widened at the sight of all her bags, but he politely helped lift them inside the vehicle. The man from Chitina already occupied one of the seats, not moving to assist as they readied her for travel. "That ought to do it. Let's get after it. This is my last trip for the day."

She hopped inside and buckled her seatbelt and prayed that whatever roads they needed to cross led her to her uncle's town. She felt out of her element, and as each pitstop came and went, so did her bravado.

«CHAPTER TWO»

The shuttle pulled to a stop at the edge of what Kennedy could only assume was the main street of the town and panic set in. "This is McCarthy?" She tried to keep the surprise from her voice, but by the amused expressions of the men standing by the shuttle, she knew she failed.

"This is it," the driver stated. "I'll get your bags." He started placing her expensive luggage in the snow and Kennedy stood still, baffled that he would just leave her without helping her find where she needed to go. The stranger grabbed a giant bag rolled into a tight bundle with clasps made of leather bindings and hoisted it over his shoulder and began walking away. Kennedy stood torn between her luggage and begging the man. Realizing no one stood in the freezing streets, she started after the man. "Excuse me," she called. "Sir." The man continued walking. Her heels sank into the muddy, snowy street and she stumbled forward on a squeal, her knees and hands breaking her fall. The man turned, and she saw him look heavenward as if he needed the extra patience to deal with her. He walked back towards her and extended his hand. She gripped it and stood, her pants soaked, and her coat soaked from wrist to elbow. She shivered. "Where are you trying to go?" he asked.

"The inn owned by Neal Donovan."

He nodded in the direction he was originally headed. She looked back at her luggage and on a heavy sigh, he walked back and grabbed one of her heavier suitcases. She attempted to roll the second bag and draped her two carry-on bags over her shoulders, but she could barely move. Still, she followed him.

The inn was a simple, wooden structure, three stories tall, which made it the tallest building in town. The sign was covered with snow, as was the porch, stairs, and everything in front of it. The whole town lay blanketed in white fluff. If her teeth weren't chattering and her feet weren't numb, she would have appreciated its simple beauty a bit longer. The man pounded on the door of the inn, the glass panel shaking. No one answered. "This is it," the guy said and turned the knob. The door swung open and the warmth inside beckoned Kennedy forth. She set her bags to the side of the entry and the man released the one he was holding with a loud thud as it dropped from his hand to the floor. "Just stay here. I'm sure Stockton will be back in a few," he grumbled and headed back towards the door.

"Wait." She hurried after him and extended her hand. "I never caught your name."

"Kirk."

"Thank you, Kirk, for being a guide for me today." She nodded towards her extended hand and he hesitantly took it and gave it a quick shake.

"Best get to that fire or you'll catch cold," he mumbled and darted back out the door.

Kennedy glanced around the vacant room, its high-beamed ceilings boasting animal mounts and furs. The oversized fireplace set back in a stone hearth and its comfortable heat warmed the entire room. She walked towards it and spread her hands above the flames and felt the slow tingles bringing life back into her veins. She shed her coat and rested it on the arm of a nearby chair before sitting on her knees before the fire. She'd wait in front of the heat for whoever Stockton was and then figure out her next move. At the moment, she was in awe that the inn was now hers. That this piece of rustic property belonged to *her*.

Hours ticked by and no one came to the inn. She rested comfortably against the sofa, her legs spread out on the giant throw rug on the floor as her feet warmed on the fireplace stones. A scraping noise had her hopping to her feet. It was now dark outside, which wasn't saying much since there were currently only six hours of daylight. But she found herself reaching for the iron poker resting next to the hearth. No one entered. She crept closer to the front door, her feet bare due to her heels drying by the fire. She heard a scuffle outside and gripped the bar tighter, prepared to defend herself. As she neared the door, a figure suddenly appeared in the glass and she squealed in surprise. The knob turned, and she hurried towards the open living space and stood in front of the fire, as if the flames could protect her.

A tall man dressed in heavy coats, a beanie, and an odd face covering walked inside. She could barely see his eyes. "If you're looking for Neal Donovan, he passed away three months ago," he stated. "If you're looking for a place to stay, I'm the one you need to speak to now."

"So, this is Neal's inn?"

He nodded. "Yep."

"And you look after the place?"

He nodded. "That would be me." He walked towards the front steps. "I was heading back from chopping firewood. We are supposed to get a heavy snow tonight." He motioned over his shoulder to a truck loaded down with chopped pieces of wood in the bed of the truck. "So, what can I do for you?"

He stuck out his hand and she took it, shaking it gently. "Kennedy Donovan."

"Donovan, hm? You must be a relative. Neal said someone would show up sooner or later."

Neal. Her uncle. Apparently, this man knew him well.

"Yes, well, I was contacted by his attorney about the inn, and I was told I needed to come and see it. They did not send me a key or anything."

"Obviously you didn't need one to get inside," he pointed out.

"No. A man named Kirk led me here."

"Kirk?" the man asked in surprise.

"Yes. He was... helpful."

"Hmm. Well, I need to finish unloading firewood. I'll be back in a few." He exited, leaving her standing in the middle of the room still holding the iron poker in her hands. She heard the scuffle sounds outside again and realized it was him stacking the wood on the front porch. After a few minutes, he wandered back inside. He then began removing his layers. Layer upon layer he shed and hung on the metal hooks by the door. When he removed the beanie and facemask, dark shaggy hair brushed the collar of his blue sweater, and when he turned, a stunningly handsome face housing sharp green eyes and partially hidden beneath a day's scruff stared back at her. She tried to mask her surprise at the man that stood before her. He flashed a wide smile. "Now, I can officially greet you. I am sorry about all the layering, but as you can see, and feel, it is terribly cold out there. I'm Adam Stockton."

She smiled warmly. "Kennedy... again."

"Right. Well Kennedy, it is nice to meet you. I had a feeling someone from your family would show up sooner or later, but Neal only mentioned a Ken. Now that I think about it, that must be you. A nickname of sorts. I guess I suspected a man would be showing up.

"Yes, my family calls me Ken," she confirmed. "Though I didn't know my Uncle Neal that well."

"Uncle, hm?"

"Yes."

"Well, you must be the niece in New York, the big shot chef?"

Her eyes widened in surprise. "How would he know that? I don't understand." Kennedy lightly placed her fingers to her forehead as she tried to comprehend. "I barely knew him."

This had the man turning and studying her a moment. "Well he knew you."

"Clearly. So, who were you to Uncle— I mean, Neal?"

"Just a friend. I moved out here about fifteen years ago and he took me under his wing. Helped me adjust to the way of life here. It took a while, but now I could not imagine anywhere else to be."

"So, you live here? In the inn?"

He shook his head. "No. I have a cabin about a mile back from town. I just help out."

"So, do people stay here at the inn?"

"Not for the past few months."

"Oh right, because of his passing," Kennedy acknowledged.

"That and because it's about to be winter," Adam corrected with a warm smile. "Tourists don't venture this way in the winter. Too dangerous for their tastes. Too cold."

"And is it quite busy during the tourist months?"

"Sometimes. It is the only place they can actually stay in McCarthy, so Neal has quite the monopoly." He chuckled as he tossed a couple of logs into the fireplace and stoked the fire.

"So where are you from originally?" Kennedy asked, curious to where the sexy stranger stemmed from.

He looked over his shoulder as she awkwardly stood near her coat on the chair, trying to hide her bare feet. He then saw the stiletto heels on the hearth and bit back a smile.

"Kansas."

"Kansas?" she asked in surprise.

"Yep."

"What made you decide to come out here?"

"My folks wanted a change of pace," he answered briskly as he made his way towards her. "Want to pick a room?"

"Oh... I'm not sure which one to take."

He began climbing the wooden stairwell and waved her to follow. "I'll show you your options."

He opened several doors down a long hallway. "Neal lived on the third floor. I figure you will want to make some changes to it before you take it over. But in the meantime, you might like one of these. These are the bigger rooms." He pointed to two doors next door to one another.

"Why would I want to change his house?" she asked.

He turned to her and studied her pretty face as she surveyed the current room. "I'm assuming your tastes are different than your uncle's. So, if you're going to live up there, I imagine you will make a few changes."

"Live here? Oh, I don't plan on living here."

His brows rose in surprise. "I see."

She fumbled her hands together as if she had just confessed her deepest and darkest secret.

"So, what do you plan to do with the place?"

"Sell it, I guess. Or... something. I'm not sure. I'm not familiar enough with the place to know if anyone would even want it." Kennedy's voice held uncertainty, and Adam began walking towards the doorway.

"I guess you should get to know the place then." He began walking down the stairs. "I'm going to gas up the ATVs and have them prepared for the upcoming storm and then get home."

She hurried down the stairs after him as he began putting on all his layers. He looked up as she entered the room. "Thank you, Adam," she began. "For watching over the place."

His lips tilted into a surprised smile. "You're welcome. If you need anything, my number is on the bar." He pointed to the long hand-carved dining bar to her right.

"Thank you."

"Be sure to lock up when I leave."

"How many doors are there?" she asked with confusion.

"Three. Front, back, and one through there." He pointed to a small mudroom off the kitchen.

"Oh, okay."

Looking a bit terrified, Kennedy stood nervously watching him. "You shouldn't have any problems, Kennedy."

She nodded, her slightly panicked face told him she wasn't convinced and that she may run back to Anchorage and catch the first available flight.

"Take care." He slipped back out the front door and she quickly hurried over and locked it behind him. He flashed her a thumbs up through the window and she attempted a smile and small wave. She sighed as she turned and faced the room before her. *What was she to do now?* She ran her hand over the smooth bar and peeked into the large kitchen. The open concept main floor was stunning and could be even more so with a few touch ups. She ran her hand over the front entry, the framing around the door carved with scenes of nature, the detail astonishing. A pounding hit the front door, and she jumped behind the nearest wooden pillar leading into the kitchen, paranoid that someone was going to come breaking through the front door. She heard a light knock and slowly peered around the post and spotted Adam again. She hurried over and opened the door. "Are you okay?" She pulled him inside and quickly locked the door again and began running her hands over his arms to check for injury. "I heard a scuffle out there."

He chuckled and lightly grabbed her hands, his gloves cold from the snow. "I am fine, Kennedy. I was being greeted by an old friend." He pointed out the glass and a giant ball of fur sat patiently swishing its tail across the porch. "He's a bit... ungraceful. I didn't want the noise to scare you."

"Oh." She lightly placed a hand over her heart. "Well, it did. But thank you, for coming to tell me."

He squeezed her hands and unlocked the front door and stepped back out into the cold. "See you tomorrow." She flashed a relieved smile as she shut the door behind him.

∞

Adam knew he and Jasper had scared Kennedy, because he saw her jump into the kitchen. The sight would have been humorous had he not felt bad. But instead of worrying about herself, she was worried about him. That thought warmed his insides a bit, and he tried not to read too much into the pretty stranger or the incredible feeling her hands had given him when she sought out an injury. It wasn't every day a gorgeous female ventured to McCarthy. *No, he wouldn't go there*. But he knew he would check on her tomorrow. Neal had asked for him to look out for the place and for his family when they arrived.

Neal had known someone would come, and Adam owed it to Neal to make sure his family was seen to. Besides, Kennedy was beautiful. He didn't think his task would be all that boring when he had something so pretty to look at. But based on her wardrobe, and her luggage choice, he didn't think Kennedy planned to immerse herself into a McCarthy lifestyle. She oozed city girl, all polished and put together. And though he found her attractive, based on his first interaction, he would not be surprised if she left the following day. A long and lonely night at the inn was sure to keep her up.

He patted Jasper on the head as they made their way to his truck, the old vehicle sputtering to life as he headed towards his own house. He hadn't slept in his cabin but a few times the last few months due to maintaining the inn. In fact, he realized, most of his clothes were at the inn in one of the bottom floor rooms. But he didn't require much, and decided he'd just have to make a trip by there in the morning to gather his things and to check up on Kennedy, if she was still there. He pulled into the barn next to his house and killed the engine, Jasper hopping out of the back and hurriedly making his way towards the house. "Plan on staying, do you?" Adam asked, and the dog released a resounding bark.

Laughing, Adam opened the door to the cold and quiet. Sighing, he immediately walked over to his fireplace and set to work on warming the house. The small cabin had served him well over the last ten years, but the single-room efficiency felt stifling now that he'd had the excess space of the inn to himself the last few months. He wished he could purchase the place for himself. He'd gladly take on the responsibility and the property, but Neal had given it to his niece for a reason. Perhaps it was out of love for the niece he barely knew, or maybe it was because she was the only family member Neal had that hadn't disowned him. But not knowing him and not having anything to do with him all these years told Adam that Kennedy was much like the rest of her family. He still wasn't certain why Neal had limited contact with his family, as he never really spoke about it. And when he did, he'd always spoken highly of them. And he was always proud to talk about the niece in New York. Though he'd never mentioned her name, Neal seemed pleased that she'd made something of herself.

Watching the flames catch and the logs begin to settle against one another, Adam began removing his layers. Glancing at the clock on the wall and listening to not only the rumbles in his own stomach, but also Jasper's, he walked over and began rummaging through his cabinets for some sort of sustenance. He spotted two canned goods and pulled them out. Beans. Well, beans it was. He looked down at Jasper and held a can up. The dog's tongue lolled happily. "Alright, one for you and one for me." Adam placed a pot on the stove and began heating their dinner. "Tomorrow we need two things," he told the dog. "My clothes from the inn and food. If I'm going to be living here again, I've got to do better than just beans." The dog agreed in a soft yip. "And you will need to go home." Jasper didn't like the sound of that as he walked away and laid in front of the fireplace, placing his head on his front paws. Adam smirked. "Sorry, bud. That's just the way it is."

Adam poured a helping of beans into a bowl and set it on the floor, Jasper lazily making his way over and lapping it up in a few bites. Trying to be thankful for at least having a can of something in the house to eat, Adam followed suit.

«CHAPTER THREE»

The next morning, Kennedy stepped outside in her heaviest coat, the wool peacoat she'd worn the day before, now fully dry. Her only pair of boots with a moderate heel, a sweater, and jeans were the best she could do for an outfit. Her style was on the cutting edge for Manhattan, but by McCarthy standards, as she watched people pass by covered much like Adam had been the night before, she was lacking. She could already tell she was not dressed for her surroundings here in McCarthy. Not just based on the fact that she shivered from the cold, but by the looks she received from those passing by. *A new face*, she told herself. They're just distracted by having a stranger amongst themselves. With a robust population of 40 people, as one of the brochures in Chitina boasted, she was sure

McCarthians knew anyone and everyone. A stranger was bound to be noticed.

Not having a vehicle was a downer, she thought, as she turned and set out towards what she thought was a small grocery store towards the edge of town. The walk would do her good and she needed food in the house. As if her stomach could read her thoughts, it released a low grumble in protest at her lack of breakfast. She popped the collar on her jacket and tightened her scarf as she continued on her way. Finally, she reached her destination and made her way inside with only her toes completely numb. The store was small, quaint, and did not have much to offer, much like the small stores in the subway terminals in New York, but it would do. She grabbed a basket and began filling it with essentials. Kennedy also grabbed ingredients to make an apple pie for Adam as a thank you gift for overseeing her uncle's inn. As she made her way to the checkout, a woman around her age welcomed her with a large smile. "You must be Neal's niece," she stated.

"Yes." Kennedy forced a polite smile. "Kennedy."

"Lisa," she replied. "My brother told me."

"I'm sorry?" Kennedy asked.

"Adam. He's my brother." Lisa rolled her eyes. "He came by the store this morning to grab some things and said Neal's pretty niece had finally arrived in town."

"Oh. I see. Your brother. Yes, he was very helpful yesterday."

"I'm sure he was." Lisa smirked as she began bagging Kennedy's groceries and spouted off her total. "Just so you know, if there are any items you wish to have that you don't see, we can special order anything. We usually get a helicopter in about once a month with supplies, especially through the winter months."

Kennedy's eyes widened at the thought of having to have a helicopter bring food supplies to the small village. "Wow, okay. Thank you."

"Mr. Neal would often receive large shipments to keep a good stock going there at the inn." Lisa continued. "I know it's the slow months, but it might be nice to have a good supply in case we are snowed in for a few months. McCarthy Road only has a few more days of passability."

"Oh really?" Kennedy asked. Her hopes of wrapping things up and leaving in a few weeks were slowly evaporating.

Lisa handed her a couple of catalogs. "Here's some supply catalogs. Just make a list and I'll see what we can do."

"Thank you again, Lisa. You and your brother have been life savers."

"We Stocktons have a knack for wanting to help."

"Speaking of your brother," Kennedy continued, noting the slight mischievous smile on Lisa's face."

"He's a handsome devil, isn't he?"

Kennedy's eyes widened. "Oh, no, that's not what I was going to say. I mean, he is, but no, I'm sorry. I was just going to see where I might find him today. I found a notebook of my uncle's last night that had some listings inside I think he may be able to explain to me."

"Ah." Lisa pointed through the window. "See that trail there?"

Kennedy nodded.

"He's about a half a mile up that way chopping down a few trees for the farm."

"Farm?"

"Yes, my family has a farm about a mile or so back from the Inn. My ma asked him to stock up on wood for the upcoming months, so he's been hacking away the last few days."

"I see. Just straight up that trail?"

Lisa nodded.

"Thanks." Kennedy lifted the two heavy paper sacks full of groceries and made her way back to the inn. She would drop the food off and then go seek out Adam and pay him for the wood pile he replenished last night. She saw the notations in the notebook about how much Uncle Neal paid him, and she knew he did not ask for payment last night due to it being her first night in town. She grabbed the money from the inn lockbox and set out again towards the trail Lisa had mentioned. A half a mile wasn't too far; she walked more than that every day in New York. Her boots continued to slip on the snow-impacted dirt, and she grabbed a lamp post, void of a working bulb, to steady herself as she slowly made her way up the trail. Her breath came in smoky puffs as she went, and her toes had long gone numb as the snow now reached almost to her knees and seeped over the top of her boots. She heard the sounds of chopping and sighed in relief.

Three men split wood, and she spotted the familiar heavy coat Adam wore the night before. She watched for a moment as he swung the ax with ease. The other men, impressive in build as well, made quick work of the heavy logs and tossed them all into a growing pile. She walked forward, and their heads snapped up. She offered a frozen smile and they just stood staring at her. Adam continued chopping, and when he tossed the wood to the side and noticed no one else retrieving or chopping, he glanced up at the men and followed their gaze to her. "Kennedy?"

His voice was breathless from exertion and he walked towards her, handing his ax off to one of the other men. "What are you doing out here?" he asked, slipping down his facemask so his words would not be muffled.

Her eyes were drawn briefly to his lips and she quickly glanced back up. "Lisa said I might find you out here," she stated, her words shaking as she shivered. She crossed her arms and stuffed her hands beneath her jacket.

He looked down and inwardly cringed at the way she was dressed, knowing she must be freezing. "Is something wrong at the inn? Did something happen?"

"Oh, no. Everything is f-f-f-ine."

The other two men still stood frozen watching the two of them. She nodded their direction and Adam turned. "Hey! Get back to work!"

The two men crossed their arms in defiance and Adam groaned. "These are my two brothers. James and Eric." The two men stepped forward and each extended a hand to her. She smiled as she accepted. "Nice to meet you. Kennedy Donovan. You guys must be c-c-c-old out here. Ch-ch-chopping all this w-w-wood." She tried to stabilize her words, but her body betrayed her, and the two men chuckled. "Best get her home, Adam," one of them said.

Adam waved her towards his truck. "Oh, I don't want-t-t-t to interrupt your w-w-work. I'm f-f-fine."

Adam chuckled. "No, you're not. Come on." He grabbed her hand and led her to his truck and opened the passenger door for her to slide in. He then hopped in the other side and cranked the engine and the heat. It was a quick drive back to the inn and she slid out, her boots slipping on the ice and her hands waving as she tried to balance herself. She felt a strong pair of hands around her waist and she straightened.

"Careful." Adam's voice was beside her ear and sent a new set of chills up her arms. She tried to ignore her body's reaction to the stranger. He then walked beside her as they climbed the steps to the inn. She opened the door and walked inside to the warmth and sighed. Turning, she noticed he lingered outside the open door. "You want to come in?"

He shook his head and pointed at his muddy and snowy boots. "Best not, I think."

"Oh."

He watched as disappointment washed over her face and he felt pleased to know she wanted him around.

"You wished to speak to me about something, Kennedy?" he asked patiently.

"Oh yes." She lightly palmed her forehead and reached in her jacket pocket and handed him a pile of folded money. His eyes widened. "What's this for?"

"The wood from last night. I noticed Uncle Neal paid you regularly for restocking." She motioned towards a small notebook. "So, I wanted to make sure you received payment."

"This can wait." He offered it back, but she shook her head.

"No. I noticed you have a schedule of replenishing every month. So, I calculated how much you must not have been receiving since his death. That should bring us current."

Adam slipped off his beanie and pulled his face mask over his face until it slipped from around his neck. He wore a frown. "There is plenty of time for you to catch up on paying me. No need to give me what I'm sure is the money from his winter carryover. You will need this for supplies this winter."

"No. I ran the numbers. It's fine." She began removing her jacket and hung it on the stand next to the door. She wore a cream-colored cashmere sweater that looked softer than a new kitten's fur. She crossed her arms and waited for him to tuck the money into his pocket. "Well, thank you then, Kennedy."

"Thank *you*." She looked down at her watch. "So, do you eat around here?"

He tilted his head at her question. "I eat."

"When?"

His eyes flashed to the clock over her shoulder. "In a few."

"Then come in. I'll make us some lunch." She turned, not waiting for his answer. He shook his head at his defeat and smiled to himself at her stubbornness. *She was more like Neal than she knew*, he realized. He removed his boots outside and shuffled indoors, removing his layers of coats. He followed the sounds of her unloading grocery bags and watched as she began mixing ingredients in a large pot on the stove.

"Soup okay?"

He nodded in silence as he slipped onto a stool.

"Drink?" She asked.

"Water is fine."

She filled him a glass and laid it on the counter.

"You do not have to feed me lunch, Kennedy."

"I know. I want to. Besides, you're here already and it's lunchtime. And I don't really want to eat alone. Again." She glanced up with a satisfied smirk as she put the lid on the pot. She then began removing fresh apples from her bag and began chopping them into thin slices.

"Do you add apples to your soup?" He looked at her curiously and she giggled.

"No. I'm making you a thank you gift."

"A gift? For what?"

She set her knife down and sighed with a semi-annoyed expression at his question. "For all the work I'm sure you have done the last few months while no one has been here at the inn."

"Kennedy—"

"Don't 'Kennedy' me." She picked up her knife. "I want to. It's the least I can do. I tend to bake for people if they have done something for me or my family and I have no other way to express my gratitude. If it is not enough, let me know if there is more money I owe."

"You don't owe me money." His voice was low and when she looked up his green eyes were kind. He reached across the counter and gently laid his hand over hers, her chopping stopped. His hand was warm and strong, and she felt the light scratch of calluses, but his touch was gentle. "You don't owe me anything. Neal helped me out more than you could ever know. It was the least I could do for him. So please, consider the slate clean."

She nodded. "I'm still making you a pie."

His lips quirked as he fought back a smile. Apple pie. When was the last time he had such a delicious dessert? He couldn't remember. "Alright. But no more after that." He smiled when he saw her face lift into a grin and her eyes held relief.

"So, tell me, where do you work in New York?"

"I'm a chef for a restaurant called Petit Boutary. It's French cuisine."

"Wow. So, is this a French soup?" His brows rose in complete surprise and she laughed.

"No. It's a vegetable stew. But it will still rock your world," she stated with confidence.

He burst into laughter as she smiled at him. "I imagine it will. Anything will be better than the can of beans I ate last night."

She liked the sound of his deep laugh and when he smiled his entire face lit up as if it were meant to hold such a happy expression all the time. His words finally sank in. "Wait, beans? That's all you ate?"

"My choices were limited last night. But don't worry, I'm well stocked thanks to Lisa."

"If I had known, I would have made you something before you left yesterday."

He smirked. "No worries."

She chopped up the last of the apples and set them aside as she began mixing ingredients for a pie crust. "So, what do you do here?" she asked. "Other than chop wood. Or is that your job?"

He shook his head. "Lately it feels like it. But I farm. My family has a rather large spread."

"Oh, Lisa did mention that. I didn't realize it was a family affair."

"Well that and the grocery store."

"Is that so?" she asked.

He nodded. "I tend to work the farm mostly though. I'm not much for being inside all day."

"Even when it is freezing out there?"

"Even then." He grinned. "Speaking of which." He stood and reached for the two catalogs resting on the counter that Lisa had given her. "You may want to give some thought to this catalog." He handed her the magazine full of different clothing. She lightly frowned and then looked down at her jeans and sweater. "Oh." Her voice was low with a hint of disappointment. He realized he may have offended her. "What you have on is lovely, Kennedy, but it is definitely not warm enough."

Realization hit her, and she flushed. "Oh, right. Yes, I guess I should order a few things. Especially a warmer jacket. I did not realize it would be this cold."

He rounded the counter and stood next to her lightly nudging her with his elbow. She looked up at him. "May I?"

Her brow furrowed in confusion. "May you what?"

He lightly ran his fingertips over the sleeve of her sweater. "It's as soft as it looks." His voice softened as she looked up at him and his cheeks flushed as he realized what he had just done. "But definitely not warm enough."

They were close, *too close*, Kennedy realized, but she did not want to back away. He smelled masculine. Intoxicating. And he looked as if he stepped out of the very catalog he flipped through.
Their eyes held a moment longer before he looked back at her hands as she began rolling out the dough. "It's cashmere." Her voice was barely a whisper as her heart fluttered in her chest.

"It's nice." He watched as she expertly draped the flattened dough into a baking dish and began shaping the edges. Her hands were fast and efficient. A loud pounding on the door made them both jump, Kennedy fumbling the dish on the counter.

Adam glanced to the door and stepped around the counter to answer, thankful for the interruption, because *clearly* he had lost his mind. He swung it open and a large older man with a robust chest stomped ice and snow from his boots outside before entering. "Stockton, ah, there you are. Your sister said I might find you here."

"Hey, Tom," Adam greeted. "What can I do for you?"

"Wolves." The man pulled off his beanie and facemask, his face aged and worn, but still friendly in disposition. He nodded at Kennedy. "Ms. Donovan."

"Hello," she greeted. "Please come in." She waved him further into the room and he shut the door behind him. "And you are?"

"Tom Higgins." The man stood awkwardly in the front entry as if he were unsure if he were welcome.

"Have you eaten lunch, Mr. Higgins?"

Her question surprised him as he continued wringing his hat in his hands. "Um, no ma'am."

"Come in then. Have a seat and a bowl of soup and you can tell Adam all about the wolf issue." Her friendly order had the man shuffling forward in uncertainty.

Adam took a stool at the bar and sat as well, pleased with Kennedy's invitation to the man. She did not know the history between Tom and Neal. The history of unfriendliness. But he could tell her small act of kindness surprised Tom.

She filled two bowls with steaming soup and laid a small bowl of crackers between the two men as she continued working on the two apple pies she was making. One for the inn and one for Adam.

"So, what's the report, Tom?" Adam asked.

"Three more dogs gone. One of them my Jasper." He shook his head in disappointment. "Tracks clear for about a half mile, but then gone. The bloody creatures are slippery. We've been hunting for a week now and no sight of them. Have you noticed any at the farm?"

"A few tracks, but no animals missing yet. And Jasper is fine," Adam assured him. "He followed me home last night and stayed at the cabin. I dropped him off at the store with Lisa this morning. He's getting spoiled."

Relief washed over the man's face. "I appreciate that. But we're still down two dogs. I think it has to be a rather large pack. I mean, two dogs in one night?"

Adam nodded soberly and could tell Kennedy was listening intently as she slipped the pies into the oven and began filling herself a bowl of soup.

"The soup is delicious, Kennedy, thank you." Adam spooned another mouthful and Tom agreed.

"Yes ma'am. I don't believe I've ever tasted anything like it."

This had Kennedy's smile broadening even further. "Thank you, Mr. Higgins. That is a compliment. I am sorry to hear about your two dogs."

"Oh, they weren't my dogs," he corrected. "The Rathers boy's sleigh dogs."

"Oh, I'm sorry. I just assumed. Well, I think it's very kind of you to help him hunt down the wolves that killed them then. How sad."

Tom studied her for a moment and then looked to Adam in astonishment at her kindness towards him. She didn't notice and then began busying herself with rearranging the pantry to fit in her new groceries.

"Anyways," Tom continued with Adam. "I was thinking maybe tomorrow, since it's Saturday, that I could gather you, your brothers, and your dad to help in the search. I know they have been busy preparing for the blizzard, but I sure would appreciate the help. Kirk is leaving today to make it back to Anchorage before the storm hits, so I've lost my help."

"Kirk?" Kennedy asked, stepping back from the pantry.

Tom looked up. "Yes ma'am. He's my son."

A faint smile warmed her face. "Your son was extremely helpful to me yesterday. He led me down McCarthy road and helped me find the inn."

"Did he?" the man asked, surprised his son would help a Donovan.

She nodded and then looked for Adam to continue his conversation with the man.

"Consider us in, Tom," Adam told him. "What time is everyone starting, and what areas do you want us to cover?"

Kennedy listened as the two men mapped out a plan for the following day. An upcoming blizzard. She knew Adam and Lisa had mentioned it growing colder. *But a blizzard?* Just the word made Kennedy feel claustrophobic. She pulled the pies from the oven and the men's talking ceased. She glanced up and noticed they were both staring at the pies like children after candy.

She turned and set them on the counter with a small smile. She grabbed two small plates and sliced the first pie with two hefty pieces and brought them over to them. "You guys save room for pie?" She slid the plates in front of them and the two men stared at it.

"My goodness." Tom's voice was barely above a whisper. "I don't believe I've had a slice of pie since Annie died."

He picked up his fork and took a bite, his eyes closing in pure satisfaction. Kennedy grinned as she caught Adam's amused smirk at the older man. Adam winked at her and forked his own bite, his mouth exploding in sweet flavor. "Wow," he mumbled. "Delicious, Kennedy."

"Good."

"You could sell these for a hundred dollars," Tom stated.

Kennedy laughed. "I'm not sure about that, but I'll keep that in mind."

Both men scraped their plates clean and she walked them over to the sink. Tom stood and began pulling on his hat. "That was the best lunch I've had in a long time, Ms. Donovan, I appreciate you feeding an old man like me."

"Of course. Anytime." She smiled warmly.

"I'll see you tomorrow, Adam." Tom nodded his farewells and slipped outside.

"It was kind of you to include him." Adam stood and stretched, his desire to walk back into the cold fading as he wished to sleep off the warm filling in his stomach.

"He seems like a sweet man." Her comment made Adam laugh in disbelief.

"Why? Is he not?"

"Not always. He is rather gruff at times. He and your uncle were not exactly the best of friends."

Her brow furrowed. "Why not?"

"They never saw eye to eye on anything. Mainly, the tourist situation. Tom did not wish to bring any tourists into the town and your uncle did. Neal thought it would be good for the community and it has been, but Tom is set in his ways and liked having everything private."

"I see. So, he is probably upset to see someone at the inn, isn't he?"

Adam shrugged. "Not really sure. If he was, I am sure that has all changed now since that slice of pie." He winked at her and she grinned.

"I'm glad you liked it. I have to say I'm pretty impressed with the kitchen Uncle Neal has here. The appliances all look new. Makes cooking much easier."

"That's because they are. Neal wanted to make sure the inn was fully equipped. He loved cooking for his guests."

"To be honest, as I was heading towards McCarthy yesterday, I was scared I was venturing into the frontier. I expected zero electricity."

Adam laughed. "We aren't that backwoods."

"Well, it's marketed quite differently at the lodge in Chitina," Kennedy pointed out.

"Ah. Yeah, they like to play upon McCarthy's history a bit. In truth, it was an incredible place for its time. McCarthy had electricity even before the entire city of Chicago did because of the mines. Coal power was quite beneficial. And it's one of the only towns within the confines of a national forest.

Now, the further you venture from town you have some folks who prefer to live 'off the grid', so to speak." Kennedy watched as he walked towards the door and began grabbing his layers. "Now, there are some things that are not as convenient as life in Anchorage or New York would be."

"Like flying in supplies via helicopter," she replied.

He chuckled. "That and being remote. Winter months can get long and hard if you stay through the season."

"Which, according to Tom, I will be due to McCarthy Road shutting down today."

"You prepared for a few months of snow?"

"Me? No. My boss? Definitely not. I have yet to make that phone call and other phone calls. Make sure my mail is collected, and rent is paid. I wasn't expecting to be here but a few days. And I've never seen snow like this. Also, I have my rental car parked at the lot on the other side of the footbridge, so I have no idea how I'm going to get that back."

He held up a hand. "Wait, they let you drive a rental down McCarthy Road?"

"Yes."

His brows rose. "Normally that is not allowed because the road is so rough."

Kennedy shrugged.

"I'll talk to Tom. Maybe Kirk can tow it back to Glennallen."

Hope lit in her eyes. "That would be wonderful. Though Kirk wasn't exactly my biggest fan."

Adam smirked. "Did he hear your last name?"

She thought back to their interactions. "Well, he knew I was coming to the inn."

"Kirk has the same opinion of your uncle as Tom does. He was probably acting that way because he assumed you were a Donovan and did not want to have anything to do with you."

"Well, that's rude." She crossed her arms in offense and Adam grinned.

"Yes, well, like I said, you may have changed Tom's mind about you just by being friendly to him today. I'll talk to Tom and Kirk. We'll get the car back."

"Thank you. But what am I to do for transportation around McCarthy? I mean, I know it's not a big town, but do people literally walk everywhere?"

"We have a few vehicles here, but mostly ATVs. Neal has a couple. I gassed them up and have them prepped in the shed should you need them."

"So, no car?" Kennedy asked warily.

"You would be surprised what you can do without around here."

"But..." She trailed off. Adam did not need to hear her worries. He was kind enough already to be helping her. He did not need to know she had no clue how to drive an ATV.

He grinned as if he knew her thoughts. He slipped on his boots. She walked towards him and began buttoning his outer jacket as he slipped his facemask over his head. He shoved his hair from his eyes and tucked it within the mask, his eyes holding slight surprise at her help. Kennedy did not notice as she continued. He smiled under the mask at the small gesture of help and her comfortable attitude towards him. She glanced up and caught his gaze.

"Can I ask you something?"

He nodded.

"How does one prepare for a blizzard?"

He laughed. "Just go see Lisa. She'll help you out." She nodded as she finished his last button.

He began slipping on his gloves. "I hate that you have to go out there in this cold."

He laughed. "I'm used to it." She could tell he was smiling due to the sparkle in his eyes and she offered one of her own.

"Well, have a good rest of the day then. And thanks for coming by for lunch."

He nodded. "Thanks for feeding me. It was delicious."

"Anytime." She opened the door for him, and he stepped out into the cold wind. He turned on the top step and gave one final wave before traipsing through the afternoon snow. Kennedy felt herself sigh and then closed the door. *No warm mode of transportation*, she mused. She shook her head in bewilderment.

«CHAPTER FOUR»

It'd been a long day. Cold, wet, muddy, laborious... but Adam would not have had it any other way. He loved working outdoors. And he loved that he was able to eat with Kennedy and offer her some company as she settled in at Neal's. He'd found, too, that he liked the thought of her being snowed into McCarthy for the next few months. Yes, she could always hitch a ride on one of the helicopters and head back to New York, but she didn't know of that option yet. And he wasn't quite sure he wanted to share it. Yet. Despite the harsh treatment Neal had received from his family throughout the years, Kennedy seemed different, completely oblivious as to why her family disowned her uncle. Perhaps she was. Neal seemed to always think highly of her despite his brother's lack of love. And Neal did leave his life's work to her, which surprised everyone in McCarthy. All assumed Adam would inherit Neal's Inn. He wasn't upset that he didn't, though he loved the place, but he was surprised. Everyone was surprised Neal left it to family. But Neal had a reason for it. And Adam respected Neal too much to challenge his decision. And after meeting his niece— his beautiful and kind niece— Adam thought that perhaps Neal was on to something.

He eased onto the sofa at his parent's house and his siblings gathered around and talked of the wolf issue and, of course, the new stranger in town. Lisa enjoyed sharing her interactions with Kennedy, of whom she was now an expert. He could smell the delicious meal his mother prepared and sent up a prayer of thanks that he wasn't stuck eating a can of beans for the night. It also, however, made him think of the warm lunch he'd received from Kennedy. The soup had been incredible as well as her company. She had a pretty smile that made her dark eyes sparkle. And when she turned those stunning eyes towards him, he felt his heart do funny things. *Which was ridiculous*, he reminded himself. He easily could have blown off the rest of his day's work just to be near her, just to soak in the beauty of her. It wasn't every day a gorgeous woman came to McCarthy to stay, even for a short time. When word got out about Neal Donovan's niece, every available bachelor would be lining up at the inn's front door. He couldn't have that. He'd already heard James and Eric discussing her with his dad. They sounded almost as smitten as he was. But he also felt a slight protective streak flare up when her name was mentioned. She was his responsibility. The inn was his responsibility. Neal had asked him to look after it and all that came with it. And in Adam's mind, Kennedy came with it.

He stood, walking towards the back door.

"Adam? Where you off to?" his dad asked.

"Grabbing some more logs for the fire." He pointed to the dwindling pile on the hearth and his father nodded. He stepped out onto the cold porch and took a deep breath of the frigid air before grabbing an armload. He loved the winter months. Yes, they could be harsh, but the crisp clean air relaxed him. He heard a knock at the front of the house but continued his stacking before stomping his feet on the rug to head back inside.

"Well, who could that be on a night like this?" his mother's voice carried over to the front door as she wiped her hands on her dish towel. "Eric, grab the door. Might be Tom again about the wolves," she called to one of her sons closest to the door. Eric hurried over and lifted the bolt, complete surprise on his face at the pretty woman before him. She stood in equal surprise as if not expecting him.

"Kennedy?" Lisa's voice rang to her right and Kennedy smiled at the familiar face. Lisa walked over and lightly hugged her and rubbed some warmth into her shoulders. "What are you doing here, girl?"

Kennedy looked around at all the unfamiliar faces and felt completely out of sorts. "I, um, I thought perhaps Adam would be here. This is where Mr. Stanley, the man at the bar, said he lived. I'm sorry if I got the wrong place." She began backing up towards outside. Mrs. Stockton stepped from the kitchen and sized Kennedy up in one glance. "My goodness, did you blow in with the snowstorm? Come inside for some warmth."

Kennedy flushed. "Oh, I do not wish to intrude. I was just—" She was gently pulled into the warmth of the home and her only means of escape closed behind her. The back door opened, and a man walked in carrying an armload of wood. A man she recognized.

Adam glanced up and froze. He pulled off his beanie. "Kennedy? Everything okay?" A relieved smile washed over her face, and his mother's eyes bounced between the two in pure delight. "Come in." She hustled Kennedy softly, lightly nudging the small of Kennedy's back. Adam disposed of the wood next to the fireplace and walked towards her. "Everything okay at the inn?"

She nodded. "Yes, I'm sorry to intrude on your family time. I didn't realize they would all be here." She handed him a small box. "I came to give you your pie. You left it today."

A slow smile spread over his face as he accepted the box. "I could have gotten it tomorrow. You didn't have to come out in the cold. Did you walk?"

She shook her head. "ATV."

His brows rose.

"Yes, you should be impressed. It only took me about six tries and Mr. Stanley coming to my rescue for me to learn how to use it." She laughed nervously.

Adam chuckled, touched that she would bring him the pie all the way to his house.

"Come now. Stay for dinner," Mrs. Stockton insisted, waving for Adam to bring her further into the house.

"Oh, that's okay. I didn't mean to interrupt."

"Nonsense. Come."

Adam waved her forward and slipped his hand to the small of her back. "I'll introduce you to everyone." He began pointing. "My brothers, James and Eric, you met while chopping wood." She nodded in greeting. "And Lisa, you know."

Lisa beamed as she leaned against the stone fireplace.

"My mother, Diane." He pointed to the older woman in the kitchen and she waved with glee making Kennedy and Adam both smile. "And my dad, Richard. Everyone, this is Kennedy Donovan, Neal's niece."

Kennedy gave a small wave. "It is nice to meet all of you."

Adam grinned as he nudged her further inside. He handed his mother the pie and her face brightened when she saw what Kennedy had delivered.

Richard leaned forward in his chair as Adam escorted Kennedy to a seat on the sofa. "Your uncle was a dear friend of mine. You are most welcome in our home, Kennedy."

"Thank you." Kennedy's eyes watered a bit at the kindness. Everyone stared at her and she fidgeted in her seat. Adam cast warning looks at his siblings to give her some space.

"So, Kennedy," Lisa chimed up. "Do you plan on opening up the inn in the spring?"

"Oh, I'm not sure yet. I'm still trying to get my bearings."

"Will you stay here?" Eric asked.

"I haven't quite sorted that out just yet." Her head turned to the next voice.

"Do you plan on selling?"
"Where are you from?"
"Why did you not come visit Neal?"
"What about your family?"
Questions slammed from every direction.

"Okay, okay, okay." Adam lightly ran his hand between Kennedy and his siblings. "Enough with the third degree. Give Kennedy a break." He flashed her an apologetic smile. "Sorry, Kennedy, my family just hasn't had a new face to meet in a while."

She shyly smiled, and their eyes held a moment. Everyone noticed, and Richard cleared his throat. "Well, how about we all head to the table and sample some of that delicious dinner."

Everyone stood, and Kennedy held back, not sure where she was to sit. She felt the familiar hand of Adam and smiled in appreciation as he motioned to a seat and took the one next to her.

∞

Kennedy sat quietly as Adam reported the following day's event of helping Tom Higgins hunt wolves and several other conversations stemmed around the table. She ate in silence but felt the watchful eye of Mr. Stockton. Kennedy cleared her throat and looked up for everyone's attention. "After the hunting parties are finished in their hunt, I would like to feed everyone at the inn for their efforts."

Diane bit back a smile.

"That would be about twenty men!" Lisa's eyes widened.

Kennedy nodded. "There's plenty of room."

"I will help you," Diane offered. "I think it very kind of you to open up the inn for a warm meal after a long day of hunting in the cold. I'll be over in the morning."

Kennedy nodded her thanks. She turned and caught the impressed gaze of Adam. He reached under the table and squeezed her hand. Everyone began to rise and gather their empty dishes, and Kennedy did as well, Adam's hand sliding from hers. She walked her dishes to the kitchen and began helping Lisa and Diane wash and dry. No one said anything about her joining in, but they made sure to include her in their conversation. "So anyway, Jack has been avoiding me for days now. I mean, what does that mean? He kisses me then ignores me?" Lisa complained as she dried a plate.

"Perhaps the boy is just shy. He's always had a soft heart," Diane stated.

"Mom, he is not shy. We've been friends for years. He has no reason to be shy."

Kennedy smirked as Lisa handed her another plate to rinse.

"What do you think, Kennedy?" Lisa asked.

"Me?"

"You are the only Kennedy in the room," Lisa stated.
"What do you think?"

"Well, maybe he isn't shy per se, maybe he is just nervous. He obviously took the step towards something more than friendship with you and maybe he's just nervous he rushed things."

Lisa tilted her head. "Good point," she sighed.

Kennedy rinsed the last dish and began toweling off her hands when she felt a hand slide across the small of her back and Adam's deep voice was next to her ear. She slightly jumped but turned to find his kind gaze. "I thought I would give you a ride home."

Kennedy turned to face him, and his hand remained, sliding to her hip as she turned. "You don't have to do that. Besides, the ATV?"

"We'll park it in the barn here and I'll bring it back tomorrow. I don't want you riding that in the dark, especially with wolves about."

"Oh... I didn't think of that." Kennedy's voice held a tinge of fear and she folded the dish towel and set it on the counter. "Thank you for including me for dinner, Mrs. Stockton. It was wonderful."

"Oh, anytime, Kennedy. Like Richard said, you are most welcome in our home." Diane hugged her warmly. "I'll be over around nine tomorrow, so we can get an early start on that feast."

"Thank you." Kennedy smiled as Adam nodded towards the door. He helped her into her jacket and slipped into his own. "It was nice seeing and meeting all of you. If you are in town and would like to stop by the inn, you are welcome any time."

"I imagine you will be tired of Stocktons before you know it," Richard belted as he walked up to hold the door as she and Adam slipped through. "You two be careful."

They made their way down the front steps and Kennedy's boot slipped, Adam catching her elbow before she fell. "Don't say it." She grumbled.

He chuckled.

"No laughing," she ordered. "I marked new boots on my order."

"Good." He opened his truck door and she slipped inside. When he cranked the engine, he slowly made his way towards the lights of the town.

"Thank you for the ride."

"You're welcome. Thank you for the pie. I'm sorry if my family came on a bit strong."

"They seem sweet."

"For the most part they are." He smiled as he pulled to the front of the inn.

She opened her door and slipped out. Adam rounded the front of his truck. She turned and accepted the friendly offer of stability as they climbed the front steps. "Listen, if the men need a meeting place tomorrow, they are welcome to use the inn."

"That might be extremely helpful, actually. We will probably set out about five tomorrow morning."

"I will be up and have some coffee ready for everyone."

"That would be awesome."

"Will you all be coming in for lunch?"

He shook his head. "Probably not. I imagine we won't be in until after dark. Probably around four."

She nodded. "Right. Weird daylight hours. Sounds good. I will have supper ready then."

Adam smiled at her generosity. They stood quietly for a second and neither said anything. "Well, I guess I better head home." He slipped his hands into his pockets. "Good night, Kennedy."

"Night." She opened the door and turned. "Oh, and Adam."

"Yes?"

"Please be careful tomorrow."

His face lifted into a tender smile. "I will."

Nodding, she offered one last wave before closing the door.

«CHAPTER FIVE»

The next morning Adam opened the front door of Neal's Inn and stepped inside, stomping his boots on the threshold before entering. His gaze found Kennedy with her back to him as she turned, wearing an apron and a smile. "Morning."

"Good morning. Looks like you have had an early day of it," he commented, nodding towards the swept off porch and the long tables she had set up outside with hot coffee cisterns and thermoses.

"Well, I did some of it last night, but yes. I've been up since about three getting everything ready. I found the tables in the hall closet. And the thermoses were just stacked in the pantry on the floor. Might as well give you guys some fuel to help kickstart your hunt." She walked by him with a large basin tub that held foil wrapped packages.

"What is that?" He pointed.

"Lunch. I figured since you guys can't make it in to eat, you can at least take something with you. They're just roast beef sandwiches, but maybe they'll give you some warmth and energy today. If they stay warm. I'm not really sure if they will." Her face slightly fell, but she shrugged. "I'm still new to this type of cold. I wasn't really sure what to do."

"You've done more than enough." He stood in awe of her as she placed the tub outside on the table as well. She noted several men already gathered around the inn's front.

"You gentlemen feel free to help yourself to some coffee. And this bin has some lunch you can pack with you," she announced. She backed out of the way as they climbed the stairs and began helping themselves. Adam tugged her hand back into the inn and shut the door.

"Is something wrong?" she asked curiously. He shook his head and ran a hand through his hair. "Adam?" she asked again.

He looked up and appreciation shown in his eyes. "You are just... incredible. Do you know that?" he asked.

Her cheeks flushed, and she waved away the compliment. "You guys are trying to protect the town. It's the least I can do."

"Because you cook for people when you don't know how to thank them," he supplied remembering her previous response to him.

She nodded with a smile. "Exactly."

He chuckled and shook his head, still amazed at the incredible woman before him. "You'll freeze if you stand out there too long without a coat."

"Also on my order list," she pointed out. "My jacket is not quite equipped enough for McCarthy."

"I have an extra. If you check the room behind the mudroom. That's where I stayed while looking out for the place. I should have some extra sweaters too, if you need one in the meantime. I mean... they'll be huge on you, but it's better than nothing."

She grinned in thanks. "I'll take a look. Thank you for looking out for me. I know it's probably been a pain having to help me so much lately, but I appreciate it more than you know. I'm a little out of my element here."

"We've all been there. Your uncle helped me. I'm glad I can repay his efforts." He opened the door again and Kennedy smiled at the turnout of men and began helping serve them coffee.

Kennedy offered a warm welcome to Tom and filled his thermos. She thanked him for protecting the town and stocked up a stunned Tom with two of her foil-wrapped sandwiches. She honestly had no idea how her fresh and encouraging presence affected the man. Adam was last as all of them began heading their opposite directions. He shouldered his rifle and filled his thermos with coffee. Kennedy walked around the table and fit two foil packages into the pack he wore on his back. He heard the zipper and turned. She winked. "Please be careful today," she whispered.

He nodded and squeezed her hand. She was hesitant to let it go when he slowly pulled away and began walking away with his brothers. She offered them each a parting smile as well and then began moving the coffee urns back into the inn.

Adam turned before heading over the hill and Neal's Inn was a bright beacon of warmth amidst the snowstorm beginning to blow in. Neal would have liked Kennedy. It was a shame the two never interacted or knew one another. The more Adam was around Kennedy, the more he wished to know her more. Keeping the image of her in the apron with her hair tied up on top of her head in his mind, he trekked forward, his feet buried beneath the snow as he headed out to track down the latest predators. He felt a shove from his brother, James, as they cleared a growth of trees. James pointed down at the ground and Adam spotted the tracks. *Definitely wolf tracks*, he thought. He split off from his brother, each taking alternative trails and following sets of tracks deep in the snow.

The tracks ended, and Adam looked around to see if perhaps there were signs of life in nearby shrubs, but he saw nothing. How could the tracks just vanish? He walked up the small hill. Perhaps it was steeper than it looked, and the wolf tracks picked up on the other side, but as he stepped to the top, a crunch and snap sounded as his foot collapsed through a hole covered by thicket and snow. He did not have time to catch himself, but instead found himself sliding down the mountainside. His body flipped and tumbled and careened towards the drop off, which he would not survive if he flew off. He grasped the ground, branches, bushes, but nothing slowed him until he pounded into the base of a small tree. His ribs exploded in pain, but his hands grasped the trunk as his body had already started to drag away to keep sliding. Heaving deep breaths, he tried to calm his sprinting heart. He reached into his pant pocket and withdrew a whistle. He blew several puffs and waited. He heard an answering whistle emerge above him. James. His brother looked down the ravine and immediately withdrew rope from his pack and tied it around a sturdy tree. "Can you walk?" he called.

"Yes. Just toss it down." The rope slid to within a foot of where he held on for dear life, and he grasped it with his free hand. He then pulled it towards himself and tied it around his waist. Rising to stand, his feet shifted and began to slide. He fell to his knees and felt James' tug on the other end. Together, they slowly pulled him up the steep slope and back to safety, both collapsing from the effort.

∞

Mrs. Stockton showed up at nine on the dot with an eager knock on the door. Kennedy, thankful she'd taken a few hours to rest, felt just as eager to begin cooking. Diane bustled into the inn carrying multiple bags of groceries. "Hi, honey!" she called. Kennedy looked up from the cutting board and smiled. "Good morning."

"I heard about the nice thing you did this morning for all the men. Such a Neal thing to do," she complimented as she set the bags on the counter. "I brought a few things from the store just in case

KATHARINE E. HAMILTON

we need them. Have you in mind what you would like to make for dinner?"

"I was thinking pot roast. That way it can cook all day with little fuss."

"Perfect!" Diane beamed. "Shall I make some hot rolls to go with?"

"That would be great. Thanks."

Mrs. Stockton walked over and looked down at Kennedy's cutting board. "What do you have there?"

"Just the veggies for all the pot roasts. I was thinking five would do it, you think?"

"I imagine so. I brought potatoes."

"Oh good. I was thinking I may have to run to the store and get some."

"Why run to the store when the store can come to you," Diane chanted, making Kennedy chuckle.

"I was thinking a cheesy scalloped potato side dish," Kennedy explained.

"Oh, that sounds like just the thing after a cold day of hunting," Diane stated. "Makes my mouth water already."

"Do you think they will find the wolves?" Kennedy asked.

"I imagine so. With all those men out there, I cannot imagine them not."

"Will they be okay?" Kennedy asked.

Diane tilted her head and studied the young woman. "Of course. They are all careful out there. You have to be."

"Good. It worries me with all the snow. How easy it might be to get lost."

"True. But they're smart. They travel in pairs or teams. Believe it or not, this is quite a common occurrence during the winter months. The wolves can get quite nasty. The boys keep a good rein on them around the farm, but sometimes folks closer to town lose animals. Which is what they're dealing with right now."

Kennedy shook her head in wonder. "In New York, the only wolves are on Wall Street."

Diane laughed. "McCarthy is a bit different than New York, I'm afraid. But you seem to be warming up to it quite quickly." She began to wash the potatoes in the sink.

"If by warming up to it you mean barely sleeping because I'm terrified of the quiet, then yes... I guess so." Kennedy chuckled, though Diane could see the slight traces of truth in her worried eyes.

She reached over with a damp hand and placed it on Kennedy's. "I know it's hard, sweetie, but all new things take an adjustment period. By the time spring rolls around, you will be an expert bush country woman."

Kennedy laughed, and Diane grinned, going back to her potatoes.

"I hope you're right. I feel terrible for keeping Adam so busy. I need to learn to do things on my own around here, but I'm still learning, and I wake up and come downstairs and the fire is already started. I assume it's Adam because he's the only other person with a key."

Diane smiled. "It would be him. He loves this place. He loved your Uncle Neal, too. He'll take care of you as long as you need it."

"I don't want to be a bother," Kennedy sighed as she tossed her veggies into various roaster pans. "He's got plenty to do without worrying about me."

Diane moved the potatoes onto the counter and began peeling. "Honey, this is McCarthy. Everyone takes care of each other. We have to. It's not an easy life here, especially in these cold months. And Adam does not mind helping. Now, where do you plan on setting up the tables?"

Kennedy liked Diane. She was a straight talker, but her caring nature that made her as Kennedy could already tell, a great mom, soothed Kennedy's worries. "In the main room. I found several tables and chairs in the storage shed and brought them in this morning. It's the warmest room in the inn and I imagine they will all need to thaw out a bit."

"You are a sweet thing, you know that?" Diane smiled as she continued peeling potatoes. "Your uncle would be very proud of you stepping in and helping out."

"I wish I knew him better," Kennedy admitted. "Fact is, I hardly ever saw him. I can remember two times as a child where I saw him. I thought he was Santa Claus." She giggled as Diane hooted in laughter.

"He easily could have been."

"But I didn't know him. My father rarely spoke of him. And my mom would never tell me what happened between the two."

"I know, sweetie." Pity laced her voice. "He was a good man. Had a wonderful laugh and loved everyone."

"That's what I hear."

"You plan on running the inn or are you just waiting out the winter?"

"To be honest, I had every intention of showing up and selling it to the highest bidder. But the longer I'm here, I actually enjoy the solitude. There's a peacefulness to McCarthy. It's definitely not New York by any means, but it's nice all the same. And I—" She gasped and threw her hands up in the air as she hurried towards the telephone. "I have to call my boss. Oh my goodness..." Her fingers speedily dialed a number and she waited. Her face paled as soon as a voice fluttered over the line. "Mr. Parsons, this is Kennedy."

Diane continued her work, now slicing the potatoes into thin sheets as she listened to Kennedy's end of the conversation.

"I know sir, but it's a bit more remote than I imagined. The only passable road is closed due to the weather and the season. I didn't know that I would be trapped here until—"

Diane's lips tilted into a small smile as she worked, liking that Kennedy would be trapped in

McCarthy for a few months. She'd noticed the small glances and touches between the pretty woman and her son. And a mother's heart could hope, couldn't it?

"I understand." Kennedy's voice quieted. "Yes, sir. Thank you." She hung up and stared silently at the receiver.

"Is everything sorted?" Diane asked before turning around and seeing Kennedy's fallen face. "Oh, honey." She walked forward and offered Kennedy a warm hug. She gently rubbed her back. "I take it he wasn't very understanding."

"He fired me," she said, her voice barely above a whisper.

"Fired?" Diane pulled back enough to look up at Kennedy. "Well, that's not fair."

"Fair doesn't keep his kitchen equipped," she stated. She hung up the receiver. "It's probably for the best. I mean, it is a bit unrealistic for me to expect a job after a few months' absence."

"Sometimes things happen in our lives that we least expect, but yet they all turn out exactly how they were meant to. I'm sorry about your job, honey."

"Guess everyone in McCarthy will have to get used to me being around."

"I think that won't be hard to do." Diane smiled and patted Kennedy on the arm. "And it's not like you have officially quit cooking." Diane waved her arms around the kitchen.

Kennedy forced a smile. "I guess you're right."

"Now, come on. Those men are going to be hungry."
She went back to her potatoes as Kennedy forced herself to focus on the task at hand and not the loss of her job. She loved working at Petit Boutary. She'd worked the last four years building up its reputation, building a custom menu of her own recipes. She paused in her dicing to blink back tears. Her eyes fell upon the warm and inviting sitting room of the inn. The fire crackled, tables were set up with linen tablecloths, and the overall warmth of the place seeped into her heart. She'd be okay. Yes, her life in New York may be a mess right now, but life in McCarthy was just beginning. Whether she decided to sell the inn in the spring or hire someone to manage it, she wasn't sure. But for now, she was here, and she would take care of Uncle Neal's legacy. She finally realized Diane was speaking to her.

"Adam has always loved it here. Neal was his best friend. Most would say it odd for a young man and old man to be the best of friends, but Neal saved his life when he was a teenager, and since that time they were inseparable. I think it does Adam good to be able to stop by the inn and be close to Neal, even when he is gone."

Kennedy shook her head. "Wait, Uncle Neal saved his life? What happened to him?" Shelving her own problems at the moment, Kennedy listened as Diane told her more about her handsome son.

"Oh, Adam was being a young boy and accepted a dare to walk out on the ice of Kennecott River. He fell through. Neal happened to be walking by at that moment, dived in and saved him. Both almost lost their lives that day, but Neal made sure they made it back to town and we all tended to them."

"Oh my goodness." Kennedy placed a hand over her heart. "That is scary."

"It was," Diane admitted. "Needless to say, Adam learned his lesson and Neal became his mentor and friend."

"He does seem to fit in here," Kennedy stated. "Adam, I mean. He just seems to... fit."

Diane turned to hide her smile as she began kneading dough for hot rolls. "He was the child who gave us the most fits when we decided to move here. He did not want to leave Kansas. Now, Richard and I are trying to convince the kids to branch out of McCarthy, and none of them want to leave," she laughed. "Which is fine. But it's hard to create a life here by yourself." She paused, sneaking a glance at Kennedy as she worked. "If he could, Adam would probably offer to take the inn off your hands, but the inn is worth too much for what anyone has here in McCarthy."

"I'm surprised Uncle Neal didn't bequeath it to him. He was obviously closer to Adam than he was me. It was sort of a risk to leave it to someone in his family."

"Neal knew what he was doing," Diane said. "He was a smart man. He wouldn't have chosen you to inherit the inn if he did not have a reason for it."

"I just wish I knew what that was."

"Maybe you'll figure it out while you're here."

Kennedy shrugged. "So, do all your children work on the farm?" she asked.

"They do, though some of them have other jobs as well. Adam does the majority of the farm work with Richard, but he also happens to be the lumberjack in town. He is constantly fulfilling orders for firewood as well. He does not like the elderly folk trying to go out and chop down trees. So, he does it for them."

Kennedy hadn't asked specifically about Adam, but she was glad Diane supplied the information, because she did wish to know more about the intriguing man.

"I thought I might make several different pies for dessert," Kennedy interrupted, trying not to seem too interested in the information about Adam.

"I think that would be lovely. The apple pie you made Adam was sure delicious. He allowed his dad and me to enjoy a piece with him. Though he will not allow anyone else a sample," she chuckled. "He took it home with him so no one could even sneak a piece."

Kennedy smiled, and they worked in companionable silence as the day wore on, each taking turns for small moments of rest as they continued. When they heard the first foot stomps of the evening, Kennedy felt the slight flutter in her chest at seeing Adam safe and sound, but it wasn't him. She masked her disappointment so as to welcome the fellow hunters that looked exhausted. Several men walked in, all having shed their boots outside. She ushered them into the room and Diane filled them cups of hot coffee as they sat by the fire. More and more men spilled into the room from outside and Kennedy sought every face for

Adam. Her shoulders slightly fell when the last crew proved not to be him as well. "He'll be along, sweetie, don't you worry," Diane whispered as she walked towards her husband to chat about the success of the day.

Kennedy didn't flush this time, knowing full well Adam's mother knew she sought him out. The door opened, and three men stumbled in and she finally recognized Adam's heavy coat. Relief flooded over her as she dropped her dish towel to the counter and quickly made her way to him. Diane smiled behind her back as she watched.

While Adam began shrugging out of his jacket, she slipped her hands to his shoulders and helped him. He turned quickly at the contact and relaxed when he saw Kennedy's relieved face. He allowed her to hang his jacket as he slipped off his beanie and facemask. Kennedy gasped at the deep gash on his forehead. The smell of dried blood lingered between them. "What happened?" She lightly cupped his face and pulled it down towards her as she surveyed the cut.

"Took a tumble, found a tree. Nothing too bad though."

"You hit a tree?!" Her voice rose. and several men glanced up in amusement at her worry over something they considered a small affair. "Well, come in the kitchen and I'll clean it up for you."

"Kennedy, really. I'm fine." He looked longingly at the men who sat already eating.

"No, you aren't," she stated, pulling him towards a stool. She nodded for Diane, and his mother explained the buffet process to the remaining men, and they began filtering through the line making plates for themselves.

«CHAPTER SIX»

Kennedy searched in a cabinet for a small first aid kit and soaked a dish rag in warm water. She smoothed back his dark hair and lightly began wiping away the dried blood. Some had dripped down his temple and into his neatly trimmed beard. Adam hissed a couple of times, but the pain was more than tolerable if it meant her hands on his face. He watched as she worked, her gaze intent on her task. It gave him ample time to study her. Her face was lean, yet supple. Her skin looked smooth as silk, and her dark eyes were a blend of varying shades of brown and gold. He flinched as she disinfected the cut, rubbed an ointment over it, and then placed a bandage on his forehead. "I think you will live."

He smiled and cringed when he stood. His ribs had taken a beating during his fall, but the worry a scratch put on her face made him bite back the groan his lips threatened to release. Apparently, he was not as good an actor as he thought.

"What's that face?" she asked, her hands immediately swiping up and down his arms searching for an injury. "Where are you hurt? What really happened? Did a wolf bite you?"

Her questions had several men chuckling as Adam blushed at the extra stares. He grabbed her hands. "Kennedy, I'm fine. I bruised a couple of ribs when I fell. It's nothing to worry about. It just... pinches a bit."

"Your ribs? Are you sure they're just bruised? They could be broken. And what do you mean you fell? I thought you said it was just a tumble?" She crossed her arms and studied him with a narrowed gaze.

He smiled. "Can I please eat?"

His question had her face blanching. "Of course." She held her hands to her face. "I'm so sorry. Yes, there's plenty. Please, go fix yourself a plate and sit." She shuffled him towards the buffet.

"Good, because I think I was about to die smelling the amazing food and not being able to partake."

She chuckled nervously as she busied herself putting away the first aid supplies. He laid his hand on top of hers and she paused and turned. "Thank you, Kennedy."

"You're welcome." His eyes roamed over her face a moment longer.

"You better hurry before they get seconds." She nodded towards the food and he walked away.

Diane walked in carrying several empty plates. Kennedy stepping forward to help cart them. "You serve dessert, honey. I'll start the dishes."

Kennedy nodded and made her way to the table with the pies and began slicing pieces for several of the men, all appreciative for feeding them. She heard Adam laugh from across the room and watched as he and several men continued talking. "They are all happy and full." Diane's voice fluttered over her as she began gathering empty pie pans. "All because of you, sweetie."

"And you," Kennedy praised. "Thank you for the help. I couldn't have done it without you."

"I imagine you could have." Diane lightly rubbed Kennedy's back. "You're a sweet one, Kennedy Donovan. I hope you do plan on staying in

McCarthy. You fit right in." Kennedy smiled and began wiping down the counter tops and putting away the clean dishes.

By the time most of the men were heading home, there wasn't much cleaning up left to do. The Stockton brothers saw to taking down the tables and chairs and carrying them to the storage shed. Diane had packed up her leftover groceries and handed them to her husband. She wrapped Kennedy in a warm hug. "You get some rest Kennedy, you hear me?"

"You too," Kennedy ordered, making the older woman laugh and hug her again.

Finally, the inn was quiet, and Kennedy sighed.

The door opened, and Adam walked in carrying an armload of wood. He hadn't left yet. She smiled as he tossed the pile next to the fireplace and placed a few logs in the flames.

"Thank you."

"Hey, it's the least I can do." He brushed his hands on his pant legs. "Everything was delicious, Kennedy. All of the men felt great afterwards. And several mentioned how great it was to see the inn back up and running."

"That's good." She sighed as she sat on the couch and leaned her head back.

"You're tired. I'll get out of your hair."

She raised her head up. "No, please stay… for a bit, if you want," she added. "I just need to sit but would enjoy the company."

He nodded. "How about I fix you a glass of wine?"

Her eyes sparkled. "That would be amazing."

He trudged to the kitchen and poured them both a glass of wine and handed her a glass as he eased slowly to the sofa so as not to tug on his sore ribs.

She took a sip and sighed. "Yes, that is nice."

He chuckled. "You've had a full day."

"You too. Were the wolves found?"

"I believe so. Though not by me. Several men reported successful kills, but I did not see a one. Saw some tracks. Unfortunately, that's what led to my fall."

"So, what really happened?"

He told her of the tracks leading to the top of an incline and his misstep. She gasped as he continued telling her about James helping him climb back to the top."

"You almost died." Kennedy pointed at his head and he laughed.

"Not quite. It was just me losing my footing and sliding. The tree caught my fall, thankfully."

"Still. Adam, that's really scary. What would you have done if James hadn't heard your whistle?"

"Wait until someone else did. Do my best to climb up on my own. Not my first time to take a fall in the snow."

"That's so scary," she stated again, rubbing her arms as if warding off a chill.

"Kind of," he admitted.

She turned to face him, leaning her elbow on the back of the deep leather sofa and her chin in her hand. "Your mother is sweet."

He turned towards her and mirrored her stance. "Yes, she is. I'm glad you think so."

"I don't know what I would have done without her help today."

He smiled at that and lightly reached over, tucking a strand of her hair behind her ear. His fingers lingered a moment and softly brushed her cheek. Her eyes found his and Adam studied her face a moment. "I think Neal would be so proud of his amazing niece." His voice was husky and barely above a whisper as he continued his study. Kennedy flushed and began to lower her face, but he lifted her chin with his fingers. "I'm being serious, Kennedy. Thank you for today. You lifted everyone's spirits with your generosity. It was nice to see the town coming together again."

She shrugged. "It was nothing."

"Oh, it was more than nothing."

She lightly slapped his hand away and smiled. "Okay, but let's not talk about it anymore."

"Why? Does it make you uncomfortable to accept praise?" He teased.

"Yes," she stated, making him laugh.

She took a sip of her wine and enjoyed the sight of him relaxed on her couch. *Her* couch? Since when did she start thinking of the inn as hers?

"You spacing out on me?" he asked.

She blinked away her thoughts and smiled. "No, I was just thinking."

"About what?"

"Well, I handed over my list for my first big, and I mean enormous, order with your mother today before she left."

"Oh really? New boots?"

"Yes. And jacket," she pointed out.

"Good. What else?"

"A television."

He chuckled. "Bored already?"

"No, more like lonely. It's too quiet here at night. I need the noise."

He smiled at her honesty. "Well, if you keep feeding those pies to everyone, I imagine you will have lots of company."

"I think I would like that." She nailed him with her caramel gaze, and he found himself scooting closer to her.

"Yeah?"

"Yeah. I would like the company. I was thinking about maybe opening a small café here at the inn. To offset the winter months from the tourist months."

"A café?"

"Is there already one in town?"

"No. The store offers hot coffee in the morning, but that's about it. I think that's a great idea. But what about when you leave?"

Her eyes grew glassy and she turned her head so that he could not see. "I'll figure something out."

Not wanting to touch upon a sore topic, Adam eased back. "But where would you put everyone?"

She pointed to the large open community room next to the sitting room. "I figure I can move that large table out of there and put smaller ones instead. It would sit quite a bit, should I actually receive business."

"Oh, you would," he confirmed. "You sure you want to take that on by yourself?"

"Maybe eventually I could hire some help."

He watched as he saw her mapping out details in her head. "So now your pie will be available every day? To everyone?"

She giggled and slapped his knee. "You and pie!"

"It's only your pie." He squeezed her hand and brought it to his lips and lightly kissed her knuckles, the action taking them both by surprise. He cleared his throat and laid his glass on the large wooden coffee table. "I should probably go." He watched as disappointment washed over her face.

"Please, not yet," she said, tugging on his hand and bringing him back to the sofa. "I... can you tell me more about Uncle Neal?"

His brows rose in surprise and he settled back against the cushions once more. "Alright. What would you like to know?"

Her shoulders raised and then fell. "Anything really. The last memory I have of him was when I was about six, I guess. I honestly know nothing about him. And being here... living amongst his things and seeing and interacting with people he loved... and hated." As she thought of Tom. "I just... want to know more about him."

Adam smiled. "He was great." His voice held a fondness, much like his mother's when she spoke of her children or husband. A familial love that warmed Kennedy's heart. Though she did not know her uncle, she was glad he had a family who loved him, even if it was not her own. "He had the best laugh," Adam remembered, his smile spreading as his eyes sparkled. "A deep belly laugh," and loud." He shook his head. "Everyone knew when Neal was in the room. His presence instantly brought cheer everywhere he went. His joy was contagious. I rarely saw him in a bad mood."

Kennedy listened intently, her chin resting in her hand on the back of the sofa, her legs crossed beneath her. "Did he ever speak about his family? About me?" she asked.

He shook his head. "Well, not really. He never spoke to me about you. I remember once, when I was younger, asking him about his family." He paused and then his lips tilted into a small smirk. "He told me he had a brother and beautiful niece." Adam turned to her and patted her knee. "Guess now I know that he wasn't lying."

She playfully nudged his shoulder. "Is that it?"

"Pretty much. I remember asking him questions over the years, but his answers were always vague, or he would change the subject. I never quite thought to dig deeper. It was his business. Plus, most of the people in McCarthy stick to themselves. Not many families here that trace back generations. Just people who moved here and decided to stay."

"I just find it so crazy that he would leave all this to me." She motioned towards the room. "Not knowing me or anything. I mean, he obviously loved *you*. Why not leave it to you?"

Adam took a deep breath and she could tell she made him uncomfortable. "I'm sorry."

"For what?" he asked.

Nervously, she picked imaginary lint from her pant leg. "For taking this place from you."

His eyes widened. "Why on Earth would you think you have?"

Not meeting his eyes, she glanced into the cheerful flames of the fireplace. "Your mother mentioned how much you loved this place, and Neal, and I just— Well, I just feel like I may have robbed you of it somehow."

Adam shook his head. "You're Neal's family, it's only right it be passed to you."

"Family in blood, yes, but not in heart. To me, it sounds like you were his true family."

"Neal was a smart man, Kennedy. He left this place to you for a reason. He must have known you would come here and investigate the place. Maybe that's all he wanted. Maybe he just wanted you to get to know him, even if it was after he'd gone."

"But why?"

Adam shrugged. "I don't know."

She sighed and felt him take her empty wine glass and set it on the coffee table. "I should go."

"I lost my job today."

Her words had him turning, stunned. "What?"

"I was fired," she repeated.

"Why?"

She waved her hand around the place. "Because I'm trapped in McCarthy, Alaska." A small smile tugged at her lips. "Can't work in New York if I can't get to New York."

"Surely your boss understands this was all out of your control," Adam continued.

"He does, but he also can't go without a chef for several months. It is what it is. I've contacted my friend, Jerry, to take care of my apartment while I'm away, water my plants, that sort of thing."

"And he knows it may be months?"

"*She*," she corrected. "And yes."

"I'm so sorry." He reached for her hand and squeezed.

She threaded her fingers through his, liking the feel of his roughened palms and the immediate comfort she felt from his presence. "I haven't told my parents yet."

"They will not be upset, will they?" he asked.

"Not sure. I know my mother was a bit worried about me coming here this time of year. My father..." She rolled her eyes dramatically. "To say he wished I would never step foot here would be an understatement. He despised Uncle Neal, and the thought of me coming here to take care of Uncle Neal's things... let's just say that conversation was a bit tense. My mom convinced him, finally, that the sooner I took care of things here in McCarthy, the sooner they could be done with Neal Donovan."

"That's kind of sad."

"I agree," Kennedy continued. "That's what I don't understand though. My dad is all about family. He makes sure I understand how important it is. Me, him, and mom. But yet, he disowns his own brother? It's just never made sense. And from all accounts, even my mom's, Uncle Neal was a nice man. So why? What could have possibly come between them to make my dad hate him so?"

Adam listened patiently.

"Anyway," She released his hand and slowly eased to her feet. "I know you're exhausted and here I am casting all my worries on you."

He stood. "I don't mind. I'm glad you feel you can talk to me about this stuff."

"Me too." She smiled, a bit of shyness creeping into her cheeks. "Not sure why. Maybe because being around you and this place makes me feel like I'm getting to know Uncle Neal a bit."

"I'm glad."

"It also makes me think the next few months might not be so bad. Having a friend around would be nice."

He reached for her hand again and squeezed it. "I'm looking forward to the next few months. But Kennedy, I can't lie to you, and I feel like maybe I would be if I didn't say this now. I know we make McCarthy sound bleak and as if you have no option but to stay here these next few months. But you can get out, if you want to."

"What? How?" Her expression slightly brightened at his suggestion and his heart sank a bit at her eagerness.

"The monthly helicopter drops for supplies. You could always pay for passage on one. It's expensive, but they will transport people from time to time. So, if you think your boss would reconsider, you could always make it back to New York."

"Hmm." She crossed her arms and thought about it. "That's good to know. But even if I did fly back, I wouldn't be ready in time. Lisa said the helicopter comes in two days. There's no way I will have sold the inn by then. I haven't even gone through Uncle Neal's belongings yet. That's on my list for this week. And I know my boss would not give me an entire month to wait for the next helicopter. I think it's just a lost cause, I'm afraid. But thank you for telling me. No one has given me that option."

He nodded.

"And speaking of Neal's belongings," She rested a hand on his arm. "When you have some time, I would like to give you first pick of anything you might want that belonged to him. I'm not sure what to do with it all, but if there is anything you might wish to have, please, take it. I know he'd want you to have it."

Touched that she would consider him and swamped again with the feeling of loss Neal's death brought to his heart, Adam cleared his throat to bite back his emotions. "Thank you." His voice gruff, he redirected his now watery gaze towards the door. "I should go before the next snow starts to unload. My cabin is going to be freezing unless my dad took pity on me and started a fire for me on his way home."

Kennedy smiled. "About that..." She pointed towards the main fireplace they'd just walked away from. "You light that every morning, don't you?"

He flushed but nodded. "Helps heat the building."

"I know, but please don't feel like you have to take care of me. I know you have a lot of work to do and stopping by here each morning and tending to things... well, I can do it."

A bit frustrated at relinquishing his last bit of connection with the inn, Adam only nodded. Yes, he came so that she could wake up to a warm house, but it was what he'd always done. Even for Neal. Adam was always up and about early, and he saw to the fire at Neal's and at his mother's store so that everyone could start their day warm and ready to go. He saw the determination in Kennedy's eyes. Perhaps she just wanted to see if she could manage the inn on her own. He'd let her try. "Alright, but I don't mind. If you change your mind."

"I know. And thank you. You've made my welcome to McCarthy a bit sweeter than it could have been, I imagine."

He reached for the first of his layers and began dressing in his outer coats. She handed him his scarf and he wound it about his neck and tucked the tails into his coat before zipping it up. "Thanks for staying and keeping me company."

He paused in his movements and leaned towards her, his lips softly grazing her cheek. "Anytime. Thank you for dinner."

"Anytime." She echoed his sentiments and he chuckled as he opened the door and a freezing wind cut through the opening. She gasped. "Oh yikes. You sure you're okay to walk home in that?"

He nodded and slipped his face covering and beanie over his head. "Used to it," he reminded her.

All she could see were his eyes and knew he smiled due to the twinkle they held. "Be careful." He stepped out onto the porch and heard her parting farewell. "And watch out for wolves, please." Grinning, he clomped down the front steps and headed towards home.

«CHAPTER SEVEN»

All she had to do was turn the knob. It should be simple. But Kennedy stood, hand frozen over the brass handle, scared to enter Uncle Neal's living quarters. She took a deep breath and turned the knob, the wooden door creaking as it swung back, and the smells of musk and spice washed over her. *Funny*, she thought, *that she barely remembered the man, but that his scent brought back a distant memory of his smiling face.* She flicked the light on. It was an open space. A small living area with couches and recliners and a television hanging over another impressive stone fireplace. A king-sized, four poster bed sat towards her right, draped in heavy quilts and worn pillows, symbols of comfort and necessity. There was a small kitchenette, consisting mostly of a toaster oven, a coffee pot, and a small mini fridge nestled beneath the cabinets. Silence hung in the air. Empty. The room felt empty and sad, as if it, too, mourned the loss of such a man. She felt bad she did not feel such a loss, but then, she did not know him. She wasn't *allowed* to know him.

She walked further into the room to a large desk that sat on the other side of the bed. She turned on the desk side lamp and eyed the papers strung about. Notes for supplies, town issues, names of people with outstanding debts... a life summed up in papers. She pulled out the drawers and noticed files designated by a year dated at the top. Closing that drawer, she moved to the bottom one. When it opened, an ornately carved box sat in the bottom. She pulled it out and set it on the desk.

She felt slightly awkward browsing through Neal's belongings. Perhaps she should have let Adam do it. She shook her head at that thought. That wouldn't be fair to him after he'd done so much to help her already. With a sigh, she lifted the lid of the box and stopped. Staring up at her was her own face. Images of her throughout the years of her life. Newspaper clippings, handwritten letters, school portraits... any accomplishment she'd ever achieved was documented by some form of treasure. She covered her mouth with her hand and leaned back in the chair, silent, her mind racing. Leaning forward, she reached for one of the letters and felt her eyes water as she recognized her mother's delicate handwriting. She perused the ink, her mother's description of her as a rambunctious twelve-year-old was etched in perfect, accurate detail. She set it aside and eagerly reached for the next letter. Sixteen, and a full report. Another letter. Two years old, her first words, her favorite stories, things that would reside in her baby book were sent to a man she barely knew. A man who had nothing to do with her. *Why? Was there some secret she wasn't aware of?* Adam had mentioned Neal told him of a Ken. Maybe Adam knew more than he let on. Resolute, she replaced the lid of the box and hurried down the stairs. She would just have to ask him.

∞

Adam eased onto the worn sofa and rested his feet on the coffee table, tired from a long day of working alongside his dad and brothers and then delivering wood to fellow McCarthians. He'd had a long visit with the Stuarts, who lived about fifteen miles from town and survived solely on the wilderness for their needs. He made a mental note to introduce them to Kennedy. She'd be shocked to meet people who lived without electricity and preferred it. He smiled to himself as he lifted a cup of hot tea and took a sip to warm his bones. A pounding had him jostling his cup, spilling the scalding liquid down the front of his shirt. He jumped to his feet and yelped as he reached for a towel. Frustrated that someone would bother coming to his place this late in the evening, he stormed towards the door. When he opened it, Kennedy stood, her face pinched and eyes blazing in fury.

"Kennedy? What are you doing here?"

"I should say the same to you." She stormed past him into his house.

"Because I live here," he pointed out. "Is something wrong at the inn?"

"You could say that." She turned, her full anger and frustration hitting him square in the chest as she shoved a wooden box at him. Instinctively, his hands came up to snatch it before it crashed to the floor. She fisted her hands on her hips. "Mind explaining *that* to me." She pointed at the box in loathing.

He looked down. "I've never seen it before. Where'd you find it?"

"You've never seen it?" she asked, her question firm. "Ever?"

He shook his head. "Should I have? Where'd you find it?" he repeated.

He saw her shoulders deflate and with them her anger. Her eyes turned solemn as she forced herself to take a deep breath. "In Uncle Neal's room."

"Okay." Adam's brows rose for her to continue.

She motioned to the lid. "Open it."

He lifted the lid slowly as if something were to jump out at him. Confusion covered his face as he removed it further. "What is all this?"

"Exactly. What is *that*?" She stepped closer to him and gazed down into the box as he fingered over some of the photographs. "He has an entire box full of information and photos of me. Letters from my mom."

"Well, maybe he just liked to keep up with his only niece. And you said it was your dad and him who didn't get along, right? So maybe your mom felt bad for him."

"No. Something is off. An uncle would have a couple of school photos, *maybe*, but an entire box full of my entire life, play by play?! That's just weird."

Adam motioned for her to come further into his house. "Why don't you sit down, and I'll make you some tea or something."

"That'd be great." She rubbed warmth into her shoulders.

"How did you find my house?"

"Your mother," she replied. "I went there first."

"I'm surprised she didn't make you stay for dinner."

"Do I look like I want to eat right now?" Kennedy crossed her arms defensively. "I needed to see you. I didn't know if... if maybe there was something you weren't telling me about Neal."

"Like what?"

"I don't know." She rubbed her hands through her hair and growled. "I didn't know if you knew more about me or my family than you let on."

He shook his head as he slid a cup in front of her and took the seat opposite her. "Sorry."

"Don't be. I'm the one who should be sorry. I was all riled up for a fight about... *anything* and came blazing in here like a lunatic."

He grinned. "A cute lunatic."

She playfully punched his shoulder, but a smile peaked through her dour demeanor. Her tone turned serious. "This scares me, Adam."

"Why?"

"Because… I just have a feeling there's something I don't know and I'm nervous about what it could be."

"Why don't you ask your mom? These are her letters. Find out why she felt it was necessary to loop your Uncle Neal in on everything you've ever done."

"I'm not even sure how to bring it up to her. He's always been a no-no topic."

"You're a grown woman, Kennedy. You have questions. At some point she's got to give them to you." He reached towards her and she accepted his hand in hers. He brushed his thumb over her knuckles.

"I guess you're right. Well… I *know* you're right. I'm just nervous, I guess. I don't like conflict. Never have. And I feel like I may start one with my questions."

"But the answers are important to you, right?"

"Yes."

"Then they're worth asking."

She stared at their adjoined hands a moment before giving his a final squeeze. "You're right. Thank you." A sad smile washed over her face.

"You're welcome."

"I also found this." She reached into her coat pocket and withdrew a pocketknife, well-worn with age and use. "Thought you might like to have it."

Adam's eyes widened at the gift. "Neal's knife?" He delicately placed it in his hands and removed it from its casing. Flicking the blade out, he thumbed it to check its sharpness. "I used this once. *Once.*" He chuckled. "Neal had me cut the line on some fish. 'Grab my knife there, boy,'" he said, mimicking a deeper voice than his own. "'You tangled the line, you cut the line.'" He rubbed a hand over his smile as his laugh broke into a sad sob. He tried to clear his throat, thinking Kennedy wouldn't notice, but she quickly slid into the chair next to him, her arm draping over his shoulders. "He was a good man, Kennedy. A real good man." She leaned her head on his shoulder as he sniffed back tears, closing the knife and placing it back into its case. "Thank you for this."

"You're welcome."

He turned, her chin resting on his shoulder as he faced her. He leaned his forehead against hers and closed his eyes a moment to compose himself. When he leaned back, Kennedy swiped tears from her own eyes. "Well, I will get out of your hair. I came looking for a fight, and since I didn't find one here, I might as well go home."

Adam chuckled as he stood and handed her Neal's box. "Maybe another time."

She shrugged. "Not sure I could be mad at you. I was mad on the way over, but when I saw you it sort of dissipated. Not really fair."

Laughing, he shook his head. "Sorry I am hard to get mad at."

She smiled before wrapping her scarf around her face.

"That's your protection?" he asked and shook his head in dismay, grabbing one of his face masks off a hook by the door.

She shook her head. "I am not wearing that."

"Necessity trumps style out here, Kennedy."

Rolling her eyes, she removed her scarf. "Fine." She slid the face mask on and he grinned.

"Don't laugh," she murmured behind the fabric. "And this smells like sweat."

He shrugged, his grin making her bite back a laugh. "Okay, I'm going now. I left my ATV running, because I was afraid I wouldn't be able to start it again."

"I could have helped you."

"Not if I was mad at you."

"Ah, I see. Good point." Adam chuckled as she swung herself onto the now snow-covered seat.

"See you tomorrow?"

"You can count on it."

"If you come by early, I'll feed you breakfast."

"You do not have to twist my arm."

She tilted her head and studied him a moment. "I really am sorry I came in such a fuss. I appreciate your honesty with me. See you in the morning." She kicked the clutch and set out back towards the inn, her driving full of choppy movements and hesitant turns. Placing a hand over his heart, Adam shook his head as he smiled and headed back inside to warmth.

∞

Kennedy sighed as she tucked the tabs of the cardboard box and squared away more of Neal's clothing. It still felt odd going through his belongings. *And sad, too,* she thought. A life boxed away and moved aside so a new person could step into your role. *Or pretend to*, she thought, thinking how inadequate she felt for the part. She lifted the box and carried it down the stairs and set it on one of the foldable tables she'd brought out from the mudroom. She then unboxed it and displayed the clothing as best she could. Five tables full of clothing, trinkets, bedding, odd pieces of furniture. She'd tried to comb through as much as she could and make up her mind on what to keep and what to give away. When the box was empty, she turned to head back up the stairs to fill it again. She hoped her method of sifting through Neal's life did not rub the locals the wrong way, but it was a necessary task. And now that she would be here for a few months, if not longer now that she lost her job, she would need to convert his small apartment into her own home, so as to keep all the rooms vacant for potential paying customers.

Uncle Neal lived modestly, not that he could not afford nicer things, because he could. She'd noticed that when looking over his books. The inn was in exceptional financial shape. Even with a harsh winter ahead, and no job, Kennedy had no fear of her finances now that she'd inherited what Neal had left her. The inn could use some updates and Uncle Neal had left more than enough for her to have the luxury of doing as she pleased. For that, she was grateful, especially after placing her first order with Diane. The helicopter would arrive tomorrow, and she could not wait to receive all that she'd purchased.

"Kennedy?"

A voice called from downstairs, and she stepped to the top of the stair landing. Adam stood in the front entry, his boots covered in snow as he waited patiently on the rug. She studied him a moment, enjoying the fact he'd stopped by to see her and the way the snow lightly dusted his coat and beanie. He slipped the beanie off and his thick black hair tumbled forth and she felt her stomach tighten as his green eyes flashed up to her. He smiled, and she felt herself float down the stairs.

"This is a nice surprise," she greeted, clearing the bottom step and setting the half full box on the nearest table.

"What's all this?" He motioned to her impromptu rummage sale.

"Well, I'm doing as you suggested and going through Neal's things. Sifting, so to speak. This is all the stuff I thought people might want to look through before I send it off to be donated." She saw his jaw flex and his eyes darted about the room. "Of course, I was going to let you have first pick of anything you may want. You and your family."

Those pained green eyes flashed back to her. "Thanks." His voice was gruff with mourning as he took a step towards one of the tables and ran his fingers over one of the many plaid shirts she'd folded. "Still smells like him."

"I noticed that too. I don't know much about him, but I do know he loved butterscotch candy. Only because I found several in some of the pockets as I folded his jeans and shirts."

She heard a small snicker that ended on a cough as if he tried to hide a sob. His back to her, she saw him rub a hand over his mouth as he reached a worn-out ball cap on the table. Lifting it, he flipped it over and rubbed his thumb under the seam. A small piece of paper fluttered out and he unfolded it. Kennedy watched as his tough exterior slowly crumbled and his shoulders started shaking. She reached him in two strides and wrapped her arms around him as he eased himself to the floor in utter despair; raw pain that could not be masked as he cupped the back of his head and bent his head between his knees. "I'm so sorry," she whispered, soothingly, as she lightly kissed his shoulder. "So very sorry, Adam."

He reached up and squeezed one of the hands that surrounded him before taking a deep breath. He finally raised his face and she tenderly brushed away what tears remained. "So sorry for your loss." Kennedy wasn't quite sure what else to say or do. Here she sat, the actual relative of the man that had died, and she felt nothing but a sense of awkwardness. And then here sat Adam, a friend, a man bereft over her uncle because he was able to have the relationship with Neal she'd only dreamed about as a girl.

"He was a great man, Kennedy." His mouth tightened as he attempted to hold back his emotions. "I know... I know I keep saying that, but he *really* truly was. In ways, he was more a father to me at times than my own dad." He motioned towards the ball cap. "That's my hat." He forced a small smile as he reached for it again and the note. Clearing his throat, he opened the slip of paper and handed it to her. Scrawled in sloppy handwriting was a note that read, "*Don't be such an old man.*"

"He gave me that hat for my 16th birthday," Adam continued. "See, when I first moved here, I had an old Kansas City Chiefs ball cap that I wore everywhere. I refused to take it off. I was so angry at my parents moving us here that it was sort of my symbolic gesture of letting them know that I wasn't over it all. Neal would tease me about it. Always pretending like he didn't know who the team was or that he was as stupid as I thought all the McCarthian people were at the time. He finally wore me down one day. We went fishing and the wind kicked up, my cap blew into the river. There was no saving it. I tried so hard to catch it. Soaked myself through and through swimming as best as I could, but the current was too strong, and the hat just drifted out of sight."

"Did you ever find it?"

"No. To say I was even more bitter after that would be an understatement. Anyhow, I climbed out of the river, and Neal slapped the seat next to him and handed me my fishing rod as if nothing happened. I sulked. I huffed and puffed, kicked the dirt. He finally said, "Don't be such an old man. It was just a hat. You can always get another one. A better one.""

Adam smiled at the memory. "I didn't want to hear that at the time, but over the next few months, I slowly forgot about the hat. I'd go fishing with Neal often, and each time we'd tease each other. He always thought I was too serious. That I acted like an old man. So that's what he'd always say to me. It sort of became his way of teasing me from then on out. When he gave me that hat, he wanted me to have a constant reminder that I was young and meant to have some fun. So he put that note into my cap, a cap I wore all the time, so that I would not forget."

Kennedy gently folded the note again and grabbed the hat. Finding the small rip in the seam, she tucked it back in there. She handed it to him. "You should keep this then," she tugged it onto his head.

"I lost this, you know. About six months ago. I didn't realize he had it. He must have held onto it to regift it to me. He did that every now and then as a joke." He pinched the bridge of his nose as he closed his eyes. Kennedy immediately went back to rubbing soothing circles on his back.

"I don't think it's the only thing he planned to give you." She stood and walked over to a long and narrow wooden box. It was carved in Neal's detailed handwork. "It has your name carved under the clasp," she pointed out. "I haven't opened it. But this was taped to it." She handed him a small card.

Adam took a shaky breath. "Geez." He exhaled. "This is not how I planned for this visit to go."

Kennedy smiled and lightly brushed his hair aside so as to see his face better. He turned, and she tapped the top of the box with her finger. "You going to leave me hanging?"

He chuckled and opened the card. "An old man doesn't need all these toys. Merry Christmas,

Kiddo. Love, Neal." Adam shook his head. "He must have intended to give this to me for Christmas."

Kennedy reached for the box. "Then I guess we should wait." She pulled the box off his lap and his mouth dropped open. "Wait, what?"

"If it's meant to be a Christmas gift, then a Christmas gift it shall be."

"But—" Adam gawked as she walked the box towards her front closet and hefted it onto one of the shelves.

"It's really heavy. I wonder what's in there." She walked back to him and extended her hand down to him. Taking it, he rose to his feet.

"Kennedy—"

"Don't Kennedy me," she said and took the note from his hand. "Seems Uncle Neal had a plan for your gift. I think it would be important to him for you to receive such a gift on Christmas. And since I obviously will not be going anywhere until the spring, I can make that plan come to fruition." She gently rubbed his arm. "Alright?"

His eyes held hers. "Alright." He looked at the cap he still held in his hands. "I at least have my hat."

She smiled, and he leaned towards her, lightly kissing her cheek. "Thank you, Kennedy."

Flushing slightly at his nearness, she diverted her gaze to the rest of the room.

"And I apologize," he began.

"For what?"

"For... kind of losing it for a minute." It was his turn to blush, and she shook her head.

"You do not have to apologize for that. At all. You loved him. And well... I'm glad someone did."

Adam nodded and cleared his throat once more. "Right, well... wow... so I didn't come here to crack on you. I actually came to steal you away for a bit."

Her brows rose. "Oh?"

"I thought you might like to take a trip with me. I need to run some supplies out to one of the outlying families and thought you might want to ride along. We could grab dinner or something while we're out."

Kennedy grinned. "I would love to."

"Great. Well, suit up then. It's freezing out there."

"Literally," Kennedy said, as she hurried up the stairs to her room. "I'll be right down."

«CHAPTER EIGHT»

Adam browsed through the tables holding Neal's possessions and felt the sting of more tears behind his eyes. *Enough*, he told himself. He already lost his head with Kennedy once today, he didn't need to pawn his emotions on her for a second time. It was hard enough coming to the inn every day and Neal not being here. But to see his stuff scattered about up for the taking... it made Adam's heart sink. The truth that he was in fact gone and not just... away. The loss was still fresh, even after the last several months of trying to adjust to life in McCarthy without him. He grabbed a couple of Neal's shirts, ones he could use for himself. There wasn't much else he needed or wanted... except for the wooden box in the front closet. He wondered what Neal could have possibly placed in there. He also wondered if

Kennedy would let him have Neal's fishing gear, and his boat... she probably hadn't gotten to those yet. He heard her footsteps coming down the stairs, her high heels clicking. He grinned.

"I thought you knew it was freezing?" he asked.

"It is. That's why I'm wearing this sweater." She motioned to the pale blue number she wore and pointed towards the door. "And borrowing Uncle Neal's huge jacket until my new one comes on the helicopter tomorrow."

"And what about your feet?" he pointed towards the black stilettos.

"We'll be in your truck, right?"

He shook his head and her eyes widened. "We're walking?"

He laughed. "No. ATV."

"Oh." Disappointment washed over her pretty face. "Alright. I'll just change into my boots."

"That'd probably be best."

"You sure we can't take your truck... you know... with the heat?"

He laughed, and he caught her grin as she slipped on a pair of Neal's wool socks before climbing into her boots.

"Unfortunately, my truck is too big for some of the trails we will be taking."

"Of course it is," she stood, and Adam held out the coat for her to slide her arms into. When he rested it on her shoulders, she turned and offered a warm smile. "You know, despite the fact I know I'm going to be miserably cold, I'm still looking forward to it. Perhaps McCarthy is growing on me."

Laughing, Adam shook his head. "We'll see how you feel afterwards."

"You mentioned dinner though, right?"

"I did."

"Then that's something to look forward to. A warm meal after a cold drive."

"Let that be your mantra."

She grinned as he opened the front door. The cold gust of wind swept right through her and she groaned. He wrapped an arm around her shoulders as he led her towards his ATV. She stopped in her tracks. "It has a trailer on the back."

"Actually, it's a sled. But yes. That's how I'm carting the supplies."

"A sled?" Kennedy walked towards the ATV and stared at the attached sled in wonder. "I've never ridden in a sled."

"Maybe on the way back you can sit back there."

She looked at him with horror. "Not by myself."

He laughed at her lack of bravery. "Alright. Then it's on the ATV with me." He swung his leg over and sat, patting the seat behind him. She hopped on without further invitation and wrapped her arms around his middle.

"At least you'll block most of the wind."

Adam pulled down his face mask and cranked the engine. As they pulled through the street, Lisa stood on the porch of the store and waved as they passed by. When he reached the edge of town, he pulled through a small clump of trees and the temperature dropped even further as they slowly drove their way through the forest. He felt Kennedy shaking behind him, and she held on tight... almost too tightly, as they traveled, but she never complained. He steered towards a clearing on their right and turned down a smaller and narrower trail. He stopped a moment and let the ATV idle. Kennedy raised her head from the middle of his back and rested her chin on his shoulder. "Is something wrong?" He held a finger to his lips as he killed the engine. Silence surrounded them. "What's happening?" she whispered, her grip around his waist growing even tighter. He pointed towards the ground and the sets of tracks that looked like dark holes in the snow-covered ground. "Wolves?" she whispered.

He angled his head and grinned at her, though he realized she couldn't see because his face mask covered his mouth. He pulled it down. "No. Rabbit."

"Oh."

"We'll take a minute," he slid from the seat and reached into the back of the sled and pulled out his rifle. Her eyes widened as she watched him load five bullets.

"You're going to kill it?" she stepped off the ATV and walked towards him.

"Come on." He took her hand and slowly followed the tracks, quietly making his way through the brambles. He held a finger to his lips as he pointed towards a downy rabbit.

"Oh Adam, no," Kennedy squeezed his hand.

Though she protested, she continued to follow him, stepping where he stepped and keeping quiet. He knelt behind a tree and rested his shoulder against the trunk. He cocked the hammer back on his rifle and aimed. The rabbit was about fifty yards out and he heard Kennedy's steady breathing as he focused. He squinted down the barrel of the gun and took one last deep breath and pulled the trigger. The blast of the gun echoed in the woods and the rabbit dropped where it stood. He heard Kennedy gasp, but she remained still. He turned, beaming. "And now we have dinner."

Her brows rose into her hairline. "Dinner?"

He laughed as he stood, helping her to her feet. "Come on," he reached the rabbit and held it up, noting Kennedy's hesitancy, he bit back a smile. "You okay with this?"

She took a calming breath and nodded. "Just not every day that I hunt for my food. I typically prefer grabbing the plastic-wrapped version at the local grocery store."

He chuckled. "Welcome to McCarthy," he added, and she lightly shoved his shoulder.

"When you asked me to dinner, this is not quite what I envisioned."

He grimaced. "Did I ruin it for you?"

"Verdict's still out." Her honesty had him nervously running a hand over his face as he dropped the dead rabbit in the back of the sled. "Depends on how great your culinary skills are to take that adorable ball of fluff and turn it into something appetizing."

"You're the chef," he reminded her. "Do you not have rabbit recipes?"

"Not off the top of my head, unfortunately."

"We'll cook it together then," he hopped back onto the ATV and Kennedy slid behind him. He twisted in the seat to study her a moment. "Did I ruin our trip?"

She rested her chin on his shoulder, their faces close. "Not if you can get me out of this cold soon."

A relieved smile washed over his face as he nodded. Pulling his facemask back into place, he started the ATV and set out further into the snow.

∞

A light flickered in the window as they approached a wood-framed cabin nestled amongst snow-covered trees. A small shed was built next to it, smoke rising from several chimneys. The house boasted a large chimney as well, and it promised the warmth Kennedy needed. Adam pulled the ATV to a stop in front of the porch and a tall, lanky man stepped out. He was close to their age, though the lines on his face made him seem older. He smiled in welcome and yelled over his shoulder into the house. He closed the door as he shouldered his coat onto his lean frame. When he reached Adam, he slapped him on the shoulder in a friendly pat before bringing him in for a hug. "Good to see you, Stockton."

"Thought I'd make the rounds before the blizzard hits."

"You're right on time then. Corinth thinks it's to hit tomorrow," the man's eyes carried over towards Kennedy. "And who'd you bring with you?"

"Ah," Adam walked towards Kennedy and placed a hand at the small of her back as he nudged her forward. "This is Kennedy Donovan. Neal's niece."

The man's eyes flashed a touch of surprise before he extended a hand and shook it heartily. "Nice to meet you, Ms. Donovan. My deepest sympathies for your loss. Neal was one of a kind."

"Thank you."

"Chad Stuart." He introduced himself and smiled as the door opened and a very pregnant woman stepped out onto the front porch, her thick blonde braid draped over her shoulder and resting on her rotund belly. She waved to Adam in greeting. "Hurry up, Stockton, don't you know it's freezing out?"

Adam chuckled as he walked forward with Kennedy. "Corinth Stuart," the woman greeted by intercepting Kennedy and leading her inside. "Welcome to our home."

"It's beautiful," Kennedy stepped inside and noted the warm fire and various oil lamps settled about the great room to give light. She saw no lamps, television, or hanging light fixtures. The furniture was worn, but comfortable, and a large basket sitting next to a wooden rocker held balls of yarn in various colors and textures. "Would you like some tea?" Corinth asked.

"That'd be wonderful."

"We heard the gunshot and I put the kettle on then. I knew the only person mad enough to brave this weather was Adam Stockton." She walked over to the now whistling kettle and poured four steaming cups of hot water. She placed a tea bag in each one and brought one to Kennedy.

Her hands, though frozen, clasped the hot mug. "Heavenly," Kennedy whispered in thanks.

Corinth smiled. "You're a brave woman making the trek all this way. How did he convince you?"

"He said he would take me to dinner."

The woman's right brow rose as she smirked.

"Little did I know that was to be the rabbit he shot."
Corinth laughed. "You must forgive him, Kennedy. Poor Adam hasn't had much practice in the art of dating. He lacks... finesse. As do most of the men around here actually. They don't get out much," she grinned as she took a sip of her own tea. "I'm sorry about Neal." She added soberly.

"Thank you. I... didn't know him very well, but I'm starting to."

Corinth pointed towards Adam out the window. "He's the best one to tell you about him. They were close."

"I've noticed that," Kennedy's eyes softened as she watched Adam begin unloading the sled with Chad.

Corinth's lips spread into an easy smile. "He's a good guy."

Kennedy's eyes fluttered back to the woman in front of her and noticed the woman's grin. She flushed. "Oh, um... yes. He is. He's helped me out a lot lately."

Corinth tilted her head. "Where are you from, Kennedy?"

"Manhattan."

Corinth's eyes widened as she laughed. "Well, then yes, I imagine McCarthy has been an eye opener for you."

"Yes. In many ways," Kennedy admitted. "I had only planned to stay for a few days, but it would seem Mother Nature had other plans. I also am to blame, because I did not do enough research before traveling here. If I had known the conditions, I probably would have waited until spring."

"Ah, but then you would have missed out on the most beautiful time of year," Corinth motioned towards the heavy snow that began to fall. "Dangerous weather at times, but also the most beautiful."

"It is pretty. Though I will admit I was ill-prepared. But Adam's mother has helped me order what I will need."

"Diane's great, isn't she?" Corinth asked.

"She's wonderful. The entire Stockton family seems to be."

"They're a McCarthy staple, that's for sure," Corinth tilted her head in greeting as her husband and Adam came into the house stomping the snow from their boots as they entered.

"I hate to cut this trip short," Adam began. "But the snow has really started coming down. We should head back while we can."

Disappointment settled over Kennedy, but she set her mug on the side table.

"You're not going anywhere until you have some tea," Corinth pointed to the two extra mugs. "It's too cold out for you not to warm up for a bit."

Adam obeyed and retrieved one of the mugs, Chad taking the other as they came to sit down. Adam sat next to Kennedy and smiled. "Corinth trying to convince you she needs a hospital?"

Corinth narrowed her eyes in mock disdain. "I'll have you know I have finally come to terms with my delivery options here in McCarthy Prosper."

"Have you now?" Adam asked and then laughed at the stubborn tilt to Corinth's chin. "Did Corinth tell you she is a former city girl as well?"

Kennedy perked up at that and looked to the woman for a response. "Indianapolis," she admitted. "I fell in love with a crazy man with a charming smile and somehow allowed him to convince me to move to bush country Alaska. How? I will never know."

Chad laughed as he leaned down and kissed the top of his wife's head. "It was my incredibly good looks."

She slapped his thigh as he and Adam laughed in unison.

Corinth rolled her eyes. "These two are insufferable," she looked to Adam. "Kennedy says you've been educating her on McCarthy life."

Adam warmly gazed at Kennedy and gently tugged on her ponytail. "Trying to."

"If it weren't for Adam the inn would not be what it is today," Kennedy bragged. "He kept it up and running until I arrived." She reached over and squeezed his hand in thanks. He linked his fingers with hers, and Corinth and Chad shared a sly smile as they watched. "I look forward to keeping it that way."

Chad perked at her news. "So, you plan to stay in McCarthy?"

"For now. Things in New York have... stalled, and the inn needs me. I'd like to see more of McCarthy before I make a final decision."

"Smart woman," Corinth toasted her mug towards Kennedy and grinned. "I like her, Adam. Don't scare her away with rabbit stew, you hear me?"

Adam grimaced as Kennedy flashed him a quick horrified look. "And that officially ruins my dinner plans," he blushed under everyone's scrutiny.

Chad laughed. "Here." He walked towards the fridge and pulled out a clear container holding raw meat. "It's already been cured. I'll trade you for the fresh one."

Adam accepted the container in thanks.

"Now I'm a little nervous," Kennedy fretfully laughed as Corinth smiled.

"You're nervous?" Adam challenged. "I'm the one cooking for a chef."

"A chef?" Corinth asked eagerly. "Now that is awesome."

Kennedy shrugged. "Former chef. I was just fired."

"Only because you're trapped here. Not for lack of talent," Adam pointed out. Kennedy nudged him with her shoulder, but his compliment warmed her. "She makes the most amazing pie."

Kennedy laughed and shook her head. "You and pie."

"*Your* pie," he explained further. "It's phenomenal." He looked to his friends as if to prove his point and Kennedy just stared at him as he spoke, her eyes warming.

"We expect to sample it soon then." Chad said.

"I'll need a pie after having a home birth," Corinth cringed as she shifted on the sofa, a hiss escaping her lips as she readjusted her sitting position. Chad hopped to his feet and assisted her as best as he could.

"I'll bring you a dozen," Kennedy promised. "Because I cannot imagine what you're going through or will go through."

"It will be easy," Adam waved his hand in dismissal, but he winked at Corinth as she tossed a throw pillow at him. "Kill him, Chad. Just kill him now and save me the strength." She looked up at her husband and he grinned.

Adam stood to his feet. "On that note, we should probably head back now. For my own safety, as well as Kennedy's." He gently brushed a hand over Kennedy's hair and she felt the thrill of the contact rush down her spine. She stood to her feet and allowed him to help her back into her coat.

"Thanks for letting us visit. It was nice meeting both of you."

Corinth slowly stood to her feet, Chad helping her hoist herself up. "Pleasure is ours. We loved Neal, and I'm glad to see he has a fabulous niece. You guys don't be strangers." She hugged Adam and whispered something in his ear before she hugged Kennedy.

Adam handed Chad a satellite phone. "If you need it."

"Thanks." Worry etched his forehead as he walked them outside. "I know I put on a brave face for her sake, but I'm still a bit freaked out about it all."

"If you need us, use it, Chad." Adam told him again. "We'll come as fast as we can."

"I know. Thanks. Kennedy, it was so great to meet you. I hope you enjoy McCarthy and that this guy doesn't scare you off. Corinth needs a friend."

"She's wonderful," Kennedy linked her arm around Adam's waist. "And this guy would have to try really hard to scare me away."

Adam looked down at her and his green eyes sparkled in pleasure as she gazed up at him. She felt a shift in the air, and his eyes turned serious as he began inching closer to her. Her breath came in puffs, the effects lingering in the frosty air around them. Chad cleared his throat and had them hopping away from one another. Adam avoided eye contact as he swung his leg over the ATV and Kennedy nestled behind him. They offered waves to Chad who stood biting back an all-too-pleased smile on his face as he waved them off.

∞

Kennedy released a loud sigh of delight as they stepped back into the inn. "Electricity!" She did a happy spin and Adam chuckled as he carried the container of meat to the kitchen. She sobered and followed after him. "Are you preparing our feast?"

"I planned on it. Hungry?"

"Starving," she admitted.

He smiled. "Good. Because, Ms. Donovan, this rabbit stew is going to rock your world."

"Is that so?" she leaned onto the counter next to him as she watched him set about chopping vegetables and tossing them into a pot.

"You going to study my every move?"

She blinked. "Sorry," she playfully grimaced. "I think I will go stand in front of the fire a few minutes. I still can't feel my toes." She started to walk away, and he grabbed her hand, gently tugging her back towards him.

"Thanks for being a good sport this afternoon."

She squeezed his hand and smiled. "It was fun." Releasing his fingers, she grabbed a blanket off the back of a chair as she eased onto the floor in front of the fire.

She fit there, he thought. The flames catching the deep red streaks that hid beneath her auburn hair. Her creamy skin glowing. For her to be so displaced, she fit perfectly. He wondered if Neal had planned this. Did he know she would indeed come? Did he plan for them to fall in love? He choked on his last thought and shook his head. Whoa. "Slow down, Stockton," he whispered to himself. But as he watched her, he did indeed feel his heart trip inside his chest. Come spring, how would he feel if she left? *More than disappointed,* he realized. He thought he sensed something growing between them, but he didn't want to rush her. She was new to *everything* here in McCarthy. She may end up hating it, especially once she experiences a long winter. A blizzard was blowing in as he cooked, and that alone could change her mind. The helicopter came tomorrow, and she said she wasn't leaving on it. But his heart prepared itself for disappointment. When she saw her way of escape, would her mind change?

She looked up and caught him staring. She shyly smiled and stood, starting to walk around the tables she'd set up with Neal's belongings. She grabbed a few thick flannel shirts that were still in good condition. Walking to the kitchen, she opened a drawer next to him and retrieved a pair of scissors.

"What are you doing?" he asked curiously.

"I was just thinking about Corinth and the baby." She began cutting the shirts into large squares. "I have tons of flannel shirts at my disposal and a new baby will need a warm blanket, right?"

Adam set his knife down and listened.

"My mom has made what are called 'rag quilts' before, and I think I remember how she did it. I think it would be helpful for Corinth and Chad to have for the baby. What do you think?"

Adam's smile turned tender. "I think it's a great idea, and a sweet one."

"You don't mind if I cut up a lot of Uncle Neal's shirts."

"Not at all. It's what he'd want. He'd want them to be useful to someone else."

She grabbed a few more shirts and brought them to the small dining table inside the kitchen and sat down as he continued preparing the stew. They worked in companionable silence and a knock sounded on the door. Tom Higgins stepped inside, his face flushed in worry.

"Mr. Higgins?" Kennedy rushed forward and led him further inside. "What's the matter? Is everything alright? You're as pale as a ghost. Adam." She looked to him in a panic as Tom collapsed onto a stool.

"Tom," Adam's voice was calm as he approached the older man.

"Jasper. He's gone," Tom's eyes flicked towards Adam and he just shook his head. "I think, I think wolves got him. There was blood. So much blood. I can't find him."

Adam looked to Kennedy and she rushed away to make a cup of coffee for the man.

"I'll help you look."

"The snow's coming so hard right now, I lost the tracks. I couldn't tell wolf from dog."

"Let me get my coat," Adam walked towards the door and Kennedy ushered by him forcing Tom to take the mug of coffee. She then walked towards Adam and began helping him snap up his coat. Her eyes held worry. "I'm sorry, Kennedy." He whispered. "But that dog is pretty much all he has."

"Don't worry about me," She waited as he slipped his gloves on. "Come back when you're done. No matter the time. I'll have you something warm to eat and drink."

"It might be a while." He warned.

"I don't care," her eyes searched his and he saw the worry underneath. Worry for him. And worry for Tom and Jasper.

He leaned forward and lightly pressed his lips to hers. It was quick and meant to be reassuring, but he ached for more. He pulled away quickly so as not to get distracted by the matter at hand. He looked to Tom. "Let's go find him."

Tom stood to his feet, lost in the beginnings of grief for his beloved pet. Kennedy patted his shoulder as he passed by. "Be careful," she reached for Adam's hand one more time. "The blizzard, Adam."

"We'll be fine. It's not supposed to hit until tomorrow night," he kissed her knuckles and followed Tom out the door, their boots crunching in the fresh snow.

It wasn't exactly how he'd planned his evening with Kennedy, but Tom needed him. Jasper was the only light in the man's life. Yes, his son Kirk came to McCarthy to trade every now and then, but their relationship wasn't exactly stellar. Jasper was the only companionship for Tom since his wife died. And life in McCarthy was hard without some sort of companion. He thought of Kennedy and the sweet, but too-quick, kiss he'd given her before he left. That thought alone warmed him to his toes as he neared the boundary behind Tom's cabin and the woods beyond. He saw the blood against the white snow, what little had yet to be covered by the fresh powder. He heard Tom's boots behind him. "I tracked it through here." He led the way and Adam kept his eyes to the ground in hopes of some clue as to where the beloved dog had ventured off to.

«CHAPTER NINE»

Kennedy rested her head against the back of the couch, her eyes growing heavy as she slowly began to doze off. It was now passed midnight, and Adam had yet to show up. He and Tom had been looking for four hours. *At what point did they give up?* She thought about Tom's devastated face and prayed they found the sweet dog, for all their sakes. She pulled the blanket tighter around her and then bolted to her feet as a rustling sound hit the front door. She grabbed the fire poker and hurried towards the front of the inn. It was probably Adam, remembering him stacking wood the first night she'd arrived. She heard it again and then a high-pitched whine. She peeked out the window and saw a lump of fur on the mat. Jasper. She gasped, unlocking the door. Sad eyes looked up at her. The dog turned his head and she saw the split in his fur as his wound oozed blood. The rest of the blood was frozen to his fur. "Sweet boy," she cooed. "Come on inside." She waved him forward and he took a slow step, limping, before collapsing to his belly. She rubbed a gentle hand over his head and he whined again.

She had no way of contacting Adam. She didn't quite know what to do. She rushed inside and grabbed a large towel. She tucked it under the dog, who had just enough energy to raise his belly and paws for her to slide it under him. She then grabbed the end of it and began to pull him inside, the towel sliding easily over the wooden floor. He whined as he made it over the rough threshold, but he didn't move as she slid him towards the warmth of the fire. She patted his head. "Okay, boy. I'm going to help you, but I don't know what to do, so you're going to need to be brave for me, okay?" he looked at her with pain-filled eyes.

She rushed towards her medicine cabinet and found a low-grade pain killer. She knew this type of medicine could be used on animals, but she also knew it was not going to be strong enough for the poor dog. But it would have to do. She wrapped it in a slice of cheese and he nipped it from her hand. She then fetched her first aid kit along with a bottle of rubbing alcohol. She didn't know the dog well enough to know if he'd bite, so she reached for her boots and unlaced one. She then wrapped it gently around his jaws to hold them together. "Sorry boy," she murmured. "I just need you to relax and keep those teeth to yourself." She gently patted his head. His eyes were droopy, and she hoped it was due to the medicine and not the loss of blood. She swished a bit of alcohol on his wound and he barely flinched. She took that as a good sign that she should work fast. She'd never treated a wound of this magnitude, nor an animal, but she figured basic first aid techniques applied. She would also do her best to stitch him up, should he hold still for her.

She drenched the wound in alcohol and cleaned his fur. She was then able to see the extent of the wound. He'd been bitten, it looked like, and his skin ripped. But nothing that looked life threatening, unless he lost too much blood or infection occurred. She hoped the freezing temperatures helped him with both of those issues. She strung some thread through a needle and inhaled a deep breath, attempting to relax the tension that had settled between her shoulders. She gently poked his skin with the needle and he didn't move, his breathing was slow and steady, and his eyes were closed. She'd take advantage of his comatose state as much as possible. She completed one stitch and then had to take a calming breath again, a tear sliding down her cheek. "You can do this, Ken. You can do this." She chanted to herself and sniffled back more of her rising emotions. Her hand shook, but she forced herself to focus and continued weaving the needle and thread through Jasper. When she'd finished, she set the needle aside and rinsed the wound area with alcohol once more before rubbing an antibiotic ointment over it. It wasn't pretty, but it was the best she could do. She then took one of Uncle Neal's old shirts and tenderly wrapped it around the dog. She untied the shoelace around his snout and kissed his nose. She gathered up her supplies and carried them to the mudroom. She then walked to the kitchen and began scrubbing her hands. Her blue sweater was stained with blood and covered in fur and would most likely need to be tossed away, but if she could keep Mr. Higgins' dog alive, it would be worth it.

She heard the knob on the door turn and her eyes flashed up to find Adam and Tom walk inside, both with defeated expressions. Adam froze, his eyes roaming over her appearance. He dropped his supplies and darted around the bar in a panic. "What happened? Are you okay? Where are you hurt?" He cupped her face and confusion at her calm gaze had him pulling far enough away to survey her once more.

"It's not mine," she said looking down at her bloodied top. She looked to Tom as he still stood by the door. "Jasper turned up." She nodded towards the fireplace and both men hurried over to the large, sleeping dog. Adam knelt beside the oversized dog and rested a hand on Jasper's side.

"I cleaned him with alcohol. Looks like he was bitten. Nothing too bad, I don't think. I didn't see any marks in his muscles," she reported. "His skin was torn and bloody, but I think I stitched him up enough."

"You stitched him?" Tom asked, eyeing her.

"Yes sir. I'm sorry. I didn't know what else to do. I was afraid if I didn't, he'd keep bleeding. I gave him some light pain killers, nothing too strong. But that might be why he is sleeping. I'm really sorry, Mr. Higgins." The night's events rushed over her and she started to cry. Adam rose to his feet and wrapped her in a tight embrace. "I tried to save him." She sniffled. "But I don't know if I did."

Tom's eyes grew glassy and he turned back to his dog. He unwrapped the torn shirts and checked the wound. Adam surveyed the expertly sewn stitches as well without leaving Kennedy's side. Tom then wrapped the dog back up. He stood and rubbed a shaky hand over his mouth before he spoke. "Thank you, Ms. Donovan."

She nodded, afraid if she spoke, she'd crumble into a fit of tears again, more out of stress relief than fear.

"Couldn't have done a better job of it myself," he complimented.

"I wasn't sure…" Kennedy looked to Adam again, their faces close. "I hope he's going to be okay."

"You gave him his best shot," Tom nodded firmly, his composure slowly sliding back into place. "I appreciate everything you've done for him. You certainly didn't have to do it. Especially for me."

Kennedy opened her mouth to speak, but Tom silenced her with a firm glare. "It's no secret by now, I'm sure, that your uncle and I did not see eye to eye. He was a stubborn fool most of the time, as was I. But, if I'm being honest, I kind of miss that." His eyes carried around the room and back to Kennedy. "You're a good woman, Ms. Donovan. Kind. Even to an old man who doesn't deserve it. I thank you for tending to Jasper for me."

Adam shook Tom's hand as the older man placed his beanie back on his hand. "Mind if I let him stay here for a bit? He's probably more comfortable here than at home."

"He's free to stay as long as necessary," Kennedy told him. "We'll update you if anything changes."

He nodded his thanks and in farewell. When he closed the door, Adam pulled her into another tight embrace and she finally felt herself relax.

∞

He woke to a wet nose pressed against his cheek and a pair of joy-filled eyes as Jasper licked his face in good morning. He'd slept on the couch at the inn to watch over the injured dog, who now, seemed pleased as a peach he had company. Adam patted Jasper's head as he eased into a sitting position and noticed fresh logs had been added to the fire. He looked around but did not see or hear Kennedy. "Where is she, boy?"

As if he knew the answer, Jasper looked to the door.

"Out, huh? Bummer," he glanced at his watch. It was half past nine. He should be out working by now. He wondered why Kennedy didn't wake him. He walked towards the back room where some of his stuff still remained and was pleased to see a change of clothes still sitting in the drawer of the dresser. He then quickly brushed his teeth and ran his fingers through his hair. Not the best, but he was at a bit of a disadvantage now that he actually lived at his own house. He needed a shave, but he'd take care of that later. He was eager to find Kennedy.

He walked up the street and spotted several faces out and about, the sun briefly shining before the next round of snow blew in and with it, the dreaded blizzard everyone had been preparing for. He spotted Kennedy's coat through the window of his family's grocery store and smiled. He stomped his boots on the landing before entering to the ring of the bell above the door. His sister glanced up and a knowing smile crossed her face. "Hey there, sleepy head. I hear you are a hero."

Adam's brow furrowed. "What for?"

"Helping Tom," she motioned towards Kennedy at the back of the store talking with his mother and rolled his eyes.

"She's the real hero. So what time is the helicopter arriving?"

"In a few," she glanced at the clock on the wall behind her. "About a half hour."

"What's that?" he pointed to a suitcase and cast a nervous glance towards Kennedy.

"Clothes. What else is a suitcase for?" Lisa grinned as Kennedy walked up with Diane.

"Hey," Kennedy gave him a small hug. "Glad to see you rested."

Adam rubbed a hand over the back of his neck and nodded. "Thanks for letting me crash at the inn."

"No problem. You were exhausted. I think Jasper liked having you there. He seemed pleased this morning," she smiled, and her eyes danced. "I'm so thankful he's okay."

"You did a great job," he squeezed her hand. "You going somewhere?" he nodded towards the suitcase.

"Oh, that," she curled up her nose a bit as if she didn't want to tell him what she was about to say. "I hope you are not upset with me."

"You're leaving," he finished and tried to hide his disappointment, but he felt his heart already begin to ache. Sighing, he grabbed her hand and pulled her away from his mom and sister to a corner of the store so as not to be overheard. "I thought you were going to wait out the winter?" he asked. She opened her mouth to respond and he wouldn't let her speak. "The café at the inn? The plans to change Neal's apartment? I don't understand. What changed your mind?"

Kennedy's lips tilted into a small smile. "Are you going to let me answer now?"

Frustrated, he waved his hand for her to speak.

"I'm not leaving."

"What?" he asked, his color slowly returning back to normal.

She giggled. "I'm not leaving." She grabbed his arms and gave him a small shake to loosen him up and he relaxed with an embarrassed grin. "I packed all the remaining shirts of Neal's and am donating them to your dad and brothers. Your mom is going to take them home and let them choose what they want."

"You said I'd be upset," he pointed out.

"No, I said I hope you weren't upset because I wasn't sure if you were done picking out what you wanted first."

"Ah," he felt somewhat foolish, but he liked the way she slid her hand in his. "I just saw your suitcase and... got a little worried."

"You think?" she winked at him and he avoided her gaze a moment as she chuckled.

"I brought a ton of luggage. If I were leaving, I'd be taking it all back with me." She pointed out.

"True. I just wasn't sure, with the helicopter coming today and all. Misread the situation." He rubbed his thumb over her knuckles and suddenly became very aware of his mother and sister staring at them. He dropped her hand. "I need to head to work. Unless you'd like me to help you retrieve your helicopter order?"

"I think I can manage," she leaned towards him and kissed his cheek, her creamy brown eyes swallowing him. "I'm glad you'd be upset if I left." She whispered, and then her cheeks deepened in color as she took a step back so he could leave. It was hard for him to look at her and not pull her back into his arms. But they had an audience. And second, he reminded himself, he didn't want to scare her away by what he was feeling. Yes, she seemed to be tossing signals that she had feelings for him as well, but the thoughts in his head were for long term. And he wasn't quite sure if Kennedy was on the same page yet. Until he did know for certain, he was going to keep those feelings under wraps as best as he could.

"Did you need something, Adam?" his mother called to him, her pleased expression not going unnoticed.

"Just checking on Kennedy and grabbing some coffee," he pointed to the machine in the corner and Lisa held up a cup already filled for him. "Ah," he stepped around Kennedy and took the warm drink. "Let me know if you need any help," he told all of them. "I'll be up the path there chopping more wood."

"Will do, honey," Diane all but nudged him out the door. "Now go. You already have a late start to the day. Best chop as much as you can before the blizzard hits."

His eyes flashed to Kennedy one more time before he reluctantly stepped outside. Kennedy took a couple of steps towards the window and watched him as he made his way towards his brothers. A small smile rested on her lips as Lisa and Diane grinned at one another in hope.

∞

"Perfect timing," Lisa called as the sound of the helicopter filtered through the air. She tugged Kennedy away from the window and towards the coats. They quickly dressed and made their way outside. "You'll want to meet, Mick. He knew your uncle really well. And since you'll be taking over the inn, it's best to know your best supplier."

Kennedy nodded and watched as a wiry man in his early fifties climbed out of the chopper. He was dark headed, with a bit of gray tinging his temples, and he had a smile so large it encompassed most of his face. A single silver hoop hung in his ear. Overall, Kennedy thought him a handsome man with a friendly disposition. Lisa made the introductions and Mick sized her up. "Well, I'll be. Neal told me you'd come along one of these days." He held the clipboard out to Diane and she signed her name. "You're a lot prettier than he described, I bet you have the men of McCarthy standing a bit straighter these days."

"Just one in particular," Lisa chimed up with a grin.

Mick's face split into a smile as he began unloading crates and carrying them to the porch of the store. Lisa and Diane began helping, so Kennedy jumped right in. "You plan on staying in McCarthy, Ken?" he asked, his familiarity sounding as if they were old friends.

"For now. I'm going to sample an Alaskan winter and go from there."

He laughed. "That's a right smart idea. If you can survive the winter, you can survive just about anything up here. Looks like you got good people to guide you through it." He nodded at Diane and Lisa.

"They've been extremely helpful. In fact, most of these crates are probably for me."

"Well, anything you need, you just let Diane know and she'll get it to me."

"I appreciate that, Mick."

"And if you have the need to travel, I don't offer it to many people, but if you're needing to wrap up some things back home and need a lift into Anchorage, I can get you there."

"That might be handy as well. I'll keep that in mind."

They set their crates on the porch and Diane began doing her inventory of supplies as they continued to unload.

"Don't be giving her too many ideas, Mick. We plan on keeping her," Lisa warned him.

Mick chuckled. "I don't blame you. You married, Ken?"

She flushed and shook her head.

"Well, looks like Lisa here's got some competition now. I feel rather smitten."

Lisa playfully punched his shoulder. "Mick's just a big flirt, Kennedy. Pay him no mind."

"She says that only because she doesn't take my proposals seriously."

"Your twenty years older than me, Mick."

He shrugged. "You're only as old as you feel."

Kennedy smiled at that and he wriggled his eyebrows.

"Never trust a pilot," Lisa warned in a stage whisper. "You can't tack their boots to the ground."

Mick laughed heartily as he lifted two crates and walked them over to the porch.

Kennedy paused as she heard the sounds of chopping taking place. She envisioned Adam competently swinging his axe and felt the slight shove as Lisa walked by her and winked. "It will be an early day for them with the storm coming," she pointed towards the horizon, mostly blocked by mountains, but the dark grey clouds hovered as if just waiting until they'd reached the right heaviness before unleashing their load.

"First blizzard," Mick walked past them and grabbed several bags of what looked to be potatoes and carried them towards the store. "Best get ready to hunker down for a week or so."

"That long?" Kennedy asked. "How much snow are we talking about?"

Lisa shrugged. "Depends. Dad says it's supposed to be a bad one. You may not be able to make it out of the house for a couple days."

"It gets that high."

"Can," Mick agreed. "I'll be curled up with a warm cup of coffee."

"You live near here, Mick?" Kennedy asked.

"Nope. I'll be nice and warm and not snowed in over in Anchorage." He grinned. "But you ladies, you tough McCarthy women, well now… that's another story. Be brave, Ken," he winked at her as he accepted the clipboard back from Diane. "I'll see you in a month." He hopped back into his seat and slipped on his head gear. He gave one last friendly wave before slowly rising back up into the air and flying out of sight.

Kennedy felt a slow wash of peace flood over her. That was her last escape route out of McCarthy and she didn't leave. And somehow, she felt okay about it. She'd found that she actually hadn't missed New York that much. Her friends, yes. Her work, somewhat. But Manhattan? She sighed as she walked towards the store, her hands tucked into her elbows for warmth. She missed her lunches with her mom, but she'd be calling her tonight any way. Though she was sort of dreading that conversation. She planned to ask her mom about Neal's mysterious box of all things Kennedy. A sinking feeling settled in her stomach whenever she thought about that box. But she needed to know. She had to find answers to why Uncle Neal would choose her as his heir. And if an awkward phone call with her mom was the only way to do it, then so be it.

"Come on, Kennedy," Lisa gestured towards several opened boxes. "Your new wardrobe has arrived."

Smiling, Kennedy hurried into the store, thankful that her toes, most of all, would now survive a McCarthy winter.

∞

Adam shuffled into his cold cabin and prepped his fireplace and lit a fire. He was going to dart to the inn one last time before coming home, and he did not want to come home to a cold house. Again. He also wanted to shower before he saw Kennedy. He made quick work of that task and was out the door in less than a half hour. The first waves of snow were falling and by the time he reached the inn, his jacket had at least an inch on his shoulders. He brushed it off and stepped inside, slipping his feet out of his boots. He heard Kennedy on the phone and she turned from her seat on the sofa and offered a brief wave. He motioned that he wouldn't bother her and would be in the kitchen. Whatever she had cooking smelled incredible, and he realized she'd set the large dining hall table for a crowd. *Who was she cooking for?* He wondered.

"I know that, Mom," Kennedy's words carried over to him and then he spotted the carved wooden box sitting on the coffee table. "What I don't know is why Uncle Neal would have this and why you would send him such detailed information about me. Something's weird. You're not telling me everything."

Adam walked back towards the door and began slipping on his boots. He knew Kennedy probably wouldn't want someone eavesdropping on the conversation she was having. To his surprise, he felt her grip his hand. Her cheeks were flushed, from either frustration or her small sprint towards him at the door, he wasn't sure. He looked up and studied her worried expression. She pressed a button on the phone and a feminine voice fluttered nervously over the speaker. "Now, sweetie, your father and I feel this conversation is best discussed in person."

"And when will that be, Mom? In case you haven't noticed, I'm snowed in until spring. And the next helicopter ride isn't for another month."

"Your father will think of something. Don't fret on it though, honey. Just enjoy Alaska. Sounds like this Adam fellow is a really nice man. Perhaps he can be your friend."

Adam grinned and Kennedy rolled her eyes as she shoved him. "He's okay."

He feigned a hurt face and she bit back a smile as she tried to remain serious. "Let me know as soon as you and Dad discuss a plan to come. I would like you to see this place. It's really something."

"I hear it in your voice," her mom sighed. "I always wanted to see McCarthy. Your Uncle Neal always spoke so highly of it." Her mother's voice sounded almost whimsical, Adam noticed.

"We'll let her know," Kennedy's father's voice barked in the background and he did not sound happy about their conversation.

"Yes, sweetie. I'll call you as soon as I know something. Okay? Have fun with your dinner." They exchanged farewells and Kennedy hung up, tossing the phone on the counter.

"They won't tell me anything about the box. Just makes it even weirder. Like there's some big secret." She sighed and then offered him a genuine smile of welcome. "I was hoping you'd come by. Want to stay for dinner?"

"Looks like you have plans."

"I do. But it would be kind of weird if you didn't stay."

"Why's that?" curious, he looked down at her hopeful smile.

"Because your family is coming over," she laughed at his surprise. "Your mom's idea. That we all needed a feast before the blizzard hit and we'd have to go a few days without socialization. I think she's worried about me, to be honest." Kennedy linked her arm with his and led him further into the kitchen. "It's not rabbit stew, I'm afraid, which, by the way, wasn't that bad."

"You tried it?"

"I did. After helping Jasper, I was starving, and I didn't want it to go to waste."

He grinned. "And?"

"And it had an interesting, but decent, flavor. My compliments to the chef." She squeezed his arm and they stood a moment holding one another's gaze. He brushed a finger over her smooth cheek and she smiled. "You didn't even say anything," she whispered.

"About what?"

She waved a hand over her clothes and it was then he noticed the fleece-lined, buffalo plaid shirt she wore over her usual fitted jeans, but with thick wool socks that were not her Uncle Neal's. "Your clothes," he added. "Are new." She nodded in approval at his observation. She darted towards the door.

"And look," she hoisted a heavy jacket over her shoulders and then struck a pose. "My new jacket." The sleeves were a bit long for her, and the jacket swallowed her up, but she looked cute parading around in her "McCarthy Wear" as she called it. He grinned as she then lifted her new boots. She had chosen the most stylish pair in the catalog, expensive ones at that, but they'd serve her well.

"I think," he walked towards her and began buttoning up her jacket. "I need to see it all together." He pulled the new facemask off the hook and pulled it over her head. She coughed as her hair flew in her mouth and he laughed as she tucked her hair out of the way and her eyes sparkled out at him. He couldn't see her mouth, but he knew she was smiling. He pulled the bottom portion of the mask down to reveal her bright smile and he was tempted to press his mouth to hers, but a knock sounded on the door and interrupted the moment. As Adam's family walked into the room, Kennedy removed her facemask with gusto.

"That's the coat?" Lisa asked. "Looks good. A bit big, but warm."

Kennedy did a small spin before taking it off. "I was just showing Adam that I am now fully prepared for a McCarthy winter."

"That you are," Diane patted her arm as she crossed into the kitchen and set two pans on the counter. Clearly his mother and Kennedy had planned a mighty feast indeed. His mom swooped by him and kissed his cheek on her way to the table. "Oh, Kennedy, this looks absolutely lovely. Look Richard, look at these place settings."

"You are all my guinea pigs," Kennedy admitted. "I was thinking of this for when I potentially open the café."

"Wonderful," Diane slid into a chair and waited for everyone else to join her.

"Need some help?" Adam asked Kennedy.

"Yes, please." She ushered him into the kitchen and he watched as she pulled out two roasting chickens fully dressed and ready for serving. The incredible smell wafted over him and made his mouth water. "Take those to the table?" She asked.

He nodded and set about doing as she asked. When he placed them on the table, his mother beamed at him. "She's a real gem, Adam," she whispered. "You'd be smart to keep that in mind."

His brothers chuckled softly as Adam blushed under his mother's weighted gaze.

"Diane," Richard warned quietly. "He's his own man. Let him be."

Adam just shook his head as he walked back to the kitchen. Kennedy handed him a platter of green beans and followed behind him with mashed potatoes. She set them on the table and Adam pulled out a chair for her. She smiled in thanks and waited until he sat beside her before addressing the table. "I have a request for you all. And please, feel free to tell me it's a bad idea if you do not think it wise."

"Go ahead, honey," Diane invited, already scooping helpings of food on her husband's plate.

"I would like to host a Christmas party here at the inn for everyone in McCarthy." Before anyone could respond, she continued. "I know it's a couple of months away, but I figured that would give me enough time to get the word out, buy supplies, and plan." She nervously wound her hands in her lap.

Diane's face split into a warm smile. "I think that would be a lovely idea."

"Has it ever been done before?" Kennedy asked.

Everyone shook their heads.

"Well, we would have a few friendly meals around the holidays, but nothing that ever encompassed the entire prosper. That would be so wonderful. We'd love to pitch in."

"Oh, I don't want you to feel like you have to. Uncle Neal left me... well, there's plenty for me to do this. I just thought that if it's my first and only winter in McCarthy, I wanted to make it memorable."

"Only winter?" Lisa asked. "You don't plan on staying?"

Kennedy shrugged. "Not sure. I just thought if I don't, it would be something great to look back on. If I do stay, then maybe it will be the start of a new tradition."

"I like that idea better," Adam admitted, taking a sip of his water. Kennedy's brown eyes fell on him and she gave him a quick peck on the cheek.

"Me too," she whispered before turning back to his family.

"We can help you decorate," Lisa chimed in and clapped her hands excitedly. "And cook too, if you want?"

"That'd be great."

"Then it's settled," Diane looked to her husband and he nodded in agreement.

"I think it will be great for McCarthy," Eric encouraged. "We don't really take the time to be social unless it's work related."

"That's true," James agreed. "Will be nice."

Kennedy reveled in their acceptance of the idea and she gripped Adam's hand under the table. He gave it an encouraging squeeze.

"Now, can we sample these birds?" James asked. "Because it's killing me here." He looked down at the giant chicken sitting directly in front of him. Laughing, Kennedy nodded and bowing her head, waited to start carving until Richard's rich baritone voice had finished saying grace.

«CHAPTER TEN»

Kennedy enjoyed the Stockton family. They teased one another, and shared with her about their work and other people in the town she'd yet to meet. Every time she was in their presence, they went out of their way to make her feel welcome and comfortable. She dried the last dish and placed it in the corresponding cupboard. "I think," Diane said, "that it is time for us to head out. The snow is falling hard now." She reached for Kennedy and hugged her, resting her hands on her shoulders. "Now, you remember what Richard told you about the chimney?"

"Yes," Kennedy replied. "Not to leave the chute all the way open or snow may fall in and then I will be without a fire until it dries."

"Yes. And the wood pile is well-stocked?"

"Yes. Adam saw to that," Kennedy flashed him a grateful smile.

"And if the electricity goes out?" Diane drilled.

"Then I am to sleep down here in front of the fire."

"And water?" Diane continued.

"Mom," Adam gently tugged his mom away from Kennedy. "She's heard you. I'm sure she already wrote everything down." He winked at Kennedy and steered his mom towards the door.

"I'm just worried about leaving her. This is going to be a bad one and we are too far to come help her if something were to go wrong."

"She'll be fine. I'm not that far."

"You better not even think about venturing out in a blizzard, Adam Stockton, or I will have your hide."

He kissed his mom's cheek. "Night, Mom."

Diane cast Kennedy one more worried look, the look only a mother could give, and Kennedy felt her nerves start to unsettle. *Surely, she would be fine.*

Lisa crossed her arms. "What if I stayed here?"

Kennedy and Diane looked to her in surprise.

"Then Kennedy won't be alone, and I wouldn't either. I mean, my cabin isn't far, but at least we'd have some company."

"I'd like that," Kennedy admitted.

"I'll go grab some clothes then and be back within the hour." Lisa hugged her mother and hurried out the door.

"That will be nice," Kennedy admitted to Adam. "I was getting a bit nervous now that all of you are leaving."

He pulled her towards him and she willingly stepped into what was now a comforting embrace. She felt his breath stir her hair. "I'm not that far. If you need anything, I can be here in minutes."

"I'm not going to call upon you in a blizzard, Adam."

"If you need me, you will," he waited until she nodded before pulling away. "I'll just head o—" His sentence never finished due to an ATV pulling a small sled breaking through the tree line. It headed straight for them. Lisa sprinted back from the direction she'd gone when she saw who it was. Chad pulled to a stop in front of the inn, his face full of terror. "Something's wrong." He nodded towards the sled and Corinth, covered in blankets, writhed in pain. "She needs help."

Diane hurried towards the sled. "Boys," she called to James and Eric. "Get her inside. Gently now. Lisa, prep one of the downstairs beds. Kennedy, boil some rags. Adam, see to Chad. Richard," she turned towards her husband and he kissed her. "I'll fetch your bag." He told her and she nodded and hurried inside, helping to support Corinth as the two brothers helped her walk into the inn.

Chad's pale face held horror. "Let's get this into the shed." Adam told him, pointing to the ATV. Chad nodded, the menial task taking his attention away from his wife and giving him a few minutes to compose himself.

"We'd struck a compromise," he explained to Adam. "When her water broke, she grew more nervous about the idea of having the baby at the house by ourselves. So, I agreed I'd bring her here to town just in case we needed your mom. We were already on the way when the contractions started. But then..." he paused a moment. "Something's not right, Adam. She's in too much pain."

Adam's brow wrinkled.

"I mean, it's more than just the contraction pain."

"Well, you guys made it at the right time. My mom is here to see about her. Come on, let's get inside." He closed the door behind them and Chad hurried towards the first room on the bottom floor behind the stairwell. Kennedy busied herself in the kitchen doing exactly as his mom had asked. He walked towards her and gently rested a hand on her shoulder. She turned, her eyes glassy, but no tears fell. "I'm boiling some scissors as well. Won't they need those to cut the cord?" She asked. "I don't have anything else to help."

"It will be fine. My dad went to fetch my mom's bag."

"Bag?"

"My mom was a nurse for years before coming to McCarthy. She's sorted of acted in that capacity ever since."

His words instantly relaxed her. "That's so good to hear," Kennedy smiled nervously. "I wish I had known that for Jasper."

"Tom already had her look him over, and she was impressed with your skill."

Kennedy rolled her eyes. "I feel less impressive at the thought of a baby being born under my roof."

He smiled. "It's going to be an eventful night."

"Will you stay, Adam?" she asked. "Please don't leave. I can't imagine all of this happening and not having you here." She waited anxiously as he pondered her request.

"I'll go fetch some clothes from my cabin. I need to put the fire out as well. I'll be back in a half hour. Chad will need the company, I'm sure."

"Yes, that was my thought as well," She gripped his arm in thanks, though she also knew she would need his strength not only through the birth of Chad and Corinth's child, but also the storm.

He squeezed her hand and then lifted it to his lips. "I'll be back in a bit."

She nodded and watched him leave as Lisa darted into the kitchen. "It's almost go time." She grabbed what towels Kennedy had ready. "Mom said she needs you in there. We need to support Corinth's legs while Chad sits behind her supporting her back. This baby is coming!" She beamed and sang the last words as if cheering. Kennedy smiled and hurried after her.

∞

Adam made it back to the inn just in time to see his dad step out of the bedroom and shut the door. Chad paced the living room.

"What are you doing in here?" Adam asked.

"Corinth banished me. Apparently, I was too..." he waved a hand around in search of the word, "annoying."

Adam chuckled. "Everything okay?"

"Yes," relief settled over his friend's features. "The baby was breach, but your mother was able to turn it. Now it should be fine. Or so she says."

"Good."

"I can't imagine having done this at home. I'm such a fool for even asking it of her."

Adam patted his shoulder. "No, you're not. It's the life you two have chosen and Corinth was all for it. Maybe she sensed something was wrong and that's why she asked to come into town. Either way, you two came here and everything is going to be just fine."

"You're right. I know you're right. I just— if anything ever happened to her, I don't know what I'd do." Chad sat on the edge of the sofa but hopped to his feet as he heard a loud cry come from the bedroom. Adam placed a hand on his shoulder to keep him in the living room. Corinth's screams carried further and became stronger and Adam inwardly cringed on her behalf. He could not imagine what Chad was feeling.

A few seconds later, a shrill baby cry filtered through the air. All color drained from Chad's face as relief and joy had him smiling like the fool he claimed to be. He sprinted to the bedroom door.

"Get in here you idiot," Corinth called him on a sob. "Come see our baby girl."

"A girl?" his voice held wonder as he stepped forward as Diane finished tending to his wife. Lisa and Kennedy smiled in welcome as they moved away from the bed to give them a moment.

Kennedy helped Diane to her feet. "I will give you a few minutes and then be back in." Diane told them.

The couple nodded and then were lost in their new happiness.

As Kennedy rounded the corner, she saw Adam and ran towards him, throwing her arms around him and squealing. "It's a girl!"

He laughed and spun her around before settling her back on her feet. "She's gorgeous, Adam. Absolutely gorgeous. And so tiny."

She looked up at him and wrapped her arms around his neck. "Thanks for coming back."

Diane sat on the couch and accepted the cup of tea from her husband. "I'll be fine. The baby is fine, and the new mommy is fine," she beamed. "I'll need to stay here." Richard pointed towards a small suitcase he'd brought along with him with her medical bag.

"I'm taking James and Eric with me. Adam is staying here." He pointed towards his son and Kennedy.

Diane smiled. "It will be good for him to stay. Chad will need the company and Kennedy will need his presence through her first blizzard."

"I checked the inn. Adam has it prepped and ready for the storm. You should all be fine. We'll take care of things at the farm."

She cupped his face and kissed him on the lips. "That's a good man. I've left several stews in the refrigerator. Should the electricity cut off, you can warm them over the fire." Richard kissed her in return. "That's a good woman," she winked at his cheekiness as he stood to leave. "Before you go, move these tables into the main dining room." She pointed to Kennedy's spread of Neal's things. "Have the boys help you."

He nodded, and they made quick work of moving them out of the way. Kennedy watched and held a hand to her forehead. "I didn't quite think about the mess."

Adam pulled her hand down. "Don't worry about it. They just know we will be spending a lot of time in front of the fireplace and want to give us more room for everyone."

"I should put on some coffee," Kennedy slipped away and busied herself in the kitchen doing more than making coffee. He saw her begin the stages of baking something. He hoped it was pie, but he knew it was her way of saying thank you to all who would be staying with her through the storm. He had to admit he was glad things turned out how they did, because he did not want to leave her to fend for herself. Now he could be here for her and the inn. His mom slipped her arm around his waist. "She did wonderful in there. Calm. Collected. I think her presence helped keep Corinth calm as well. They seem to be a good fit."

"Yes, they hit it off well."

"She'll be thankful you're staying."

"She is," he admitted. "As am I. I hated the thought of her being scared by herself."

Diane's smile softened. "Neal would be proud of you and how you've seen about her."

"I wish I could say it was only out of obligation." Adam watched as Kennedy slipped a dish into the oven.

Diane grinned and patted his cheek. "She's a sweet one. Lots of unknowns for her right now, but you don't have to be one."

"I don't want to pressure her into staying if she ends up wishing to leave." Adam ran a hand through his hair and over the back of his neck.
"You've got a few months yet," Diane told him. "Plenty of time to win her over to McCarthy."

Adam chuckled at his mom's confidence. "And to me."

"Oh, I think you've already done that." Kennedy glanced up and her eyes immediately gravitated towards him, her dazzling smile melting him. "See." His mom added and gently squeezed his arm before walking back towards Corinth's room.

Kennedy eased onto one of the couches and patted the seat next to her.

"So, you've made a friend out of Tom Higgins, you've saved a dog's life, you've helped bring a baby into this world... tell me, Kennedy Donovan, is there anything you can't do?" He asked as he eased onto the cushion next to her.

She laughed and shook her head. "I will admit I feel as if I could quite possibly conquer the world." Her smile wavered as the first fierce winds hit the windows of the inn and whistled. "Well, maybe."

Adam draped his arm around her shoulders and snuggled her into his side. She rested her head comfortably against his chest. "It will be over before you know it."

Lisa emerged and sat on the couch opposite them giving her brother a smug smile as her eyes darted to an aloof Kennedy. "I think I want to have a million of them." Lisa announced.

"A million what?" Adam asked.

Kennedy's head turned to listen to his sister as well.

"Babies," she stated confidently and had them all laughing. "I mean, the pain looks like it completely sucks, but that little girl is amazing. Her little fingers and toes." She held hands to her face. "So stinking cute."

"You realize she will grow up, right?" Adam asked.

Lisa rolled her eyes. "Yes. But think of all the fun they will have while she's small," she sighed. "I need to find a man."

Adam choked on the sip of his coffee and Kennedy patted his chest on a laugh. "There's always Mick," She reminded Lisa.

Lisa wriggled her eyebrows as Adam seized in a fit of coughing. Kennedy patted his back. "Good 'ol Mick," Lisa said. "Seriously, if he were twenty years younger, I would totally consider him."

"Does he have a son?" Kennedy asked.

Adam swiped his hand through the air. "Whoa, why are you even encouraging that idea?" He looked at Kennedy in surprise. "You've met Mick, right?"

Kennedy shrugged. "Yes. And he was nice. Funny. Handsome."

"Handsome?" surprise lifted Adam's brows.

"Yes," Kennedy admitted, and Lisa agreed.

"Plus, he wears those tight jeans," Lisa pointed out and Kennedy nodded in agreement.

"What?" baffled, Adam's gaze bounced between the two of them as they giggled like school girls. "I didn't realize Mick was such a catch."

"And he flies a helicopter," Lisa continued. "That's kind of sexy."

Kennedy nodded. "That is true."

Adam just shook his head and closed his eyes. He felt Kennedy playfully poke his side and his lips twitched into a grin. "Though *this* guy can handle an axe like it's nothing."

Lisa rolled her eyes. "Right, yay, Adam knows how to chop wood. We're talking about a helicopter here, Kennedy. A giant, helicopter." She held her arms out as if to encompass the room.

"And he can shoot a rabbit."

"Big deal," Lisa baited. "I can too."

Surprised, Kennedy sat back impressed. "Well then... I give up. I didn't realize that was a common skill." She sat back up quickly and held her finger in the air. "Oh, I have one. Annnnnd," she continued, "he cooks a mean rabbit stew."

Adam threw back his head and laughed, gently tugging on her ponytail as Lisa bit back a grin herself. He threw his arm around Kennedy's shoulders and pulled her to him, kissing her temple. "Thanks."

Winking up at him, she rested her head against his heart. He found his younger sister's gaze and grinned proudly as she hopped to her feet. "I'm going to pick out a room. Enjoy your snuggles with my culinary artist brother."

He felt Kennedy chuckle, but she didn't move away when Lisa left. Instead, she tilted her head up to look at him again. He felt her lips lightly graze his jaw and they fell into a comfortable silence staring at the flames in the fireplace.

∞

Adam sat on one of the stools at the bar, sleepy-eyed next to a half-asleep Lisa as Kennedy finished preparing the breakfast casserole she'd planned to feed everyone. All were weary. Not only did the blizzard keep everyone awake, but so did the new baby. Kennedy's limbs felt sluggish as if every movement required climbing out of quicksand. She slept more than the others, but she woke throughout the night to terrifying sounds of wind and trees snapping. She'd slept in Neal's apartment on the third floor and therefore did not hear the baby crying throughout the night. Adam and Lisa on the other hand, were on the first floor and within earshot. Kennedy refilled their cups of coffee. Adam grunted in thanks as Lisa just eyed it with loathing only because it meant she would have to move her hand from beneath her chin to reach for it. The extra effort was not worth it at the moment. Adam sighed as he stood and stretched his back. "I'm going to make the rounds and see how much snow we have outside." He shuffled to the door and groaned as the baby let out another cry.

"I take it back," Lisa whined. "I don't want a million babies anymore."

Kennedy chuckled as she slipped from around the bar to walk towards Adam and help him with his coat. She hadn't realized the moment it became her routine, but she liked that it was something he allowed her to do. As if it were a special and brief moment for them to share before going their separate ways. An excuse to be close to one another. Well, that's how she saw it any way. She straightened his collar as he reached for his gloves on the entry table, her fingers lightly brushing his neck. "Breakfast is almost ready," She told him.

"I won't be long. Just want to move some wood around. Clear a path to the shed just in case we need to reach the ATVs for any reason."

She lightly brushed his hair from his forehead her fingers lingering as they brushed his lightly bearded cheek. "You should be sleeping still. Lisa told me you guys were up almost all night."

"While you slept like a baby," Adam taunted.

"Actually, I don't think that saying is very accurate." Kennedy giggled. "Considering I slept and the baby did not."

"Good point. I'll try to catch a nap or something today. It's not like we can do anything with all this snow out."

"That's true," Kennedy looked out the front window of the inn and gasped. "Oh my." McCarthy was covered in blankets of snow. She couldn't even see where the road had been. The inn's porch held at least two feet along it's front awnings and steps. The wind continued to rain down flakes, the skies not promising any signs of stopping. "It makes me want to run and jump in it. It looks so smooth and soft."

Adam grinned as he opened the door and stepped onto the porch. "Might want to put on your new clothes before doing that or you'll freeze before you get the chance." He reached for a shovel he'd brought up the day before, and Kennedy thanked the heavens again for his preparedness and willingness to take care of the inn. "Give me a few minutes and I will come help."

"I'm fine. No sense in us both getting cold."

"I want to," She told him, her eyes serious.

He paused in his scooping and nodded. "Very well then. I'll be here or working my way towards the shed."

Kennedy sprinted back inside. "Lisa," the sister still sitting at the bar now seemed more alert as she topped off her coffee with cream. "Can you take the casserole out of the oven in five minutes?"

"Is there a timer set? Because I'm terrible about that sort of thing."

"Yep," Kennedy pointed to the small apple-shaped timer on the counter. Lisa shot her a thumbs up. "Thanks. I'm going to go help Adam." She ignored the sister's sly smirk as she donned her new coat and boots. Reaching for a beanie, she slid it over her hair and wrapped a scarf around her neck. When she stepped outside, Adam was already to the side of the building, slowly making ground in creating a walkway towards the shed. The snow was an impressive two to three feet deep. "Is there an extra shovel?" Her voice had him jolting in surprise and she bit back a smile as she approached him.

He pointed to the side of the inn and she saw he'd placed one there for her. She grabbed it and began scooping beside him. "I've never seen snow like this. It's beautiful."

"Can be."

"We should make a snowman."

Adam looked at her and laughed. "A snowman?"

"Yes," beaming, she leaned on the top of her shovel. "It's the perfect type of snow."

"And it would be covered up by tomorrow."

Disappointment fell over her face. "Oh. That's a bummer." She grabbed a handful of snow and packed it together in her hands into a perfect ball. "See. It holds together. Imagine how big a snowman we could make."

He shook his head as he continued scooping. She tossed the snowball at him and it shattered against his shoulder. He turned in surprise. "What was that for?"

"For being a party pooper," she grinned as she began shoveling again.

"A party pooper? I'm being a realist." He pointed out. "I'd hate for you to go through all the trouble of building a snowman and he just disappear in the next wave of the blizzard."

"But you're forgetting something."

"And what's that?" Adam asked, his brows arching as she took a step towards him and smiled with a mischievous gleam in her eye.

"All the fun we would have," Kennedy's breath fanned out in a frosty puff as she stood only inches from Adam. His green eyes were vibrant amidst the startling white surroundings, and she couldn't help but wish he would take the time to build something as foolish as a snowman with her. Because all she wanted to do was spend every second she possibly could with him.

"Maybe once we're done shoveling a path," he went back to work and Kennedy rolled her eyes behind his back.

"And don't be sassy about it," he said, without turning.

"Wha— How did you know I was being sassy?"

He laughed. "I could sense it."

She grabbed another handful of snow and quietly packed it together. "Well, sense *this*," she tossed it hard towards the middle of his back, but he turned at the last second, the snowball landing right in the middle of his chest. He tossed his shovel aside and ran at her. She squealed as she tried to gain traction to flee, but he grabbed her around the waist and tossed her into one of the fresh piles they'd shoveled. She landed in a cold cloud of fluff, Adam landing next to her, grabbing snow and rubbing it against her cheek. She swiped her hands in defense as he laughed. Her hand grappled around her side and she felt the slush in her hand before slapping it over his face in revenge. He nudged her hand aside and pinned it beside her head, her other arm trapped by her side. He looked down at her, his body sheltering her from the current snow fall as it grew heavier by the minute.

A flake landed on her lashes and she blinked it away. Adam's eyes grew serious as he studied her face. All she wanted was for him to close the gap and kiss her. She couldn't remember the last time she'd ached for a man's kiss. But with Adam, it's all she could think about since the moment she'd met him. When he'd given her a peck on the lips before helping Tom find Jasper, she'd been slapped with complete awareness of him. Only him. When he shifted so as to stand, she gripped the lapels of his coat and those radiant eyes found hers again. "Please kiss me," she whispered, inwardly cringing at being so bold. Thankfully, Adam didn't make her repeat the request. His lips, surprisingly warm despite the weather, found hers in a gentle, patient caress. The tenderness flooded through her veins, heating degree by degree until her hands lost themselves in his hair, and their pace quickened. He hijacked her senses, her chest pounding, as she tried to satisfy the longing in her heart.

"So, the timer didn't go off," Lisa's voice drifted from the porch, followed by a short. "Oh. Wow... Um..."

Kennedy reluctantly pulled her lips from Adam's and turned her face towards his sister. Lisa wore a cheeky grin as she crossed her arms expectantly. Adam glanced over at his sister, he and Kennedy both wearing a new shade of scarlet that they'd soon blame on the cold winds instead of the passion of the moment. "Anyways," Lisa continued. "I went ahead and took it out. I *think* it's done, but you might want to take a look at it... when you can..." She chuckled as she turned and walked back into the inn.

Adam dropped his forehead to Kennedy's, his breath still recovering. She cupped his face and lifted it just enough for her to see his eyes. A slow smile spread over his handsome face before she planted one last, long and satisfying kiss on his lips. "Don't stay out here too long," she pointed at the heavy snow falling down around them.

"I'll be back inside in a few minutes," his voice, gruffer than usual, had her biting her bottom lip to attempt at hiding her pleased smile as she pulled herself away from his embrace. "Just need to cool off a bit."

She laughed and held her hands to her flushed cheeks in response and he watched as she happily scurried her way back into the inn.

«CHAPTER ELEVEN»

He opened the door to laughter and a proud Chad as he walked around carrying a small bundle in his arms. "Hey Adam, want to come check out my little angel?"

"Angel, is she?" Adam eyed the baby with doubt as she snuggled beneath the flannel blanket Kennedy had made. "I will admit that was not my first thought this morning."

Chad grinned. "She does have some lungs on her."

"What are you guys naming her?"

"Ivy," Chad answered with a hint of awe in his voice as his little girl gripped his thumb. "Want to hold her?" he held her towards Adam and Adam took a cautious step back. "She doesn't bite, man."

Adam pointed at his coat. "I've been outside. Give me a minute."

"Which means no," Chad pointed out. "You want to distract me. But I get it. She's so tiny I'm afraid I'm going to break her."

"I'll hold her," Lisa walked up and extended her arms. "You should get some sleep, too, while you can. You and Corinth are both going to need it for tonight."

Chad delicately released his baby girl into Lisa's capable hands. "You're probably right about that. Kennedy fed me some delicious breakfast so now I think I can fall asleep completely content. Until Ivy decides to cry."

"We'll try to keep her satisfied in here so you guys can have at least a couple of hours," Lisa told him.

Adam's gaze had wandered towards Kennedy when Chad mentioned her name and his sister and friend noticed his distraction.

"I just caught them mugging down outside," Lisa stage-whispered towards Chad.

Adam avoided her comment and shed his coat and boots at the door before heading towards the kitchen. He hadn't meant for the kiss to happen. But when she'd looked up at him and asked, he couldn't resist. She'd slowly maneuvered her way into his heart and he'd be a fool to deny his feelings had grown over the last couple weeks. And as the days wore on, when she'd lived in McCarthy for several months, he already knew he would not want her to leave. He was falling in love with Kennedy. His heart stampeded at the idea. But his brain needed more time to compute the situation. He couldn't fall for her right *now*. He shouldn't let himself fall for her at all until she decided what she aimed to do with the inn come spring. But as she laughed with his mom in the kitchen, sitting casually on the counter as his mom stirred her coffee, he knew he was officially done for. He wouldn't pressure her to stay when the time came. He'd just take the time he'd been given and enjoy every second. When she spotted him, her smile turned shy and her face flushed at the memory of what they'd just shared outside.

"Hey honey," His mom greeted. "How's it looking out there?"

"Like a blizzard," he reported dryly reaching for his own cup of warmth. "I'd say we have another day at least. It's coming down hard now."

"Kennedy, how are we in food preparation?" Diane asked.

"Well, I have plenty of groceries."

"We should make some dishes that can be cooked or heated over the fire just in case we lose power."

"Oh," Kennedy's face fell. "I didn't even consider that. I could have been doing that all morning."

Diane patted her leg. "No worries. We still have time yet."

"I'll do it. You need your rest. You had an eventful night last night keeping tabs on Corinth and the baby," Kennedy suggested.

"Oh, I'm fine," Diane waved away the concern. "Besides, Corinth is sliding right into motherhood like a professional. She doesn't need me in there much anymore." A touch of remorse hid in her tone.

Adam hugged his mom towards his side. "But we still need you," he winked at her as she rolled her eyes.

"Thanks for making me feel better, honey. Now what are you doing since Kennedy and I will be cooking? Do you plan to help with that? Or do you plan on standing in the way gawking at her?" Diane challenged.

Adam lightly shoved his mom out of his embrace as she chuckled her way to the pantry. "I happen to like gawking at her," he called after her.

"I noticed," Diane's voice drifted out of the pantry as Adam stepped towards the counter Kennedy perched upon. He stood in front of her, their eyes even.

"Hope you don't mind my gawking."

She grinned. "Not at all."

He grabbed her hands and kissed her knuckles. "I'll leave you to cooking. I'd only be in the way, as my mother so kindly put it, and I could be useful elsewhere."

"It's a pity we can't go for a walk or ride somewhere," Kennedy hopped off the counter. "I've started like freezing outside with you."

"I'm glad," he smirked.

"But duty calls," she pointed to his mom setting canned goods on the counter.

"Maybe later we can build that snowman," he offered.

She crossed her arms. "I thought you said it would be pointless?"

He shrugged. "Maybe I just like the thought of having you out in the snow again."

She turned crimson and started nudging him out of the kitchen as he laughed. "I don't trust you in the snow," she murmured. "My hair is *still* wet."

But knowing her thoughts had turned towards their kiss had her eyes softening when she looked up at him. "I'll catch you in a little while?" she asked sweetly.

"Kennedy Donovan," he whispered as he kissed her cheek. "You've already caught me." He heard her sharp intake of breath as he lingered next to her ear a moment longer before drifting away and towards a rocking Lisa in front of the fireplace.

∞

The electricity lasted until two in the morning, that was when Kennedy noticed the chilling temperatures in her room. She flashed an accusatory glance at the little wood burning stove in the corner. She held a hand to it and felt barely enough heat to warm her palm. She opened the cover and saw the dreaded fluff of white that now resided over the wood inside. *She'd forgotten to check the flute. Wonderful.* She tiptoed down the stairs, a blanket wrapped around her shoulders, into the living room. Lisa lay curled in a ball on the rug in front of the fireplace one of the heavy comforters from a bedroom draped over her. Diane slept gracefully in one of the leather recliners, and Adam stretched from one end of the couch to the other, all perfectly warm and sound asleep. She glanced at the clock on the wall and noticed it was half past two. It was too early to do anything around the inn, and she wasn't quite sure what she could manage in the dark any way, so she fetched a floor pillow and a book off the shelf and propped herself on the rug near the fire, her back resting against the couch Adam slept on. She'd made it to page twenty-three before Adam's foot accidentally bumped her head. She held still, hoping the contact didn't wake him up, but she felt the cushions behind her shift. "Ken?" He asked, his voice groggy.

"Hey," she whispered, holding a finger to her lips and pointing towards his mom and sister.

"What are you doing down here?"

"My fire is out. So is the electricity."

He rubbed a hand over his tired face. "I can fetch you some more wood." He started to rise, and she held a hand to his knee.

"Don't bother right now. I accidently left the flute open and it's full of snow. I'll just stay down here, and I'll worry about it in the morning."

He pointed to the couch. "You want this to sleep on? I can sleep on the floor?"

"No," her eyes widened. "I am not taking your bed. I'm fine down here. Not even that tired, really." She motioned for him to lay back down, which didn't take much convincing. Within minutes, she heard his steady and even breaths. All was calm inside the house again, but outside, Kennedy heard the whirling of the wind and the whispers it carried through the awnings. Trapped by snow was an interesting dilemma. Trapped with a handsome man made the situation seem much less dire. A good man at that.

The golden hue of the fireplace warmed the surrounding circle of its light and the warmth of the inn itself enveloped her. Uncle Neal cherished the place. And the people of McCarthy. He'd also cherished her, by proof of what resided in the mystery box upstairs. And though she questioned his devotion towards her, the longer she stayed in McCarthy, the less she questioned why he'd chosen such a place to live. The people were amazing. Not just Adam, though he granted them a thousand points in their favor, but also Corinth and Chad. Tom Higgins, the gruff old man who'd been her uncle's enemy even seemed to like her.

And she saw underneath his tough façade. He was just lonely. And wouldn't that be a problem here in remote Alaska? Could anyone fault Tom for feeling that way after losing his wife? And what about Uncle Neal? Was he not lonely at times? She shook that thought away because she knew he wasn't. Adam made sure of that. Affectionately, she eyed the sleeping man behind her. And what would life in McCarthy be like if she chose to stay permanently?

Yes, she'd have to lose some of the luxuries she was used to in the city... like a vehicle or restaurants and entertainment venues. But would those things matter if she had no need of them? She'd been in McCarthy for almost three weeks and she'd yet to even think about her latest sitcoms or plays. In Manhattan she worked around the clock it seemed, so she never took advantage of all the wonderful places to eat or go out. Would she really miss that? She had her handful of friends that she'd miss seeing now and again, but wouldn't they just love coming here? She grinned at the thought of her friend, Jerry. The adventurous Jerry would eat McCarthy up, and that was what mattered most. She'd keep in touch. No matter what. That's how Jerry was. Kennedy sighed. Putting the book aside and walking towards the kitchen to fetch a pot of water to heat over the fire for tea, she ran a hand over the smooth bar top as she passed. This was hers now. Completely hers. Was it something she wanted to sell? Could she leave this place now that she'd discovered how amazing it really was?

Her parents would flip. Of that, she was certain. But it was her decision. Her property. Her life. Her heart. Her eyes carried towards Adam again. Did Uncle Neal consider the possibility of them falling in love? Did he plan for it to happen? Not that he could control them once she was here, but he *did* actually get Kennedy to McCarthy by way of will and testament, so that was at least impressive. Did he hope that Adam would connect with her? That the boy he cherished would fall for his long-lost niece and therefore the inn would be passed to both of them? Or was Uncle Neal even that savvy? She didn't know a thing about the man except for the legacy he left within Adam and the inn. *But what a legacy it was,* she thought. A place of refuge during a blizzard. A place to call home when she no longer had one. A new job when she'd lost one. A love... a love when she hadn't realized she needed one. Perhaps Neal was as smart as she started to believe he was. And perhaps, despite not knowing her personally, he knew her better than anyone else. Because for a stranger, he seemed to know exactly what she needed.

∞

The blizzard only lasted three days, and the heavy-laden snow still blanketed the town. But people were finally stirring, and work needed to be done. Paths were cleared, roads uncovered, and electricity returned. Chad and Corinth were packed up with baby Ivy, and to everyone's regret, they were heading back to their cabin. Though Corinth wished to indulge in modern technologies a bit longer, she and Chad wanted to check conditions on their homestead. Adam watched as Kennedy hugged Corinth close before the new mom climbed into the sled and Chad tucked her and the baby warmly with blankets. Kennedy handed him a stack of foil pans full of meals she'd prepared for them and he graciously set them in the sled as well before hugging her. Chad started at the clap on his back and Adam pulled him into a brotherly hug. "You guys be careful. Call us if you need us," he pointed to the satellite phone tied to Corinth's bag.

"We will. Thank you all again," Chad accepted the hug from Diane as Richard and Adam's brothers made their way into town on ATVs.

"Seems paths are pretty clear for you guys to make it home if these guys can make it in, Adam pointed out.

Chad offered a grateful and final wave as he cranked the engine and slowly made his way through the tree line, pausing briefly to talk to Adam's dad.

"And all was quiet," Lisa sighed. "It's a little bittersweet. I kind of like that little runt."

Kennedy shook her head on a laugh at Lisa's fickle relationship towards Ivy.

"I'm going to go check on the store," Lisa made her way, hands in pockets, towards the grocery market, the bell above the door singing as she walked inside.

"I'm going to borrow an ATV, if that's alright?" Adam asked. "Need to head back to my cabin and check things and then help dad at the farm for a bit."

Kennedy nodded. "That's fine. I—" Her words trailed off as the sounds of a helicopter could be heard coming towards McCarthy. "Is that Mick?"

Lisa darted out of the store and sheltered a hand over her eyes as all stood and watched Mick expertly land the helicopter in his usual spot. All darted towards him, his unexpected arrival causing worry amongst other residents as well, as several walked out of their homes and businesses. Mick hopped out all smiles.

"What has happened that you would be here so soon?" Lisa asked as she walked up and accepted the friendly hug around her shoulders. "Did you bring me a husband?"

KATHARINE E. HAMILTON

Mick waved a hand over himself. "Always ready and waiting, sweetheart." She rolled her eyes. "Actually, I brought Kennedy a surprise."

"Me?" Kennedy eyed him curiously as did Adam.

Mick wriggled his eyebrows before opening the small door of his helicopter. A high-heeled boot stepped over the side, and Mick held up a hand as a delicately framed woman stepped out onto the snow in a designer peacoat. "Mom?" Kennedy's jaw dropped as she ran forward and enveloped her mother in a tight hug. Her father followed his wife and Kennedy stood back dumbstruck. "Dad? What are you guys doing here?" she hugged her father and gave Mick an appreciative nod.

"Your mother felt we should come to visit you while you were here," her father's no-nonsense tone told her he'd disagreed with the idea.

"Look at all this snow," Veronica Donovan held a hand to her chest and turned in small circles to soak in the small town. "My goodness, it's absolutely stunning."

"We did just have a blizzard," Kennedy added. "I can't believe you came. And I can't believe you convinced this guy to give you a ride," she pointed at Mick and grinned.

"Money talks, sweetie," her dad replied, and Kennedy felt the flush of embarrassment at the insult towards Mick. The friendly chopper pilot gave her a small wink of assurance that he didn't take offense.

"I've also brought a bit of supplies," Mick reported to Lisa and Adam. "Your mom had already placed a small order for next trip. Figured I might as well bring it along with these folks. Here we go," he reached into the chopper and retrieved the Donovan's suitcases before taking out various crates for Lisa. She signed his clipboard. "Thanks, Mick."

"Anything for you."

"Charmer," Lisa just shook her head as she walked the crates to the store.

"Appreciate you making a special trip," Adam told him.

Mick tilted his head with a tinge of a grimace. "Don't thank me yet," he murmured. "That guy's a piece of work. The woman's friendly enough, but they argued most of the way."

"It will be interesting," Adam agreed. "To see how he feels about the place."

"Best of luck," Mick tapped his fingers to his head in a salute before walking back to his chopper.

Kennedy gasped and waved him down. "Mick! Wait!" The man stopped in surprise as she handed him a small note. "I'm hosting a Christmas Party at the inn and would love if you can come. I know it would probably be a special trip out, or maybe we could plan it around the time of one of your deliveries. Just let me know. We would love to have you join us."

Mick slipped the envelope in his shirt pocket. "I wouldn't miss it, Ken. Sounds like a great time. See you in a few weeks."

She hurried back towards her parents. "Let's get you guys inside. Mom, I love your jacket. Is that new?"

Adam watched as she steered her parents towards the inn and pointed. She then lifted her mother's suitcase and reached for her dad's, the man not even concerned that his daughter hefted the heavy luggage herself. Adam rushed forward and intercepted both the bags and Kennedy sighed in relief. "Thanks."

She led the way and proudly opened the door of the inn. Her mom gushed about the 'quaint' and 'homey' interior and her dad stood silently surveying the place. Adam placed the luggage inside the door, the sound bringing her parent's attention to rest on him. Kennedy beamed as she stepped beside him. "Mom, Dad... this is Adam Stockton. He's—" she paused as if trying to think of the right term to call him. "My friend. And he was a dear friend to Uncle Neal." Adam extended his   hand.

"Veronica   Donovan,"   Kennedy's   mother introduced herself first and then lightly elbowed Kennedy's father to be polite. "Keith. It's a pleasure."

"You've sort of caught me on an odd day," Kennedy explained as she walked further into the room. Blankets were still draped over former sleeping areas and on the floor, and the tables full of Uncle Neal's belongings were crammed into the formal dining area. "See, with the blizzard, I had several people staying here. A new baby was born just a few days ago. It was magical," she rambled as she hurriedly picked up blanket after blanket and folded them neatly or draped them to look less messy. She sent an imploring gaze to Adam, but he stood still, not wanting to track snow into the room on his boots. He pointed down at his feet. Understanding dawned on her face. "You heading out now?" she asked, rushing towards him. He squeezed her hand and felt her nerves.

"I am. I need to check on things."

"Right. Of course," she held a hand to her heart and whispered. "I'm freaking out a bit. What if they don't like it?" her hushed tone full of worry.

He smiled tenderly at her and gave her an encouraging hug. He caught the curious stare of her mother before releasing her.

"Will you come for dinner later? I'd love for them to get to know you better. You were special to Uncle Neal, and I think it would be good for them to s—"

He held a finger to her lips. "Sure."

A relieved smile washed over her face. "Thank you."

He nodded over her shoulder towards her father, who'd already started investigating some of the downstairs rooms. "You better offer a tour."

She grimaced. "Right. Well..." Regretfully, she pulled her hand from his. "I'll see you in a bit. Be careful today."

"I will," she nodded and turned to face her nosy parents as they investigated the place. He saw her draw one last deep breath before walking towards them and hated leaving her to what felt like the wolves. Realizing that the sooner he completed his tasks the sooner he could come back, he silently exited the inn.

«CHAPTER TWELVE»

Keith Donovan excelled at almost everything, but hiding his emotions was not one of them. Kennedy could see the disdain written on his face as his eyes continued to size up his new surroundings.

"I can place you guys in a room upstairs on the second floor. Those rooms weren't used the last few days," she began hefting her mother's suitcase up the stairwell, her mother following close behind her. "You have your own bathroom in the suite." She pointed out.

"With running water?" her father asked in genuine concern.

"Yes, Dad, with running water. And we have electricity too, believe it or not."

"You make me nervous when you say 'we.'"

"I meant, McCarthy in general," she ignored his prying eyes and headed down the stairs to grab his suitcase next. When she returned, her mom had shed her coat and rolled up the sleeves of her sweater. "I have dinner planned around six. Adam should be back by then."

"He seems like a nice man," her mother prodded, her leading tone had Kennedy quickly diverting her attention to the thermostat to check the heat.

"He is," she said, and then motioned towards the stairs. "You guys want some coffee or tea?"

"Coffee," her father requested.

"Alright." She hurried down the steps and to the kitchen. Her mother slid onto the stool Adam normally occupied and watched her.

"Well, it's a nice kitchen isn't it, Keith?"

A grunt was all Kennedy heard as she busied herself at the coffee pot pouring cups.

"Adam said Uncle Neal had this updated a couple of years ago. I'm glad he did. It's been a nice surprise for me here. After all, I feel most at home in a kitchen." Kennedy forced a smile as she slid the mugs to her parents. "So..." She took a deep breath, dreading the answer she would receive. "What brings you guys here?"

Her father eyed her mother fiercely before turning to her. "I thought you knew we were coming."

Kennedy shook her head and then looked at her mom's guilty face. "Mom?"

"Oh, I just couldn't stand not knowing what your life was like here," she admitted and then pointed a finger at her husband's frown. "And I knew you would never agree to come if I had not made it sound like Kennedy was having an awful go of it."

"What?" Kennedy gasped. "Mom... I've loved it here."

"I know, sweetie, but I felt our conversation on the phone a few weeks ago needed to happen in person."

A stone-faced Keith straightened in his chair. "This conversation should not be happening at all," he growled. "Neal brought this upon us."

"Oh shush. It's a conversation that should have happened a long time ago. We've discussed this."

Her tone held warning and Kennedy leaned against the counter.

"What in the world is going on?" she asked.

"Let's go sit by the fire," her mother hopped from the stool, her heels clacking against the wood floors as she made her way towards the comfortable living area. Kennedy tossed a couple of extra logs into the fireplace before sitting across from her stiff-backed father and eager mother.

"That box you found," her mother began. "Where is it?"

"Upstairs," Kennedy answered.

"Go fetch it," Her mother ordered tenderly.

Kennedy hurried up the stairs and came back down, placing the carved box on the coffee table. She saw her father's frown waver a bit before his eyes hardened again.

"Isn't that something?" Veronica ran a hand over the box and looked at her husband. "Your dad made this."

"You did?" Kennedy asked. "When?"

Hesitantly, Keith responded. "A long time ago."

Eyes searching, Kennedy looked at her mother as she lifted the lid and filtered through the years' worth of memorabilia. "Your Uncle Neal was a good man." Her mom stated, and her dad avoided eye contact with her as her mother continued. "He had the best laugh, didn't he Keith?" she reached for her husband's hand and it was then Kennedy finally saw that his refusal to speak was more for composure than for spite. He gave a brief nod in agreement.

"Everyone here has told me the same thing," Kennedy added. "And that he was kind."

"He was," Veronica smiled, her lips quivering a bit. "You see, honey... well... your Uncle Neal... well, he's not... he's not really your uncle."

Kennedy's eyes bounced to her dad, his jaw tightening. "Okay, then who was he?" she asked.

"He was your dad's college roommate," her mom replied.

Surprised, Kennedy straightened in her seat. "So why did he leave me all this? And why have you told me all these years that he was my uncle? We have the same last name," she pointed out.

"You do. Yes. Back then, at college, housing was sorted by alphabetical order. Your father and Neal were in the same dormitory and were placed together as roommates because they were both Donovans. They became fast friends," she squeezed Keith's hand as she spoke. "Two jokers, really." That statement had Kennedy's eyes popping as she turned them towards her father.

His resolve slightly melted. "Don't find it too hard to believe, Kenny." His special nickname and his small smile at her disbelief had her worries somewhat dissipating.

"That's how I met your father, actually. I was dating Neal."

Kennedy's mouth dropped open again as she turned her attention back to her mom. "What?"

Veronica chuckled as if the memories were just as funny as Kennedy's stunned expression. "Don't look so shocked. I was quite a catch back then, wasn't I, honey?"

Her father gave a clipped nod and Veronica patted their conjoined hands. "Neal and I were quite serious. High school sweethearts. Then attending the same university. We had big dreams. We were going to get married and settle outside the city to raise a family. He'd commute into the city and I'd raise our children in a quiet suburb."

"Whoa... this is the same man who owned this place?" Kennedy asked. "What was he planning on doing in the city? They don't exactly need wood-chopping inn owners there."

Keith snickered at his daughter's response before her mother silenced him with one of her looks. "Your Uncle Neal was an accountant."

"That explains his bookkeeping here," Kennedy told them. "So, what happened? Why did you marry Dad? And why did you guys make me believe he was my uncle?"

Her mother's eyes turned sad which then melted what was left of her father's resolve. He took over the conversation. "When I first saw your mother, I fell for her instantly."

"That's not true," her mom sniffled as she reached for a tissue that Kennedy offered her.

"It was," he affirmed. "But I knew I could never have her. The more I got to know her through Neal, the more I was sure of it. But she was dating my best friend. They were in love. All four years of school they dated. There was nothing I could do about it. When graduation rolled around, Neal wanted to take a trip. He was always the adventurous type. We usually went skiing on our breaks from school, but this time he wanted to come to Alaska. So, we did. We actually stayed in this very inn, though it did not look like this back then."

Kennedy leaned forward in earnest for him to continue. "One trip was all it took. Neal was convinced he could make a life here. That it would be better than any life he'd have in the city." Her father heard her mother's sniffle and he squeezed her hand. "By this point, I'd accepted a job in New York as was the plan. Neal and I wished to work together. But for Neal, his mind was made up. He was going to marry your mother and move here to McCarthy. At that time, he didn't even have a plan. He just wanted to go on an adventure. Your mother, however, had different plans."

Veronica patted his hand that she'd take over the explanation. "I was not interested in a life in Alaska bush country. To be honest, the thought terrified me. I could not fathom why Neal would even want such a thing. We fought about it, in great depth, for weeks. This life was just not in the cards for me. Neal would not be swayed though. He was determined. So, he wished to take a break. Go our separate ways."

"Just like that?" Kennedy asked. "You were together for years."

Her mother nodded sadly. "That's how badly he wished to come here. Something about the place bewitched him. He absolutely loved it, and there was no replacing it. I loathed the idea, and we were young and selfish so neither of us wished to give up on what *we* wanted."

Kennedy crossed her legs underneath her and nestled into the corner of the couch and pulled the nearest blanket over her lap for added warmth and security as she suddenly grew chilly.

"It was a month later that I realized I was pregnant." Her mother's words dropped like a bomb within Kennedy's stomach.

She blinked. "I'm sorry, what?"

Her mother's shaky smile had tears rushing to Kennedy's eyes. "What did you say?"

"Neal was not your uncle, honey. Neal is your biological father."

Kennedy's eyes sought her father's face and the truth shined there in its rawest form. "But— You're—" She pointed to her father and he reluctantly shook his head. "How? I mean—" She pinched the bridge of her nose. "Why? Why lie to me all these years?"

"When I found out I was pregnant, I was so distraught." Her mother waved her hands as a plea. "Not because I didn't want you, baby, but just because I did not know where to turn. I knew if I told Neal he would want me to move here. If I told my parents, they'd have me move back home. But I wanted life in the city. I wanted what I'd always dreamed of. That's when I bumped into your father again. We ran into one another at a small restaurant in East Village that we both love to this day." She smiled tenderly at Keith and he rubbed his thumb over her knuckles. "I hadn't planned to tell him, but seeing him again and remembering how close we three were in school, the truth just tumbled out of me. That was when your father proposed."

Kennedy released a loud laugh of shock.

"Oh, it was sudden." Her mom chuckled behind her tears. "But he told me of his feelings all those years we were in school and I'd always thought him a good friend. And handsome." She smiled shyly at her husband before continuing. "It was then we came up with how we would handle the situation and how we would tell Neal."

"And you were fine with her carrying another man's child?" Kennedy asked her dad. "Your best friend's child?"

He nodded. "I loved her. I didn't care whose child it was, it was Ronnie's." The affectionate nickname he'd called her mother for years had Kennedy's heart softening. "I didn't care what problems we'd face down the road, as long as I had her, we'd face it together."

"But your name is on my birth certificate." Kennedy pointed out. "Not Neal's."

"That was part of the agreement." Her mother continued. "You see, when we told Neal about the pregnancy, he of course, offered what we thought he would. He would pay to move me here to McCarthy. Marry me. The whole works. When I refused, he didn't quite know what to do. When I told him I was engaged to your father, his temper cooled long enough for me to talk sense into him."

"He wasn't mad you were already engaged? It had only been a month or so." Kennedy sat shocked.

"Oh, he was upset. But when we were truly able to talk it out, shelve our pride and selfishness, he realized it was a blessing. We didn't want to cut him out of your life, but we all agreed it would be hard on you growing up if you had two men in the role of father. So, he relinquished his parental rights. He was fine with your father being your dad as long as he could still be in your life. That is when we decided he would be your Uncle Neal."

"But you disowned him." She looked to her dad for answers.

"You were such a precious girl," her mother complimented. "So fun and full of joy. And you loved your Uncle Neal. He spoiled you rotten." She took a deep breath. "But as you got older, Neal grew discontent. He saw the relationship you had with your dad and felt like that role should be his. He wanted to tell you the truth. We disagreed. Like you've pointed out, your dad's name is the one on your birth certificate. He was the only father you'd ever known. We didn't want to confuse you or worse... upset you. You were only six years old at the time. All of this would be too much for a six-year-old to handle. So, we told your Uncle Neal that he was not allowed to see you anymore if he could not keep his identity secret. And that's when he stopped coming to see you. He'd send cards every now and then, but through the years, those slowly started to trickle down to nothing. I kept sending him updates on you, not knowing if he ever received them." She motioned towards the box. "Clearly, he did, but he honored his word. If he could not keep it secret, he was not allowed to see you. I guess he felt if he ever saw you again, he'd confront the issue. I think, too, that he did not want to disrupt your life."

Kennedy stared absently at the fire. Neal was her father. Not her uncle. Not some random guy who'd left his fortune to her. But her father. Pity hit her full force at the loneliness he must have felt living with such a secret. Living alone in McCarthy knowing he had a daughter out there.

"I'm sorry." Her father's voice interrupted her line of thought. "When you received the documents about his passing and what he'd left you..." He looked away a moment.

"Dad," Kennedy's voice drew his eyes back to hers. She walked towards them and squeezed between them on the couch. She grabbed each of their hands. "You're my dad. Even now, knowing all this, you're still my dad. You always will be." She bit back a sob as he pulled her into a tight hug. She felt his shoulders shake as she and her mother cried too. They sat there, the weight of their announcement sinking into their lives. Nothing had changed with their announcement, and yet, she did feel different. Not towards her parents, but towards Neal. Now she finally knew why he left her the inn. His life's work. His life's love was this town and this inn. He was giving her himself and his love in the best way he could. And she counted herself blessed to have not one, but two loving fathers who cared for her.

∞

Adam knocked on the door of the inn, and for the first time in years, he felt like a stranger standing on the front porch. What would her parents say about her life here in McCarthy? Were they here to take her back to New York? He prayed not. When Kennedy opened the door, her reddened face and swollen eyes had him stepping forward in concern. She smiled, the radiance of it surprising him as he studied her. She pulled him inside and helped him with his coat. Smells of what promised to be a delicious dinner wafted through the air. Her mother walked forward, a glass of wine in her hand as she smiled in greeting. "Adam, I'm so glad you were able to join us for dinner."

He nodded politely as Kennedy linked her hand with his. Her mother's eyes darted down towards their hands and back up to his face. "Would you like some wine?" She asked.

"Yes, thank you." Kennedy gently rested her head on his shoulder as she led him further into the inn. When they reached the kitchen, she relinquished her hold on him so he could slide into his usual spot at the bar to watch her work. Her mother placed a glass of wine in front of him as her father made his way down the stairs. He slid onto the stool next to Adam and nodded in greeting.

He wasn't quite sure why he felt awkward, but it was as if there was something amiss amongst the Donovan's. He was still concerned about Kennedy's tear-stained face, but she acted as if nothing was wrong. She lifted a lid from her pan on the stove and stirred. "I think we are ready. Mom and Dad, you guys want to go to the table. I'll have Adam help me bring it over."

Her mother smiled as she linked arms with her dad and walked towards the dining table. Kennedy leaned towards Adam. "I have so much to tell you." She whispered, her eyes dancing.

"Good, I hope." Adam gently brushed his fingertips over her cheek. "I'm a little concerned about this."

She smiled. "They're happy tears, I assure you."

His shoulders relaxed. "That's good to hear."

"Come on." She pointed to the pan on the stove for him to carry and she carried a platter of green beans to the table. They slid into seats across from her parents. Her mother said grace and Kennedy served them a roasted lemon chicken with rosemary and new potatoes. His mouth watered. As he picked up his fork to take that first satisfying bite, her father cleared his throat.

"So, what is it you do here in McCarthy, Adam?"

He paused, inwardly disappointed that the fragrant food had to sit on his plate a few minutes longer. "I farm. Mostly." He replied.

"Farm." Her father repeated, his lofty attitude slipping through.

"His family has a farm about a mile outside of town." Kennedy explained. "Adam also supplies most of the residents of McCarthy with wood."

"A wood chopper?" Her father asked, shooting a curious gaze to his daughter.

"Not to mention he saw to the inn until I arrived." Kennedy continued. Adam reached under the table and squeezed her hand. He appreciated her trying to make him sound good to her father, but he also did not want her father to think he couldn't speak for himself.

"And have you always lived in McCarthy?" Keith asked.

"No sir. My family moved out here when I was fifteen."

"And you've been here ever since?"

"For the most part." Adam answered. "I had a brief couple of years at university, but ultimately came back here."

"College?" Her dad's brows rose in surprise and Adam felt Kennedy cringe next to him.

"And why did you choose life here in McCarthy?"

"It's where my family is. I love it here. I love the way of life, the people... it's in my blood, I guess you could say."

Her father grunted in acceptance of his answer as he forked a bite to eat. Adam took the lull in conversation as a chance to take a bite. Kennedy's mother then stepped in to take over the inquisition. "We saw your family when we arrived. Kennedy said your mom used to be a nurse and helped deliver that sweet baby during the blizzard."

"Yes ma'am. Though Kennedy and my sister, Lisa, helped."

Her father's brows rose at that bit of news.

"'It takes a village' takes on a whole new meaning here," Kennedy chuckled as she beamed at Adam.

"Adam and his family are helping me plan the big Christmas Party I aim to throw here at the inn in a few weeks. Please tell me you guys are staying that long."

"We are here until that helicopter comes back." Her mom grinned. "So, I would say that's a yes. I would love to help you, sweetie. This place would look lovely with some Christmas decorations."

"I know. I'm not sure if Uncle Neal had any. I haven't found them yet though."

"They're in the shed." Adam told her. "I'll fetch them for you before I leave. And if you want a tree, just let me know how big and I can find you one."

"Maybe we could look for one together." She suggested. "When we build that snowman." She winked and he just shook his head as he smirked.

"You know, Kennedy, the helicopter pilot said there is room to transport another person on the trip back to Anchorage. We'd be happy to escort you home." Her father took a long sip of his wine.

"I don't plan on leaving until spring." She reported.

"But why?" He asked. "You've come and assessed your inheritance. I say we list it while we can and then come spring you can wash your hands of it."

"Dad," Kennedy's tone held surprise. "I don't plan on selling it."

Keith seemed surprised. "Why not?"

"Because Neal left it to me."

Her father's face clouded.

"It has potential. Everyone tells me it does quite well in the tourist months. I think I could keep it running."

"By yourself?" Her mother asked.

Kennedy shrugged. "I planned to open a small café here as well."

"Wait." Her father held up his hand. "You planned on staying? Not hiring a manager, but actually staying here?"

"I planned to see how it goes for a while." She admitted, though with less confidence than she'd shown the last few weeks. Adam's eyes bounced between her and her father.

"Kennedy, you can't be serious. McCarthy is no place for... you. You've a life in New York. You're a chef at one of the finest restaurants."

"Was." Kennedy told him. "I was fired."

"What? When?" Her mother asked.

"When I found out I was snowed in at McCarthy. They can't go without a chef for three or four months. So, they fired me."

"But there is a way out." Her father added. "The helicopter. Or did they not tell you." He fired a hot stare at Adam and pointed. "This was your doing, wasn't it? You withheld that information from her, didn't you?"

"Dad, stop. No. Adam is the one who told me about the helicopter. It's been my decision. I've chosen to stay. There was just too much to go through. I'm still sorting through Uncle Neal's belongings. I have yet to even inventory the rooms."

"Then we will hire someone. I don't want you staying in McCarthy."

"I thought... everything was fine now." Kennedy's voice quieted.

"Just because you now know... everything." Her father continued. "Doesn't mean I want my daughter living in the God-forsaken Alaskan wilderness. You're young. Single. This is no place for a beautiful and talented young woman."

"Dad." Her voice held warning.

"Don't 'Dad me.'" He ordered. "That's just how it is. This place is best... forgotten."

Adam felt Kennedy's grip on his hand relax. She reached across the table and gripped her father's hand. "Dad." Her voice was calm. "I think we both know this place will never be forgotten. As much as we may like for it to be. But it holds a place in our hearts. It doesn't upset me being here. I love it. I've felt happier here than I have in the city in a long time."

"We just... don't want to lose you, sweetie." Her mother's smile turned into a firm scowl as she held back more tears. Kennedy placed a hand on her heart. "Please... you two could never lose me. I'm just asking for a chance. I want to give this a go. If it turns out to be a complete disaster, then so be it. But I have to try." She grabbed her dad's hand as well and both her parents reluctantly nodded.

Adam shifted uncomfortably in his seat and Kennedy softly chuckled. "I guess we should fill you in on what's going on." She said. She looked to her parents and they nodded.

Adam leaned back in his chair and Kennedy grabbed his hands in hers. "It would seem, Adam, that Uncle Neal had some secrets."

Adam's brow furrowed as he waited patiently for her to continue.

"I'm his daughter."

«EPILOGUE»

Kennedy took Tom's coat as he and his son, Kirk, who'd flown in with Mick, walked further into the inn, both still a bit awkward with being openly invited inside by a Donovan. She waved towards Adam and he walked up carrying two fresh cups of punch for the two men and gave them the brief breakdown of where all everyone was gathered. The tree that she and Adam had chopped down stood proudly in the corner of the main room, rising up to the second-floor landing, its looming presence adding rustic charm to their Christmas celebration. Her mother had wrapped the stairwell banister in homemade garland and ribbons that Diane had donated to the cause. Kennedy had spent the last two days preparing appetizers and a buffet to feed the masses. Diane had helped while Lisa helped her mother decorate the main floor. All was perfect, and Kennedy felt her dad had found a friend in Richard. Adam's dad's knowledge of the banking industry proved to her father there was hope for McCarthy yet. She accepted a hug from Corinth as she and Chad walked into the house. Adam's hand slid to the small of her back as he greeted his friends as well.

"It looks phenomenal in here." Corinth complimented. "I don't think I've ever seen Neal's inn so festive."

"There's much to celebrate this year." Adam winked at Kennedy as he pulled her closer to him. Telling him of her true connection to Neal had only strengthened their bond. And Neal's reasoning for leaving Kennedy the inn now all made sense.

"I heard some interesting news on the way into town." Corinth reported.

"Oh?" Kennedy asked curiously.

"Mick was spreading the rumor that you were staying in McCarthy."

Kennedy bit back a grin as she nodded excitedly.

Corinth cheered and hopped as she hugged Kennedy close. "I'm so glad!"

"Me too." Kennedy beamed as she motioned them further inside so as to close the door behind them. Chad held Ivy in the crook of his arm. Kennedy peeked down at her as they passed by and went about greeting others in the room. Adam shifted Kennedy to where she stood fully in his embrace. He looked up at the mistletoe that hung from the door. "How'd that get there?" He asked.

Kennedy draped her arms around his neck. "My mother insisted."

"Should I be offended?" Adam asked.

"Why would you be?"

"Because you were to greet every person who walked in the door. Therefore, you would have had to kiss everybody. Did you kiss Mick?" He angled his head and his right brow lifted.

She playfully punched him in the stomach as he laughed. "Either kiss me or not, Adam Stockton."

He grinned as he placed a tender kiss on her lips. "You don't have to tell me twice." Tugging her hand, he led her towards the center of the room and hailed everyone's attention. He then waved a hand for her to welcome everyone as was her plan.

"I'm so excited all of you came to join us tonight. I'm so thankful for all of you." Kennedy beamed at all the familiar faces and some of the new ones that surrounded her. "As you all know, Neal left this inn to me in his will, and over the last couple of months I've been trying to decide what I ought to do with it. My first instinct was to come and sell it off as quickly as possible. However, the longer I've been here, and the more people I've met," she nodded a head towards Corinth's direction and grinned. "I fall more and more in love with this place. So, I wanted to officially welcome you to the new Donovan's Inn and Café, because I will be staying here in McCarthy to run the place." Murmurs of surprise filtered through the crowd. "Merry Christmas." Kennedy raised her glass and toasted to her new friends as they clapped and cheered in response. She then let the music and chatter take over once more as she clasped her hand with Adam's. "Come with me a minute." She told him and led him to the mudroom off the kitchen.

"Everything okay?" He asked.

"More than okay. I have a promise to keep." She lifted a blanket revealing the long box that Neal had carved and left for Adam's Christmas present. "I thought you might want your gift."

He held a hand over his mouth.

"You don't have to open it right now, if you think you'll need some time." Compassion had her resting her hand on his arm. "But I wanted to give it to you now so as not to forget before the night was up."

He walked towards the box and flicked the clasp. "Now's fine." He pulled her with him as he knelt in front of it. Opening it, a small gasp of wonder left his lips as he stared down at several of Neal's guns and fishing tackle. Amidst the belongings was his old ball cap. The Kansas City Chiefs emblem faded and worn. "He'd found it."

Kennedy reached for the hat and turned it over in her hand. "He knew if he gave it back to you that you'd never give McCarthy a chance. Maybe that's why he hid it all these years."

"You're probably right about that." Adam's fingers traced over several of the contents. "These were his favorite fishing leers. And look," he pulled out an old pistol. "He loved this thing."

Kennedy tenderly brushed Adam's hair aside as she stared at the side of his face as he peered into the box. "You were special to him. It's only right he leave you some of his prized possessions."

"And knowing who you are now, it was only right for him to leave you the inn." Adam pointed out. "It would seem Neal had all of us figured out and seen about long before we even knew up from down." He chuckled to himself. "I wonder what he'd think about me now."

"What do you mean?" Kennedy asked. "He loved you then, he'd love you now."

"But I wonder if he'd feel that same love towards me knowing I'd fallen in love with his daughter."

Kennedy's mouth gaped a moment before splitting into a giant grin.

Adam reached for her left hand. "It's true." He continued. "I've fallen completely in love with you Kennedy Donovan. And I know we haven't known each other long, and I know some people may doubt what we have. But—"

His words were cut off by Kennedy throwing her arms around his neck and planting a firm kiss on his lips. He pulled her away on a laugh. "Wait, I'm not done." He kissed her gently once more before continuing. "Marry me." He added, between kisses.

Kennedy leaned back to study his face, his eyes growing serious as he waited for her response. His brows slowly rose as the silence stretched between them. "I love you too." Kennedy kissed him again, long and slow.

"Is that a yes?" He asked.

"It's a most definite yes." She felt his shoulders relax in relief as she melted into his embrace. As his lips neared hers once more, Lisa walked in.

"So, we're almost out of pun—" They heard her sigh as she crossed her arms. "You know what? Never mind." She laughed at their embarrassed expressions and made her way back into the kitchen announcing that Adam and Kennedy were making out in the mudroom.

"I'd hunt her down, but I need her to be a bridesmaid."

Tossing his head back on a laugh, Adam helped her to her feet. "Come on, let's go give them something to really talk about." She felt him slip something on her finger and looked down to find a simple solitaire resting there. Beaming, she nodded for him to lead the way to their friends, family, and to their new future.

All titles in The Lighthearted Collection Available in Paperback, Ebook, and Audiobook

Chicago's Best
https://www.amazon.com/dp/B06XH7Y3MF

Montgomery House
https://www.amazon.com/dp/B073T1SVCN

Beautiful Fury
https://www.amazon.com/dp/B07B527N57

INTRODUCING THE FAMILY

THE SIBLINGS O'RIFCAN SERIES   KATHARINE E. HAMILTON

The Complete Siblings O'Rifcan Series

Claron

https://www.amazon.com/dp/B07FYR44KX

Riley

https://www.amazon.com/dp/B07G2RBD8D

Layla

https://www.amazon.com/dp/B07HJRL67M

Chloe

https://www.amazon.com/dp/B07KB3HG6B

Murphy

https://www.amazon.com/dp/B07N4FCY8V

The Brothers of Hastings Ranch Series

Graham
https://www.amazon.com/dp/B08777YG9R

Calvin
https://www.amazon.com/dp/B087N9DL7T

Philip
https://www.amazon.com/dp/B08B2QZZSB

Lawrence
Coming 12/30/2020
PreOrder Here:
https://www.amazon.com/dp/B08JWT8Y8N

**Check out the Epic Fantasy Adventure
Available in Paperback, Ebook, and
Audiobook**

U<small>THE</small>NFADING
L<small></small>ANDS

The Unfading Lands
https://www.amazon.com/dp/B00VKWKPES

Darkness Divided, Part Two in
The Unfading Lands Series
https://www.amazon.com/dp/B015QFTAXG

Redemption Rising, Part Three in
The Unfading Lands Series
https://www.amazon.com/dp/B01G5NYSEO

Find out more about Katharine and her works at:
www.katharinehamilton.com

Social Media is a great way to connect with Katharine. Check her out on the following:

Facebook: Katharine E. Hamilton
https://www.facebook.com/Katharine-E-Hamilton-282475125097433/

Twitter: @AuthorKatharine
Instagram: @AuthorKatharine

Contact Katharine:
khamiltonauthor@gmail.com

ABOUT THE AUTHOR

Katharine E. Hamilton began writing in 2008 and published her first children's book, <u>The Adventurous Life of Laura Bell</u> in 2009. She would go on to write and illustrate two more children's books, <u>Susie At Your Service</u> and <u>Sissy and Kat</u> between 2010-2013.

Though writing for children was fun, Katharine moved into Adult Fiction in 2015 with her release of <u>The Unfading Lands</u>, a clean, epic fantasy that landed in Amazon's Hot 100 New Releases on its fourth day of publication, reached #72 in the Top 100 in Epic Fantasy, and hit the Top 10,000 Best Sellers on all of Amazon in its first week. It has been listed as a Top 100 Indie Read for 2015 and a nominee for a Best Indie Book Award for 2016. The series did not stop there. <u>Darkness Divided: Part Two of The Unfading Land Series</u>, released in October of 2015 and claimed a spot in the Top 100 of its genre. <u>Redemption Rising: Part Three of The Unfading Lands Series</u> released in April 2016 and claimed a nomination for the Summer Indie Book Awards.

Though comfortable in the fantasy genre, Katharine decided to venture towards romance in 2017 and released the first novel in a collection of sweet, clean and wholesome romances: The Lighthearted Collection. <u>Chicago's Best</u> reached best seller status in its first week of publication and rested comfortably in the Top 100 for Amazon for three steady weeks, claimed a Reader's Choice Award, a TopShelf Indie Book Award, and ended up a finalist in the American Book Festival's

Best Book Awards for 2017. <u>Montgomery House</u>, the second in the collection, released in August of 2017 and rested comfortably alongside its predecessor, claiming a Reader's Choice Award, and becoming Katharine's best-selling novel up to that point. Both were released in audiobook format in late 2017 and early 2018. <u>Beautiful Fury</u> is the third novel released in the collection and has claimed a Reader's Choice Award and a gold medal in the Authorsdb Best Cover competition. It has also been released in audiobook format with narrator Chelsea Carpenter lending her talents to bring it to life. Katharine and Chelsea have partnered on an ongoing project for creating audiobook marketing methods for fellow authors and narrators, all of which will eventually be published as a resource tool for others.

In August of 2018, Katharine brought to life a new clean contemporary romance series of a loving family based in Ireland. The Siblings O'Rifcan Series kicked off in August with <u>Claron</u>. <u>Claron</u> climbed to the Top 1000 of the entire Amazon store and has reached the Top 100 of the Clean and Wholesome genre a total of 11 times. He is Katharine's bestselling book thus far and lends to the success of the following books in the series: <u>Riley</u>, <u>Layla</u>, <u>Chloe</u>, and <u>Murphy,</u> each book earning their place in the Top 100 of their genre and Hot 100 New Releases. <u>Claron</u> was featured in Amazon's Prime Reading program March – June 2019. The series is also available in audiobook format with the voice talents of Alex Black.

A Love For All Seasons, a Sweet Contemporary Romance Series launched in July of 2019 with

<u>Summer's Catch</u>, followed by <u>Autumn's Fall</u> in October. <u>Winter's Call</u> and <u>Spring's Hope</u> scheduled for 2021 release dates. The series follows a wonderful group of friends from Friday Harbor, Washington, and has been Katharine's newest and latest project.

Katharine has contributed to charitable Indie Anthologies as well as helped other aspiring writers journey their way through the publication process. She manages an online training course that walks fellow self-publishing and independently publishing writers through the publishing process as well as how to market their books.

She is a member of Women Fiction Writers of America, Texas Authors, IASD, and the American Christian Fiction Writers. She loves everything to do with writing and loves that she is able to continue sharing heartwarming stories to a wide array of readers.

Katharine graduated from Texas A&M University with a bachelor's degree in History. She lives on a ranch in south Texas with her husband Brad, sons Everett and West, and their two dogs, Tulip and Paws.

Made in the USA
Las Vegas, NV
02 December 2020

all you
hold on to

all you hold on to

By K.T. Egan

GenZ
The Future of Publishing

For my mother, who, while even watching over me now, has always inspired the stories in my heart.

Anderson Creek Kids

Roxanne Wortham

Maverick Sterling

Cheyenne Anderson

Silas Montgomery

Wesley Carmody

Connor Carmody

Prologue
August 2002

It was going to rain; all the mothers on Anderson Creek Road said so.

.   They muttered this to their husbands as they peaked out their kitchen windows, taking in the golden hour glow that had crossed their little corner of Northeast Pennsylvania.

They said it while they strained pasta and potatoes for dinner or sliced a freshly cooked pot roast into perfect portions. They said it while they put plates and napkins in their husbands' hands to set the table or called out to them as they watched the nightly news. They said it while they checked the time on the stove clocks and counted the minutes until they would pry open the screen doors and call straggling children to dinner.

As they said it, their husbands rolled their eyes and went about their evening routines. They set tables, watched the news, graded summer school tests and quizzes, or finished the last page of the daily newspaper or their newest bookstore find. They had to get it done before the kids came rushing in and they had to devote time to be the parent that was never home during the summer days.

The glow had done nothing to deter the wills and wanderings of the children who lived on Anderson Creek Road.

1

They played soccer in large front yards or raced bikes up and down the cracking pavement, avoiding the small potholes that would only get bigger. They waded knee deep in the creek, splashing at jean cut off shorts and tie-dye t-shirts and helping the smaller ones make mud pies for dessert.

All but six of the street's young residents used the last golden hours to play before the storms rolled in and they were left inside their houses for what the forecast deemed the rest of the week.

Those six friends had gathered deep in the woods on the hill at the back half of Caleb Anderson's property. They were seated at a large, semicircular, round stone that the leader of the group, one Maverick Sterling, had deemed their Round Table.

He was a handsome boy of twelve, with curly black hair and chocolate colored eyes, who had a habit of staring for far too long. From his spot, at what he deemed the head of the table, he watched the other five chatter excitedly. His best friend Silas was trying to balance a stick on his nose while Connor, the youngest of the group, urged him to drop it. Connor's older brother, Wesley, was talking to the two girls to Maverick's left. Cheyenne, carrot haired and fair skinned, was nodding, and Roxanne was trying not to laugh by muffling her face in a handful of the springing brown curls that framed her face.

Maverick smiled and clapped his hands together, trying to gain everyone's attention. They all had a bad habit of not paying attention to him.

"Hey!" he called out in his most glorious timber. It fell weak on the ears of everyone but Roxanne, who shot him a smile before gathering the attention of the other four. Once they were all paying attention to him, he nodded shortly and stood up, crossing his arms over his chest. "I asked everyone to come meet me here because summer is almost over."

"So, why are we wasting time here?" Silas chirped up. He'd wanted to teach Connor how to climb trees, mainly so he could watch the ten-year-old fall on his back a couple of times.

"Chey is going home soon, and I figured that, since she has made herself a member of our group, we'd say goodbye?" Maverick grinned at his friends, including their newest addition, and grabbed the sharpest rock he could find. "I want us to make a promise to each other, including Chey."

"Oh, boy. What's this promise, Rick?" Wesley rubbed his hands together in excitement. The last time Maverick had made them make a 'promise,' he, Silas, and Maverick had all been grounded, to varying degrees, for the better part of one month.

Maverick grinned almost wickedly at the group and walked to the old oak tree that completely shaded their corner of the world. He pressed the tip of his rock into its peeling bark and slowly, meticulously, carved his name in giant, scraggly letters. 'Rick,' he spelt. Grinning over his shoulder, he gestured the other five forward.

"Each of you." He held the rock out to Roxanne, with the most unbelieving look of them all.

She shook her head, and her curls bounced. "You've lost your mind." She tsked and took the rock. "What's the 'promise'?"

"To be friends. No matter what." His grin then was innocent, his eyes warm. "Martin said that some of his best friends, he doesn't talk to them anymore. I don't think I ever wanna not talk to you guys."

He smiled in earnest at all of them.

Roxanne mulled over what he was asking and then shrugged her shoulders. He had asked for weirder, more dangerous things. Things that she had willingly complied with because, at ten years old, she knew she would follow him through pretty much anything. She took her time carving the seven letters of her name into the bark. Hers was a much smaller script than Rick's, positioned slightly to the left and underneath his.

When she was done, she handed the rock to Cheyenne and then backed up. While her friends wrote, she toed the grass, kicking up clumps of leaves and damp earth. Maverick shot her a quick wink, and she pinked in the cheeks.

When six names were etched into the bark, they returned to the "Round Table" where Maverick had set his six pack of soda cans on the rock surface. "A toast. To friendships that will last through anything."

Six hands clunk together six cans, and the five others mirrored his cheer—if for no other reason than Maverick had said so.

Roxanne's mother called her name loud enough to break through the quiet ring of trees that they had been situated in. It

4

was their cue to disperse and head home to their mothers and their fathers and their siblings. They headed out, toward their dinners and their chores. As the six walked almost in unison, the golden hour broke, and the heavy nimbus clouds shattered. It began to pour.

They hit the pavement and ran as a group.

It was a cold rain, the kind that fell heavy and without mercy for the people underneath them. Maverick shed his sweatshirt and draped it over Roxanne's head in a failing effort to keep her dry in the downpour. Wesley and Silas shoved at each other while aiming for the deepest puddles. Cheyenne caught hold of the sleeve of Maverick's sweatshirt and used it on her face. Silas shoved into Maverick and acted as an usher, moving them along.

Cheyenne was the first to break away from the pack of running people. She waved her hand at her friends and started up the wide, dirt driveway toward her grandfather's retirement house. Roxanne stopped to wave after her before Maverick wrapped his arm around her shoulders and herded her along. They said goodbye to the Carmody brothers, and then Maverick made sure Roxanne got into her house before he followed Silas to their corner of the cul-de-sac.

The two boys nudged and shoved at each other, Silas picking on Maverick's need to protect Roxanne. They parted ways in front of the two almost-identical two-story houses at the opening of the street. A quick wave at each other and then they were inside, headed toward their own dinners and their own evening routines.

Chapter One
November 2012

Roxanne watched her shadow collect snowflakes, like little balls of frozen precipitation piling up on the outline of her figure on the sidewalk. She could count them, each fluffy flake that fell from the moment she'd run outside, and Maverick had followed her. She sat on the curb while he watched over her, thousands of flakes falling all around them and neither of them saying a word as they clung their eyelids and melted on the tips of their noses.

He stared at the top of her head, mute.

Roxanne licked her lips, hunting for words to say.

"Do you remember," she finally said, after what felt like hours in the still gray evening, tilting her head back to look up at him. "Do you remember when Sid broke up with Callie? And we thought he was the biggest idiot in the world?"

Maverick's face shifted, from an almost blank anxiety to confusion. There was nothing left in him, nothing left in either of them, to continue the fight. Not after he'd just burned their entire world down.

"I do." He lowered himself onto the sidewalk beside her and looked over at her, his dark brown eyes blood shot.

In his face, she saw the years of knowing each other that had all just been thrown away. She saw the seven-year-old boy who had held her hand on the slide and the thirteen-year-old who had caught his first fish and nearly kissed it in excitement. His face showed the lines of the high school senior who had big dreams of law school and had never made it on the football team. In those dark brown eyes, which she'd spent almost twenty years loving in every way under the sun, she saw the man she'd thought she was going to spend the rest of her life with.

That thought made her throat catch and caused a soft burn to start in her eyes, once again.

"We were wrong." Her voice caught on the last word, and she patted him on the knee affectionately. "I don't think either of us had ever been so wrong before."

Roxanne pushed herself to her feet and swallowed back a sob.

"Rox." Maverick reached out and caught her hand in his.

When she looked back at him, she saw the sadness she felt written across his face, and she couldn't help the confusion and the betrayal from touching hers. "I'm sorry."

Roxanne tugged her hand away, not to punish him but rather to save herself, and she turned her face up into the light snow.

"I am, too," she said after a moment, and ended their conversation with a soft step away from him.

She was sorry, sorry that their entire lives had been thrown aside over something that felt so small. To Maverick, obviously, it'd been so much. So much more than the sum of their relationship, the sum of their past. While they had burned hot, hotter than she'd ever thought possible in her young adult life, they had fizzled out so quickly that she started to puzzle the probability of the sun making another rotation around the earth.

Roxanne didn't turn back around until she was at the door of their apartment building, making eye contact with the same doorman who had let her in and out every single day since they moved in a couple of years before. They'd shared a conversation nearly every day, a smile whenever possible, and Christmas cards and cookies every year. The man's concerned stare was nearly the breaking point as he pushed the door open for the twenty-two-year-old woman. Her eyes filled with tears, panic burning up her throat as it first occurred to her that she was entirely on her own in the situation.

"Tell him when he comes back in...tell him. I'll be out by dinner time."

She hugged the older man quickly, a final goodbye for someone who had acted as a protector and a friend.

Then, without another look behind her, she took the stairs, two at a time, and let herself into their apartment for the last time.

Chapter Two
August 2016

Autumn had lost its wonder a year after Roxanne Wortham had moved to the Nevada desert. Admittedly, it could have been the fact that she had turned twenty three that year, and with the knowledge that she had lived for more than two decades thrown into her face for the third time, she could have felt a new sense of adulthood with the passing of this latest birthday. An adulthood where wonder, where magic, where the possibility of something more, blended into the dull, nine-to-five routine of capitalist adulthood.

She didn't tend to think so. Rather, she blamed the loss of magic that met her the end of that September—after she had relocated to Las Vegas, Nevada—on the fact that the desert sun scorched the earth long after September passed through the calendar year. Instead of the crisp falls she had experienced for most of her life in Penn Ridge, Pennsylvania, or the beautiful, colorful falls of the small town in New York where she had traveled every other weekend to visit her best friend, she was left with the dried-up earth of a desert that saw very little weather. She missed preparing for winter and the smell of dampness in the air before the first heavy snow of the season. She craved the cold blanket covering the earth and reminding her that time was passing. The chill that hardened the ground underfoot the passing of September used to mean that the world was still moving underneath her and no matter what, there was still a tomorrow waiting to happen.

Now, after three years of watching the summer sun slip into seasonless fall and winter months, Roxanne took the passing of September to mean that the weather cooled down a fraction and that the tourist season was done. For a brief moment, anyway.

If she hadn't kept a steady eye on the calendar at her desk, and the accumulation of hair (and curls) that came with avoiding a hairdresser for months unless absolutely necessary, Roxanne might not have ever known that time was passing at all.

Of course, it was an absolutely *romantic* notion to think that time didn't pass at all in the Nevada desert. Other than the end of tourist season, the end of the summer also meant slightly longer nights and the promise of an occasional cool breeze sweeping off the desert around ten at night. It was with the promise of a cool breeze to alleviate some of the summer sweat off the back of her neck that Roxanne sat, pen pursed between her lips, reviewing a page of writing she had been working on for the past week. Her eyes stared blankly at the sheet of paper while she thought about the silly notions of time passing and her own romantic misconceptions.

If only they translated so well onto the creamy, yellow legal pad pages spread out around the metal patio table. Roxanne was about to make a note, in the margins of the page she held, about the romanticism of fall, when a sour twisting radiated through her abdomen. It was a deep, sudden sense of dread that she had become well acquainted with over the last twenty-six years of her life.

See, Roxanne did not believe she was omniscient in any way, let alone could she predict the given outcome of anything. (Her excursions to the casinos on the Strip when she had first relocated proved this.) But this gut feeling, she knew all too well. It had come right before her father suffered a heart attack two years prior and had nearly plowed her over when her grandmother had passed away six years before that. She had woken up from a deep sleep in an absolute panic the night her brother had gotten into a fatal accident, almost an hour before they got that late-night call; and when her life fell apart, four years prior, she had felt it for days.

She sat upright in her seat, her teeth gnawing away at the end of her pen, and went through the list of people in her life. She had spoken to her parents the day before, and Silas just that morning. Connor had checked in the Friday before, and Wesley had been more or less MIA for the better part of the past year, something about photography and birds. Cheyenne, her best friend, was in Penn Ridge vising her grandfather – she'd texted her a couple of hours before she went to bed. Her cousin, Cynthia, who was six months pregnant, had been texting her nonstop with baby name ideas. Ethan's sister, Isabelle, was accounted for, and his parents in Colorado were as well. That was everyone they talked to; but knowing where everyone was didn't make her feel any better.

Roxanne went through the list and checked off each named person temperamentally. This should have eliminated the stress building in her stomach, but instead, it made the stress in her shoulders tighten even more. She kept chewing on the end of her pen, her eyebrow twitching, and her obsessive tendencies causing tension to spark in the back of her head.

Just when she felt the bubble of dread start to morph into something darker and her skin subsequently felt like it was crawling, a noise behind her drew her back into reality.

Her partner of almost three years was just opening the sliding glass door that separated the high rise from the Nevada ending when the feeling struck. He caught the look of surprise that flashed across her face and furrowed his orange eyebrows together.

"You knew I was making tea," he teased while she set her pen and the legal pad on the table.

Roxanne shoved both of her hands through the mess of chestnut curls that framed her face before responding.

"You didn't startle me." She sighed, forever trying to dispel the awkward humor Ethan used in his day to day life. "Did my mom or dad call?"

She had left him her cellphone in an attempt to cut back on outside distractions.

"Nope." He set her purple mug down on top of the legal pad, in the same spot where her fifth cup of coffee had left a ring on the page an hour ago. She was making such great progress. "What's up?"

"I was just wondering," she said quietly. He'd just mock her if she told him about the twist of her gut and the anxious drip coming down between her shoulders.

"How's the great American novel coming?" he asked playfully, giving her an affectionate pat on the shoulder. "You haven't turned the page."

"I'm aware," she griped. "I've been staring at this for what feels like forever, trying to figure out how I wanted to word this one thought and... well...I think I just decided."

Ethan raised an eyebrow at her, sitting at the table across from her. "What did you decide?"

"That I'm taking the line out. And then rehashing the entire piece." Her lips curled in frustration. "Or just throwing it out."

Ethan laughed and reached across the table to put his hand over hers.

"It's really okay," he assured her softly. While her greatest critic, Ethan was often her biggest fan. "Have you tried walking away and coming back to it?"

Roxanne laughed. This was a short yet still explosive laugh leftover from the still present tension that was rock hard in her gut.

"If I walk away from it anymore, I might as well not finish it." She took a sip of her tea, the scalding liquid sliding over her tongue and down the back of her throat. "It's not like crunching numbers, Ethan. It takes...patience."

"And 'crunching numbers' does not?" His voice was soft, not quite playful but not angry.

When she didn't laugh, he resigned himself to scrolling through his phone and drinking tea, while she stared in frustration at her legal pad. They sat in silence, tea burning their lips, their tongues, as the warm desert night relaxed around them. It was nearing eleven when she sighed in frustration, dropping her head onto the glass table. The legal pad landed with a 'thud' on the patio's concrete floor. She still felt the uneasiness in her gut, but her overall frustration was paramount.

Ethan chuckled, only quietly, at her and stood up.

"C'mon. Let's go to bed. You'll feel better when you get back at it tomorrow after work." He gathered their mugs and went inside before her self-deprecation could morph into an argument.

Glumly, Roxanne picked up her legal pad and followed him inside.

Chapter Three
August 2016

Despite the knot of discomfort in her stomach, Roxanne made love to Ethan that night. It was quick, as it always was, and her brain wasn't in it, but it was the exercise she needed to fall into a dead, briefly dreamless sleep.

Roxanne had a complicated relationship when it came with her dreams and despite never truly knowing it; she knew that no matter what the circumstance was, there was always something looming over the horizon. A handful of hours watching the time pass on their analog clock kept her from going insane. The small reprieve she had gave way into something horrid. This was something that made her brain throb.

That night she dreamt of being cold. Of lying in a stream of cold water, stained red, covering her entire body. She was lying on her side, her head resting on the sharp corner of a rock while another stabbed her in the kidney. The water washed over her face, tangled her hair, and made it hard for her to breathe.

She lay there, barely aware that she was half drowning and probably in the position of eventually bleeding to death. Her discomfort, the pain and the cold, were drowned out by the realization that she was still alive.

Alive and fully capable of understanding the vibration that was drumming all over her body. After a moment, the vibration ended and she was washed anew with the silence of the stream, running over her ears and flicking the corners of her eyes. Her eyelids flickered open and she was staring at a blanket of stars, unencumbered by city lights or desert heat waves. Trees, instead, marred the corners of her star lit night, their leaves waving in a soft, chilled breeze that washed over her. Cold. Sticky. Red.

The vibrations started again. This time, Roxanne felt her body shifting toward them, the cold water slowly warming. And a weight, draping itself across her abdomen, also responded to the vibrations in the air. She and the weight shifted toward the source of the vibrations as her eyes drifted closed once more.

In the silence of her bedroom, she let her eyes open to the whisper of Ethan's breath across her face and the vaguely lit atmosphere the Las Vegas neon signs provided, even through the curtains. She laid there for a heartbeat, listening to her boyfriend's half-conscious breathing, until it dawned on her that the vibrations in her dream had followed her into their waking world. Semi-waking world, considering she still had Ethan's snoring breaths on her skin.

When the third round of vibrations started, her side of the bed lit up, her phone spamming on her nightstand. Ethan groaned in his sleep and rolled over, his back to the light, while she fumbled in the dark for her phone. The time on their cable box read a little after five in the morning, meaning that he would be up for work soon. She could feel the exhaustion of the late night and rising

16

anxiety perpetuating her sense of unease as she slid out of bed and all but limped out of their bedroom.

Their living room was just starting to fill with light from the desert, the sun rising slowly over the still vibrant Las Vegas skyline and filtering slow orange and honeysuckle colored light through the sliding doors that led from the apartment onto their balcony. Her writing desk, which was positioned by the door, still held her yellow legal pad from the night before. Her phone had stopped vibrating in her hand by the time she made it to the kitchen, and she wasted no time getting out the coffee grinds and a filter from their cabinet.

As she scooped coffee grinds into the filter, her phone screen lit up, for a third time, with a '570' area code flashing across the screen. Roxanne shoved her hand through her messy curls as she looked down at the 'Scranton, Pennsylvania' that was positioned under the phone number, and her stomach twisted. Her throat felt tight, and the pit that had made her sleep uncomfortably all night returned with abundance.

"Hello?" She fought to keep her voice even upon answering the phone, dumping water into the reservoir of the coffee maker.

"Hello, is this Ms. Roxanne Wortham?"

She didn't know the voice on the other end of the line, but it definitely did not sound like the automatic voice of a telemarketing scheme.

"Yes, this is Roxanne." Roxanne kept her voice at a miniscule pitch as to not wake up Ethan. She knew that her mom and dad were in South Carolina at this time of year, not

Pennsylvania, and that if she was getting a phone call from Pennsylvania for Silas, Nancy, or the baby, it would have had a Philadelphia area code.

The Scranton area code could only have belonged to a crisis involving Cheyenne and her grandfather, and either outcome made Roxanne's chest hurt.

"May I ask who's calling?" she asked around the knot of anxiety in her throat.

"My name is Kayla, and I'm calling from the ICU of Moses Taylor hospital." Her voice was clinical, short. Roxanne's eardrums throbbed, but she kept quiet. "I am calling on behalf of Maverick Sterling."

Roxanne's blood went cold. Her pulse thundered in her ears.

"I-I'm sorry? Could you repeat that?" she squeaked out.

"I'm calling on behalf of Maverick Sterling," Kayla repeated. "You're listed as his emergency contact?"

Emergency contact. Something was wrong. Roxanne forced herself to breathe evenly and ignore the storm in her ear drums. She hadn't seen him or heard from him in years. Somehow, that didn't matter. The thought of him being hurt, or worse, had caused her body to jolt awake with panic, and the world stopped moving.

"Is he...is he okay?"

"He was in an accident this morning, at a little after six," Kayla started. "You're the only person listed in his file, and we've been trying to get in touch with you for over an hour. He's just gotten out of surgery."

"Did you call anyone else?" Roxanne asked numbly. Maverick was in the hospital. Alone.

"You're the only person listed as his emergency contact." Contact. Singular. Not Sid. Not even Silas.

She rubbed her face, her hand shaking. "There's no one else who can...okay. Okay. I'm in Nevada right now. So, I won't be there for a couple of hours. He's out of surgery?"

"For now. They're going to bring him in for another round in a few hours."

"Is he...?"

"He's not in good shape."

"What can I do?" There was no point in arguing about the emergency contact or the phone call, despite the irritation coming off of Roxanne in waves.

"I would get here as soon as possible," the woman replied.

Roxanne murmured a pleasantry in goodbye and hung up before all but dropping her phone on the counter.

"What's going on?" Ethan put his hand on her shoulder, feeling the tension resting there.

"I, uh, I have to go home." Roxanne looked up at her partner, taking in the concern in his dark eyes. She felt herself shuddering involuntarily at the concern situated in them. "There's been an accident..."

"Is it Silas? Cheyenne?" He looked panicked.

"No. It's Maverick."

Chapter Four
August 2016

Ethan couldn't believe his ears when he heard Roxanne say she was going back to Pennsylvania. Part of him thought that it was a joke, a nightmare, or a hallucination—the product of her uneasiness on the patio and the stress of his job. He followed her down the hall to their bedroom and opened his mouth to speak, only for her to slam the bathroom door in his face between them. He stood there with his hand raised, one finger extended and his mouth open for nearly a whole minute before he backed up.

"Roxanne." Ethan knocked on the door. "Roxanne what do you mean it's Maverick?"

"He was in an accident," she called back.

"Okay? What are you doing?" He stepped back when she yanked open the door, wearing soft blue jeans and her plain sweatshirt.

"What are you doing?" he asked again, firmly.

"I need to go back to Scranton." She brushed passed him and yanked her little blue carry-on suitcase out from underneath their bed. "I need to go."

Ethan's jaw ticked. "What do you mean you need to go back?" He stepped in her path, blocking her from her dresser.

"I mean I have to go." Roxanne dodged around him and yanked open her underwear drawer.

Ethan grabbed her arm. "What are you talking about?"

Roxanne looked up at him, her blue eyes rimmed with moisture. "He's unconscious and really hurt, Ethan."

"Okay but one of your friends can go hold his hand. Hell, he's a grown ass man. He can be there by himself." Ethan relaxed his grip around her arm, trying to quell the anger burning inside of him.

Maverick had been a sore spot their entire relationship, at least on his end, and the man wasn't even around. Unless they were with her friends, the group of people she had, in his honest opinion, unhealthily dependent relationships with. Then it was like Ethan was the interloper in his own relationship.

"Roxanne c'mon."

She stopped grabbing underwear and socks to look up at him. "Ethan, he doesn't have anyone else. I need to go."

Ethan dropped her hand and shook his head.

"Do whatever the fuck you want," he growled before storming out of the room, slamming their bedroom door behind him.

He slammed around the kitchen, making coffee and unloading the dishwasher just so he'd have something to do. His mind raced, thinking of all the ways he could justify her staying. Or, at the very least, take him with her. He had as much of a reason to go to that hospital as she did, even if the reasons weren't in sync with each other. While Roxanne could go out of a sense of duty to the man who'd broken her heart, Ethan could go out of a sense of possession. He could stand by her side while she did whatever she felt like she needed to do and make sure that the thorn in his side stayed just that and not a full-blown infection.

Early sunlight started to make its way into the apartment through their terrace doors, raking its long fingers across the clean, sterile surfaces of their dining room and kitchen area. Ethan looked out at the still bright Vegas skyline, the strip's vibrant, colorful lights still a beacon in the mostly gray morning. He rubbed his fingers against his jaw. The anger had begun to boil down to just tempered annoyance. He didn't think he could stop her from going, and asking to come along would just seem desperate. He didn't have to be happy about the situation

He brought her a cup of coffee and a resolution he could live with.

"I don't like that you're leaving," he said gruffly and offered the mug to her.

Roxanne stopped packing and gave him a slight smile.

"I think you'd be crazy if you did." She set the mug down on the nightstand and went back to folding pants. "I need to finish packing."

Ethan bit back the rest of what he wanted to say, trying to keep from saying something that would make their situation more tense. He stalked out of the room and eventually settled on the couch, staring blankly at the television in silence when he found himself thinking about the night that they first met.

K.T. Egan

Chapter Five
January 2013

"The Las Vegas skyline, long story short, is one of my favorite views." Ethan gestured behind him, toward the wall of windows overlooking Fremont Street, sending a wink in the direction of the leggy blonde draping herself across his best friend's lap.

He had been rambling on for the last half hour in an attempt to make Liam look better, although the conversation had drifted from the press firm he worked at to his copious amounts of international travel at the expense of said firm. The blonde was more interested in the stories than the person and acted seemingly content to be all over the other man. Ethan leaned back in his seat, draping an arm over the back with a chuckle to himself at the blissful expression in the other man's eyes.

Their eyes met over the table, and Liam laughed and drained the contents of his bottle while trying to navigate the woman's attention somewhere other than the front of his jeans.

The bar was very, very full. People jostled, jeered, chatted, and drank; the sounds of Vegas locals on a Thursday night, enjoying the less touristy season that filled the air of the dim bar. With a wink in the direction of the couple, Ethan stood and gathered a handful of empty bottles from the table's top. A promise to return with more drinks passed his lips as he departed into the crowd; although, he half hoped he would return to an empty table. Liam seemed to be doing just fine on his own.

At the bar, Ethan deposited his armful of glasses and requested three more. The bartender closest to him, a man Ethan knew very well, nodded and gestured to the crowd surrounding them. With summer over and the drop-in tourists giving the city a chance to breathe before the holiday season, locals were given the chance to roam their favorite haunts again, giving both Liam and Ethan the perfect opportunity to attend their favorite bar without having to deal with that many obnoxious, littering tourists. So, he nodded his head in understanding and turned his back to the bar top, leaning his back against it to take in the crowd.

He knew some of the faces in his immediate area, strangers he had become acquainted with on nights like this, but for the most part, the faces all blended together. Except for one pretty face, sitting by herself at the other end of the bar. She had dark hair that was half hiding her face as she sat hunched over, busily writing in a notebook. There was an empty wine glass to her right. Ethan turned back to Bill, gestured down to her to indicate he wanted her glass to be refilled, and pushed off of the bar.

Through the crowd he could see Liam and the blonde, still huddled at the round table where he had left them. He squared his shoulders, politely moved through the crowd, and took up the empty stool beside the mysterious woman. She didn't look up, just inched her glass a little bit closer to her notebook, although it was empty, as if she was containing herself. He watched her write for a moment, amazed at the way her pen glided over the page. In the dim lighting, he couldn't read what she was writing, but her words flowed in an elegant script.

"Writing a book?" He leaned on his elbows on the bar, craning his head toward her.

She didn't bother to pick her head up. And she didn't respond. The bartender set another glass of white wine in front of her, taking away her empty glass, and she didn't so much as say thank you.

Ethan turned back to the woman. "I'm Ethan."

He extended his hand in the hopes she'd take it.

While she didn't do more than pick up her head, he had at least gained her attention. The bartender set his beers down beside him, and he gladly took a long pull before trying a third time. He couldn't help but catch the arched eyebrow, at the amount of drinks before him, no doubt. He held up both hands to gesture to the fact that not all of them were for him; he probably looked like an alcoholic. Not exactly the first impression you wanted to make.

"You don't look like a local," he offered, although he could tell how lame of a reach it was and mentally kicked himself. "This is kind of like an unofficial local's night, so…"

"You are exceedingly bad at this." Her voice was almost as beautiful as her face, and he was beyond himself the minute she opened her mouth. "Rox."

She shook her head dismissively at his hand and picked up her pen again.

26

"Got you to respond though." Ethan felt himself grinning. "Again. Writing a book?"

Roxanne snorted, tilting her head to the side as she continued to write.

"Nope." Her hair slid back from her neck, revealing a row of small, jeweled earrings in her left lobe. "Drunk?"

"Nope," he mimicked her disinterested tone. "You?"

In the dim lighting he couldn't tell what color her eyes were, but she definitely rolled them at him as she lifted her glass to her lips. "Thank you."

"For?" He puffed up his chest, sure that he could recover from the mocking tone of her voice and the quirk to her lips.

Roxanne rolled her eyes again as she took a sip. "The refill."

She set her glass down and picked her pen up again. In the time he had been sitting beside her she had written two things on her paper, which as he looked closer, he realized was a list and not a paragraph.

"What brings you here on a Thursday?" she asked as she continued to jot down words. It was too dimly lit, and her handwriting was too messy, for him to see what she was writing.

"Dedicated wingman." Ethan jerked his thumb toward himself as he shot a look across the bar, toward Liam and his blonde-haired groupie. They were still at the table but looked less and less decently placed by the second.

She followed his gaze and flat out laughed; it was a sound that he decided he liked. A lot. "What brings you in here on a Thursday?"

Roxanne sighed and capped her pen, turning to face him. She crossed her legs delicately and tilted her head to the side to make eye contact with him. "You're not going to go away until I bare my soul to you, are you?"

Ethan sat up straight and took another pull from his beer. "Nah, I'm committed now."

She snorted again and finished the contents of her glass. Before responding, she checked the time on her watch and shook her head in a soft of abject resignation.

"Then I'm going to need at least one more." Her smile in his direction was small but genuine, and Ethan couldn't help but smile back.

He finished his beer, gestured Bill over to refill her glass, and leaned against the bar once more with his head turned to her, his chin resting in his palm with his undivided attention on her. Roxanne ran a hand through her hair, the dark waves tumbling back over her shoulder.

"Well, I just moved here," she started with a sigh.

"From?"

"Just a small rural town in Pennsylvania that no one has really heard of. It was that fancy of a place."

"Why Las Vegas?" Ethan offered, to which she smiled ironically.

"It seemed like as good a place as any for a new start" — she shrugged her slim shoulders— "and I was able to find a job."

"A new start, huh?" Bill had set her wine down, but she hadn't touched her own glass, instead she was looking him in the eye. He took the chance to let his eyes wander over her features, taking in the softness of her cheeks and the way her eyes filled her face. He wished he could see the color of them, but he could definitely note the fact that there were deep bags under them. "What are you running from?"

"Why do you assume I'm running?" she asked, her voice muted, her head tilted to the side as they continued to stare each other down.

Ethan leaned closer until he could feel her breath on his face so that the words out of his mouth would sound fractionally less harsh despite the crudeness in them.

"Because, darlin', no one comes to Las Vegas for 'a new start' unless they're running from something." It was a truth he knew all too well. "So, Rox, what are you running from?"

"The explanation could take a while," she said, sounding less than impressed. "You might have to buy me another drink."

She raised her wine glass to him before taking a long drink. He was already waving the bartender over for a refill.

Chapter Six
August 2016

Roxanne finally left their bedroom with her little suitcase in tow and her untouched coffee in hand. Ethan got to his feet and met her in the kitchen, his annoyance fizzling out to a sad resignation.

"Were you able to find a flight?" He licked his lips.

"Yeah." Roxanne set the mug down and reached out to wrap her arms around his waist.

Ethan put his left arm around her shoulders and rested his chin on the top of her head. "When do you have to be to McCarran?"

"My flight leaves at nine," Roxanne said into the fabric of his t-shirt. "I should get going."

"I could…I could drive you." Ethan stepped back to look down at her. He adjusted the strings of her UNLV sweatshirt, the one she usually wore when she had to travel, and tried to smile. If he could just keep his hands on her a little bit longer, then maybe she would change her mind. Maybe she would stay.

Something in her blue eyes told him that changing her mind was impossible, though. He couldn't put his finger on it, but it worried him more than he ever knew something could.

"I already called a car," she replied softly.

Her hand, so much smaller than his, reached up to cup the left side of his face. Her soft fingertips touched the rough stubble there in an act of pure affection. "Besides. If you take me, you might miss your workout this morning."

It was an attempt at alleviating some of the stress of their situation.

"I'm going to London tomorrow," he reminded her as he wrapped his hands around her waist and pulled her close. "Will you be here when I get back?"

His breath was soft on her face as he leaned down. Roxanne stood on her toes, wrapping both of her arms around his neck, guiding his face closer to hers.

"I'm going to try," she whispered.

In truth, she didn't know how long she was going to be needed. It all was determined by whether or not Maverick left the hospital in a wheelchair or a body bag, but such morbid thoughts could only bring bad karma, and she didn't want to dwell on it.

"I'll call you when I land." She tilted her head to the left, curls tumbling over her shoulder with a little smile popping up on her lips. "And when I get to the hotel I'll be staying at, I'm going to have to sleep on it."

Ethan offered a strained laugh and planted a soft kiss on her forehead. "I'll talk to you this afternoon?"

He gave her a tight squeeze before letting go and stepping back.

After the door closed behind her, Ethan made his way into their bathroom and turned the shower on as hot as he could make it. He stared at his reflection in the mirror while he waited for the shower heater to catch up with his mood and scowled back at the man staring at him. The man who should have told his girlfriend not to go.

Steam started to cling to the glass, clouding in slowly around his face.

"Fuck." He scraped a hand down from his hairline to his chin while the other gripped the edge of the black vanity top. "Shit."

Roxanne was going back to Pennsylvania, back to *him*. And he'd barely tried to stop her—hadn't even bothered to try and make her see the reasons why this was not a good decision. He hadn't voiced all of the rational thoughts racing through his head right then, hadn't vocalized all the anger boiling under the surface. It bothered him that she didn't seem to understand, or even care, how he felt about what had just transpired.

Didn't she get that going back to Maverick put Ethan in a terrible position, even if it was just to keep the waste of space from waking up alone in a hospital room? How was he supposed to be okay with the fact that she was going back?

Angry thoughts shifted to paranoid thoughts in an instant, and Ethan found himself imagining Maverick waking up in his hospital bed just to kiss her. That smug glint in his eye as he stared Ethan down behind her while she fawned over him. Their friends laughing at Ethan until he left, feeling the fool. It was enough to make his gut clench.

He pounded a fist on the vanity and cursed once more before forcing himself into the shower. He still had to face his day, his job, and his coworkers, while she ran across the country for the person who still joined them in bed every night.

Chapter Seven
August 2016

Cigarette smoke and lilacs clung to the woman sitting next to Roxanne. It was a heady mixture that had been making her stomach churn since they'd boarded the plane in North Carolina. She rubbed at her nostrils for the tenth time in less than five minutes and laid her head back on the headrest. While she tried not to gag on the scent wafting between their seats, she trained her eyes on the window beside her, looking out at the mid-North Carolinian morning.

It was nearing noon on the east coast, and her body was adjusting to the time zone slowly. If she was at home, she'd be on her way to her third meeting of the day as a research and marketing analyst for Embrion International, one of the medium-sized hotels in Las Vegas. She was always bouncing back and forth between people's offices.

Instead of running errands or trying to figure out the best way to say 'free internet for guests' in eight different ways, she was sitting on a plane, chewing on her thumbnail, thankful they had given her a handful of days off to make the trip.

The woman beside her was still getting situated when the plane started its trip down the runway. She had yellow, painted nails and was wearing what looked like a velvet track suit, her short gray hair wound into tight curls around her wrinkled face. When she smiled at Roxanne, her teeth were almost as yellow as her fingernails, and her red lips split across in an awkward half circle. Roxanne scooted closer to the wall of the plan and turned her attention back down to the yellow legal pad on her lap, taking notes on the woman beside her in a small, effective shorthand.

"Where are you off to?" The woman had noticed Roxanne's little notes, unable to read the messy scrawl, but she smiled at the ambition in the notes anyway.

"Scranton." Roxanne knew the dialect of her seat mate and had grown up hearing the soft 'yak's' and the lack of t's in her words. It made her feel like home. She forced herself to put her pen down to really look at the woman. "What about you?"

"Easton." The woman licked her upper teeth. "My kids sent me to Las Vegas for my birthday. What a city."

She sounded like she was star struck; the same star struck that Roxanne had felt when she first explored the city with her cousin three years before.

"Yeah," Roxanne smiled. "It never stops being a madhouse."

Her smile turned into a smirk, her thoughts traveling back to that trip she and Cynthia had taken through Cesar's Palace on her first excursion into the city. She'd almost puked at how big it was, at how loud it was, at how much she loved the rush of people moving around inside the building.

"When I first moved there…I was all alone, on my first big adventure. And I felt like I was dreaming for weeks," Roxanne added.

The woman laughed beside her, shaking in her seat. "It's definitely a dream."

"Lately it's been feeling like a nightmare," Roxanne said quietly as she tapped her pen on the legal pad.

And going home…going back to Pennsylvania could either be the worst part of it yet or the wakeup call that I need, she mused to herself as she wrote the thought down, her mind going back to the stagnant life and the four walls that she lived in.

Roxanne was looking out the window, her mind lost, when the plane touched down on the cement tarmac. Her seat mate, Karen, as Roxanne had later learned, was leaned over her once again to look at the small runway. Roxanne couldn't help but watch as well, caught up in the foliage that surrounded them; the lively trees sporting green and full leaves, the hills they'd flown over that boasted life of all kids, the occasional cellphone tower that slowly grew larger as they loomed over their sections of the earth.

Somewhere in her chest it resonated that she was, in fact, home—that the desert she had grown accustomed to being indentured in was nothing compared to the beautiful piece of the world that she had loved. That she had missed.

36

"I always forget how green it is," she mused to the older woman as the plane touched down. "Which is weird 'cause I grew up here."

Karen laughed beside her and checked her reflection in her makeup compact. "I go away for a weekend to see my sister in Delaware, and I come back and forget it too. It's always a great gift, to pass into the state lines and get sucked into the beautiful thickness of it."

Roxanne nodded. "It's always like another world," she mused and tapped the tip of her pen against her fingertips.

They exchanged a knowing look, and Karen went back to primping. Roxanne felt at home, sharing secrets about the beautiful, green world of Northeast Pennsylvania that could only be shared with someone who had lived in the area long enough to see its splendor—to catch a nautical twilight while standing in the middle of a field, watching the clouds overhead. The area was like a whole nother world, an entirely different place that Roxanne had missed entirely too much. And someplace she'd been away from for entirely too long.

Roxanne switched on her phone to notice that she had two missed text messages from Ethan and a missed call from Silas. A number she didn't recognize, from South Dakota, had called her. They'd left a voicemail, which she'd check when she was at the hotel.

She and Karen parted ways at the luggage claim, where the older woman was greeted with a banner and the squealing of her grandchildren. Roxanne watched the woman be surrounded by people she loved after only a week away, and she felt something akin to sadness deep in her belly. Her own grand return to NEPA, the first time she'd been back in four years, was to the cramped baggage terminal with its two carousels and car rental desk. Roxanne called herself a car and stepped out into the hot August afternoon, soaking in the gentle sun as it touched her skin and listening to the subtle sounds of Avoca, Pennsylvania.

While she waited for the Uber to pull up in front of the small airport, Roxanne called Silas to let him know she'd landed.

"Hey," his grainy voice greeted her on the second ring.

"Did you know that Avoca is tiny as hell?" she retorted and adjusted the strap of her laptop bag.

"One of the many marvels of NEPA." Silas chuckled dryly on the other end of the phone. "Any news?"

"Yeah, I called for an update while I was waiting in North Carolina. He was going into surgery again."

"Surgery for what?"

"Something about his knee. They're not super big on giving details over the phone." Roxanne dug her notepad out of her purse and skimmed through the notes she'd made on the fourth page. "I've got a mountain of paperwork calling my name when I get there."

A black Mazda pulled up to the curb in front of her, the white and black "U" on the back window. She waved briefly at the driver before sliding into the backseat. "I'll call you after I see him?"

"Yeah…just let us know."

Roxanne sent two long messages to Ethan as the car wove through the small highway that connected Avoca to Scranton, telling him about the woman she'd met on the plane and the conversation they had. It was hard to focus on the words while her driver chatted about his Psychology class at King's College and the familiar thrush greenery of her home state flashed by the windows. Eventually she stowed her phone in her laptop bag and rested her head against the glass, just in time to see the exit for Penn Ridge streak passed them. Her heart ached for home and childhood and all of the things that moving away had taken from her.

She let the driver talk, offering very little in the way of response, stopping him only when they passed by the Electric City mural on their way into Scranton to ask how much longer until they'd get to the hospital. In all that time, she thought about the Ridge. About the sunny Main Street which fed into Route 6 on either side, the colorful old buildings that sported diners and one-of-a-kind boutiques and cramped offices. She could practically taste Lorenzo's greasy, delicious pizza and hear the excitement of the Town Square Farmer's Market. If she closed her eyes, she was right back in the late summer rush of Penn Ridge and that small comfort helped alleviate some of the anxiety about what she was about to do.

Before she knew it, the driver was calling her name, bringing her back to attention. They had pulled up to the Emergency Room entrance of Moses Taylor, and he was looking at her through the rearview, his young face full of concern.

"I hope your friend is okay," he called after her as she got out, dragging her small suitcase with her.

"You and me both," she grunted at the car's back bumper.

The last time she had been in Moses Taylor hospital, she was twenty and had broken her wrist at a frat party. Maverick had almost punched the ER nurse that had checked her in, his drunken, panicked brain convinced that she needed to be seen first, before even the five-year-old girl waiting ahead of them. She could remember him telling Silas frantically that her wrist was not going to kill her from where she stood, looking at the Emergency Room entrance. A tight, albeit fond, smile slowly found its way creeping across her face, and she shook her head before heading into the building.

At the desk in the ICU, Roxanne had to twice calmly explain to the tired eyed nurse behind the computer that no, she was not married to the patient and yes, she was the woman they had called. The first time, the words had fallen out in a rush, making her hands shake as she got them off of her chest; the second time, she'd had to raise her voice and annunciate as best as possible. She got results that time. Instead of the initial shock of paperwork, which she had been expecting, hoping for, since she got off the plane, she was deposited into the hands of a young nurse with a round face and kind eyes.

She introduced herself as Layla and took it upon herself to lead Roxanne down the long hall to room 310. The door was partially open, and the curtain was drawn over the outside window.

From the doorway, Roxanne could see a pair of feet, one wrapped in a white cast

"You can go in, but he was still out when they brought him back from surgery." The nurse had a soft voice, a comforting voice that did nothing to quell the tension building in Roxanne's shoulders.

Roxanne stopped, one foot in the doorway to the dimly lit room. She turned to look at the nurse and swallowed back the hundred questions that sat on the tip of her tongue. "What...what really happened?"

She'd gotten a brief note about the accident when she called with her layover—she couldn't bring herself to step over the threshold without knowing.

Layla smiled and put her hand on Roxanne's shoulder.

"We've had a couple of rainy days over the weekend. He was driving back from what we assumed was a campground in New York, on the Casey, and hydroplaned. Spun out of control and drove into one of the embankments right before the Scranton exit," the nurse spoke.

When Roxanne flinched, the nurse started to sympathetically rub her back.

"There was a tractor trailer behind him. The driver called 9/11 and pulled him out of the car. It took a while for the paramedics to get there, so he was in rough shape when he got to us. His left leg is completely shattered, and he's pretty severely concussed."

"Campground?'" Roxanne asked numbly, biting at her lower lip.

"He was wearing hiking boots and had this ID badge in his pocket." The nurse gave Roxanne a laminated green card with the name of Maverick's favorite camping spot in Narrowsburg.

Roxanne licked her lower lip. It was raw from her constant worrying. She held the card by its corners as if it would break should she wrap her fingers around it. Maverick would collect a pass every year—and they'd go together, Roxanne and Maverick together under the stars. A lifetime ago.

"Did he wake up at all?" Roxanne croaked around the small lump forming in the back of her throat.

"No, but he will. When he's ready." Layla dropped her hand and gave her a wink. "You should probably go in there. They always do better when someone speaks to them."

"What am I supposed to say to him?" Roxanne looked up at the nurse, panicked. It'd been four years since the two of them had had a conversation. How was she supposed to interact with him when he couldn't interact?

Layla gave her a broad smile as she picked up a chart. "Whatever comes to mind. Just hearing your voice will help."

Roxanne made her way into the room slowly, deposited her bag and jacket and suitcase on the floor by the sink and counter combo in the corner diagonal from the bed without turning to look at it. She smoothed her hair down in the reflection of the glass door separating her from bandages, gauze, tongue depressors, and suture kits. The woman who stared back at her was frazzled, curls crazy around a face that was tired with eyes sporting stress and a headache. Her plain sweatshirt, an old American University hoodie that her brother, RJ, had bought when he'd committed in 2004, was sporting a new coffee stain by her collarbone and was half tucked into her leggings.

She sighed at her reflection and raked her hands through her hair before twisting it up into a knot at the top of her head.

"Okay. Okay. We can do this," she whispered under her breath and smacked her cheeks, lightly. "Until we can get ahold of Sid, we can do this."

Still, she took another long look at her reflection before turning to look at the narrow hospital bed. The body that laid underneath the weak hospital lights was fuller than she was used to, half wrapped in the pale colored blanket. His left leg stuck out of the thin, rumpled fabric, wrapped in white plaster and elevated in a sling. His hands were covered in scratches, stitched but still red and raw. The blanket sat around his waist like he did when he was sleeping. Her eyes stopped at the top of it, and she steeled herself for a breath before continuing the silent excavation upward.

Over the collar of his blue and white hospital gown, his neck was also sporting raw lacerations, not deep enough for even a bandage but long enough to hurt. There was a clear tube protruding out of his cracked lips, snaking up to a handful of machines clouding around the back of his hospital bed, that helped him breathe. A jagged cut sported around his left eye, sneaking toward his left lobe. His face was sporting a handful of days of growth, and his hair needed to be cut, badly.

43

The breath in her lips stopped, and she choked on a wealth of emotion and a moment of weakness. Hot tears sprung to her eyes as she looked at the small man, the strong man, the man she had thought she was going to spend the rest of her life with and had learned to live without. She took in how he looked so small underneath that thin blanket.

Roxanne sank into the orange, plastic chair by the bed and groped for Maverick's right hand, careful of the IV that sat poking out of it. She shook her head, sniffled, and squeezed it tightly. All the anger she'd been feeling, all of the panic over the right words to say, and what would inevitably be the wrong ones, fell away to the sheer relief that he was alive. He wasn't the man she'd known, at least, he didn't look like the man she'd know. The one she'd grown up loving. But there was something in his peaceful face that touched her to the core – the sweet innocence in his expressionless lips and eyes that reminded her so much of the boy he used to be. And of the man that she'd once thought she was going to spend the rest of her life with.

Roxanne was struck by the man laying in the bed before her, her heart sinking to the bottom of her stomach as the realization washed over her that this was, in fact, Maverick. And that he was hurt, so hurt he might not ever wake up. A world without Maverick was a world Roxanne wasn't sure she'd be able to live in – no matter their history.

"Maverick…what have you done?" she whispered and squeezed his hand in both of hers. "What did you do?"

44

Chapter Eight
August 2016

Ethan couldn't focus on anything. His mind wouldn't stay locked-in on the desktop screen in front of him or the client who was all but shouting in his face. All morning he'd been struggling to find meaning in the numbers that usually ruled his life or to find reason in the ingoing and outgoing emails passing through his fingers.

He hadn't been able to focus all day. It was hard to care about something as benign as an angry old man's retirement account when your girlfriend was on the other side of the country with her ex-boyfriend.

"Mr. Cole? Are you listening to me?"

Ethan looked up to the man sitting across from him. "I'm sorry. I was paying attention. Bali, right?"

Carver rolled his eyes at the man and jabbed a finger at his portfolio. "Do the numbers mean that I can go or not?"

"Without seeing a difference in your charts, you will be able to make the trip. You could even take your wife *and* the kids with you." Ethan clicked his pen and dropped it on the folder. "But I think our meeting is over."

"It's only been an hour," Carver protested as the accountant stood up and adjusted his sleeves.

"An hour is all I can give you today, Roland." Ethan offered his hand to the man, a fixed grin on his face. "I have another client coming in a half an hour."

Carver grunted but shook hands with the man and proceeded to leave his office. Ethan's head wasn't in the game—it really wasn't. His thoughts wouldn't stop hovering towards Roxanne, smiling back at him from the framed portrait next to his monitor, somewhere in Pennsylvania while he sat and tried to make it through the workday.

"I'd get my head out of my ass if I were you, Cole." Carver grinned as he said it, his beefy neck all but swallowing his chin as he grinned at the other man. "Whatever she's done, whoever she's done, you've got a solid head on your shoulders and a bank account that can support any mistakes."

"I'll see you in a month, Roland," Ethan grumbled as the door shut between them. He picked up his phone for the third time and tapped out another quick message to her. *Just checking it. Hope he's okay.* The text would go unanswered, probably for hours, but he felt a little bit better once it was sent.

"Do you know how fast he was driving?"

"Nope." Roxanne stopped fidgeting with the blue pen long enough to turn to the next page of paperwork and squinted at the small print. "The police officer I talked to wouldn't give me any information that the nurses didn't already fill me in on."

She took a deep swallow of the coffee that sat on the nightstand next to the hospital bed and massaged her eyelids. "His insurance is going to cover everything and then some, thankfully. But he needs to wake up because I don't know any of his passwords."

Silas almost chuckled but caught himself at the last second, making a disgruntled coughing noise instead. "He hasn't even woken up yet?"

Roxanne ground her teeth while also rubbing her fingers against her forehead. She hadn't moved out of the uncomfortable, plastic chair for hours, since the last time she'd allowed herself a coffee break. She'd alternated between filling out the paperwork given to her by the nurses and scolding him for getting himself into the hospital in the first place. Six hours of staring at the hospital bed had given her a headache; six hours of waiting for something to happen, slowly filling out paperwork, and yelling at a half corpse (well, fifth of a corpse) sporadically was giving her a hard time.

She sighed again, turning her attention away from his fuzzy face and back to the phone call.

"No. No he's been pretty much out of it." She glanced up at the man on the bed and pushed her glasses into her hair. "They took the breathing tube thing out an hour ago. According to the neurologist, his brain is concussed but not bad enough that he shouldn't be awake."

"So, he's being stubborn."

"Yup. What else is new?"

"Cut him some slack, Rox. He just got into a car accident."

"Where he got off easy. He needs to stop being lazy and open his eyes so I can go home!" she nearly yelled the words at the body on the hospital bed. When all that happened was the monitor beeping back at her, she dropped her thumb and drained the contents of her cardboard cup.

"I'm gonna go, Si. See if the nurses can help me fill out any of these forms."

They said their goodbyes, and Roxanne ended the call. Her phone buzzed with another message from Ethan, checking in on her for the umpteenth time. She was tempted to turn the damned thing off, just to get away from his constant texting and hovering. Instead, she tapped back a short response, telling him that she would call once she got to her hotel room. She looked up at the hospital bed again. The various monitors showed that his heart rate was unquestionably okay. The nurses had told her this several times. This gave her a good enough incentive to leave, closing the packet of papers she had on her person.

Layla was standing at the nurse's desk, chatting with a woman in orange scrubs whose hair was almost the same color. They were animated; they were laughing. They reminded her of conversations she'd had with Cheyenne, moments that had come easier when she was living on the East Coast. She felt stupid, lost in her thoughts and thinking of the past as Maverick laid in the bed, unable to move.

48

"I think...I think I'm going to go check in to my hotel room," she interrupted quietly and scratched at the back of her neck. "He's not going anywhere anytime soon."

Layla gave a soft chuckle. "No, he probably won't be."

Her friend nodded a happy agreement and went back to whatever file she was electronically updating.

Roxanne nodded and hugged her jacket to her chest.

"You'll call me if anything happens or if anything changes right?" her voice clotted, touched.

"Absolutely. Go on. Try to shower and get some rest. Visiting hours end in a few minutes anyways. But you can come back first thing in the morning." Layla patted her shoulder and smiled.

Roxanne hitched the bag over her shoulder and started toward the elevator, a weight lifting the further she got from his room. She didn't need to know what he was dreaming, not even what he was thinking when he took the Casey too fast like the same idiots they had mocked as children. All she needed was a chance to shut her brain down for a few hours and catch Ethan up on everything that had happened thus far.

She looked back at his door as the elevator opened and smiled meekly at the nurses standing across from it. Maverick was in the best room on the floor, the closest to anyone should something go wrong. She didn't feel much better, but she got into the elevator and tucked her phone between her shoulder and ear, calling Ethan.

Chapter Nine
August 2016

"His name is Rupert. And he's kind of a dick. But there's this one woman who makes him not so much of a dick. And that's about all I've got."

Roxanne looked up from the blank Word document on the off chance that Maverick had decided to open his eyes, and she let out a frustrated breath. She hastily tapped out the sentence she'd told him before picking her head up again.

"Cheyenne thinks he kind of sounds like you," she added, "only taller."

The jab made her smile, even if he wasn't awake to hear it.

"And less annoying."

Although, how annoying could you be if you were completely silent? It'd been four days since the accident and Maverick hadn't so much as twitched. Even his broken leg, ensconced in heavy plaster, didn't seem to so much as itch.

Roxanne had never seen Maverick so still, nor had she ever felt so alone in his presence. While sitting with him the past four days, she'd been able to get a lot of brainstorming done for her book. And a lot of research done for the hotel. Her spine was stiff from sitting most of the day, but she was still so afraid of leaving him alone, even for a minute. Just in case something happened and she wasn't there; just in case something happened and he was alone.

"I'm sure you'd like Rupert." Roxanne closed her laptop and got to her feet. She stretched her arms over her head and then rolled her head on her neck. "Maybe more than you like me."

Maverick still didn't respond.

Roxanne walked to the singular counter with the sink on the far end of the room to pick up her phone. She had four missed text messages from Ethan and a new email from her mother. She didn't acknowledge any of them. Rather, she sent a text to Cheyenne asking her if she was coming anytime soon.

Then she turned back to the hospital bed with a huff. "You could wake up at any moment now, Rick."

The body on the bed breathed steadily. Roxanne rolled her eyes and flopped back down in her seat, scooping her laptop up off the floor.

"Where was I?" she asked him. "Right. Rupert is a dick."

Roxanne sat by Maverick's bedside every day for the better part of three weeks while they rebuilt his left leg and kept on eye on his neurological responses. His condition stayed more or less the same, despite everything that Roxanne and the doctors did. There was a neurologist who came in twice a week to check on his brain function, and the orthopedic surgeon who had reconstructed his leg continuously checked his leg's function. Both of them reassured her that he was fine, and he would wake up when he was ready.

The Tuesday after the accident, the neurologist had pulled her aside and told her that he wasn't sure why Maverick wasn't waking up, that when he was ready to, he would open his eyes. The best thing she could do for him, from the doctors' and the nurses' mouths alike, was to talk to him. She should sit by his bed and talk to him about as many things as she could come up with. So, she did.

Roxanne read to him, every page of every cheap book she picked up in the hospital gift shop, every page she herself wrote, every tweet whether they made her laugh and shake her head. They watched reruns of *Gilmore Girls and NCIS* off her laptop, and she even talked to him about the short text messages and snippy phone calls she exchanged with Ethan. When she was really tired, she stopped trying to make it back to her hotel room before falling asleep, and she would rest her head on the pillow beside his and rest. It wasn't an intimate gesture at first, but she could hear his artificial breathing and was able to pretend that he was just asleep beside her.

The third Saturday after the accident, while her head rested beside his on the flat pillow, she thought about the sound of his breathing and the last time they were that close. At first, she couldn't place it—their entire lives together lost to the sound of him breaking up with her, running through her head for the millionth time. A stray ray of sunshine flecked through the curtains, beaming across her face to remind her of the actual last time that they had been together.

Chapter Ten
April 2014

Had she ever felt so hot before? No, no she definitely had not. She was sure of that as she stood with her back to the dance floor, in the itchy blue taffeta Nancy had picked out for her bridal party to wear, keeping her gaze steadily on the wall behind the bar. Beside her, Cheyenne drunkenly crooned at Wesley over something to do with his most recent magazine shoot. Roxanne should have been paying attention, should have been actively engaged since she didn't get to see them often anymore, but she couldn't focus. Ethan's warm hand on the small of her back only added to the heat coursing through her body while he actively listened, trying to keep up with the drunken giggles and coils of Cheyenne's voice.

It was Silas's wedding, and she should have been there, really been there. In the moment, she should have been celebrating with her closest friends the first of what she hoped would be several weddings—several blissfully happy moments where she could stop stifling smiles for Ethan's work posse. Instead, she found herself sneaking glances at the dark-haired man who had shown up without her even knowing he was invited. Of course, she should have seen that one coming. He was Silas's best friend,

54

no matter how strong the bond was between Silas and Wesley, or even how often Silas had stuck up for Connor in their youth, he and Maverick were as close as you could be without being blood related.

Maverick had stood respectfully at Silas's side throughout the entire ceremony, despite having missed the rehearsal dinner the night before. He looked like a near stranger with his haircut that was too short for his face and a crisp, unwrinkled suit. His head remained high, and he looked stoic, if dryly bemused to be at the wedding. Their eyes had met for the briefest of moments when she'd walked down the aisle on Connor's arm. Maverick hadn't smiled, but he hadn't looked away either. Roxanne had been the one to break contact, shifting her gaze from Maverick's dark stare to the smiling face of the groom to whom she offered a thumbs up before she made her way to stand behind Nancy's cousin.

There hadn't been anymore eye contact, although she could feel someone staring at the back of her neck when she wasn't looking. The stares had gotten more intense since Ethan had come to stand by her after the first dance, trying to coerce her onto the dance floor. It made her feel hot, uncomfortable and attended, but she wasn't sure she wanted the attention to stop.

"Earth to Rox."

Roxanne blinked, shaking off her stupor to look at Cheyenne, her lips pursed. "Mhm?"

"I didn't think you'd had that much to drink." Her best friend giggled. "Where'd you go?"

"Nowhere. I was right here." Roxanne smiled thinly and turned away. Turning directly into Maverick.

He reached out automatically to steady her at the same time Ethan caught her by the arm.

"Careful." His breath smelled like hops. "Didn't think you'd make it."

"Nice to see you, too." Roxanne's heart skipped a slight beat and she hated it. Hated the way there was a soft warmth in the back of her throat. "You making a speech?"

Maverick glanced over at Ethan and took a bemused sip of his beer. "Mhm." He thrust his hand out. "Maverick."

Ethan shot her a helpless glance, to which she shrugged and groped for Cheyenne's hand. The two women watched Ethan and Maverick shake hands, collectively holding their breath. "Ethan."

"And how do you know the bride and groom, Ethan?" Maverick's eyes never left the taller man's face. "I don't think I've seen you around."

Ethan shot Roxanne a helpless look. Roxanne let out an awkward cough and tucked herself underneath Ethan's arm. It wasn't something she'd have had to do if she was with Maverick, bur Ethan liked to keep her close. Sometimes uncomfortably close.

"Ethan is uh…my boyfriend," Roxanne said firmly.

Maverick nodded.

"I heard you were dating someone. I'm just surprised you brought him here." Maverick eyed Ethan skeptically. "To each their own right."

He nodded at Cheyenne.

Wesley clapped a hand on his shoulder and gave it an almost aggressive squeeze.

"C'mon. Let's go find Si," he urged his friend, his dark eyes imploring her to move on from the conversation.

Cheyenne, biting her lip, nodded enthusiastically and looped her arm through Maverick's. "Yeah! And I need to find the ladies' room. Come help me."

Maverick made a grunting sound but let the two of them lead him away. Roxanne heaved a hard sigh, unsure of when she'd started holding her breath. She looked up at Ethan. Her boyfriend was glaring in the direction Maverick, Cheyenne, and Wesley, Ethan's face turning red at the collar of his white button down shirt. Roxanne squeezed his bicep affectionately, panicking a little at the redness creeping into his face.

"Hey, hey." Roxanne tugged at the sleeve of his jacket. "I'm sorry about that. He's an ass when he's drunk."

Ethan looked down at her, something murky and angry in his face. "Yeah. An ass."

She shrugged weakly and hooked her arm around his waist and gave it a light squeeze. Ethan's jaw was locked in annoyance, but he let her lead him back to their table. They'd just sat down with new drinks when Maverick grabbed the band's microphone and, very loudly, cleared his throat into it. The reception's hundred plus guests all turned to pay attention when someone tapped on the side of their glass with a spoon. The clinking brought a lull to the conversation.

"Hey, everyone." Maverick had lost his suit jacket and undone the top two buttons of his shirt. His short hair looked like someone had ran their hands through it a couple times, and he looked so much more like the man she'd known and loved. So much more like the Maverick she'd known her entire life, not the man he'd been when he walked in.

"I guess first and foremost, congratulations Silas and Nance!"

Maverick bowed his head at the hearty applause he received. "Now, I know, we're all starving, and this free-range table arrangement thing is kind of confusing, but it's fine. Nancy does this for a living and hey, we've all met some new people!"

Maverick's face was turned directly at Roxanne and Ethan. None of the three smiled, despite the chuckles that went up around them.

"I've known Silas my entire life. He's been my best friend since we were, what, four? I don't know. The first time I tried to steal his Tonka Truck ended up in a lifelong friendship. The kind that gets you through the ups and downs. Losing family members. Moving to a new state. Breakups."

Silas, standing with his new wife by their parents, stiffened a little at the word. Roxanne frowned at her friend's back. Ethan, staring directly at Maverick, dug his fingers into Roxanne's thigh lightly. She put her hand over his and squeezed her eyes shut, hoping the speech would end soon.

"But wow. Who knew this fucker was going to get married. Especially before I did." Maverick laughed dryly, and the energy in the room crackled with uncomfortable interest. "But here we are. Here. We. Are."

Wesley tried to snatch the mic from him, but Maverick had hit his speed.

"For real though. Look at him all cozied up to Nance—love ya Nance—acting like he's got it all together. But they didn't even screen their guest list. I mean, there's a couple people here who…eh I don't know…maybe shouldn't be?" Maverick's eyes searched Ethan out again before Wesley managed to get the microphone away from him.

Roxanne jumped to her feet, apologizing to Ethan profusely, before she raced out of the ballroom behind Maverick and Wesley. The two men struggled against each other in the hall in front of the bathrooms, Maverick grumbling about the mess Silas had made of something while Wesley begged him to be quiet. Her eyes met Maverick's over Wesley's shoulder, and she just shook her head in disgust, turned on her heel, and left Wesley to quiet him.

Chapter Eleven
August 2016

Roxanne spent that Sunday evening ripping up pages of legal pad paper that she wasn't satisfied with, grumbling to Maverick's unconscious body while she did so.

"I named her Jane, which is kind of boring." She sighed and threw the legal pad on the floor. "But do you know how hard it is to name characters?"

The body in the bed did nothing but breathe.

Roxanne shot him a dirty look and tore another page into shreds. "The least you could do is wake up and give me a hand ya know. You always had…interesting ideas if nothing else."

Layla dragged in her cart, interrupting the aggravated writer.

"How's he doing this morning?" she asked in her cheerful tone. This had been the same routine they'd been experiencing for the past three weeks and Roxanne had just about had enough to the point where her rage was boiling over.

"No change as far as I can see. Dr. Keffler was already in to check on his head and said that he looks fine. He has *no reason* to be unconscious right now." Roxanne shot a pointed look at Maverick, who didn't react. "He's just being stubborn. As always."

Layla laughed as she checked his machines and made notes in the chart. "Hear that? Your friend here thinks that you're being lazy."

"Not lazy, stubborn." Roxanne gave the bed a soft kick to emphasize her point to the unconscious hunk of meat existing on it.

"What she doesn't understand, Maverick, is that I'm surviving off of bad hospital coffee and food that shouldn't really be called food, and I am missing my glorious triple headed shower. So, do us all a favor and wake the fuck up, Maverick Thomas Sterling."

Roxanne shot Layla a smirk and leaned down close enough that her lips almost touched his ear, and she whispered. "Or, so help me, we both know I will aggressively wake you up."

Layla began to laugh while she made some notes on the clipboard at the foot of the bed. "Why don't you go get some rest?"

"Because someone is being stubborn." Roxanne shot the bed a dirty look.

"Go to the hotel. Take a shower. Get some 'real' food, too. I'll call you if anything happens." Layla pointed toward the door. "Go." She gave Roxanne a reassuring nod. "Go on."

Roxanne sent one last scathing look at the man in the hospital bed, whose limbs were healing but who refused to wake up.

"Something better happen, Maverick. I would like to go home." Still, she stopped to squeeze his fingers before picking up her purse and slipping out of the room.

On her way to the elevator she tugged out her cellphone and dialed Ethan's number, hoping that he wasn't in a meeting. They had been arguing since that first night in the hospital, from passive aggressive text messages to short phone calls, and it all seemed to do more harm than good. When he didn't answer, for whatever reason, she closed her eyes and left a soft message for him to call her back while waiting for the elevator.

As the doors opened, she heard a loud crash and systematic beeping going off down the hall. Roxanne turned in time to see Layla's peach colored scrubs disappearing into Maverick's room on the tail of another nurse in similarly bright scrubs. Roxanne dropped both her purse and her phone and sprinted back to the window, just in time to see Maverick shoot straight up and lock eyes with her through the glass.

Chapter Twelve
August 2016

Wake the fuck up.

The words were stuck in his head, echoing around in his skull as he tried to stay as still as possible because moving anything hurt. Breathing hurt. His leg hurt. His chest hurt. Everything hurt, the worst pain that he had ever felt. He knew he was hallucinating the voice, urging him to get up, and he betted it on the pain. Or maybe it was one of the nurses who was speaking, and he'd just been too distracted to distinguish the difference between the two voices.

Maverick tried to move his left leg and let the pain shoot up through his spine. He ground his teeth and cursed.

When he opened his eyes, it was to a group of people standing over him. None of the faces were familiar; none of the panicked voices were the same.

"What...what happened?"

His chest was on fire. His throat was so dry that when he spoke, it felt like it was grating together like sandpaper. There was a headache behind his left eye, throbbing with each breath to the point that it made him want to throw up. When he finally cracked his eyes open, irises and corneas blurring with dryness, he was nearly blinded by the fluorescent lights overhead.

The nurse closest to his bed, a woman in coral colored scrubs and a kind smile, filled him in on the accident in short, soft sentences. She stayed by his side while a flood of doctors in white coats and more nurses in vibrant colored wears spoke to him. Most of them spoke medical jargon, words he only knew from reading client medical records and the stint Silas had done as a pre-med student. While the nurses spoke to him, speaking circles around what had happened to him weeks before, Maverick digested as much as he could and tried to place the voice that had woken him up.

He knew he was missing something; the longer he spoke to the nurse, the less sure he was that she'd been the one to wake him. And even the doctors seemed to think that he knew more than he did, or maybe they just didn't care.

As a surgeon came in, the smell of eucalyptus and mint soon swam through his nostrils, putting him at ease and making the itching in his throat and the pain in his left leg feel a little less cumbersome. Maverick continued to focus on the smell while the orthopedic surgeon checked his leg and his arm and talked to him about the recovery process. And as he fell asleep, trying not to think about what had been described as 'weeks of physical therapy,' he breathed in the eucalyptus and mint one more time.

When he woke up again, after a period of blackness that he wasn't sure had existed at all, the silence in the room made him feel like he wasn't actually alone. It wasn't the kind of silence that he'd gotten used to in his apartment, or even his office at the firm at the end of the day; it was the kind of silence that was filled with pages turning and someone else's breathing. The smell was stronger—so strong it burned a little. It prompted him to pick his head up from the pillow and look around the dim room.

At first, all he could make out was a pair of green painted toes propped up against the edge of his bed. There was a freckle on the side of the right foot, the size of a pea. When he recognized the foot and the delicate ankles that were half hidden by faded blue jeans, he had to believe he was dreaming again. Without moving too much, in the hopes of not alerting her to the fact that he had woken up, Maverick eased his head back and swallowed hard as he gazed at the springing brown curls and heart shaped face he'd seen in his dreams for years.

Roxanne didn't look up, her nose buried in a tattered copy of *The Rescue* by Nicholas Sparks. She was wearing a purple long sleeve shirt that had seen the washing machine a thousand times. She had glasses on—he'd never seen her wearing glasses before. His dried lips and sore throat winced as he coughed and tried to speak. Her eyes flickered up from the page at his harsh exhale, and she rolled them before closing the book and standing up.

Roxanne picked up the cup of ice chips Layla had left and scooted her chair a little closer to the bed. "The nurse said it might be a little difficult for you to speak, so don't push it." She fed him a spoonful of ice chips.

Maverick let the ice melt in his mouth before he tried to speak.

"What...what are you doing here?" The words were still rasped and hard to force out, but the sound he made was stronger than a puff of air.

She raised an eyebrow at him. "I could ask you the same question."

He tried to sit up, his whole-body creaking with the movement. Pain shot up and down the left side of his body anytime he so much as thought about moving his arm or leg, and the pain medication they had him on made him foggy. It was a terrible combination, and he had never been in so much pain in his life.

"Remember...when you...broke your ankle?" he asked to fill the awkward silence between them.

Roxanne's eyes flickered up from the page of her book again. She held his gaze, her lips pressed into a firm line while its corners twitched upwards in a fight for a smile. They had been fifteen when it happened. Maverick and Wesley were lapping Roxanne on their skateboards while she, more or less, threw a tantrum over a joke Maverick had made. To make it up to her, he'd insisted she take a turn and let her go down the hill of the Anderson's private drive on her own.

It got hazy after that—the memory. Maverick had been answering something Wesley had asked and looked away from her for a minute when he heard her screaming at the base of the hill. The whole drive to the hospital, RJ had yelled at them from the front seat for being stupid, and Maverick had held her hand and told terrible jokes and fought to make her smile. It wasn't the last time, or the first time, they had been in Moses Taylor for something one of them had done, but it was the first time, for Maverick anyway, that the time they spent together felt like more than an affectionate friendship.

His dry lips smiled, painfully. Roxanne shook her head and closed the book again.

"Yeah, I do." She sighed and closed her eyes. "Do you remember when I snapped my wrist at that party at the university?"

Maverick coughed on a dry laugh. "Yeah…God, yeah. I was such a jackass."

Roxanne laughed despite her hardest efforts not to and tucked her chin into the neck of her purple sweater. They both succumbed to the silence of their memories, of the awkward and quiet laughter and the bags under Roxanne's eyes and the casts on Maverick's body.

He let the silence sit between them for a few minutes before he spoke again, laying his head back on the pillow. Despite the pain his body felt and the awkwardness that ruminated between them, having her there was a salve he was grateful for, if only for a second—especially since he didn't deserve it.

"Have you been here this whole time?" Maverick squeezed his eyes shut while he said it. "I thought I saw you when I woke up."

Roxanne leaned forward to give him another spoonful of ice chips. "I've been here the whole time."

Her confirmation made him feel guilty. "Why?"

"Again. I could ask you the same thing." Roxanne propped the book back open and glanced back up at him. "You need to go to sleep. We can argue about this tomorrow."

Maverick tilted his head to the side. They would more than likely argue about it in the morning, or the moment when Maverick showed any signs of feeling even a little bit better. For now, though, Roxanne was there. With him. He tried to settle back down, his aching leg and arm shifting on the mattress and causing a stab of pain to rake through his body.

"Read to me," he grunted after a moment of swallowing back the pain. "I hurt too much to sleep."

"Are you five?" She turned the page without looking back up at him. "You don't get special treatment. You were driving too fast. You know how that road gets when its wet, so now you get to suffer in silence."

Maverick stared at her, his dark eyes boring into her while she slowly ran her eyes over the page. She let out a loud sigh and frowned up at him. "You should be trying to sleep."

"If you're...gonna be stuck here"—he licked his lips—"with me, you should at least read to me."

He tried to put on his most appealing smile. The pain medication dripping into his body through the IV made it harder for him to work his lips, and he already felt his eyelids drooping. But he grinned up at her anymore.

"Read to me," he begged again.

"If I read to you, will you please stop talking?"

Maverick nodded lightly.

Roxanne looked up at him from the rim of her glasses and sighed before going back to the page she was working on. "Do you remember when Taylor picks her up from work the first time?"

"Of course. Iconic." Maverick fought the grin and worked up his best peaceful face for Roxanne's benefit. He closed his eyes again and settled back once more.

While he adjusted the thin blanket and itched at the tender skin above his cast, she started to read again. Her voice was soft, and the words she read were familiar, bringing him back to an earlier chapter in their history. And as he fell asleep, listening to her tell him a story he'd heard from her lips a thousand times before, the pain stopped in his limbs.

Chapter Thirteen
August 2016

Roxanne woke up with a kink in her neck from sleeping in the hard chair by Maverick's bed. She coughed and stretched in the chair, her bones cracking with each move. He was asleep, still in the same position she'd watched for the last three weeks, but this time his head was turned towards her. Roxanne got to her feet and quietly fished her phone out of her purse—she had three missed calls from Ethan and one from her mother.

The missed call icons on the screen made her shoulders hunch and her heart have palpitations. She and Ethan had been missing each other on the phone for four days, the calls wavering from long messages to short snippets of conversations via text and email. Roxanne wanted to believe that she missed him, that her growing frustration over the missed calls and snappy text messages was a sign that she missed being with him. But seeing Maverick animated, talking to her like he had the night before, made her feel things she didn't want to acknowledge. So, she swallowed them down and stuffed her phone and jacket in the oversized purse she'd brought with her and slipped out of the room.

Roxanne managed to slip her way into the elevator and pressed her phone to her ear to listen to the multiple messages that Ethan had left her. In the first message, Ethan was telling her that he missed her and that he was going back to London for another round of meetings. When he trailed off right before the beep of him hanging up, he asked her when she was coming home. In the second message, the sounds in the background suggested that he was hastily walking and fidgeting with unknown objects. In truth, he was walking her through his packing process for London. It was easier for him to pack when he talked out loud, floating ideas into the space around him and picking clothes he thought she would have. The third and final message told her that her mother had called the apartment's landline looking for her—he apologized for answering, and for telling her mother where she was. At the end of the message, he'd said goodbye and told her he'd talk to her before his flight took off.

Roxanne put off calling her mother the entire walk back to the hotel. She sent out a few messages to the group chat of their friends to update everyone on Maverick's waking and his pain levels, took a shower, and made herself a cup of weak coffee before she even thought about calling her parents. It wasn't that she didn't like talking to Ralph and Rhea (Roxanne and her parents were close); it was that she didn't want to be the one to tell them that Maverick had gotten hurt.

When Rhea answered on the fourth ring, Roxanne forged a smile and sat on the edge of the unused bed. "Hi Momma," she used her sweetest voice.

"Hi baby." Rhea Wortham sounded agitated, as agitated as Roxanne was ever aware of. "Ethan said you were back in Pennsylvania. Is everything okay with Caleb?"

"Caleb is fine. Cheyenne is fine." Roxanne picked at the dry skin on her lower lip and stared at the harsh pattern on the carpet. "There's been an accident."

"An accident? Are you okay? Should I call your father?" She could hear the agitation switch to panic and smiled a little.

The tremor in her mother's voice was something that Roxanne had heard only a handful of times in her entire life. Rhea was an incredibly strong-willed woman, although it didn't come without some compromises on the side of her husband and child. The last time Roxanne had heard the tremor, it was in the hospital, when her parents had fought the surgeon who had slipped out of the operating room to tell them that her older brother's misfortune had cost him his life.

Roxanne swallowed back a soft tremble, the feeling in her gut brewing. *This is exactly why I didn't call*, she thought to herself as she heard the word's coming out of her lips. "Maverick got into a car accident a couple of weeks ago. A pretty serious one. He's okay, but I've been here waiting for him to wake up—he woke up last night."

Rhea was quiet for a minute. Roxanne could have sworn she heard her mother pacing on her new hard wood floors, heels clicking softly and stressfully back and forth. "Ethan did not mention that when I talked to him last night."

"Ethan's not too happy that I'm here." Her lip was bleeding. She tucked it underneath her upper teeth and sucked on the iron tasting drops.

72

"Mhmmm. I'm not surprised." Rhea sighed on the other end of the line. "Do you know what you're doing for Thanksgiving? That's why I called. To see if you were coming for Thanksgiving this year."

"I don't...I don't know, Momma. I have no idea."

"Tell Maverick I hope he feels better, darling. I have another call on the other line. Can I call you back later?"

"Yeah, yeah. I'll let him know."

"I love you, and we miss you Rox. You being this far away isn't easy."

"Miss you too, Momma. I'll talk to you later."

Maverick was sitting up in bed watching the local news on the small TV over his bed when Roxanne got back from the hotel. As Roxanne walked in, he looked over at her and waved in her direction before turning back to the screen.

"I heard from Si this morning," Roxanne started.

Maverick turned the volume down on the screen and scooted back down against his pillows.

"He's coming this weekend." Roxanne dropped her purse on the chair and opened the curtains to let in some sunlight. "We talked about it last week, before you woke up. I'm getting tired of sleeping at the hotel, so he was going to take a shift so I could go home. But you're awake now. And that changes things."

"You don't have to stay." Maverick shrugged. "I'm awake now. The doctors assured me that the worst part is over now. You don't need to stay here."

"Why am I here, Maverick? How come I was the person they called? Why not your brother? Or one of the guys?" Roxanne watched the cars below them. "Why didn't you take care of the power of attorney?"

Maverick looked up at her and sighed. He didn't have a correct answer. He'd never have a correct answer for her about any of the mess they found themselves in. If he told her the truth, that he never thought of it, she'd get angry. But that was it. When you're twenty-six, you don't think you'll need someone to pull the plug on you; you think you're invincible, made of steel, going to live forever. You have all of the time in the world to make these decisions—decisions he had already made when he was nineteen years old and had never once regretted or overthought.

When Maverick had given Roxanne power of attorney privileges, they had just started their sophomore year of college and Sid had decided he was going to go fight disease in other countries. The decision had come after they'd bought tickets for a trip to Europe. It'd dawned on Maverick when he and Roxanne were looking into travel insurance for their bags that, if something had happened to him, no one would be able to make a decision for him. They'd done their due diligence on how to fill out the proper paperwork and had gone through the motions of having the POA drawn up and documented by her father's law firm.

With that single decision, Maverick had given her total control over making decisions for the quality of his life, or death, despite the urgings of her parents, his brother, and the lawyer who handled the paperwork. He'd done so because he'd been so sure that their lives together were going to be forever. In all the time since the paperwork was filed, he had almost forgotten about it. It'd just about disappeared in the last seven years of being alive. Almost. Despite everything that'd happened between them, despite them going down to just him and her based on a stupid decision he'd made when he felt they were too young for forever, he'd always trusted that Roxanne would be the one he'd want to make those decisions.

"It...didn't come up at the time," Maverick said finally. "I'm sorry, Roxanne. It just...wasn't a priority."

"Maybe not for you, but my boyfriend is furious, my mother is probably worrying sick, and our friends are all trying to rearrange their lives to be here with you and me." Roxanne dropped into the plastic chair and forced her legs crossed.

Maverick snorted and turned the TV back up. Roxanne snatched the remote from him and turned it back down; she didn't want to be ignored. "I will go to my lawyer first thing on the day I'm released, and I'll get the paperwork fixed. I promise."

"Rick...Maverick...that's not the point." Roxanne tugged at the end of her braid. They sat in silence, looking in each other's directions while their eyes explored the room.

She sighed and squirmed around in her seat. "Look, I'm sorry for fighting with you about this. I'm just...not sleeping here. And the hotel is too quiet."

"So, stay at my place. I'm obviously not using it. Besides, my plants are probably dying." Maverick felt the argument shift away from them and relaxed. "C'mon, Rox."

The removal of full names had been a signal since they were kids that there was no anger in the room. Or at least no anger over present issues. He could tell she recognized it too by the way her defensive scowl had slipped away.

"I'll have to talk to Ethan, but I'm sure your bed is at least more comfortable than the one I've been trying to sleep on." Roxanne fidgeted with the strings on her hooded sweatshirt. It was the American University one she had loved to wear when she was traveling. He smiled at the coffee stains on the sleeves and the frayed strings, the memories. All the memories.

Seeing her, focusing on her instead of the pain in his bones, had inundated him with feelings and memories that he had once thought were long gone. She evoked in him something that he had thought was dormant, or dead, lost when he made the biggest mistake of his life.

"Don't chew on the strings," he urged and coughed into his elbow. "Call Ethan, go get your stuff. My keys and wallet are on the counter. And have the nurse bring me whatever paperwork needs to be filled out."

"I'll call him later. You should be resting. I'll take care of the paperwork for now." She set her lips in a stern line and settled back in the chair with her book. "Do you want me to read to you again?"

"Please. There's nothing interesting on 16. Not that romance novels are interesting."

Maverick winked at her and closed his eyes again. He wasn't necessarily tired, despite the urging from her and the nurses to rest as much as possible. He was just glad that she had come back in the morning.

Chapter Fourteen
August 2016

"I don't think you staying in his home is a good idea Roxanne."

Ethan thought his brain was going to explode. He'd made Roxanne repeat the statement three times, thinking he'd misunderstood her. Nope. Nope, she'd really told him that she was going to move out of her hotel room into her ex-boyfriend's apartment. After she'd already flown out there on the drop of a dime because the jerk had gotten into a car accident. His head was definitely going to burst open.

He paced around their bedroom, still cluttered with the clothes she had left out after the last bout of laundry she did before going to Pennsylvania, his phone on the bed. He'd put her on speaker because the timber her voice was reaching was giving him a headache and when they fought, he liked to be as far away from her as possible. Ethan hated fighting, thought it was stupid and didn't actually accomplish anything. For the last two years, he'd been battling Roxanne's outright bullheadedness with silent stares, passive aggressive dinners, and the accomplishment of her admitting defeat and approaching him calmly—usually days after the offense.

This fight was a little different. He had to bring himself to raise his voice, to hold out on affection and kindness in return for her speaking to him.

"I don't think you should do it." He begged himself to be calm, forcing his words to come evenly. "And...you know what...I don't think it's such a good idea. It's weird and creepy. And besides, he's awake now. Can't you come home?"

"He's not out of the hospital. Or out of the woods. He starts with the physical therapist on Monday, but it could be weeks before he gets home."

Ethan sifted through a handful of wrinkled t-shirts sitting at the bottom of his clean laundry basket. "I still don't like it."

"I know..." Roxanne sighed. "Make sure you bring your gray sweater, the one with the ribbing on the sleeves."

"Don't change the subject. I do not feel comfortable with you staying in his apartment, Roxanne."

"I don't have the money to keep staying at the hotel, and no one knows how long I'll be here."

He threw the t-shirt he was holding on the floor and balled his free hand into a fist. "You don't have to stay. You shouldn't have been there in the first place."

"I don't disagree; I just feel like I can't leave." He heard a car horn honk somewhere behind her and rolled his eyes while he fished t-shirt off the floor. "I'm sorry, I really am."

Ethan sighed. He was sure she felt bad, that she felt like she was stuck between a rock and a hard place. He knew well enough that Maverick lived up to his name, was the glue that had once held her world together, and she had to go because he'd put her name on a piece of paperwork. He didn't like it. But he understood it.

"My flight leaves around midnight your time. Can I give you a call at the airport?" He rubbed the back of his neck, at the knot that had formed from the nights of not sleeping in their empty bed.

"Of course. I'll leave the sound on."

"I'll talk to you later." Ethan swore hard once the phone was hung up. He dropped the smart phone on the bed and eased himself onto the ground, his head propped in his hands.

When Ethan had met Roxanne, he'd felt like something that was missing had been dropped into his lap, unceremoniously, messily, and loudly. Roxanne was a mess when they'd met. Ethan hadn't been much better, but they'd somehow found a way to make it work. Until it stopped working anyway—until they woke up one morning to a phone call that changed their lives. A phone call that unstitched a wound from her past that had almost healed.

The stitching was unraveling, the wound opening wider with each second they were apart.

She didn't know what she was expecting when she unlocked Maverick's front door, but it wasn't what she got. He lived in an old building with gray stone edifices and a lobby that had seen better days; she'd taken the stairs because the elevator looked uncomfortable and the lights overhead blinked enough to give her a partial anxiety attack.

The hallway carpet was old, the kind of old that she'd imagined she'd see. She was used to the history of the area, of the desire to keep things as old as possible for as long as possible. The paint was green and peeling at the molding, and the air smelled like a mixture of must and lemon. Roxanne had stopped just outside of Maverick's door, thinking about the first apartment they had lived in with a similarly dingy looking hallway and triple bolted door. It had smelled of must and lemon cleaner as well, although their next-door neighbors smoked cigarettes like chimneys.

She shook herself out of the haze the memory brought and steeled herself for the penultimate bachelor pad awaiting her on the other side of the door. What met her eyes was nothing she'd imagined before. It was everything she could picture Maverick living in and nothing she could picture him in at the same time.

The walls were a soft blue gray, painted to reflect the natural sunlight that came in through the French doors leading to a small patio with an iron railing. His living room was comprised of a leather sectional and dark wooden furniture. He had a TV mounted on the wall and three floor-to-ceiling bookshelves chalked full of paperbacks and hardcovers and binders. Roxanne set her jacket and purse on the back of the couch and tucked her suitcase against the back of it before exploring any deeper than the open living room area.

She wandered around the galley kitchen, the black counter tops and pale wooden cabinets clashing in a way that worked with the open space and the walls were the same color as the living room. It all worked. He had a silver teapot on the stove and a French press on the counter. There were two black mugs in the sink and a miniature fern sitting on the back of the sink below a small window. The apartment was lived-in; there was a worn gray t-shirt slung over the back of a chair at the high-topped kitchen table and a pair of running shoes thrown haphazardly by the patio doors. The kitchen table had coffee mug rings on it, and the couch had a throw blanket Roxanne was sure she recognized balled up by the one arm.

Roxanne smiled as she crossed back into the living room. She'd forgotten what an apartment that looked lived-in felt like. An entire apartment—not just the bathroom counter where her makeup and hair boxes were and the bedroom where she threw her clothes and was picked up after. Maverick's book shelves were cluttered, a history of someone, she noted when she saw a handful of paperbacks that she'd read (and a few that had solely been hers), something that Ethan didn't have before they'd met and Roxanne had gradually gotten rid of her belongings.

Her fingertips ran over the titles of several colorful paperbacks that had been hers in another lifetime, and she felt the smile slip from her face. He'd kept books she'd read as a teenager and books they'd collected during her years as an English literature major, with water stained and worn out spines. She stopped on her battered copy of *The Secret Garden* and tugged it out of its spot. The fourth chapter was still dogeared from her last time through, the week before they'd broken up. Roxanne shook her head and popped the book back into place. She left the bookshelf of memories after fondly running her fingertips over the frame of Maverick's high school diploma.

The guest bedroom had a desk in the same style of the living room furniture. She noticed the bed that sported a wine-red comforter that looked fairly familiar to her. She dropped onto the bed, sank into the soft mattress, and fingered a small tear in the surface of the comforter. It was definitely memorable, even if she couldn't place it.

There were a couple of pictures in the guest room, she guessed it doubled as his office when he worked at home. On the wall over the desk was a dated picture of Maverick and Sid and their parents, from when Maverick was four or five. Roxanne knew the picture. It had spent years by his bedroom in his grandmother's house and had traveled with them to college. In their first apartment, it sat by their front door and said goodbye to her every time she left. Noelle Sterling's brilliant white smile and Stewart's quiet grin were comforting. It was one of the only pictures that Maverick had of his parents, and while he'd always hated the bowl cut and the checkered bow tie he sported in the picture, he'd always kept it close.

Seeing the picture again brought hot tears to the surface and Roxanne had to blink them back. When Roxanne's brother had died, Maverick had consulted the picture, asking his parents to keep an eye out for the brother that Roxanne had to identify in the hospital. When they'd started dating, she'd promised them that she'd take care of him. When they broke up, they were the last thing she saw before she left the apartment.

"He's okay," she reassured the image as she stood up. "Stubborn as always, but he's okay."

Chapter Fifteen
September 2016

"Okay Maverick. We're going to get started with some exercises to get the strength back in your wrist."

Maverick scowled at the physical therapist sitting across from him. Their third session was going much like the last two—with Maverick experiencing pain he'd never thought imaginable and the therapist giving him quippy, hearty grins that he didn't think he deserved. Maverick wasn't sure if he liked the man, hated the man, or just needed some fresh air. The furthest he got out of his hospital room was the therapy suite, where he got to sit across from his bearded torturer and pretend his muscles were getting better.

At least he was getting space from Roxanne and her tense, unhappy expressions or the long silences they'd been suffering through since he'd woken up. Sure, there'd been a few soft moments where he'd made her laugh or she wasn't swamped with work or Ethan, but the majority of the time they spent together was in a tense, sad silence. It was heightened by the intense itching in his left leg from the heavy cast – sometimes it itched so much he begged Roxanne to shove a pen down it and scratch for him (that never ended well) – and the fact that neither of them was getting a lot of time outside in the fresh air, or away from each other.

Maverick sat up straighter in his chair when he thought about Roxanne's face the last time he'd asked her to scratch his leg and sent his physical therapist an impatient look. "How long until we can start working on my leg?" He rubbed at the raw skin with his right hand. "I mean, my hand isn't really all that important right now but my leg –"

"—is still in a cast and just had major surgery. So, let's focus on the things that we can help. Which, right now, is your left wrist." The therapist, Marshall, handed him a stress ball and showed him a couple of exercises to help gain back motor control.

Maverick flexed his wrist weakly and squeezed the ball. The strain it put on his arm muscles and his brain made him squirm. He heard the cracks in his joints, and the stiffness fought against him as continued to squeeze the ball. "When are they gonna let me go home?"

"I'm sure they will soon. I think the biggest concern is just that you need someone to take care of you." Marshall counted the number of times he squeezed the ball, his red pen making little ticks on the white sheet of paper on the table between them. "Have you found a counselor yet?"

"I was wondering if that was going to come up." Maverick winced as he flexed with the ball again. "I don't need to talk to someone."

"You were in a major accident. You need to talk to someone." Marshall held his hand out for the ball. "How does that feel?"

"Really stiff. My wrist feels all locked up. Is that normal?"

86

"You haven't used it in a month." Marshall handed him a two-pound weight. "Inward flexes with it. Toward you. Three, and then a minute of rest."

"Okay. So, when will it stop feeling like this?" Maverick turned his wrist up so he could see his scarred knuckles. "If I can go back today with some improvement, it'll make my life a hell of a lot easier."

"Your girl will stop yelling when you get home. That's kind of what they're supposed to do." Marshall made another note in his neat shorthand. "I can't tell you how many wives give their husbands a hard time for getting themselves into these situations. By the time they're coming to me for outpatient therapy they've got pleased women and half of them end up as fathers."

Maverick couldn't help the laugh that came from his chest. "Yeah well. That'd be a damn miracle."

"She'll come around. Accidents like this scare people. Especially when it's with someone you love." Marshall held his hand out for the weight. "Speaking of scared."

Maverick looked over his shoulder to see Roxanne weaving her way through the PT room, holding a bag of takeout food and two coffees. She looked great. She'd been teasing him for the five days he'd been awake by looking amazing the entire time. Sleeping in his apartment was helping. Even though she left late at night and came as soon as she could in the morning, she looked well rested and always put together. Today she was wearing light colored blue jeans and a vibrant orange t-shirt with a scoop neck that hung off of her in a way that hinted at curves but didn't cling.

"I brought real food." She beamed at him, eyes wrinkling at the corners under her glasses. "And I just found Layla. If everything checks out on Friday, they're going to send you home."

"Awesome." Maverick looked back at Marshall. "Am I good to go?"

"Alice will wheel you back up to your room." Marshall capped his pen and stood up to address Roxanne. "His wrist is going to need these exercises, as indicated. Make sure he's doing them in his room *and* when he gets home."

Roxanne took the paper and slipped it into her back pocket. "He will."

Once they were back in his room, she dragged over the wheeled table and set up the contraband food she'd brought. A breakfast burrito and vanilla latte, solid food that hit his stomach and tasted like Heaven. He inhaled the meal quickly, even though the burrito was the spiciest thing he'd had in weeks, and the coffee burnt his tongue and incinerated his stomach on the way down. He didn't mind.

Roxanne watched him eat with a smile on her face and her feet propped up on the edge of the bed. "Your fern is doing well, and the cactus is blooming. I brought in your mail and went ahead and cleaned up around your apartment last night. You're welcome."

"Couldn't sleep?" Maverick offered her a potato wedge.

"Ethan and I were on the phone." Roxanne waved his hand away and scooted a little lower in the chair.

Every time she'd talked about the redheaded man, her voice became clipped, and her shoulders tensed. He'd noticed it and found himself secretly relishing in the fact that things weren't going well for them. He felt terrible for being relieved that her relationship wasn't sustaining her journey to help him.

She shut down any further conversation about it by pulling out a worn legal pad and pen. Maverick rolled his eyes and popped the wedge into his mouth before he turned the TV on.

"Si will be here in a few hours," Maverick winced. "You can go home now if you want." He tried to put the words out in a nice way—a way that would be least likely offend her. If he touched too close to having a real conversation about something other than the car accident and his medical care, she'd shut down on him. Or yell. The last yelling match had been bad enough that the nurse on duty had asked her to leave until she calmed down.

"I'll go home when you're discharged." She didn't look up, her delicate scrawl on the page coming out in harsh movements. "When I can trust that you're going to not be an idiot and will take care of yourself. Or I can find you a permanent babysitter. Silas is *not* the one to do that because, well, he has a wife and baby on the way."

"I am fully capable of taking care of myself." Maverick took a long swig of his coffee.

"Maverick, you were driving 90 miles an hour on the Casey Highway in the rain. You are not capable of taking care of yourself at this point."

Neither of them had heard Silas Montgomery walk in. Nor did they notice him standing in the middle of the doorway, watching the two of them interact the same way they'd been ever since they were kids. In that moment, it truly felt like he was back in high school watching his two best friends fight it out over dinner plans. The residual guilt that always slammed to the surface when he saw Roxanne or heard Maverick talk about the woman he had lost swelled in Silas' throat. He forced himself to swallow it down with the taste of mint toothpaste and airport coffee.

Seeing them together like they were, bickering intently with each other and occupying the same space without any harmful words or actions, made Silas see, if only for a second, the future that could have been. He'd always felt silly, being as invested in Maverick and Roxanne's relationship as he was, but when he saw the two of them in that moment, it kind of made sense. Roxanne and Maverick had been the king and queen of their congregation— had been the ones who had inevitably belonged together. Silas loved his wife and thought the world of her, but when he thought of Nancy, he didn't think of a soul mate. He thought of a choice he'd made which had led to a world of the right choices. When he thought of his best friends, of the couple they'd been as kids and the adults they'd become, they were soul mates. And he and Cheyenne and Wesley and even Connor when he was around, they were the fates who had been responsible for keeping their lifelines tied together.

When they both looked at him, he smiled and dropped his jacket and overnight bag by the door.

Roxanne got to her feet and wrapped her arms around him, her face tucking into his shoulder. She squeezed for a little bit longer than she needed to, and he pressed his hand over her curls to keep them from attacking his nose, letting her hold on. He could tell that she was holding up better than expected, and that seemed to ease his guilt. Maverick reached over to bump fists with him and gave that same enigmatic grin that had caused Silas to break two bones and almost crash his car when he was seventeen.

"Is he giving you a hard time?" Silas asked her fondly when he let her go and propped himself on the foot of Maverick's bed beside his good leg.

"He's trying to send me home. If I'm not here, then he doesn't have to take care of himself." Roxanne gave Maverick a wicked grin, the kind she'd once have thrown his way so easily and picked up her empty coffee cup. "I'm going to go get a refill. Can I trust you two not to burn the place down while I'm gone?"

"I'll hold the fort." Silas saluted her.

The two men waited for her to walk out in silence. When she was clear from the door, Silas smacked Maverick's leg and got to his feet. "I understand you miss her, and you fucked up, and it's my fault, but you can't go and try to get yourself fucking killed."

Maverick swatted back. "It's not like I planned to get in a car wreck. Or that I was aware that she'd come if I was." He rubbed the spot on his right leg where Silas's blow connected and scowled.

"You had us all worried. Wesley dropped a job so he could come out in two weeks and babysit you. My wife nearly had a miscarriage when she heard that you were in an accident. And Roxanne? Did you even think about how she would react?" Silas was pacing back and forth while Maverick tried to sit upright. "She dropped everything and came across the country because she was terrified you were going to die."

"I was just driving a bit too fast, Si. Sometimes we all take the Casey a bit too fast. You know the Casey, the turns, the no shoulder areas. It was raining, and I guess I underestimated how fast I was driving. It was an accident. You know damn well I wouldn't try to kill myself just to get her back. I gave up on the idea that she was ever coming back when she brought that…that guy to your wedding."

They were fate, Silas thought again glumly and looked at Maverick with a scowl. "You're an idiot." Silas had stopped his back and forth and stared down at his best friend. He'd been the one to clean Maverick up off the bar top after he broke up with Roxanne, had helped move him out of their home, had taken the verbal abuse when it clicked in Maverick's head that Silas was the reason he and Roxanne had broken up. He'd told him countless times that he was an idiot for ending the relationship and then for not moving on. And his heart had stopped when he got that call that his idiot best friend had almost died in a car crash. He stooped down and wrapped his arms around his friend in a tight, quick embrace before he punched him in the arm. "You're a fucking idiot, Rick."

"Yeah, but I'm alive and my ex-girlfriend, the love of my life, is here fawning over me while her relationship goes down the tubes." Maverick grumbled. "So, yes, Si, I am an idiot. I'm a guilty fucking idiot. But I am a guilty, pampered, kind of smug idiot who is most definitely going to hell."

"She came," Silas observed. "She's still here."

"And he's not happy about it. They've been fighting, but she won't talk about it."

"I'll talk to her. Once she knows that Wes is coming, she'll probably take the option to go home."

Maverick nodded. Silas's plan was logical, sound. But it caused him pain to think about her going back home to Ethan. He'd thought that when he woke up, he'd felt the worst pain of his life. Up until that moment, the worst pain had been watching her walk away because he'd made a mistake. Up until that moment the worst pain had been knowing that he'd ruined something that was good, that was pure, because he'd gotten caught up in being stupid and twenty-three.

Sitting there with his leg in pieces and her sweatshirt with the frayed strings and coffee stains across the foot of his bed, he knew that waking up still wasn't the worst pain he'd ever felt. The worst pain Maverick would ever experience in his life would be the pain of having to watch her walk away again.

Chapter Sixteen
September 2016

Roxanne and Silas stayed until Maverick fell asleep that night. They played Monopoly—Layla had swiped it for them from the children's ward—for six hours and pretended they enjoyed it, talking about anything but what was happening around them. Roxanne told them about the novel which sat nowhere near finished in her purse, and Silas caught them up on his prenatal research. Maverick did the least amount of talking, which Roxanne thought was weird, but she stayed out of it. It made beating him at the board game, after forty minutes of going back and forth with fake money, less entertaining, but she no longer knew him well enough to know if he talked a lot.

It didn't come up until they were walking to Maverick's apartment and she was grasping at straws for conversation with one of the closest people in her life. She blurted it out while they turned the corner away from the hospital.

"He's usually not that quiet." Roxanne looked up at Silas in the streetlamp light. "He's never been that quiet when it's just him and me."

"He goes through periods of quiet and loud. That much hasn't changed." He shrugged and draped an arm around her shoulders. "How are you?"

"Good. Culture shocked. It feels weird being back here after so long. I mean, I don't think three years is 'long,' necessarily but…" Roxanne shrugged.

"And how have you been handling…?"

"He's okay. He's alive. We've been…getting along." Roxanne rubbed her arms against the chill of the night air. She'd left her sweatshirt with Maverick. He'd been using it to prop his head up while they caught the tail end of *Beetlejuice* on the small TV in his room and had fallen asleep to it. "I was so ready to be mad at him. When I got here, I was furious. And kind of scared. But more furious. And then I get up to his room, and he's breathing, and he's alive, and I just…I was so thankful." Roxanne stopped to dry the stray tears that were bubbling up in the corners of her eyes. "I was so relieved I felt sick. And he woke up, and I couldn't be mad. Not really. Not yet."

Silas hadn't said a word while she'd tried to get the words out. He'd let them into Maverick's apartment with his key and filled the tea kettle while she sat on the corner of the island and continued.

"But he kept me as his power of attorney. And he's the one who broke up with me. Ethan's mad at me." Roxanne tugged at the end of her braid. "Being here has brought up a lot of issues for everyone involved. It's just an impossible situation."

Silas found the box of decaffeinated Earl Grey he'd been hunting for in the cabinet above the fridge, and he popped a bag in the two mugs he'd laid out on the counter. "Wesley is coming out in a week and a half. He's doing some sort of freelance assignment that he said he can do from anywhere. He's coming to keep an eye on Maverick, so you can go home."

"He called me yesterday and told me." Roxanne took the mug of hot tea from Silas with a grateful smile and kicked her foot against the island. "Is it weird if that doesn't make me feel any better? Like…the knowing that someone else is coming to do the thing that I should be doing. Or should not be doing, I guess, so I can go back to my life. It's not helping." The words, when they started to come, didn't stop, wouldn't stop. She couldn't explain it to herself or to the man who stood patiently waiting for her.

When she didn't say anything else, he gently prodded her. "What do you mean?" Silas fidgeted with the string of his teabag and looked at his friend.

"I can't, Si. It's all just so complicated." Roxanne set her tea down, untouched. "I think I'm going to go grab a shower."

"You can go home," he said with assurance that time, as if he was forgetting that he was supposed to be an impartial bystander to the situation. "You can go home right now."

"I don't need to go home, Si. I need to shower."

She waited until she was in the bathroom to exhale a shaky breath and sink to the floor. Having the company, having the guys, it was supposed to make it easier, but she was feeling overwhelmed. She smacked her head back against the bathroom door and squeezed her eyes shut. "Damn it, damn it, damn it." Her palm hit the tile with each burst, the cold sticking the center of her hand. "Damn it."

Silas stayed for three days.

Three days of watching his best friends silently interact around the elephant that sat in the room of antiseptic and white. They moved in tandem. Whenever Maverick twitched for a drink of water, Roxanne stopped what she was doing to hand him the cup, and any time she picked up her pen to write, Maverick would turn the TV down. She would pick up food for them for dinner instead of letting Maverick eat the hospital food, and the physical therapist would give her a rundown before he left the room. Roxanne made Maverick exercise his arm on the physical therapist's orders like clockwork and whenever she was writing, he would perk up and ask her to write out loud. They worked together in everything they did, despite what happened in the past.

The breakup had put all four of them in an impossible situation. Cheyenne had just moved to Albany and Silas was on his way to Bethesda for a new job. Connor was barely home from basic training, and Wesley was still trying to figure his life out. None of them had been in the right space to pick sides or to suddenly pick up the pieces of two of the people that they cared most about. They'd discussed it before: who would get who if Roxanne and Maverick broke up. They joked about it when they were all drinking or when something stressful happened and everyone needed a break. It had been a joke, something that no one saw coming or believed could happen. When it did, they'd all been in disbelief. But they'd stuck to it, stuck to both of them.

There had been no awkward fight. No one picked sides based on knowing each other or spending time together. They'd stayed friends and had even had moments where Roxanne and Maverick had to be in the same part of the equation because they were all friends. Even when Roxanne had started dating Ethan—none of them had approved of the man then, and none of them approved of him now—or when Maverick had started to parade girls around post-Roxanne, they'd stuck with both of them. It boiled down to more than just wanting Maverick and Roxanne to be together. It'd become a way of being, believing that they were meant to be and doing everything in their power (the power of the four fates, as Silas often saw them) to keep them on their own course once they'd broken up.

The group didn't think that the two would ever get back together—but that had started to matter less and less as the months had blended into years, and Maverick and Roxanne turned into two totally different people. All six of the Anderson Creek kids had turned into different people. Over the last four years, it'd become less about trying to get the two back together and more about keeping the six friends together, despite the breakup.

Still, it was hard for Silas to sit with them, to interact with them as if nothing had ever happened. Of course, their breakup had only caused a few moments of drama for himself and the others in the grand scheme of things. But seeing them together now made him feel like a kid whose parents, already divorced, were seeing each other again. He was filled with both excitement and trepidation and wasn't sure which feeling to give in to. And it was even harder to discern between the two of them when Roxanne would ignore a phone call or text from Ethan, and Maverick would grin like he'd just won the lottery. Or when Maverick would stare at Roxanne a little too long, and she would pretend that she just hadn't noticed, slightly pink with pleasure at the attention.

The morning Silas left, he waited until Roxanne went to pick up salads from the place she'd found down the block around lunchtime. He waited until she was gone to bring up his concern to Maverick. He'd wrestled with it for three days to try and figure out how to say the words, whose side to pick. So, when the words came out, he had a headache and felt like the worst friend imaginable.

"What are you doing?"

Maverick looked up from the email he was reading on his laptop. "Trying to catch up on work because Rox said my email was overflowing."

"You can go home tomorrow. And Wes will be here in a few days. So, why don't you just let her go home?" Silas eased off the counter where he'd been sitting. "If you send her home, she will go."

"I told her she can go home already," Maverick argued as he pushed himself as upright as he could get with the leg cast. "She doesn't want to go."

Silas rolled his eyes. "If you tell her to go, which you've had practice with, you and I both know she will go."

Maverick shook his head at Silas and looked out the window. His arms crossed against his ribcage, and his lower jaw stiffened. Silas waited for Maverick to say something, anything. Maverick sighed, finally able to feel Silas's disapproval on his face, and he turned his attention back to his friend. The look on his face said it all.

Silas sank down into the chair Roxanne had been occupying when he saw the hopelessness on Maverick's face. "What are you uh…gonna do?" He'd seen the look; he knew the look. It was the same face Maverick had come to him with when they were fifteen and he realized he had a crush on Roxanne. Of course, Maverick had been the second to last to know, and Silas had been naïve enough to laugh at his friend over that tidbit. This wasn't a laughing matter, though.

"Do you think she knows?" Maverick pushed his hands through his hair, only wincing slightly at the strain in his wrist. "I feel like I'm sixteen again."

"You're acting like you're sixteen again," Silas shrugged. "She doesn't know. She didn't know then, and she doesn't know now."

Maverick nodded. "Good. Good. You're right. I should tell her to go home. To go back to…him."

Silas laughed at the wrinkle in Maverick's face and shook his head. "We are sixteen. It is ten years ago, and we are sixteen and any second now, Wes is gonna walk in with that awful mullet and tell us about Connor's pubic hair because we are sixteen."

"Why are we sixteen?" Roxanne walked in on the tail end of the conversation with their lunches.

Maverick smiled coolly up at her and reached out for the bag. "Wesley texted Silas about Connor's love life. Or lack thereof." His grin broadened when she laughed, and he shot Silas a look, begging him to not say anything.

Silas sank down in the chair and shook his head. It was really   an   impossible   position.

Chapter Seventeen
September 2016

The day that Maverick went home was the day that he promised himself he was going to turn his life around for the better. It hadn't started when Roxanne wheeled him to the car, nor had it started when he signed the hospital discharge papers. It started when she helped him hobble into his apartment, smelling just like how the hospital smelled, like eucalyptus and mint.

She'd made herself at home, and that made him happier than he could have put in words. There was an extra throw blanket on the couch, one that he'd never seen before, and dishes were in the sink. Papers, a laptop, pens, and post-it notes were strewn across his kitchen island. Her sweatshirt was on the back of a chair, and he could already see the strands of curly brown hair that were imbedding themselves in his carpet. Maverick took one look around the space–his space—and felt at home in it for the first time since he'd bought it. It was in that moment he decided that his entire life was going to change. He was going to find a way to get her back. To put their lives back on track.

He would start slow, rebuild their friendship, get to know the woman that she had become. Then, when things felt right on track, he would tell her how he felt, how he'd known he'd still felt before he opened his eyes and she was there, waiting for him to wake up. Before he told the guys or dealt with the reverberations of her relationship with the ginger falling apart, he would make sure she felt the same way. Maverick shot Silas a text telling him not to worry about him and Roxanne, that he had figured out where his head was at. Silas' quick reply, a four-line text message telling him not to do anything if he wasn't ready to follow through, made Maverick smile. He texted back just as quickly, telling Silas he was ready to fix what he'd broken.

The whole exchange had happened while Roxanne moved around the apartment, tidying it up subconsciously. "I went to the grocery store last night and picked up some things, eggs, bread, coconut milk, you still drink that right? I also got a ton of turkey, sausages, and some fruit. It'd really help you if you ate fruit, you know. The basic fruits like apples, bananas, and oranges. I just wanted to make sure there was something in the house. But you have to do at least some of the cooking, got it?" She shoved curls behind both her ears and looked at him expectantly.

Maverick hated fruit. But they both knew that. He lowered himself onto the couch, his leg smarting as he bumped it against the coffee table. He hid the soreness with a terse grin.

"I'll do my best to eat fruit," he promised as he propped his left leg on the coffee table. She picked his foot up and set it on a pillow, which he didn't recognize either, before she went back to tidying.

"Why don't we order something tonight? There's a Chinese place down the block that delivers until ten," Maverick suggested as he watched her clean up the apartment, a smile brewing on his face. It made him feel things he'd thought were buried down deep.

"Sure. Sure." She smiled at him. "You still eat dumplings?"

"Steamed. Their egg rolls are to die for. We should get some of them." He turned the TV on and closed his eyes, listening to the faint murmur of the Channel 16 news and Roxanne ordering dinner. He waited until she got off the phone to break the silence. He twisted himself around so that they could see each other over the back of the couch.

"When are you uh…. when are you going home?"

"Oh. Well, Ethan's in London for the next three weeks, so I'll probably go back when he's done." She frowned at him, suddenly so unsure. "If that's okay?"

Maverick nodded a little too eagerly. "Yeah, sure. No. I'm definitely going to need help getting around."

Neither of them said anything for a few minutes. Maverick lounged on the couch, smugly looking at the little throw blanket out of the corner of his eye. It was disarmingly nice to have some things that were hers in his space.

Roxanne continued to putter in the kitchen, putting her used coffee mug from the morning in the cabinet as quietly as possible. Maverick craned his head back to look at Roxanne when he heard the mugs clank together.

"Do you wanna watch a movie?" he asked.

"What did you have in mind?"

"You pick." Maverick turned back to the TV and held the remote over his head for her to grab. She plucked it out of his hand and flopped down on the couch next to him. He noted the two pillows she stacked between them and rolled his eyes. "Just no girl movies."

"And what, per say, is a 'girl movie'?" Roxanne handed him the phone that she had used to order dinner.

"Movies that you like." Maverick nudged her teasingly.

She rolled her eyes but left his elbow close to her arm, seemingly unbothered by their proximity to each other. Maverick tested his luck by scooting down further into his cushion so that they were closer to each other. Roxanne rested her head against the side of his arm as she hit play on a movie and tucked the lap blanket firmly around her. He closed his eyes. It was all too easy to pretend that things were the way they should have been—the way they had been before he'd ruined all that they had worked toward, all that they held on to.

Slower. Take the turn slower. Road is too wet. Take the road much slower. There's a truck, headlights in the rear-view mirror. Phone's buzzing in the console. Don't check it. Road's wet, truck behind, driving too fast.

Silas's name flashes across the phone screen in the dark. Could be the baby.

Why won't the Bluetooth pick up? It's five in the morning. He wouldn't be calling unless something was wrong.

Don't check it.

Turn coming up. Once the road merges into four lanes, it's smooth driving.

Phone's stopped buzzing.

It's started raining again. Make sure the high beams are on.

Foot on the gas, not on the brakes, trying to beat the storm. The road's familiar.

Pick the phone up to check Silas's message. It could be the baby.

Tire just slipped, taking the turn.

Shit. Shit. Shit.

Brace for impact; hold on to the wheel.

Maverick woke up in a cold sweat right before he felt the crunch of his steering wheel press into his rib cage once again. It took him a second to get his bearings straight.

He was laying in his bed with the mauve sheets and the weighted comforter that had been a gift from Cheyenne tangled around him. He sat up slowly, groping in the dark for the switch of his bed side lamp. The harsh onslaught of light made him flinch, the movement causing his raw skin to rub uncomfortably against his cast. His skin was soaked with sweat, and there was pain in his leg, his arm, and his ribcage. The phone Roxanne had gotten to replace his, which he vaguely remembered crushing in his palm upon impact, told him it was only a little after one. He hadn't even slept three hours.

K.T. Egan

Maverick carefully swung out of bed and made his way with the support of a crutch. The door to the guest room was closed, prompting him to take extremely slow steps in an effort not to wake Roxanne. It wasn't that she was necessarily a light sleeper. He'd just forgotten what it was like to live with someone else, to have someone else sharing his space and needing their own quiet. When they had lived together, Maverick would always be in bed before her, and she would always wake him up when she climbed into bed. In the mornings, he'd sneak out, somehow without waking her up. They had lived in harmony on each other's sleeping schedule, and it had been a long time since Maverick had ever felt that sort of unity with someone else.

Maverick stuffed an eggroll and bottle of water from the fridge into his short pockets and made his way to the couch. He almost tripped over the leg of the coffee table and recovered by rolling into the back of the couch, at the expense of a lot of noise. His leg, which had been aching through the entire process, screamed when the cast hit the edge of the couch. He stuffed his face into the cushion and groaned.

When he looked up, his eyes watering still from the pain in his thigh and shin, he could see Roxanne peaking around the corner at him. They made eye contact, and she smiled only a little as she stepped out into the soft light from the kitchen. She was wearing a pair of paisley pajama shorts and an oversized t-shirt. Her hair was a mess, and she looked like Heaven.

Maverick pushed himself up and shot her what he hoped was a genuine, comfortable smile. His blood was racing. "Did I wake you?"

"No. Yes." Roxanne ran her hands through her hair. "I'm not sure. The room was really cold. Are you okay?"

"Yeah. I just got into a fight with the coffee table. The table won. Do you need to adjust the thermostat?"

She chewed on her lip. "I don't think so."

Maverick let her continue, watching her fidget with her shirt's hem. If he could have, he would have wrapped her in his arms and let her work through her thoughts. They'd spent hours in that position, at various stages of life, for reasons that they experienced both together and apart. It was their comfort to spend that time embraced, listening, and learning. "I'm not...used to being cold. It's so much hotter back home."

"Turn the air conditioner down." Maverick held the lap blanket out her. "There's some tea in the kitchen. Although you probably knew that."

Roxanne rolled her eyes at him but migrated toward the stove. "What are you doing awake?"

"I had a...uh nightmare."

He could hear her puttering around behind him, like she had been maneuvering his kitchen for years. She didn't comment on the arrangement of half empty tea boxes in the cupboards or the fact that he'd had a bad dream.

"Tea?" she offered.

He twisted around to look at her over the back of the couch and let himself smile. She looked so at home in his kitchen, so much like the Roxanne he held onto in his memories, that his smile faltered at the corners.

"You know it."

"Was it about the accident?" She looked up at him, her blue eyes riddled with concern and the kind of domestic care that he used to incite. He wasn't sure how much longer he could keep up the pretenses and the pleasantries when looking at her in those shorts, making herself right at home in his home, made him boil. "Rick? Earth to Maverick?"

"Yeah. Here." He rubbed his face and propped his chin on the back of the couch. "What were you saying?"

"That if it was about the accident, you should think about talking to someone. I mean, you should really talk to someone anyway. That's what the doctors suggested when you were discharged, remember?" She leaned against the counter and frowned at him. "We can look tomorrow?"

"I don't think I need to talk to someone." He rubbed at the tender skin on his leg. "It was just a nightmare."

"About the accident. If you're having nightmares about the accident, you should be talking to someone."

"Roxanne you don't have to worry about it." She shouldn't be worrying about it. "It's not really something you need to worry about."

She rolled her eyes again. "You need to talk to someone."

"You need to stay out of it." Maverick turned his back to her, crossing his arms like an irritable child. It'd been a long time since she'd worried about him.

"Please stay out of it," he said uneasily.

"If you wanted me to stay out of it, you would have taken my name off of your power of attorney. But I'm here. Because you didn't. So, I think I have the right to have an opinion. And my opinion is that you need to talk to a therapist if you are having nightmares about the severe car accident you were in." She slammed down the teapot after filling their mugs, the metal causing the entire stove to vibrate.

Maverick flinched at the scrape of ore against ore. "I told you that you could go home at any time. I woke up, and I'm alive, so you're not needed here."

Roxanne threw the box of teabags at the back of his head and stormed out of the kitchen. Maverick jumped when the guest room door slammed shut and rubbed his face. The argument was nothing like the blow ups that they used to have. He wanted to believe that they had both matured enough for the fight to be nothing more than a short spat. Still, he got up and hobbled to the door and tapped on it until he heard her get off the bed.

She opened it and scowled up at him, her head tilted back so that her dark curls fell past her shoulders. "What, Maverick?"

"I'm sorry." He bared his teeth in a half-smile and leaned against the door jam. "That was a really stupid statement."

"Yeah. It was." She rolled her eyes and slunk back to the bed. He watched her curl up on the left side of the bed and peak out at him from the blanket cocoon. "I'll leave in the morning."

Maverick licked his lips before he sank onto the bed by her feet. "I don't want you to go. Not yet." He put his hand on her ankle. "I mean...I've been home for less than twenty-four hours, and I'm going to need the help."

She sniffed and tucked the blanket over her head. He tugged it down and gave her a small smile. "Just stay until Wes gets here. We'll reassess then?"

"You need to see a therapist." She sounded so small in her blanket puddle. Her wide eyes, still so blue in the light coming in from the hallway, made his lips soften. He nodded his consent, and she held her hand out. They shook, and Roxanne scooted toward the right side of the bed. "Tell me about these girls you've been dating."

He laughed and stretched out beside her, his arms folded behind his head. "Uh. Sure. Tell me about your book in return?"

"Sure," she replied. They shook on it again before she snuggled back into the mattress and pillow, the blanket tucked up underneath her chin. "But you have to go first."

"You're sure you really want to hear it? There's been a...few of them." A few too many in the space between them. "I'll start with the first one-night stand then?" he teased and had to fend off her pillow attack.

Once she'd settled down, Maverick indulged her by starting with the story of his love life since their breakup. He told her

111

about Maura, the wannabe dancer, and Crystal, the law student. He went on and on about all of the countless times he found himself going to the mountains just to get away from it all. He even humored her with the weirder cases he'd had since becoming an associate, including the man who tried to steal his ex-wife's fine china.

While he talked, she laughed and made soft interjections, usually to point out all of the bad decisions he'd been making. He didn't stop, not even dissuaded by her lack of approval, until she was breathing softly. Maverick tucked the blanket around her, to keep her warm, before settling down beside her for the night.

And when he fell asleep, he didn't have another dream about the accident. Instead, he dreamed about the last vacation they took together and the hours they'd spent on that sandy beach, trying to figure out the rest of their lives. His dream self-wondered how they could have ever been so wrong.

Chapter Eighteen
September 2016

"I'm picking up a prescription for Maverick Sterling. Date of birth March 23rd, 1990."

Roxanne stood under the artificial light in the pharmacy around the corner from Maverick's apartment, listening to a toddler scream incoherently behind her while a headache formed in the back of her head. She had been in line for twenty minutes while the child freaked out, and her tired mother tried to console her. She was tired, tired for herself and the young mother who she could hear on the verge of losing her temper. While she tried to tune the child out, she found herself thinking about that morning and the heart attack that had nearly killed her when she woke to Maverick's snoring face, two or three inches from hers.

They'd slept in the same room for the last six nights. Maverick had been waking them up with accident-related nightmares. The first three nights, they'd both ended up falling asleep on the couch on accident—but the last few, he'd ended up just coming into the room she was in and depositing himself onto the other side of the bed. Roxanne had pretended to be asleep the first time, relaxing only when he built a wall of pillows between them, turning her head to peak at his silhouette in the darkness.

He'd looked so young that she hadn't had the heart to push him away with the knowledge of what the nightmares were doing.

Even though he respected her personal space, it was hard to sleep next to him at night. It wasn't that he snored any worse than he had five years ago or that he'd suddenly turned into a sleep talker. But she found herself waking up in the middle of the night, every night, just watching him sleep. After a while, it dawned on her that she was still in shock over the fact that he was alive.

The last two nights, she'd laid in bed restlessly, satisfied with her midnight vigil, and she wondered what it meant to be so grateful that he was still breathing. Still breathing and a pain in her back end when he was conscious because Maverick hadn't changed in the twenty years that she'd known him.

She shook her head out of the stupor, thinking about how Maverick almost ended up dead after the accident, and the fact that she had traveled all this way just to help him made her exhausted. While the pharmacist gathered his prescriptions, all but the pain killers because Maverick had given her such a hard time about it, she tuned back into the child's argument behind her. They were negotiating whether or not the toddler needed candy, and the mother was sorely losing.

Roxanne couldn't help but wonder if she would have been in the other woman's position had things ended up differently. They looked similar in age, and the woman was dressed professionally, and the child could have been no more than three. Had Roxanne stayed, had she and Maverick been able to work through whatever had caused him to renege on their relationship all those years ago, would they have somehow found a way to set aside their differences and raise a child? A child with dark hair and dark eyes, the same smooth, almost cacao colored skin of its mother and aloofness of its father. She knew Maverick would have loved it and that she would have adored it. Everyone in their lives would have been engrossed in its very existence. But would she have been so tired?

Roxanne rubbed her eyes as she thought about the child. A future child. The pharmacist handed her a paper bag with the two prescription bottles in it, and she turned to let the mother and her toddler take her place in line. As she passed the other woman, she threw her a smile in solidarity and caught a glimpse of the blonde haired being as she screamed at her mother. Definitely a dark-haired beauty, with her mother's skin and her father's eyes.

Outside the pharmacy, the early September evening had set in full force around the little city. Roxanne let herself daydream as she walked back to the apartment, crunching on the first of fall's leaves that had fallen underfoot. A warm, soft breeze raced around the buildings to lift her hair and tickle the hem of the borrowed sweatshirt, a relic of Maverick's law school days that she had swiped from the closet on her way out. While she walked, enjoying the coolness of the night, she let herself think about the child that might have been and the life she would have had, had she stayed. She wouldn't be writing copy and marketing campaigns for a resort, that was one thing she knew without a moment to second guess. She might have actually finished the novel—something about the Pennsylvania air had her inspired in ways that her time in

Nevada hadn't done—and maybe they would be in a house instead of her sterile apartment or Maverick's warm, probably a little crowded, two bedrooms.

Roxanne didn't feel guilty for the thought process, even when her call to Ethan's phone went straight to voicemail. She stood outside the apartment, shaking her head at his contact profile, while the initial sting over being ignored dissipated. He wasn't happy with her. Really wasn't happy when she'd answered his call last night and he'd heard Maverick's offkey singing in the background.

They'd had a very calm argument about when she'd be home, ending with her reminding him that he'd been in London for a week and a half longer than he'd initially told her. At the end of the call he'd snapped that he'd be staying even longer, citing that he had no reason to try to go home to their quiet apartment and then disconnected before she could rebuff. He was angry; she understood that. What she didn't understand was his insistence that she go back to Las Vegas and sit in the empty apartment waiting for him to get back from his trip. It wouldn't do either of them any good for her to just sit and wait, and she'd been making steady progress on both her work and the novel while she was away. She'd hoped he'd understand that her progress was as much incentive for her to stay until Maverick was able to function completely on his own as was the man in question's health.

When she entered the apartment, still obsessing over Ethan's lack of understanding of her situation, she was met with something that had not been a part of her routine since she'd gotten on that plane a month prior. Silence. The apartment was quiet and warm, very warm. Its owner was nowhere to be seen. Not draped across the couch or practicing his hobbling around the room without any crutches despite his physical therapist's best efforts to not let him do it. Roxanne set the bag from the pharmacy on the kitchen counter and headed toward his bedroom.

She passed the open bathroom door, caught a whiff of rosemary and thyme, and backtracked. Maverick was standing over the bathtub, dumping the contents of her body wash bottle into the tub as it filled with steaming water. He was naked from the waist up, his skin already covered in a light sheen of sweat from the apartment's warm temperature and the steam coming off of the tub. Roxanne started to say something but was cut off when he straightened up and the muscles in his back reacted to the movement.

He'd put on some muscle mass since they'd seen each other last, filling out his 5'7" frame with additional, hard, smooth muscle. She'd noticed it in the hospital, along with the hair that he refused to cut (which was now worn in a knot at the nape of his neck), but there had always been at least a layer of fabric between her eyes and the byproduct of his new life. Now, with nothing separating her eyes from the supple definition of his upper half, her mouth had gotten a little dry.

Maverick must have heard her swallow because he tilted his head toward her.

"Hey." He set the bottle on the edge of the tub and stretched again.

117

"What're you doing?" Roxanne found her voice with enough dignity to be a little annoyed over his use of her soap.

He smirked at the indignation in her voice as he turned to look at her. "The hot water is supposed to help relax my muscles. After PT today, Marshall told me to take a forty-five to fifty-minute soak. I was gonna wait for you to get back, but you took so long." Maverick shrugged.

"I was there. I heard," she huffed. "I meant, what are you doing with my soap?"

"Oh. Bubbles. It smells good and makes really great bubbles." Maverick's grin was infectious. She found herself trying not to reciprocate. "I'll replace it," he finished.

"Mhm." Roxanne shut the faucet off and pointed to the stack of clean towels she'd put on the shelf above the toilet that morning. "You flood, and you're cleaning it up."

"Yes, mother." He started to undo the tie holding his gym shorts up, making direct eye contact with her. "Can I have some privacy? Or do you wanna climb in there with me?" He winked, caught a washcloth to the face, and laughed her out of the bathroom.

Once she heard him get into the tub, and the 'sploosh' of water that inevitably had poured out onto the bathroom's tile floor, Roxanne pressed her forehead to the door and squeezed her eyes shut. She was getting into dangerous territory, territory that was further expanded by her boyfriend's immature need to play the silent game. Thankfully, Wesley was supposed to get in at any time, and she would have a hand with Maverick. And with herself. A mitigator.

With her pulse calmer, her head clearer, and the knowledge that the sense of impending doom in the pit of her stomach was soon to be rid of itself, Roxanne went back to her writing boot camp at the kitchen table. She waded through the legal pads she'd filled out since they had gotten out of the hospital until she found the half empty one that had the last of yesterday's pen scribbled in the margins. A blue pen with a fine tip and the stereo pumping out a mix of SoundCloud rap and country music helped her bunker down and enjoy the fifty-two minutes that Maverick spent flooding the bathroom.

She was about three lines from the end of the chapter she was working on when Maverick let out a holler, right before she heard a loud crash coming from the bathroom. He was hunched over in front of the sink, dripping wet with his red boxers clinging to his legs, wrestling with the plastic bag he'd so carefully wrapped around the cast. In his struggles, he had knocked over her travel bag on the sink's ledge and had spilled the cup of Q-Tips all over the floor. There were three towels on the floor underneath his feet, trying to soak up as much of his mess as possible.

Roxanne couldn't help but laugh at both Maverick and the mess from her stance in the doorway. "Do you need some help?" she asked him, half a tease in her voice.

He looked up, his face still full of concentration, and gave her a sheepish smile. "Could you?"

"One sec," she answered as she turned her back.

Maverick watched her slip out and back in with a pair of scissors and crouch in front of him.

"I'm going to try not to stab you," she said and began to hack at the plastic wound around his leg, her lower lip tucked underneath her top teeth.

"Do you, uh, do you know what you want for dinner?" It was his turn to cook. Thinking about the food in the kitchen was sure to help him feel less concentrated on the feeling of her hand on his bare thigh. "I was thinking I could make ravioli or something?"

Roxanne nodded thoughtfully as she leaned forward to get a better look at the plastic twisted around the top of his cast. Her dark hair was hiding her face, the curls keeping her expression a mystery to him.

"That works. I picked up some spinach and onions at the store yesterday so we could probably cook them up too, huh? With a little bit of that Paleo spice?"

"The one I put on the broccoli?"

The conversation was held in soft tones, soft breaths that passed through the still steamy air in transgressive throws. Maverick was supporting himself on the sink, his knuckles turning white with the death grip he had locked on the counter's edge. Roxanne's lip was starting to tear from the pressure of her teeth in the soft skin. She nodded, and her hair tickled the bare skin of his thighs, causing his back to stiffen.

"Yeah. It was good," she spoke.

He could feel her breath and willed himself not to react.

120

"Okay. Just about done."

"Good cause I need you to finish up," Maverick hissed through his teeth, and Roxanne's head snapped up.

His face was red, and he was holding himself so rigidly that he looked like he was going to pull something. "Rox," he started and shifted his weight in preparation of her reaction to the thought that needed to be expressed. It was a bad decision. His knee started to buckle—if it weren't for the death grip on the counter, they would have ended up on the floor.

Roxanne jumped up and offered him her shoulder, helping him sit on the toilet. "What happened? Is it your leg?" she questioned.

Maverick cursed a string of sentences that were held together by their common anger. "Yeah," he managed once the pain started to subside. At least it had taken his mind off of her proximity and all of the things that he wanted, needed, to do to her. "I guess I was on it too long."

Roxanne continued to worry at her lower lip, this time from anxiety over his leg and not the heat coming off of his skin. "I'm sorry. I tried to work as fast as I could."

"No, no it's not your fault." He squeezed her hand as the knot in his thigh began to work itself out. "I'm just dying on the inside." His teasing smile made her roll her eyes and release her hostage lip.

"I'll let you get dressed." *I also need to cool down*, she thought as she fanned her red face. "And then you can mop up the mess you made."

He waited until she was about to close the door to speak, his own flustered pulse trying to find a way to control itself. "Hey, Rox."

She turned and smiled at him, the tiniest curve of her lips. "Yeah?"

Maverick worked up the courage to give her a lopsided smile, and she grinned back at him, the reaction as easy as breathing. "Thank you," he said in earnest.

Roxanne touched her fingers to her collarbone in a sign of gratitude they had worked out a decade plus before. "I'd say anytime, but let's not make a habit of any of this. Okay?"

"Deal." Maverick's smile slipped when the door closed between them, and he pressed his forehead into his hands, calling himself any and every name in the book.

On the other side of the door, Roxanne did much of the same.

"Okay. So. We don't ask *anything* about how they're doing. We keep them separated as much as possible. And if Maverick looks like she's been beating on him, we pretend we don't see."

Cheyenne Anderson had gotten the brief in a short text message from Silas shortly after he left Scranton, calling in reinforcements. He hadn't been clear on what he was worried about—telling her that she would need to see their friends together to understand for herself. She had chosen the week that Wesley would be out to make the half hour drive out from Penn Ridge, deciding that they could each tackle one half of the situation. If anything, she was sure that Roxanne and Maverick were on the brink of committing homicide and needed a refresher from each other.

Wesley Carmody glanced down at her, his hand posed to knock on the door to 6C, with his lips pursed in a straight line. "I think you and Si are being more dramatic than necessary. If things were that bad, Rox would have been on a flight back to Vegas before Maverick got out of the hospital."

"Si was convinced that something's up. He thinks Ethan's giving her a hard time about being here." Cheyenne adjusted the strap of her purse and shrugged. "I just want to be prepared to pull them off each other."

Wesley chuckled and kept his own thoughts about pulling the two of them apart to himself. He knocked twice and bent to pick up Cheyenne's suitcase. "I just want to know where you think all of us are going to be able to sleep."

"Rox and I can share the guest bed. And you can sleep on the couch." Cheyenne painted a grin on her face when Maverick opened the door, quelling her anxieties for the preferred joy of seeing him in one piece. His surprise at seeing her on his doorstep quickly faded into the brotherly grin she'd been so sure she'd lose when he and Roxanne broke up, and they wrapped each other in an embrace. Cheyenne regretted not making the drive down after the accident, but her grandfather wasn't in great shape, and Roxanne had assured her that the two of them would be fine. It wasn't until Maverick was hugging her that she realized how worried about him she'd been.

Maverick let her go and shook Wesley's hand before they too hugged.

"You've lost weight," Wesley observed when he stepped back. Since the accident, Maverick had slimmed out. "You look much better."

Maverick rolled his eyes and limped backwards. He was only out of the hospital for a few days and was already trying to by-pass the crutches. "Some things never change I suppose," Wesley remarked as he gestured for the red headed beauty beside him to follow their friend inside.

"We weren't expecting you," Maverick said to her as he supported himself on the back of the couch. "Rox is going to lose her mind."

"Where is she?" The last time they had seen each other, Roxanne and Ethan were moving into the apartment, and Cheyenne had chin length hair. Two years had gone by way too fast. While interested and concerned about the pair of exes, she'd chosen the week's retreat as the perfect excuse to see her best friend again.

"I may or may not have flooded the bathroom earlier. She's doing damage control right now." Maverick scratched the back of his neck. "How was your flight, Wes?"

"Good. Good. The flight to Denver wasn't nearly as smooth." The taller man deposited their bags on the floor by the kitchen table and rolled out his shoulders. "You should see this apartment. It's great."

"I'll come out in January. By then I'll be done with the therapy, I hope."

"Why don't you sit down?" Cheyenne dropped her purse on the couch and flounced down the hall to the bathroom.

While the two women squealed and shouted over their 'surprise' reunion, Wesley helped Maverick make himself comfortable on the couch. He settled down next to his friend and flipped on the TV. "How're you feeling?"

"Glad to be alive. I can't believe it's been over a month already."

Wesley nodded, flipping through channels. "When is Rox going home?" He hadn't been through the apartment yet but based on the mess on the kitchen table and the shoes by the front door, he could tell that she had made herself at home. He felt justified knowing that he'd been right, that Silas had been overreacting way more than he needed to.

"Soon, I think. Ethan's been on her to be home by the time he gets back from London." Maverick scratched at the dry skin above his cast. "It does help that his business trip keeps getting extended. Less incentive for her to go home."

Wesley saw it in that moment, what Silas had been so concerned about. It wasn't that Roxanne and Maverick were on the verge of killing each other. It was the fact that they weren't. He didn't say anything, just made a mental note for there to be a later conversation. If Maverick had sensed the concern in his friend's face, he didn't let on, instead opting for a cheeky grin.

"Connor extended his tour," Wesley offered by way of conversation and let the topic fill the space between them.

Maverick nudged Wesley with his arm, an act of affection. "He was gonna do this no matter what. We can't be cranky with him for choosing to go over there more. He's a hero."

Wesley rolled his eyes ceilingward, but the big brother in him relaxed a little as Maverick switched the TV over and handed him an Xbox controller.

Chapter Nineteen
September 2016

Roxanne and Maverick were doing much better than Silas had let on in his frantic text messages to Cheyenne and Wesley. They were a unit. A unit that had once worked so well together and was doing its best to not get too comfortable in that estranged rhythm. All through dinner, Maverick kept a steady eye on Roxanne while she spoke or laughed, passed her food when she reached for it (even if it was right in front of her), and did his best not to stare at her. Cheyenne had noticed too because she'd excused herself to the bathroom and sent a text to Silas asking him why he'd made such a big deal over their situation if they were getting along—very well.

Silas' response said that it concerned him, and he revealed in the tirade of messages that almost vibrated Wesley's phone out of his pocket that Maverick was still *in love* with Roxanne, and Roxanne *probably was* too. Wesley wasn't inclined to agree, but Cheyenne's disposition when she came back to the table proved that he was the only one sitting in that room who didn't see the damage that could be done.

"Hey, Rox, when did you say you were going home?" he asked while Cheyenne carried the last of the dinner dishes into the kitchen. She all but threw them in the sink in a useless signal for Wesley to stop talking.

"Soon," Roxanne replied with a raised eyebrow. "Maverick's still having a hard time getting around, so I'll probably wait until he gets into the walking cast before I make any decisions about when to go back."

"What about work?" Maverick's pained words and Cheyenne's attack on the tea kettle and mugs didn't dissuade Wesley. He smiled instead and took a sip of his wine.

"They've been really great about me working from here. All I need, really, is an internet connection and my laptop."

"And Ethan's still in London, right?"

"Uh, yeah. He'll be back, hopefully, the week after next."

Wesley nodded.

Maverick shot him a dark look. "What's with the inquisition, Wes?"

"I'm in between contracts right now, and the apartment won't be ready for at least a month. They're renovating the entire space, so I was gonna try to crash here again."

After the breakup, when Maverick had been on the brink of failing out of law school in his last semester, Wesley had volunteered to stay with him and help him get back together. It had been four months since the breakup, a week after he found out that Roxanne had moved to Nevada, and he'd nearly fallen into a barrel of whiskey a night. Wesley had the most fluidity in his life and had been more than willing to stay until things had calmed down. He'd only moved out six months before the accident, after finding out that he really enjoyed the peacefulness of the Colorado mountains from his last assignment.

"You can stay." Maverick softened, the perceived slight having been cleared up.

"Won't it be a little crowded?" Cheyenne asked. Wesley shot her a look, her dark scowl eating through his skull.

Roxanne smiled as she got up from the table. "I'll only be here for another week or two, just until Maverick's in the walking cast. I think we'll survive until then."

Wesley nodded and settled down his questions before Cheyenne broke something in the kitchen. The subject was dropped for a moment which took the tension out of Maverick's shoulders and put Cheyenne back into a good mood.

They convened in the hallway after a suggested midnight snack run, Cheyenne's angry footsteps making it hard for Wesley to keep up with her.

"I don't understand why you're so angry," he called after her as she took the steps two at a time to stay ahead of him.

She whirled on him once they'd left the building, a hallow of bright rust following the movement. "Because you're going to ruin everything!"

Wesley stuffed his hands in his pockets and started down the street. "I don't think I'll be ruining anything. If it was meant to work out, it would have worked out, Chey. And it didn't. If you don't recall, Roxanne lives in *Nevada,* and Maverick's stuck his dick in half the city by now."

"He's still in love with her. He told Silas as much." Cheyenne had caught up. "And did you see the way they were around each other? I'm sure she feels the same way. I can just ask and then—"

"Then what? They live happily ever after? That didn't work, Chey. She's dating someone else. Hell, she lives with the guy."

"The guy that neither you nor Si like. Nor her parents."

"It's a relationship regardless."

"With a jerk," Cheyenne grumbled.

Wesley stopped walking and caught her arm. "Why is this so important to you?"

Cheyenne shrugged, her eyes oddly red in the dim street light. "I just...I want to believe in forever, Wes. I mean, my parents have been together for almost thirty years. But only after my dad was divorced. And if Rox and Rick can't make it, then maybe forever doesn't exist at all." She looked down at his hands and pursed her lips. "My love life is enough of a shit show that I just need this win."

Wesley dropped his hand. The past between them only further helped her case.

"I just...I think we should leave it alone. If it happens, then it happens. But if we push...well...then we'll probably end up with drama. Which we've been lucky enough to avoid...for the most part," he whispered.

Cheyenne shrugged. "He does seem much more relaxed with her around."

They'd come to a stop, waiting to cross the street, and he peered down at her in the streetlight's cool glow. Wesley gave a begrudging nod. "It feels like it used to."

They walked a few feet in silence, Wesley with his hands stuffed in his pocket and his head tipped up toward the star-filled sky and Cheyenne scurrying to keep up with his six foot seven gate.

"We shouldn't meddle," Wesley said eventually, with less reserve than he'd gone into the conversation with. "Especially since neither of us knows why they broke up in the first place."

"Si does," Cheyenne responded as the pair crossed the street.

Wesley shook his head. "It's been four years, and he still won't tell us what happened. I doubt we'll get it out of him now."

"So, what, we just stand around and do nothing?"

"We let what's going to happen, happen."

Cheyenne rolled her eyes and followed him into the bakery. "That's boring."

He snorted at her. "That's life. What kind of cupcake do you want?"

Chapter Twenty
September 2016

The two extra bodies in the apartment had turned in to a lot more work than Roxanne had anticipated. She'd forgotten how hard it was to live in a space with more than one other person, or how crazy things could get when you lived outside a bubble of sterility. By day three, her exhaustion had taken center stage. She had to cart all of her writing and work materials back and forth from the library in order to get anything accomplished. And coming home to clean up after the three people was an exhausting line of work.

She was grateful for the extra company—having the two of them in the apartment meant that they'd been sleeping separately, which was helping to clear her head, and she didn't have to cook dinner or worry about laundry. But the apartment was more of a wreck than usual when she got home.

Wesley helping to take Maverick to physical therapy and being willing to work with the man had given her more time with the manuscript—time that it had desperately needed. In Vegas, she'd had a hard time putting words to paper. She couldn't find the thoughts that she so desperately wanted to scribble down, nor could she find the kind of ear she needed in Ethan to bounce ideas off of. Her late nights with Maverick and Wesley and Cheyenne, when they had arrived, helped her bounce ideas around. She had to make three runs for new legal pads and a new pack of pens and was nearing what she felt in her gut was the end of the story.

It was a liberating feeling and almost as addictive as the mountain of baked goods Cheyenne had been destroying Maverick's kitchen with.

Maverick was sitting on the couch while Wesley snored on the other end, reading a book while the end credits of a movie rolled across the screen. He was shirtless again, his hair loose and falling around his face. She clicked the door shut as quietly as possible behind her so not to wake their sleeping friend, and she set her bags down by the door.

"Hey." Maverick smiled at her, and her heart nearly skittered. "How was work?"

Roxanne smiled and headed for the kitchen. "It was good. I got a lot done and was able to send in a handful of posts for the weekend already, so we're looking good."

She'd also reached what she believed was the climax of her work, the moment where Rupert and Amelia finally held each other in an embrace that she'd scantily defined for the world to see. It had elicited passion in her stomach that had only intensified when she'd seen Maverick's bare torso. Instead of responding to it or stifling it, she rolled her shoulders and hoped that the spark would inspire her to finish the novel. Perhaps once it was done, she would feel less compelled to stay in Pennsylvania.

"I'm stiff," Roxanne whispered aloud. "I was going to change and go for a walk. It's finally starting to get nice and crisp out there." And she'd truly missed the bristling NEPA autumns.

"I'll come, too." Maverick got up carefully and reached for the crutch leaning against the couch. "Marshall said I should be getting out more now anyways."

"Yeah, sure. I'll be ready in five minutes."

Once alone in the guest room, Roxanne tried to reach Ethan one more time for the day. After being sent straight to voicemail again, she rolled her eyes and set the phone on the charger, knowing that her time for needing it was well over. If he wanted to talk, he'd get to play the waiting game. She changed into a pair of sneakers and a long sleeve shirt, the same shirt she'd worn twice already that week. It was starting to stretch from being washed so much. Roxanne fingered the longer than normal sleeves and twisted her mouth into a small scowl.

One more week.

Maverick was waiting for her in a t-shirt and track pants with the leg rolled up to reveal his entire cast. He had his crutch wedged under his left arm and a smirk on his face. They made their way out of the apartment without saying anything, walking side by side but not close enough for their arms to touch.

"How was physical therapy?" Roxanne smiled up at him as they trekked around the park.

"It was good. My arm's already getting up to function. Marshall says it's because I've been working on it." Maverick flexed his left wrist, the skin tensing around the plate. "My leg on the other hand is not so good."

"What's wrong?" Roxanne let him guide her down the street, toward the park.

"Not healing as fast as I had wanted it to." Maverick leaned on the crutch to take some more weight off his leg and shrugged. "I'm just in a lot of pain still. The best thing I can do for it is to keep moving, supposedly, but I don't think it's helping me much."

"If it wasn't helping, you wouldn't be able to get around without the crutch as much as you do." Roxanne smiled and nudged her arm against his. "You'll get there in your own time, Rick. You can't just push yourself."

He snorted, and the two of them moved in tandem around the small park.

"I'm thankful to be here, grateful that my biggest issue after the accident is waiting for my leg to get used to the metal rod in it." Maverick let out a hard burst of air.

They were moving slowly along the tough concrete sidewalk, his steps still halting enough that Roxanne took one step for every two he managed. He looked up at the sky, watched the hint of autumn rain blow in over their heads, and sighed again. "I just can't believe that I put myself in this situation."

"I can't believe you put either of us in this situation," she responded honestly as she helped him settle on a wrought iron park bench. "Did you talk to O'Neil about changing your POA?"

While being in Pennsylvania had been a blessing in disguise for Roxanne, her work, and her mental health, she couldn't shake the feeling that being there had just caused more issues for everyone in the long run. Maverick changing his POA back to his brother or one of the guys would hopefully alleviate some of that tension staying rooted in her scalp.

"Somehow, when my boss called me asking if I was coming in to work next week, that wasn't a part of the conversation." Maverick scratched at his leg, irritated. "I'll talk to him about it when I go in on Tuesday."

"You know you don't have to. You can take more time off." Roxanne tucked her lip underneath her top row of teeth.

Maverick shrugged. "It'll get taken care of. This will never happen again."

"You'll never get into a life-threatening car accident again?"

Hearing him confirm that he was going to take care of the POA should have made her feel better than it did. A strange, crushing weight had rooted itself in her chest—not dissimilar to the one she'd felt the night before she got the phone call about the accident. She offered Maverick a weak smile and rubbed at her arms, still chilled despite the thick layer.

Maverick looked out at the empty park, stiff. "You won't be the one who gets called if I do."

They sat in silence, his words leaving a soft, ringing feeling in her ear drums.

"You can go home, y'know," Maverick said finally. "Wes's staying so that you can go. And Chey's not going back to Albany until the end of the month. If something happens, I'll be with people who can help." In their silent repose, the park had become

136

dark, the sun disappearing behind fluffy gray clouds that worked to cloak the last rays of their September night.

"I'll leave after you go back to work. Like we had originally agreed on. I have a couple weeks left of remote-work time, so it shouldn't be that big of an issue for me to just stick around for a little while longer." She toed at a crack in the sidewalk in front of them.

Maverick nodded. "That works for me. I just don't want you to feel like you're being held hostage."

He saw a storm brewing on Roxanne's face and held his hands up in self-defense. "Oh no, I was just saying I…"

Her eyes scrunched, and he flinched. She wasn't liable to yell at him in public—causing a scene was just not her way—but he knew that he'd never hear the end of the comment. Instead of giving him a hard time about it in the park, she tucked her legs up and rested her chin on her folded knees.

"I forgot how comfortable fall is here," she mused. The one-eighty in conversation caused him to look at her, his head cocked to the side. "In Vegas, we don't have a touch of cool weather until December at least. And even then, it's not the greatest."

"I couldn't do it. I mean, when I heard you'd moved to the desert, I thought they were just messing with me. But you did. And you…like it?"

"I mean. I don't necessarily like the heat. Or the lack of grass. Our complex has this little yard area in the center of it with turf for grass, which is the closest we get to grass unless we go to the park that's a half hour drive away. And all of my houseplants died within a week because the air conditioning dried them out." Roxanne shrugged and rubbed at her shins. "We really don't do much either because it's so hot. Like, he works most of the day, and I work most of the day, so there isn't much time to do anything during the week or even on the weekends. He'll go hiking with some of his buddies from college on the weekends in the winter. And I have a couple of girlfriends who really like the shop but…"

"But it's not like you can just get in the car, drive a couple of miles, and be in a forest?" His teasing made her lips quirk, even if he had hit the nail on the head.

"Hiking the desert when the sun is setting is beautiful. Horseback riding in the mountains is an experience like no other. But living in the city, in the heat, every day without any real escape is…suffocating."

"So why don't you guys move closer to your parents? Or his family? Where are they?"

"His job is in the city, and he's much less flexible than I am. I brought up moving out to Henderson once when he asked me to move in with him, and it was the first fight we'd ever had. And the worst. Until I, well, until I came out here."

"It's nice to know I can elicit so much passion out of the carrot man."

Roxanne burst into a fit of giggles. "The 'carrot man'?"

Maverick's bashful grin made her laugh harder. She knew that he'd been trying hard to keep his opinions to himself when it came to Ethan, especially when he'd caught them bickering in the hallway a few days before, and she appreciated it. But she could also appreciate the childishness of calling him stupid names and the mischievous glint in Maverick's eye when he said it.

"I didn't start that one," he defended himself, relishing the sweet sound of her laughter.

"I wouldn't be surprised if you had. Although, I bet you're the one who uses it the most." She was still hiccupping on giggles, although they were coming slower. "Which one of you did?"

"Connor."

Roxanne laughed outright, shaking her head. "He's such a child."

Maverick chuckled, too. He was cut short when she rested her head against his arm, still giggling.

"An absolute child," he agreed and rested his cheek against the top of her head.

She smelled like rosemary and eucalyptus, the same smell, he'd bet the same brand of shampoo, she'd had for most of their adult lives. He'd relished how it filled the apartment after she showered, and it made all of the sense in the world to him to have it fill the air.

"But none of them like him." He'd already overstepped by calling him 'carrot man' in the first place. He might as well keep rolling out the punches until she punched him.

She didn't get upset, just shrugged against his side. "I know. Chey tries really hard. But he's not y-he's not what they think I need. What I needed."

Maverick nodded. He didn't feel the need to say anything because he knew, just as she did, the words that she'd tried to say and the way they had been caught in her throat. He hadn't had a much easier time with any of the girls he'd seen, casually or not, after the breakup. But she knew that. He'd told her all about it the first night back from the hospital.

They sat in the comfortable silence, Roxanne scooting closer to Maverick to monopolize his body heat and Maverick resisting the urge to wrap her in him for a while. The soft grayness of the park air had leveraged into a deeper, smoother darkness, filled with intermittent streetlights popping on. His phone buzzed at one point, a text from Wesley asking where they were. He'd showed it to her, and they'd agreed silently to head back.

She hopped up and offered him her hand, not that she'd been able to really help him up, but he let her try. Once he'd gotten on his feet with the crutch wedged underneath his armpit, they took their time walking the perimeter of the park before leaving. As they'd reached the sidewalk, a clap of thunder sounded overhead, urging the two to quicken their pace.

Halfway back to the apartment, with just enough time to duck under an awning at the first touch of fat raindrops, they got caught in what felt to Roxanne like a torrential downpour. Maverick had tugged her under the awning when he felt the first couple of drops on his head and had backed her against the door, making the most out of the minimal coverage. She had started to protest when a third thunderclap preceded the downpour.

After it started, with a partial pout on her thin lips, she stared over his arm at the stoic gray buildings, dripping with water.

"Did you know it was supposed to rain?" She had to yell to be heard over the storm's torrent.

"No," he turned, winced. "I guess my leg isn't healed enough to be a functional weathervane."

Roxanne rolled her eyes. They were crowded together against the side of the building, a bank, under the narrow awning's shadow. He was standing close enough that she could feel the heat off of the entire length of his body and if she moved any closer, she would have been met with the hard lines of his figure. He was looking down at her as if he was also aware of the space that barely separated them, a darkness in his eyes that she never thought she'd see again.

She swallowed, pressed herself closer to the wall, and looked out over his shoulder once more. "I wish your leg was in one piece."

"You and me both." He laughed, but she couldn't force herself to join in at that particular moment.

"Once it lightens up, we'll make a go for it," he promised.

Roxanne nodded firmly and squeezed past him, the momentary shock of his body pressing against hers enough to make her hope the storm would let up soon. She looked over her shoulder at him once and was relieved to see that, based on his expression, he seemed to feel the same.

Maverick didn't sleep a wink that night. His whole body was chaotically aware of the woman sleeping down the hall. He could feel her softness all around him in ways that he used to dream about at a distance. Their chemistry had changed. She didn't shy from him, but she hadn't pushed to be near him either while they cowered from the rain. And her closeness drove him crazy in what was a different kind of passion from what he could remember— the kind of passion that had built itself up since he drove her away.

He caught a few winks in between sultry dreams of Roxanne contorting herself for him and distressing thoughts of her leaving again. The worst dream came around three, when he was in the middle of imagining the way her body would bow for him, and it wasn't him anymore. He was watching her with the carrot man, hearing and feeling everything the other man did but forced to watch from the outside. He woke up in a cold sweat, his leg aching.

By the time his phone screen told him that it was morning, even before sunlight had started to drip through the curtains, he knew that he couldn't just watch her walk away. Maverick eased himself out of bed and looked at his haggard reflection in the dresser mirror. The man who looked back at him needed a better plan and fast.

Chapter Twenty-One
September 2016

Ethan stared at his silent cellphone, occupying the empty space where Roxanne should have been laying in their bed, trying to muster the courage to call her. His trip had ended a few days earlier than he'd expected and brought him home to their quiet apartment a week before he was ready. He hadn't spoken to her since he'd found out he'd be home early, avoiding all of her calls and text messages to assuage the sinking feeling in the bottom of his stomach. Liam had spent the better part of the trip, between meetings, trying to convince Ethan that the storm would pass. He'd argued that relationships went through rough patches and that Roxanne's trip was going to still, somehow, bring her back. Ethan wasn't as optimistic.

He rolled onto his side, his back to the phone, and stared out the window at the sun as it rose. It was a little past five in the morning and late enough in the year that the sunrise actually woke with him, not before him. As the light streaked in through the open curtains (there was no need to black the room out if Roxanne wasn't in it) it stroked over the shorts she'd left on the floor by the dresser and her pile of shoes outside of the closet. He made a note to pick up the clutter that afternoon.

Ethan rolled back over and turned the phone on, waiting while the screen came to life. The screensaver, a picture of his nephew and niece from the last time he'd seen them, smiled up at him. He should give his sister a call, he knew. She'd have an idea or two about what he was supposed to do with Roxanne. Instead, he hit his iMessage icon and wrote her a quick text asking for new pictures of the kids. When it sent, he switched to the contact list and found Roxanne's name.

Her phone rang three times, giving him three chances to abort. He waited. It clicked over, and he could hear breathing on the other end—but it didn't belong to her.

"Hello?" He sat up in bed, the hairs on his arms standing up. "Rox?"

"She's asleep."

The voice on the other end of the line wasn't familiar, not that anyone from her life had a chance to get familiar with them. Her friends hated him about as much as her parents did. It was the cross he'd had to bear as he'd come in off the heels of what he'd once heard Cheyenne describe as her 'big love' when she thought he wasn't home.

"Who is this?"

The man on the other end of the phone was silent for a minute. Ethan swung his legs over the edge of the bed while he waited, doing his best to keep from jumping to any bad conclusions. Ethan had become a master at watching his temper. He and Emily had spent years watching their parents bounce back and forth in the middle of fight after fight after fight, and he'd

144

promised to never get that bad. He wasn't so far from being sorely tempted though.

"It's Maverick," he heard finally, and his blood ran cold. "Rox left her phone in the kitchen last night."

He was explaining himself, which Ethan did not think was very good.

It was possible that she had forgotten her phone in another room though. She was never too good at keeping the device within arm's reach, especially if she was inspired.

"You said she's asleep?" Ethan asked calmly as he made his way into the kitchen.

"We were up pretty late. Cheyenne's heading back to Penn Ridge this afternoon, and we lost track of time."

Ethan rubbed his face, staring at the floor. "It's only after eight. She wouldn't be awake anyway," he said more to himself but heard Maverick's soft agreement in the background. Neither of them knew what to say to each other so they were in silence while Ethan made coffee and Maverick puttered.

"So...do you want me to tell her you called?" Maverick asked finally.

Ethan had filled his mug and was staring at the black liquid. He inhaled the steam and rubbed at his eyebrows. "No. I'll call her back later."

"Yeah sure." Maverick popped a short burst of air out.

"Hey...is there...something going on between you two?" Ethan heard himself ask it and wished, almost instantly, that he could have seen the other man's face. The silence that met him at the other side of the call made him antsy. He took a sip of his coffee while he waited for Maverick to answer.

"Ya know, I don't have to like you. I don't have to care for you being with…Rox. Hell, I don't even have to give a damn whether or not you even exist in my eyes." Maverick's cold temper filled Ethan's ear. "But you're on the phone with me asking me if my ex-girlfriend and I are seeing each other behind your back?"

"Look. I was just asking—"

"You were just asking if she was cheating on you. Which, if she was, I would sure as shit not tell you. Not that I should have to because you should know her well enough to know that she would never. Now, I am going to hang up this phone, and I am going to tell Roxanne you called. And I will definitely *not* tell her what you just asked of me. Because I give a damn about her and her feelings."

Maverick disconnected the call before Ethan could get another word in edge wise.

Ethan stood, staring at the kitchen backsplash, while the little bit of coffee he had in his system started to mix with the acid and race up his esophagus. All he'd done was make the situation so much worse by asking the wrong person the right question.

Chapter Twenty-Two
September 2016

Maverick never told her about his phone call with Ethan. He stewed in the annoyance all morning and barely spoke to her in his aggravation. He didn't say a word about it to anyone until he and Wesley left for his physical therapy appointment the next afternoon. By then, he'd had enough time to sit on it—and think about it—and come up with some sort of action plan.

Wesley let Maverick finish the story, his eyes firmly on the road in front of them, without a word. When Maverick was done speaking, he tilted his head to the side and shot a quick look at his friend.

"If my girlfriend ran across the country to go help some guy I'd be pretty upset too," Wesley responded, hands stuffed in his pockets. Maverick shot him a sour glance, to which he shrugged again.

Wesley continued, "I don't like the guy. But I can understand where he was coming from. The real question is, why the hell did you answer her phone?"

"It was ringing! I thought it was her parents. Until I saw the name." It was Maverick's turn to shrug, shifting awkwardly around the crutch. "I was curious. The only other time I've seen the guy, I was knee deep in a bottle of tequila."

"In a bar's worth of tequila," Wesley corrected.

Maverick grumbled his agreement and rubbed at his knee, which had been smarting since he'd gotten into the car. "Do you think I should tell her?"

With a grunt, Wesley turned into the parking lot of the professional block where Marshall's non-hospital office was located.

"I don't think so. If they're having issues on their own, you bringing this up—and pointing out that you don't think he trusts her—will only make matters worse. Which, in turn, will only make her more upset." Wesley turned the car into a spot and cut the engine. "If she asks, then sure, tell her the entire conversation. But…"

"But don't bring up how insecure and boring her boyfriend is?" Maverick reached for his crutches in the backseat.

"I wouldn't tell her you goaded him on either."

"I didn't! He was angry all on his own."

"I mean, you answered her cell phone—while she was still asleep."

Maverick waved his hand at Wesley and climbed out of the car. "What's he like?"

Wesley shrugged. "Ethan? He's…quiet." He held open the door to the office for Maverick. "I've only met him like twice. And the first time he was on his way out the door for a meeting." The second had been Silas' wedding, but the both of them knew how that had gone. "Chey says that he's really boring. Super stiff."

Maverick nodded his agreement. He could see that the man would come off as boring to Cheyenne. From the little bit Roxanne had told him, there wasn't much to Ethan's personality past numbers and his fraternity friends. "I think Roxanne would agree with that."

Wesley gave his friend a dark look. "I don't know if you should think things like that. It'd stir the boat."

Maverick snorted, maneuvering his way to the elevator. Maybe he wanted to stir the boat; after all, there wasn't anything he wouldn't do to get Roxanne back. Aside from, well, hurting her. And despite what he wanted to believe, all the evidence pointed toward the fact that the two of them breaking up would cause her pain.

"Yeah. You're right."

Wesley patted hm on the back and clicked his tongue. "Things'll get back to normal soon."

Maverick sighed. That was what he was afraid of happening. Instead of telling Wesley, he shrugged off his friend's hand and tapped his brace. "I hope things get back to normal soon." He forced himself to smile. "I'd like to be able to walk again without these damn things."

Wesley grinned and pressed the number for Marshall's floor. "You'll get there."

Chapter Twenty-Three
September 2016

The end of September was nearing, and Roxanne had been with him for nearly two months. Maverick had no idea what to feel about it, nor did he have any idea what to do about it. After Cheyenne had gone, giving him a prompting from the doorway, and Wesley had made himself at home, it seemed like Roxanne's leaving was on the horizon. Of course, he knew it was because she'd always planned on waiting for him to get back to work. But it was coming, and he felt powerless.

He'd taken to spending more time with her alone since he'd spoken to Ethan, asking her to walk with him in the evenings and bunkering down with her in the guest room to catch up on the shows they used to watch before he'd retreat to his room. It was something but not enough to keep her from talking about moving back home.

Maverick went back to work on Tuesday, just as they had planned, and while he wanted to celebrate, he couldn't help feeling a little disappointed that it had come so soon. It came with the knowledge that she was leaving soon, that his plan, their friendship, while it was better than nothing, was all that could be. Still, he drove himself to work in his new car, enjoyed the bagels and coffee in the break room while the firm welcomed him back, and settled back into what was once his routine.

By noon he was exhausted. Reviewing case files and sending emails from the comfort of his couch was nothing compared to dealing with the partners, the interns, and the other associates who circulated in and out of his office daily. In the lull from eleven to twelve when he'd had a chance to think about something other than cases, he let himself think about Roxanne. He wondering what he could to make her stay—to make her let go of the carrot man and his uncomfortable need to know that whatever was happening between Maverick and Roxanne was nothing more than a forced friendship.

He'd figure it out. He had another couple of days to get in closer, to talk to her more, to try to find some crack in her own relationship, or to realize he needed to let her go. Whichever one came first at the end of the day. After, of course, he ate lunch.

He'd just set his mind to ordering a sandwich and avoiding everyone but Nick when he heard a tap on his door.

"It's open!" he called out while he opened a new case file, trying to pretend that he'd been productive for the last half hour since the last time someone had bothered him.

"It's a cozy office."

Maverick looked up and smiled at Roxanne, who was standing in the doorway with a takeout bag and two bottles of sparkling water, checking up on him.

"Your dad set me up well before he sold the place." He pushed the file to the side.

"You set yourself up well. They got you during the sale, which made the firm's cost go up." Roxanne sashayed in and dropped down in the stuffed black chair on the other end of Maverick's desk. "I was out at the library and figured you might be hungry."

Maverick fished a couple of napkins out of the top desk drawer and reached for the bag. "Whatcha bring me?"

"Burrito." She twisted the cap off her bottle.

"A burrito and a welfare check. I'm a lucky man." He winked at her as he unwrapped the lunch. "How was the library today?"

"Good. I didn't get much done but I figured out which flight I'm going to take home. And Ethan actually talked to me today."

Maverick snorted. He'd just about had enough of hearing Roxanne lament over the guy.

"I'm sure he was so happy to hear from you," Maverick said sarcastically.

"Be nice." Roxanne popped a tortilla into her mouth. She spoke around the mouthful.

"No. No, I think I'm just about done being nice." His mind had been made up. He'd made it up when he saw her standing in the doorway to check on him with lunch in hand and a ready smile on her face. There was no way he was going to let her go without a fight.

"Whataya mean?" He'd caught her attention, enough that she'd put down the taco she was about to bite it into. "'Done being nice'?"

"Ethan called you the other day, and he and I spoke on the phone." Maverick picked the file folder back up and started to leaf through the case documents to keep his hands busy. "He's a dick, and all wrong for you. And your relationship is a joke."

"Excuse me?" Roxanne's voice had that edge to it. The fighting edge. "What did you two talk about?"

"He asked me if you were doing me behind his back." Maverick didn't bother to look up from the case folder he was leafing through, despite the sharp 'hurung' she made when he spoke. He did brace himself for her reaction, though, sure that what she was going to respond with was going to cause him physical pain. "Which leads me back to my original argument that your relationship is a joke."

Roxanne took a minute to formulate her thoughts but stood up from the plush chair on the other side of his desk.

"What do you mean?" she asked calmly, not quite the reaction he was expecting.

He looked up then and took off his glasses. "I mean, your relationship with that ginger haired dope. It's a joke."

The parsed words, the carefully thought out delivery, were sure to buy him some more time before the attack. He knew she had it in her, even if it had been a long while since he'd purposefully pushed the buttons of a full-blown attack. "You're wasting your time."

153

Roxanne popped her lips. The hollow sound filled the office, and Maverick eased himself out of his chair, worked slowly around the desk (and her), and closed the door.

"You don't know anything about me, my life, or my relationship."

He didn't like the unnerving calm in her words. It wasn't the fight he'd been so used to having, the battle he'd crafted and lost so many times. It was as if she had given up, had lost some her ability to pose an argument. He found himself musing over how quiet their home must have been for her to get so good at so carefully composing her words.

"I do, though." He pushed and eased himself onto the corner of the desk. "I know everything about you, Rox."

Maybe not everything single solitary detail, but he knew her for decades. He knew her strengths and her fears and the dreams she'd had as a child. He knew the ink stains on her fingers and how she got the burn on her left elbow and how now, as she stood staring at him, she was resisting the urge to bite her fingernails. He couldn't help but wonder if Ethan knew her like that. Knew her well enough to see that she was on the tipping point. That she was angry, even if her mouth didn't move and her eyes barely showed it. What Maverick did know about Ethan was that he didn't trust her, not even enough to know that nothing could have happened between her and Maverick with him still in the picture. It was the ammunition that he'd needed to push his attack and head for war. "And I know that your relationship is a hoax."

"And how is that?"

He heard the strain. Heard the careful composure starting to slip through. She ran her hands down her thighs once, as if her palms were sweaty, and balled her hands into fists. Her lower lip had jutted out, and her eyes were furious.

"Because..." Maverick took a breath, knowing he had to get the words just right. "Because it's not real. It's not where you should be."

She didn't respond.

"Because you should still be with me." It was out. A flood of emotions broke free. It was a hard push. "It should always have been me. I should have been all you held on to for the rest of your life."

He pushed himself off the desk and passed the space between them. His fingers ran along the soft curve of her jaw, and he tipped her head back. "Because I am all you can hold on to, the only thing you need to hold on to, for the rest of your life."

And he kissed her. A soft kiss. An unassuming kiss. A kiss that she melted into. Her arms wrapped around his neck, and she pushed into him like he was a well, and she was a body lost in the desert sun. And as they kissed, he felt grounded, he felt whole.

Maverick didn't push for more than their lips meeting. He held back all of the urges and emotions he'd felt since he'd woken up in the hospital to fold her into him as gently as he could. But his arms, steel bands around her frame, shook her back into reality. She stepped back, her hands firmly planting on his chest to keep them apart. Her chest heaved; her eyes filled. There was no explosion. No shout or scream. Just a softly heard whimper before she grabbed her bag and borrowed jacket and left.

"You could have been. You should have been." Roxanne let out a shaky laugh as she yanked the door open. "But you messed that one up, didn't you?"

Chapter Twenty-Four
September 2016

Roxanne stood on the front step of Caleb Anderson's house, her hands trembling as she tried to get the courage to knock on the front door. After what had happened in Maverick's office she'd just gotten in the rental car and drove away. She didn't really see the road until she'd ended up at the outskirts of Penn Ridge, staring at the blue and red welcome sign. At that point, she was too far to turn back and yet, she was still not close enough. She had no answers for herself and a sea of anxiety still pulsed in her gut. She'd driven up the familiar roads until she'd come to a stop at the Retirement House, her car parked behind Cheyenne's Cherokee.

On that drive, she'd tried to work through what had happened. How she felt. How kissing Maverick had awoken something in her that Ethan's touch never did. She was still burning, her body still feverish from the simple kiss when she cut the engine and spent fifteen minutes freaking out about it. She hyperventilated and let herself shake it out.

She'd still been in shock when she wandered up to the door.

Roxanne forced herself to take a deep breath before she knocked softly on the door. Two minutes passed without any acknowledgement, and she stiffened her shoulders, rasped on the door harder. In response, Cheyenne yelled that she'd be right there.

Cheyenne opened the door to Roxanne's red eyes, finally filling with tears. Her warm smile soured in an instant, and she reached for the other woman.

Roxanne went willingly into the embrace. Cheyenne held her while she stared at the fireplace and tried to figure out how to speak the words out loud. She felt like she was falling apart on the inside. Caleb had wandered into the living room to see who was at the door, took one look at the sea of emotion that was threatening to flood his house, and retreated upstairs.

Eventually, Cheyenne led Roxanne into the kitchen and sat her at the island with a bowl, a whisk, eggs, and sugar.

"Whisk," she commanded softly. "It will help your mind for you to work."

Roxanne did what she was told, whisking the bowl's contents together. Cheyenne mixed dry ingredients in another bowl while Roxanne's sobbing subsided. They worked in silence, the same silence that had filled the familiar kitchen for three days after RJ had died and another twelve hours before Roxanne had admitted that Maverick had dumped her. Cheyenne's need for soul food had left Roxanne plenty of room to calm down over the years.

"Maverick kissed me," Roxanne said finally.

The other woman stopped stirring and took the bowl from Roxanne.

"He kissed you!" she said levelly, trying to keep her excitement in.

K.T. Egan

"Yeah. Like. It was kind of like an *I'm just gonna do this, and we'll see what happens* kind of a kiss. In his office!" Roxanne reached for the bag of melting chocolates Cheyenne had had on the counter.

"How did it feel?" Her friend swatted her hand. "Wait."

Roxanne shrugged. *How did it feel?* She wanted to shout that it felt like home, like warm afternoons in grassy fields and cold winter nights in front of a movie with a blanket and a cup of cocoa. She wanted to say that it felt like it had never changed, like they had never changed. She wanted to scream that it felt so *unfair*. That he'd had no right to kiss her, to push her over the precipice that she'd been balancing on since she'd returned. One foot in the old life he'd shattered, and one in the new life she'd built without him. He had no right.

"It felt...the same but different at the same time," Roxanne opted for finally. "It was like riding a bike. Something you just don't forget how to do."

Cheyenne nodded, still whisking. Roxanne could see her lips twitching like she was pleased with the events of the afternoon. "And how do you feel?"

"Angry. Annoyed. Confused." Roxanne dropped her head onto the counter, barely cushioning it with her folded arms. "He had no right. We've been over for a long time now. I have a whole new life and a whole new relationship. Oh God, Ethan already thinks I'm cheating on him with Maverick." She banged her fist on the island.

"More like cheating on Rick with him," Cheyenne muttered.

Roxanne's head whipped up. "What?"

Cheyenne pursed her lips. "I just think that, if you really wanted to be with Ethan, you would have gone home sooner. Obviously here with Rick is where you wanted to be. It's been almost two months. He's alive, he's up, and he went to work today. And you're still here. Taking your time. And to what? Write? You can write anywhere. You proved that by moving to Las Vegas in the first place."

"I love Ethan," Roxanne shot back.

She did. She'd loved Ethan from the moment he'd kissed her. Just...in different ways than she'd loved Maverick.

With Maverick, her love had been consuming in the best way. He'd filled her days with friendship and companionship, had fit in seamlessly with her family, and had been the one thing that stayed constant. From friendship to romance, they'd been a duo from the start. With Ethan, she'd had to learn how to think outside the box, to build herself up because the person who was supposed to didn't see the same end goal—to exist on her own. It'd been a learning experience, one that she'd needed and would forever be grateful for.

"I love Ethan," she said again, this time weaker.

She knew, just as her friend's knowing gaze knew, that the love between them had been something much different. Something that hadn't been enough to keep her from going back to Maverick. "I just...don't know if I'm in love with Ethan.

"I know." Cheyenne squeezed her hand. "He's not Rick."

K.T. Egan

"Rick and I have been over for a long time," Roxanne said again, although she wasn't sure which of them she was trying to reassure.

"So, you say." Cheyenne dumped the contents of her mixing bowl into a flat dish.

"We have been."

Cheyenne shook her head. "If that were true, you wouldn't still be here, Rox."

"I have a good man waiting for me back home." Roxanne rubbed her face. "A good man who won't just throw our life away because he gets in a bad mood. A man that doesn't fight, a man who likes sterile, neutral colors." A man who had never filled her with passion in the same way Maverick had; a man who stifled her more than he inspired her. The words sat on Roxanne's tongue but were swallowed down for fear of what would happen if she said the out loud.

"I'm sure there's more to it than either of us know." Cheyenne was convinced Silas knew the real reason, even if he'd hid behind half-baked excuses since the breakup. "Have you ever thought to just ask Rick?"

"No, and it doesn't matter. He was pissy. We had a little disagreement about dinner. He walked out. I followed. He dumped me." The bitterness in Roxanne's voice physically hurt Cheyenne. "It's over. It's been over. And I just…I need it to stay that way."

Roxanne looked out the bay windows over the sink, into the woods where they used to play as kids and shook her head. "I didn't see it coming, you know."

161

Cheyenne nodded slowly. "We all knew. No one saw it coming."

"And now…"

"And now?" Cheyenne prompted.

"Now I'm starting to wonder. And think about it. And it makes no sense to me because me being here has literally changed nothing. It's like I never left." Roxanne stood up in her frenzy and was wringing her hands.

"I even caught myself, the other day, thinking about where he and I would be now if we had stayed together." Roxanne laughed at herself and shook her head.

There was only one thing she could do. She'd known the answer before she'd gotten in the car. She'd known the answer as soon as he'd woken up in the hospital. She needed to go back to her life, to her life without him. The life she'd built. Because he'd broken her once so hard that she'd never thought she'd recover. And she wasn't going to put herself in that position ever again.

Roxanne dried her eyes with the sleeves of her sweater and stood upright. "I need to go home."

Cheyenne had started to argue but closed her mouth when she saw the sureness in Roxanne's eyes. There was no way to change her mind. Maybe, just maybe, if Roxanne went back to Ethan, she'd see what Cheyenne had seen, what Wesley and Silas had seen, when they all saw them together. That Roxanne belonged back home with Maverick, building the future they had taken a break from. She hoped so for the sake of the both of them.

Chapter Twenty-Five
September 2016

Maverick and Wesley were sitting on the couch, in the middle of an episode of *Mad Men*, when Roxanne made her way through the door. They were stretched out on the large leather structure, a bowl of popcorn between them and Chinese food containers and a wing box scattered around the kitchen counter.

They both looked up when she slammed the door behind her and dropped her purse on the hall table. One look at the scowl on her face and both men slunk lower onto the couch as if to hide behind the back of it. She was having none of it. She'd spent the entire drive back from Penn Ridge struggling with herself, trying to argue against the voice telling her stay.

In the end, her decision had stayed firm. It was with the anger of that decision that she stormed around the couch and shut the television off. Her hands planted firmly on her hips, she leveled both of them with a forceful glare. It was a look they knew well. It was the "someone is in trouble" look that had been spearing them since they were kids.

It was the look Maverick had gotten when he got gum stuck in her hair and that Wesley had earned when he struck a baseball into her mother's kitchen window. At twenty-six years old, it was fair to say that they were both still terrified of it. Although

Maverick's guilt-ridden face and Wesley's pure confusion proved how much further removed from that reality they were.

"I'm sorry for the mess. We were gonna clean it before you got home," Maverick started while struggling to get to his feet to go take care of the trash in the kitchen, acting as if nothing had happened because he hadn't bothered to tell Wesley about the incident at the firm. He'd still been reeling from the fight and from the feel of her kiss when he'd gotten home.

Wesley tugged him back down when they caught a fresh glare from Roxanne and gestured to him to stop.

She sighed at the two of them and sat on the coffee table. "I need to talk to you guys." Her blue eyes turned to Maverick, and she gave a halfhearted shrug. "Mainly you, but Wes can be here, too."

"Should I be worried?" Maverick tugged at the collar of his t-shirt.

"I don't know. Probably...not."

If he was going to act like nothing had happened, then Roxanne, feeling validated in her decision to leave, would do the exact same thing.

"Okay. Let us have it." Wesley nodded at Roxanne.

"I need to go home." Roxanne had put a lot of thought into this next move and how to tell him them, and it would save them all a lot of pain if she just got it out there. "I've been here for two months, and Maverick is obviously fine. He went back to work today, didn't he? It's time."

Going back to Las Vegas meant going back to the life she had made for herself. To the man who had helped her when she was falling apart and to the life that they had built. It meant that she had to figure out her relationship with Ethan and her job and her life. It meant that, when she and Maverick said goodbye, this time it was for good.

Roxanne heard herself explaining her thoughts to both men, walking them through the anger and the pain that had driven her home.

"I think, it would be best if, when Rick and I said goodbye this time…it was for good," she finished on a half-whimper, her hands trembling at her sides. Despite her emotional frenzy, she'd managed to keep the kiss out of the equation. It wasn't the time to talk about it, especially not in front of Wes—that would just leave too many questions.

She couldn't bring herself to look at Maverick or Wesley, instead focusing on the space between the two men on the couch.

Maverick didn't say anything. He let her speak her peace, his chest aching. When she seemed to be done, he got to his feet and disappeared to his room without a word. Roxanne rushed after him, stopping at the closed door. On the other side, she could hear him throwing clothes around and let it go. It was for the best, for her, for him, for Ethan. That's why she was doing this.

"You're just gonna let her go?"

Maverick hadn't looked up when Wesley had stalked into his room, the door slamming shut behind him. He was lying over the foot of his bed, tossing a baseball up and catching it. The room was in shambles from the tornado of clothes he'd created, and his bed was a mess of half ripped off sheets and pillows that had seen better days. No matter how bad it looked, it didn't match the hurricane happening inside his head.

He tossed the ball up again instead of responding to his friend.

"She's packing still. You can go stop her," Wesley suggested.

"I kissed her, Wes." Maverick shrugged as he said it. Once out in the open, it didn't feel like such a big secret at all. It hadn't mattered enough to her to change things, to make her see, so why would he continue to feel guilty about it. She was leaving.

"I kissed her, and I told her it should be me, and she's leaving anyway. I have no more. Nothing left." Maverick tossed the ball again. It was a weak attempt but playing it slow, being her friend, had gotten him nowhere. Except asleep beside her.

Wesley laid down on the bed next to Maverick and crossed his ankles. "You kissed her?"

Maverick nodded and threw the ball toward the ceiling. "I kissed her."

Wesley caught the ball when it bounced back and glanced at his friend. "Do you really think it should have been you?"

Maverick chewed over that while Wesley took a turn throwing the ball up at the ceiling.

"I do," he said finally, exhausted. "I really think that breaking up with Roxanne was the biggest mistake of my entire life."

It was, Wesley thought. He didn't say anything else, because he didn't know what to say. There were never any words to express how he'd felt about the breakup between Maverick and Roxanne because sometimes, he didn't know how he felt himself. The break-up had taught Maverick how to be self-sufficient, a skill he hadn't had before. But it'd also changed Maverick, dulled some of the spark his friend had in a way that'd made him truly one of a kind. Having Roxanne back had brought back some of that spark, without the volatility that had made Maverick so hot headed when they were younger.

"Well, we all make mistakes," Wesley said finally. He sat up and shrugged at his friend. "C'mon. Let's go shoot some artificially intelligent robots."

Chapter Twenty-Six
September 2016

That night, after Wesley had finally left Maverick to himself, he sat on the floor and dug through a box of pictures underneath his bed. When he found the Polaroid he'd been searching for, dated December 1997, he eased himself back to look at the image. It was of two kids, one with curly, dark hair and the other with two missing front teeth. They were wearing backpacks and parka jackets, and she was proudly holding up a snowball the size their heads combined.

Maverick smiled and ran his finger along the edge of the photograph. Sometimes it was hard to remember that he and Roxanne had been friends first—good friends, part of a group of great friends who had etched their names on a tree and promised to never leave each other behind. Another picture, dated from the spring of the following year, showed the two of them with Silas and the Carmody brothers. They were all in swimsuits, standing on the edge of Anderson Creek. Roxanne's mother had taken this one, her delicate script on the back of the picture with their names and ages. It was hard for him to believe that Connor had only been six at the time.

The pain in Maverick's leg reminded him that the floor was hard and that he wasn't in the position to stay bunked down against the hardwood. He heaved himself up onto the corner of the bed and dragged the box of pictures back up with him.

He pulled out another picture with the back dated 1997, this time an image taken on a disposable camera and not a Polaroid. It was an early fall picture. If he had to guess based on the color of the leaves on the apple tree in the Wortham's front yard, it was still September. In it, he and Roxanne were sitting on the ground underneath the tree having a tea party. Sid was standing not too far off, talking to RJ and Ralph.

Maverick could almost remember the day. He and Roxanne had known each other for a handful of weeks, and it was their first playdate. He remembered begging Sid to let him go and pouting the whole walk to the Wortham's because his brother had insisted on joining him. That was as far as the memory went.

At the bottom of the box of pictures, underneath four albums and dozens of loose prints, Maverick found the picture from Roxanne's first day of the first grade.

September 1997

The first grade was going to suck. Maverick was so sure of it that he fought Sid the entire way to Penn Ridge Elementary, starting with the large rip he put in the t-shirt that Sid had originally chosen for him. His brother was patient, on the border of kind, while their grandmother tried to mitigate it on the drive to the school. She'd dropped both boys off, hugged Maverick for good luck on his first day, and entrusted his safe deposit on the middle schooler who had a death grip on his shoulder.

Sid walked him all of the way to his classroom's door, holding onto his shoulder and the backpack. Maverick's arms were crossed over his chest, and he was ready to fight Sid. His brother stopped them outside the classroom door and squatted so that they were eyelevel. He tried to calm his brother's mess of hair while the seven-year-old glared up at him. His brown eyes were full of affection and kindness. The child started to relax his shoulders, and his arms dropped to his sides.

"I don't wanna," Maverick said finally, looking up at Mrs. Karlile's classroom door. "Can we go home?"

"You know that we can't. You have to go to school. *I have to go to school.*" Sid messed up his hair. "Besides, don't you want to make friends? Have someone to play with?"

"I play with you. And Gram." It all made sense to Maverick. Go to school, meet other kids, go home. It would be the same as at Mom and Dad's house. He just…didn't want to.

"Rick, buddy, we gotta do this." Sid held out his fist for Maverick to tap. "I'll be with Gram to pick you up after school."

"Promise?" The seven-year-old sized his brother up with suspicion, his dark eyes furrowed. "Pinky swear?"

The thirteen-year-old smirked and held out his pinky. With the seven-year-old's little finger wrapped around his, he bent his forehead down, their faces close so that he could whisper and only the child could hear. "Triple pinky swear. With a double ice cream scoop."

"Mint chip," Maverick agreed and nodded against his brother's forehead. He had relaxed enough to look at the door and not feel scared anymore. "Can we go for some after?"

"I'll talk to Gram. But you gotta get in there, kid." Sid stood up and messed up his brother's hair again. "Ready?"

Maverick nodded sharply and let himself in to the classroom. He'd looked over his shoulder to make sure Sid was waiting for him to get inside before he walked in and let the door swing shut between them. The whole class stopped talking when he stood in front of them, and Mrs. Karlile had gotten up from her desk to say hello.

She introduced him to the class and asked him if he had anything he wanted to share with his new friends. The seven-year-old had fought to not roll his eyes because it would have been rude. He told the entire class, in plain words, that he was an orphan. Mrs. Karlile had laughed awkwardly and ushered him to his desk while the class whispered about the weird word and what it could mean.

Maverick sat, stuffing his backpack under the desk like the girl sitting on the other end of the table. She smiled at him with super blue eyes. Maverick didn't smile back.

"Hi," she said happily, kicking her foot under the desk. "I'm Roxanne."

"Hi," he watched her kick her foot, watched her smile, and found himself smiling too. "Rick," he held his hand out like he had seen his father do anytime he'd met someone new. "I'm new."

"I know." The girl giggled and high-fived his outstretched hand. "I'm not."

Maverick had laughed at the high five. Maybe the first grade wouldn't be so bad after all.

Maverick woke in the morning in a cold sweat, the feel of Roxanne's little hand in his so real he had to curl and uncurl his fingers a half dozen times to make it go away. He turned his head to see the baseball on his pillow, lying on a pile of photographs. The adhesive of the broccoli and sun stickers on the baseball, another relic of his childhood, beginning to wear. Maverick focused on smoothing them down. His brain woke slowly while he smoothed down the stickers and fixed the little pile of photographs into a neat stack.

It was right then and there that something clicked. He got out of bed as fast as he could manage and limped out of the room and down the hall. The guest room door was wide open, and its guest was no longer inside, the bed primly made, and the piles of paper and used pens that had once sat on the writing desk all vanished. The only thing that Roxanne had left behind was a little note on the comforter and the American University sweatshirt she had borrowed.

He didn't read the note, instead crumbling it up in his hand and throwing it on the floor before leaving the room. He almost collapsed on top of Wesley when he found his friend, snoring on the couch. The emotions that flooded through him were akin to those he'd felt the first time he'd let her go. And it all but broke him.

Maverick noticed, struggling to hold himself together, that even though Wesley snored like a train behind him, and even though he had lived alone in the two-bedroom space for over two years, that the apartment had never felt so quiet.

Chapter Twenty-Seven
September 2016

Rupert realized, as the plane hit the tarmac, that we don't know how far we have to travel until we feel so alone.

Roxanne underlined the final period, her fingers achingly clinging to the Bic ballpoint pen that had long since indented her middle finger. It sunk in slowly that it was the final period as she shifted around in the hard, plastic seat in the terminal. As she sat there staring at it, she felt an uneasy sensation in the pit of her stomach thinking of all the periods she had put on the yellow legal pads that had been stuffed in her suitcase and her shoulder bag. She stared at it with a detached sense of satisfaction, short of pride, wishing that she had someone to tell the news to.

She never thought that she would have finished her first novel sandwiched between two strangers in a crowded in an airport in North Carolina. Nor did she ever think that when the time came, she would be avoiding turning on her phone because she knew that she couldn't tell the one person she really wanted to. Texting Maverick about this triumph would only make her leaving sting so much worse—for both of them.

Roxanne had resigned herself to scribbling the time that she'd written the last word in the upper right-hand corner, capped the pen, closed the worn pages of the legal pad affectionately, and

174

rolled her head. Each vertebra in her neck cracked blissfully as she moved around in the seat. She tried to snap the tension out of her lower spine, but she had been waiting for her flight from Charlotte to Las Vegas for too long, and the rigidity was wearing on her spine. She stuffed the last legal pad, half-filled, into her worn out shoulder bag and wrapped her hair in a knot, shoving the pen through it to try and hold the curls in place.

The woman to her right shifted out of reach of her elbow while impatiently cleaning the face of her toddler. The child was giggling, her mother's onslaught with the wet wipe almost as amusing as the cartoons on her mother's phone. To Roxanne's left, the man in the wrinkled business suit tensed at the child's eruptions. Roxanne rolled her eyes at him and got to her feet, her tired muscles screaming.

She wandered to the flight tracker, hoping that the twice-delayed flight was still having issues. Another half hour until boarding but it looked like the rough weather that was keeping her grounded had finally passed.

Turning from the board, Roxanne caved and turned her cellphone on. While it booted up, she found a coffee shop and scooted into line, scrolling through the four missed calls, eleven text messages, and two calendar notifications that sported through her phone screen. Ethan had texted her twice, asking if her flight was still delayed, and Cheyenne had given her a detailed outline of Connor's latest escapades.

While she scrolled through the mini essay Cheyenne had sent, parsing through spelling mistakes and awkward phrases that indicated she had been using the speech to text while at the bakery, the line moved forward. Roxanne stepped forward without looking up and collided into the back of the man in front of her.

"I am so sorry," she squealed quietly, fumbling with her phone and the paper ticket that fell on the ground.

He turned around and stooped to pick it up while she just stared at it senselessly.

"Las Vegas?" He stood, holding the boarding pass out to her.

She took the ticket and took him in. He was unruly, with black hair that was graying at the roots and a lined face that watched her as she watched him.

"Yes," she said with a short nod.

He didn't speak until she had stuffed the paper into her shoulder bag. "Business or pleasure?" His voice was an octave she'd only heard on the west side of the country.

Roxanne quelled the eye roll that his question prompted and took a step forward. "I live there," she responded.

He nodded. "So do I."

He fished in the side pocket of his jacket and pulled out a bent business card. It read "Dr. T. W. Khan - Full Professor, Literature. UNLV" in a small script. She took the card, the colors similar to her airplane sweatshirt, and then looked back up at him.

"UNLV?"

Ethan had taken her to the campus before, had shown her around the narrowed halls of a state education, and had boasted about his time as a student there. She'd felt stifled but amazed because she'd never been in a university so large.

"I've been teaching there twenty years. Have you ever been?"

"My uh...my boyfriend went there. Graduated in 2012, Finance."

He was next in line, and the barista cleared her throat twice before he turned to order. Without asking or even directly offering it to her, he told the barista he was paying for her drink, too and gestured her forward. Roxanne tried to protest, took one look at his disapproving scowl, and shuffled up to the counter to order.

When she offered Professor Kahn a five-dollar bill for the iced drink, he waved her off and directed her toward a small bench near the terminal.

"A drink for a bit of conversation?" He smiled and sat down, balancing his hot coffee on his knee to fish a pair of glasses out of his jacket pocket.

"Uh, sure." Roxanne wiped the condensation off of the side of her plastic cup while he perched a pair of glasses on his nose. The professor smiled at her while she nodded and rubbed at the ink on her fingers. "Where are you coming from?"

"Visiting family in New York. My son and his family live in Orange County." He took the lid off of his coffee cup. "What about you?"

"Home." She wrapped both of her hands around the cup. "Well, the town that I grew up in. Kind of."

"Visiting family? Writing the great American novel?" His tone and the way his lips and eyes upturned in tandem opened her up like a fresh sheet of paper or a new pack of pens. She could see in his eyes the same thing she saw in her own.

"No. A... friend of mine was in a really bad accident a couple of months ago and I... had to go back and help him out."

If Kahn had noticed the shrill turn in her voice or the way she continued to rub at her fingers, he didn't let on. Instead, he took another sip of coffee and waited.

"He's okay." She picked at the plastic lid. "More okay than we thought he was going to be, so I spent a lot of time being at home."

Her fingers stopped picking, rested around the base of the plastic cup. "It was really great to be back home, seeing people that I haven't seen in years, being in the same area that I grew up."

Roxanne shrugged her shoulders and started to peel at the base in earnest. It bugged her, sat heavy in her shoulders that the history between her and Maverick could be boiled down into a singular timeline. No misconceptions, no alternate endings—they had been a comet that had missed its mark.

As she sat, talking with a total stranger in a crowded airport terminal, it was all laid out in front of her. A beginning and an end. Ideas that had both been calming and unnerving once now made her feel numb.

Could Maverick have been thinking the same things? Or was he focused on getting better? Walking with a purpose, his apartment empty and quiet, the way he had grown accustomed to it. Was he searching for the woman who had left the tea bags in the kitchen? Was he looking for somebody new? Was she a fool for even wondering it?

Dr. Kahn was watching her with a bemused expression on his lips. "Are you sure you want to go back to Las Vegas?"

He had heard the drop in her voice, the shadow in her gaze. The prying question made her head shoot up, a certain sense of self-preservation filling her being. When their eyes met, his shoulders hunched defensively, and he held his hands up. "I'm not trying to pry…"

"I left some unresolved business in Pennsylvania," she offered and took a swallow of coffee, the smoothness of the soymilk and the beans filling her with a small notion of warmth. "The friend I left behind…he was the one person I thought I was going to spend the rest of my life with. We uh…we have the same group of friends, and I think they all saw it going in another direction, too."

The professor nodded, waiting for her to continue.

"He broke my heart. Which is how I ended up in Vegas in the first place. And I started a new life with a new group of friends and a new boyfriend. And then, out of the blue, almost four years later, I get a phone call saying he's hurt."

Telling the story to someone else made it seem more real. Aside from the small glances and encouraging nods from her friends, the idea of she and Maverick being anything more than the past had never felt real. Kahn made it real.

"So, I picked up and went back."

"Why?"

"Great question. I have no idea. After going there and being there and helping him, I still have no idea."

Before he could respond, their boarding call sounded. A sigh of relief came up through the crowd. Kahn stood and offered his hand to help her up.

"It's a short flight," he mused to her as they got in line.

She needed anything but a short flight.

Professor Kahn had turned into a crafty confidant and an excellent listener. Roxanne hadn't fully realized how much she needed an outsider's perspective until she had finished pouring her heart out to the man. He had given up his business class ticket in exchange for the seat next to hers, giving a nineteen-year-old boy the flight of his lifetime in the nicer cabin. He took notes while she talked. Every once and a while, he chuckled or clucked his tongue and would occasionally read back something to her if he wasn't sure he'd noted it correctly.

When her story was finally done, her exasperation palpable with the slump of her shoulders, he closed his little notebook and laced his fingers together.

"My wife and I met when we were in high school," he said after a moment of looking at her from the bridge of his glasses. "We didn't get married until after she had gotten divorced…in our thirties. By then, she already had two kids, and we'd fallen out of touch for a decade. As a matter of fact, Facebook reconnected us if you can believe that."

He chuckled before digging a picture of his wife and their five kids out of his wallet and held it out to her.

"After we got married, I adopted Mike and Leah. I wouldn't have my amazing oldest son and daughter if it weren't for the fact that we had our fair share of struggles. These things happen for a reason."

Roxanne puckered her lips. "I hope that someday I'll have that kind of wisdom to give to someone else."

"That someday might be closer than you think." He put the creased, but beloved, picture back into his wallet. "When you type up your manuscript, I'd love to read it."

And just like that the conversation had ended or moved to somewhere else. Kahn jotted down his email address on the airplane napkin and handed it to her.

"And I hope you use this story to inspire you. I know that my family inspires a lot of what I write."

"It does all sound a little crazy, doesn't it?" Roxanne smiled at the professor, crossing her legs as best she could in the stiff seat. "Kind of Romantic in a very Hawthornean sense."

"That's the English major in you." Kahn grinned at her. "It honestly doesn't sound as crazy as you think."

They had spent the rest of the flight talking about lighter topics like the classes he taught and the odd jobs she had found since graduating from college. The conversation calmed her nerves and made her feel more well-rounded, a gift after the tension in her shoulders for most of the day.

She learned that he had been in New York, spending time with his oldest son and his wife. They were expecting a baby, Kahn's first grandchild, and had asked him to fly out to help them buy a house. His youngest was six years old, their other two children eight and ten, and so his wife had to stay at home. Kahn was excited to be home with her and back to his classes, having taken a long weekend to help the young couple house hunt.

They exited the plane and meandered through the terminal, still talking about the curriculum he had created. Roxanne was wistful, hanging on to every word he said.

Part of her wished that she had gone back to school already, had continued her education after finishing her undergrad. Part of her hoped to start again soon, getting a master's in literature. She voiced the idea to him as they made it to the baggage claim, and he nodded in encouragement. He told her it didn't matter how much space was in between, she just needed to find the right program for her. On the escalator he told her not to think of the school first because she still needed to figure out where she was going to choose to live.

Kahn's eyes told her that it was more than just where—it was possibly who.

At the luggage carousel, just as Roxanne caught sight of Ethan, Kahn smiled at his wife, a soft pressure built in the back of her neck, and anxiety swept through her sternum. She watched the elderly couple embrace, smiling and holding onto each other. If only Ethan's embraced had caused her the same amount of comfort Kahn seemed to draw out of his wife's.

Chapter Twenty-Eight
October 2016

"I don't think me showing up is going to make him feel any better." Silas was packing even as he argued on the phone with Wesley, his hands shaking in spite of himself as he moved from dresser to bed and back again.

"Things have been funky between you two for years now, Si, I don't think you coming out here is going to make things worse. And I can't deal with him alone. He's been in such a funk since she left."

Silas could hear the sounds of Maverick shouting profanities in the background, profanities that Silas could assume were either related to a work case file or a video game. Considering the shock and awe he was sure Roxanne's departure had left in Maverick and considering the colorful language spouting out of his friend's mouth, Silas would have assumed the latter of the two options.

"They sure as shit won't make things better."

"Look. The man's a wreck, and I don't know what to do. Roxanne isn't even answering my texts. I need help."

"I'm coming."

When Silas had told Nancy about Roxanne leaving, about the moderately tense conversations he'd been having back and forth with Maverick (the most the two had spoken since before the wedding), and the fact that Wesley was dealing with a sober but devastated Maverick, Nancy had all but packed Silas' car herself. Nancy had asked him to stay out of the mess, sure that his involvement would just make things worse, but the nuclear fallout was his place to clean up.

"Thank God. I don't know what to do with him," Wesley responded with relief.

"I'll be there tonight."

"You're a God send."

"I don't know how much better I'm going to make it, but I'll be there."

After he hung up with Wesley, he left his bedroom and found his wife rocking the baby and watching the news. She smiled and leaned into his arm when he wrapped it around her.

"It's time you and Rick made up for what happened," she informed him. "Maybe you can help him work through it this time?"

"Wes said he's a mess." Silas rested his head on his wife's head. "At least this time it isn't my fault."

"The first time wasn't your fault either, Si. Rick just needed someone to blame." Nancy handed him their son and kissed his cheek. "I'm baking cookies for you to bring with you." Her pale face, dimples and all, smiled up at him before she disappeared into their kitchen.

Silas rubbed his son's back while the infant cooed in his ear. He'd gotten the best end of the stick, at the end of the day. Nancy had been a blessing to his future and his friendships but had come at a cost. When he'd asked Maverick to be his best man he'd agreed, although there was a ton of bitterness in the exchanges that followed. Silas knew that Maverick still blamed him, and he had a hard time not blaming himself for it too.

"Do you think they'll work it out?" His wife's voice tugged Silas out of his own head. Nancy stood, holding a plastic spatula with a smile on her face.

She answered her own question, "I hope they do. I liked Roxanne a lot when I met her."

"I hope so, too. We've all been rooting for them for the last decade," Silas chuckled. "It's kind of been consuming, to a point. Whenever they get near each other, it's all any of us can think about."

"Pack mentality." Nancy perched on the arm of the couch. "The six of you are such a tight knit group of people that when something threatens you, you all get a little crazy."

There was her psychology degree coming to play. Silas knew she'd seen similar things at the high school she worked at, and it made him turn red at the collar.

Nancy continued, "We don't like when the status quo is changed."

"So what you're saying is that it's juvenile."

"Only if you can't acknowledge it." Nancy took the baby, who had fallen asleep on his father's shoulder and laid him in the playpen. "And only if you can't focus on other things." She smiled as she wrapped her arms around his neck.

"The cookies?" Silas nuzzled his face into the crook of her neck and planted soft kisses along her jaw.

"They need twenty minutes to cool," Nancy hummed.

Silas grinned and guided them onto the couch.

"I don't want him here."

Maverick had said it so firmly that Wesley nearly dropped his phone from the startle.

The two friends were sitting as far apart as possible on the L shaped couch, waiting in a silence that Silas was less than comfortable with. Maverick had been pissed when Wesley told him their friend was coming. He had slammed a door in Wesley's face and had stayed locked in the room until right before Silas had been expected to arrive. Then the owner of the castle had stormed out of his den, grabbed a yogurt, and took up a majority of the couch space. Silas had had to deal with Maverick's petulant scowl while he ate and had fixated on a mindless mobile game in order to pass the time.

"It's a little too late for that." Wesley checked his phone again, waiting desperately for a response from Cheyenne about the situation. "He'll be here any second."

"You shouldn't have called him."

Maverick was staring at Wesley expectantly, his hands folded in his lap and his brown eyes wide, innocent, needy.

"You weren't handling things well," he pointed out dully as he responded to Cheyenne, confirming that they might need a mediator.

"I'm fine." Maverick stood up, wincing at the feeling of putting his weight on his left leg, and made his way around the couch.

As he was walking when the doorbell rang. Maverick shot Wesley a look over his shoulder and huffed, brown eyes holding back anger. "He's sleeping on the couch."

"I'm sleeping on the couch."

"You can have the guest room"—Maverick continued his slow march toward the kitchen—"since that's empty now."

He leaned against the counter for support, flexing his ankle tensely. Two days without the cast, and he still found it hard to put weight on the limb or use the joints in it. And the rash, the God forsaken rash that had sprouted up at the top of the cast and agonized him for a month, was still there. It rubbed against the leg of his sweats, the first real pants he'd worn since the accident, and made walking worse.

Wesley got up shaking his head. "That's Roxanne's room."

Despite her being gone for a week already, Wesley felt weird sleeping in the room even if the couch was starting to put a crick in his neck. It felt weird being in the apartment in general since Roxanne had left.

Wesley let Silas in, rubbing at the back of his neck. "Hey."

Silas stood in the hallway, wincing at the sound of things slamming on the kitchen counter. His hair was unkempt, shirt hanging loosely over the pockets of his jeans and unevenly rumpled, and he looked as if he hadn't slept.

Wesley thought he fit right in but didn't voice that tidbit out loud. Instead he offered his friend a smile and shut the door behind him. They both flinched at the emphatic drop of the teapot in the sink.

"He's in a mood," Wesley said softly to Silas, offering to take the other man's duffle bag.

Silas dropped his bag in the hallway and shouldered past Wesley. He stood just on the threshold of the kitchen, watching Maverick scrub at the teapot with a sponge, his shoulders tense.

Wesley watched, unsure of the reasons behind the hesitance in Silas or the anger driving Maverick to hand wash the dishes in the dishwasher, his phone still clutched in his hand.

"Hey, Rick," Silas finally spoke.

The water from the sink was shut off, and the scrubbing stopped.

"Did you say something to her?" Maverick demanded of the other man without looking at him. Instead, he had braced himself on the sink and was staring at the suds and water before him.

"I haven't spoken to her since Wes got here. I swear." Silas held his hands up in surrender and took a step into the kitchen.

Maverick nearly barked on a laugh and pushed himself off of the sink. "If I find out you had a hand in this…" he all but snarled as he pushed past Silas. "I swear to you, Si, that's it. We're done."

189

Wesley stood helpless and confused as Maverick shoved past him as well. He barely heard Maverick declare he was going for a walk before the door slammed shut and he and Silas were left to their own devices.

The two men looked at each other, and Silas shrugged before entering the kitchen to finish the task Maverick had started.

"What was that all about?" Wesley asked, finally putting his phone down on the counter.

"It was about the breakup." Silas put the cup he was rinsing in the sink and looked at Wesley.

"What do you mean?"

It was an agreement between he and Maverick that they keep it between the two of them for as long as it made sense to. That no one needed to know why Maverick and Roxanne had broken up because it didn't matter. In the long run, as Silas had reassured Maverick when it happened, it might be the best thing if no one knew why. It didn't seem to be the case anymore.

"I mean, it's about the reason they broke up." Silas sighed and hung his head, until his chin nearly touched his chest. "It's because of me."

Chapter Twenty-Nine
October 2016

Maverick had texted Cheyenne when he'd left the apartment, asking her to meet him at Sadie's, the diner they used to frequent as teenagers in Penn Ridge. He'd spent the drive working through the storm in his head, alternating between hoping Cheyenne had heard from Roxanne to just hoping he could put the newest chapter of the mistake behind him as soon as possible. He knew she'd gotten back safely—she'd texted him a couple of days before to let him know she was alive and to congratulate him on the cast coming off. Maverick hadn't responded but kept pulling the message up. Just to see her face in the contact icon on the top of the message.

He was fiddling with his phone, her contact profile up the screen when Cheyenne slid into the booth across from him. Her hair was in a knot at the top of her head, and she had flour streaks on her t-shirt.

"Hey." She smiled at him as she grabbed the menu he'd left for her.

"Were you busy?" Maverick took a drink of his coffee. Arguably not the best.

"I've been spending a lot of time in the Ridge, so Grandpa and I have been selling at the farmer's market." Cheyenne sent

Maverick a wink. "There's a whole apple pie waiting for you and the guys in the backseat of my car."

"With the Taste of Celeste logo on it, I'm sure." Maverick smirked. He could taste the buttery crust on his tongue, and his mouth watered.

"Just on the box. I don't have the brander here." Cheyenne didn't even bat an eye. Maverick had taken a couple of trips up to Albany to see the bakery she'd opened the year before, especially in the beginning when she'd asked him to help her with the bank paperwork.

"What's up?" she asked.

"I wanted to know if you've heard from Roxanne?" Maverick smiled at the waitress when she stopped to refill his mug and ask if they were ordering food.

"Since she got home?" he repeated while waiting for her answer.

Cheyenne tightened her lips. "How is your leg feeling?"

"Cast is off." Maverick settled back against the orange vinyl booth. "But you knew that."

"She told me. She was worried you'd have a hard time adjusting to it being off."

"No. It's been going alright actually. Marshall, my physical therapist, says that the leg is healing well on its own. It's skinny, and I lost a lot of muscle when they had to cut in and reconstruct it." Maverick rubbed at his knee, resisting the urge to itch through his pants. "So…you *have* heard from her then?"

"Yeah. Briefly. She went back to work in the office on Monday, and that's really helped her."

"Helped?" Maverick couldn't help the way his shoulders jumped. "Is she okay?"

Cheyenne hesitated, as if she was parsing out what to say to him. "Things are…tense between her and Ethan," she said finally. "And leaving wasn't easy for her, Rick. I know it wasn't easy for you, but you weren't the one who had to leave home. Again. Because of the same person."

"She could have stayed."

"Could she?"

"I kissed her. But you knew that. Did she tell you I asked her to stay?"

"She did before she left. And she was terrified."

"Of?"

Cheyenne didn't say anything. Maverick fought the urge to roll his eyes and propped his elbows on the table.

"What was she scared of, Cheyenne?"

Cheyenne's only response was a hum at the back of her throat while she held her coffee cup below her nose. Neither of them spoke. She made a point of turning her cellphone face down on the table surface, as if she was giving Maverick her undivided attention. He noticed the action but ignored it, thinking back to all of the abstract times she had inserted her nose in business that wasn't hers and how, when he needed her to do just that, she'd clam up.

When their waitress dropped off their food, Cheyenne shot her a dazzling smile and dumped a pile of ketchup on the spare plate they'd been given. She broke the silence that had settled between them first, as Maverick knew she would, after she'd worked through two onion rings.

"So…" Cheyenne began.

"So?"

"Silas is here."

"Mhm."

"And Roxanne is gone."

"Mhmm."

"And suddenly it's 2012 again."

"Oh?"

"Only this time she got to walk away. Instead of being forced to."

"Now wait a minute—"

Cheyenne raised both her eyebrows at Maverick, patiently waiting while the man sank down in his seat, shoulders hunched in on himself. When he didn't say anything, Cheyenne touched his wrist again, lighter this time, and pushed her hair back from her eyes.

"It feels eerily similar, doesn't it?"

"Cheyenne." His temper had soured even more than the sight of Silas in his doorway. "What do you want?"

"I want to know what happened."

"I broke my leg in a car crash. Roxanne flew out 'cause I was an idiot and didn't update my paperwork. She stayed for a

194

while. I got the wrong idea. I kissed her. She left." Maverick ticked off each blow on his fingers. "And now you're giving me a headache."

"Do you agree?" Cheyenne tossed her red hair over her shoulder and gave Maverick a cheeky smile. "That it was time for her to go?"

"What I think isn't important anymore, Cheyenne. It hasn't been for a long time." Obviously, it wasn't important at all, or she'd have talked to him instead of running away.

"Right. Not since you broke up with her out of thin air."

"Cheyenne."

"That's what I really want to know about." Her green eyes winked at him, half in mischief and half in amusement, as she sipped her drink. "The reason why."

"Christ. It's been four years. You'd think you would have moved on with your life by now."

"Have you?"

"I was *in it*, Cheyenne." Maverick slammed his hands down on the table hard enough to cause their cups to rattle. The couple of tables around them all looked over in surprise, and Maverick shrunk down in his seat. Maverick slumped down in the booth and bit his tongue. "I am still in it, Chey," he said weakly, shaking his head.

Cheyenne smiled and waved at their audience as if nothing had happened before she turned her attention back to him. "We were all *in it*, Rick. We were all invested. And then it just ended."

Her green eyes dulled a little, as if they were starting to burn from tears. "And none of us know why."

"Silas knows why." Maverick put his hand over Cheyenne's as it sat on his wrist, half to reassure himself and half to comfort her in the process.

She was right. They had been invested in the relationship, just like Maverick and Roxanne had been. From the moment he was thirteen and realized he had a connection with Roxanne that surpassed friendship, and even before that, all the way back to the first time he met Roxanne as a first grader. Silas and Wesley had opened his eyes to what he was feeling toward Roxanne and helped him cover it up as he bounced from girl to girl for almost three years after. Cheyenne had been the one to help him pick out the tulips he bought her on their first date. And all the years since, the six of them had been a court, a collective, when it came to the relationship. Even when Maverick and Roxanne had moved into their first apartment in college, the thin lines that blurred their romance from the group's collective got thicker.

They had all been in the relationship from the start. The difference was that they weren't as in it as Maverick had been—as he still was.

Cheyenne caught Maverick's far away stare and gave his wrist a squeeze. "What happened?" she asked again.

"Back then?" Maverick licked his lips when she nodded. "I was going to propose."

He settled back in his seat again and started out the window, shaking his head. "I was going to ask her to marry me," he mumbled, lost in what had been and what could have been.

Chapter Thirty
November 2012

Maverick checked his watch for the third time before popping another piece of nicotine gum in his mouth. Waiting for Silas had him stress craving a cigarette—of course, he was the one who had chosen to quit smoking just days before making the biggest purchase of his life. He chewed on the gum and stewed in his irritation, his back hunched against the cold wind blowing in from the valley. He'd give Silas two more minutes before he went in without him.

While he waited, he turned back to the storefront windows and tried to assess the jewels they had on display. It was mostly necklaces. Not really her thing. He checked his watch and then spat the gum into the curbside trash can.

"I am late!" he heard Silas shout from behind him just as he went to rip open the door. His best friend sprinted down the sidewalk, his shiny brown loafers and fitted suit pants making it hard for him to be careful in his rush. "Traffic was ridiculous."

"Uhhuh." Maverick tapped the face of his watch. "I need to get back in fifteen minutes."

"Well you didn't plan on buying one today. Right?" Silas' chest heaved as he spoke.

Maverick rolled his eyes as he yanked the door open. "I did. But it's fine." He could always come back after work and finish his mission alone. He should have just gone on his own in the first place. Silas had insisted, threatened to tell Cheyenne if Maverick didn't take him along for the trip. That would have been a whole different excursion that Maverick, while he loved the redhead, could not have handled.

A bell rang over Maverick's head when he and Silas entered the shop. The older woman at the front counter beamed a hello to them, and Silas pushed the shorter man forward. "This man wants to buy a ring."

He should have gone alone. "Uh…hi. I'm looking to buy an engagement ring."

Maverick fished the Post-It with Roxanne's ring size on it out of his jacket pocket. "She's a size six. Likes rose gold. I uh…I don't think she'd want one with a super big gem."

He'd done a lot of research into ring types over the past few weeks, trying to figure out what would be the most functional for Roxanne. She typed a lot, and he'd read that heavyset bands were harder to type with. Avoiding that was the only real inkling he had. Roxanne wasn't one to frequently wear jewelry, if any at all. She didn't even wear makeup. He relayed that information to the woman behind the counter while Silas examined the nearest ring display.

The woman's eyes sparkled at the utter nervousness written across his face. "How wonderful. Let me see what I've got in the back with a smaller stone." She sent him a wrinkled smile before disappearing into the back storeroom.

"Have you thought of how you're going to ask?" Silas looked up at his friend, a quick grin on his face.

"Nothing super complicated. She'd hate that." Maverick wandered along the display counter, stopping at a section that bore the placard vintage rings. "I was thinking of taking her up to Auburn to go camping. And then I'd bring her down by the river and just ask her. Or maybe we'll go out to Texas to see Connor?" He shrugged, his hands stuffed in his pockets. "I can't think of a way to ask her where she'll get her picture of it, but it won't be super conspicuous."

Silas chuckled. "If only your romance writer girlfriend actually liked romance. Maybe you should ask Chey. She'll know."

"I wanna do this on my own."

Maverick had stopped at a bronze band with three opals inlayed in it. The stones weren't too flashy, but they shone in the light overhead and had some small diamonds placed around them. It was the kind of ring that had a sturdy band and some flash sparkle, but all the stones were set in a way that they were low to the band's center.

"I wonder how heavy that one is," Maverick mused, gaining Silas' attention.

The two men bent together to inspect the ring and passed back and forth comments on whether or not Roxanne would wear it. Maverick wasn't inclined to think she'd wear any ring that he got her, but Silas had voted confidently for the opals. His argument, that Maverick had wanted to buy her a ring regardless of whether or not she'd wear it, didn't fall on deaf ears. Even if the ring turned out to be nothing more than a symbol, she was sure to like it well enough.

When the woman came back out with a tray of similar rings, Maverick almost panicked. He knew it was irrational, but there was something at the back of his head telling him that maybe, just maybe, he needed to put more thought behind the decision. Silas kept him in good spirits, agreeing with him that Roxanne was going to love the ring.

Maverick and Silas parted ways in the jeweler's parking lot. Silas clapped his hand on Maverick's shoulder and gave him a brotherly smirk.

"Don't overthink it too much." Silas gave him a knowing look. "You and Rox are solid."

Maverick scratched the back of his neck. He was sure it was written across his face—the pure panic coursing through his veins at the realization that he was about to change their lives.

"You ever wonder what life would be like if she and I didn't get together?"

Silas stopped, his hand in mid-air toward his driver side handle. "What?"

Maverick chewed aggressively on his piece of gum. "Like...I dunno. Maybe if she had dated a little when we were kids...or I'd waited a little longer to ask her out."

Silas laughed and cracked open his car door. "Cold feet's not a good look on you, Rick. You've always done better with certainty."

Maverick faked a grin and ducked his head. "Yeah. You're right." He fingered the ring bag in his pocket. "We're solid."

If only he could make himself feel sure of that.

October 2016

"I couldn't get the thoughts out of my head. Like…maybe Roxanne needed to experience more of life. Or that we were too young to get married." Maverick raked his hands over his face. "And Si, well, he was getting ready to propose to Nancy, so he was a bundle of nerves about getting married, too." He grinned wryly. "He convinced me that asking Roxanne to marry me was going to be the biggest mistake of my life."

"He what?"

"He kept giving me statistics about people who got married in their twenties and were divorced by the time they turned forty. All of these statistics. Statistics on high school sweethearts and divorce. And annulment." Maverick couldn't remember why he'd been so angry at Silas at the time—why all of the information had put a wedge between them. He'd been so angry for so much time. He'd made a complete ass of himself at his best friend's wedding. "It seems so stupid now. Breaking up with Roxanne, getting mad at Silas because I had cold feet."

"We were kids." Cheyenne gestured toward the waitress, for another cup of coffee. "We all made mistakes."

They both smiled at the woman in thanks, the smell of partially burnt coffee spreading over the terse air they'd created with their conversation.

"I made the biggest mistake of my life because I had cold feet and an attitude."

"You've come a long way since then."

Maverick snorted, dumping two packets of sugar into his fresh cup of coffee. "By the time I was ready to tuck my tail between my legs and get her back, she'd moved to Las Vegas and started seeing that man. Felt like I'd dodged a bullet 'cause she gotten over it so quickly."

It had killed him to know that she'd moved on, replaced him, while he'd nursed their breakup with a diet of tequila and ninety-hour workweeks. Seeing her at Silas' wedding had caused the wound to reopen and led to a very bad choice on the basis of it, but he'd bounced back. Until the accident.

"And now she's back with him." He pushed the plate of onion rings away.

"Does she know? About the ring?"

"Never came up. Only you and Si know about it."

Cheyenne frowned at him, her brows furrowing. "What the hell is the matter with you?"

"What?"

"She was out here for months. For you. With you. And you couldn't be bothered to…oh…I don't know…tell her that one of the worst days of her life wasn't actually her fault?"

"She thinks it's something she did?"

"Well, yeah. Any woman in her situation would think it was her fault." Cheyenne rolled her eyes at him.

Maverick scowled at her. "What does it matter to you?"

Cheyenne rolled her eyes once more. "You guys are two of my best friends. It matters to me because I want you to just be happy."

"She's happy with Ethan." He took a long drink of coffee. It burned down his throat, hot, sweet acid that hit his empty stomach heavily. "Do you think she's happier with him than she was with me?"

Cheyenne rolled her eyes again and swatted his hand playfully. "I'm not dishing on Rox's relationship with you." She bit her lip. "But I will say this…he and Rox don't click together the way you guys do."

"Used to."

"No. You guys still click."

Maverick couldn't fight the flutter in his chest. He'd hoped there'd still been something between them but knowing that Cheyenne had seen it—that Roxanne had possibly even talked to Cheyenne about a spark between the two of them—had his pulse racing. There might still be hope for the perfect future with the woman he'd loved since he was a child. If only he could show her he'd changed—that the cold feet that ruined his life had evaporated the moment he realized he lost her for good, and she was the only thing he needed for his entire life.

Chapter Thirty-One
October 2016

While Maverick and Cheyenne talked, Wesley and Silas had their own small conference. The two men, over a couple of beers at one of the Irish pubs near the University of Scranton, hashed out Roxanne's abrupt departure.

"What does this mean for the rest of us?" Silas asked, running his finger down the line of the pint of beer in front of him.

Wesley could see his tired eyes in the puddle, sporting the same look as the last time they sat together in the dark corner of the bar.

"I don't know." The photographer shrugged and shoved his hand through his hair. "You didn't see Rick after she left. He—I guess he kissed her. Asked her to pick him over Ethan."

Silas laughed, a cold chuckle. "That's not what I expected. Obviously, she said no. No wonder Maverick freaked out. The man had no idea what he was doing or thinking."

"It's probably for the best." Wesley took a swig of his beer and kicked his foot against the leg of the table. "There's no way that you can spend four years apart from someone and then just pick back the fuck up where you started. They're two totally different people."

K.T. Egan

Yet, somehow, they had managed not to kill each other and instead, they moved pretty much in sync, even after all this time.

Silas nodded.

Wesley eased away from the table to grab two more beers and caught sight of the picture of the five of them that was pasted to the wall behind the bar along with a collection of images from other patrons over the years. It'd been Silas' birthday, the last to turn twenty-one that year. They were all standing together in matching orange shirts, blood shot eyes, and tooth eating grins. In it, Maverick had his arm securely around Roxanne's waist, and she was looking at him like he was the greatest thing in the world. He had multiple images of them in the same pose—pictures that sat on SD cards and in his school portfolio.

Wesley had also seen the pose multiple times when he was with the ex-couple.

"Maybe they'll work it out," he said when he returned to his friend and set their cold beers on the table. "You didn't see them together but man, I'll tell you. It was like nothing changed."

"Maybe that was part of the problem." Silas hated to feel guilty about it. He wasn't the reason any of this had happened. But the sinking feeling in his gut was written all over his face.

Wesley tapped his bottleneck against Silas'. "You wanna tell me what that was all about earlier?"

The switch in gears came with a wave of loud music. He waited for the noise to quiet down before he pressed on. "Why did he think you had something to do with her leaving?"

Silas tried unsuccessfully to wipe the scowl off his face. "Just some shit that went down way back when. He needed someone to blame when they broke up, and I was the best target. Far enough removed from the situation at that point that he didn't have to interact with me daily, but close enough to him that it was easy to lash out."

And Silas had been the only one who had known the reason behind the break up, making it easy for Maverick to pin all of the blame on him. Despite the strain it'd put on their friendship, Silas had taken the brunt of Maverick's aggression without complaint because, at the end of the day, he'd gotten off better.

"When Nance and I got engaged, Rick didn't take the news too kindly either."

"Is that why he lost it at the wedding?"

"Part of it, I think. Part of it had to do with her bringing Ethan. Most of it had to do with the fact that I haven't been as good a friend as I could have been and neither has he." Silas chuckled and shook his head. "We've been trying to patch things up. Before the accident, we were in a pretty good place."

"You can't just leave because he was in a piss-ass mood."

The photographer nudged his friend and took a long pull of his warming beer.

Silas shrugged and looked down at his empty glass. "How's Connor doing?"

The change in subject was refreshing for both of them. Wesley shrugged, a proud little smile creeping across his face.

"He's good. He's got another three months or so. He extended his tour. And then, I have no idea what he's going to do after that. Probably try to go back again."

"He can't like it that much over there." Silas didn't know much about being a soldier, or being in a family of soldiers, but he was convinced that the soft dip in Wesley's voice sounded almost jealous.

Before the other man could say anything, they were interrupted by a stampede of college co-eds who had just stormed in through the bar's front doors. They were a mess of laughs and shouts and an obvious oblivion of people who didn't have much to worry about.

Wesley bent his head toward Silas' so he could be heard over the noise, even as the two men caught glimpses from their new section mates. The wedding ring on Silas' hand couldn't deter a few flirting giggles from girls who had obviously pre-gamed before their mid-week adventure; however, the attention that Wesley garnered was unparalleled.

Silas gave his friend a good-natured grin. "Maybe you should start thinking about settling down."

Wesley groaned at Silas and raised his beer in a mock salute. "I've got some time before any sort of decision like that has to be made."

Silas shrugged and brushed his thumb across his wedding ring affectionately. "It's not the worst decision I've ever made. In fact, I might even say that it's the best one."

Wesley shook his head. He gestured for another round from their waitress and diverted the conversation toward topics he felt more comfortable with.

Chapter Thirty-Two
October 2016

A hot breeze kicked up the desert sand and blew it into the horizon, marking the setting sun's orange glow as it descended slowly over the mountains. Roxanne watched its disappearance reluctantly, her fingers hovering over the keys of her laptop. Ethan looked up when she sighed and started to say something, only to jump up when the next breeze blew through stronger and knocked her papers all over their balcony. The couple scrambled to scoop up the yellow pages before another breeze blew through and knocked them over the edge.

Roxanne tucked as many as she had grabbed back into the accordion where she kept them and started to thank Ethan when she caught his confused look. He was holding the last page, dated with her flight and the finish line, his eyes fixed on it.

"You finished it," he said slowly, as if the words made him sick. "You finished it?"

"Yeah. Didn't I tell you?" Roxanne tugged the page from his grip and stuffed it in with the others. "I'm still a long way from 'finished' but the first draft is done."

Ethan looked up at her, a half scowl on his face. "It took you three months to get through four chapters and you finish it in, what, two?" He wasn't asking her exactly, even as his face searched her for some answers. "While you were there. With him."

Roxanne felt her defenses rising and tried to squash them. Ethan had been nothing but accommodating in the two and a half weeks that she'd been home. He'd helped her get back to her sleep schedule. He'd been willing to cook dinners and do laundry while she got caught up at work. He'd even been understanding when she didn't want to go to dinner with him but met with her new friend, Professor Kahn, for late night editing help. He'd done everything in his power to make the transition back easy for her. Getting mad at him for his concern was going to do nothing but make his efforts feel useless and possibly cause an issue.

"I had a lot of time to write," she answered instead and closed her laptop.

Ethan followed her inside, still hung up on the finished manuscript.

"This boils down to more than just having a lot of time to write, Roxanne. You were inspired. You were inspired there in Pennsylvania, inspired with him. You couldn't even find that here with me? What's the difference?"

"Ethan, don't do this to yourself."

Roxanne set her laptop and papers down on the kitchen counter and crossed the space between them. As she laid her hands on her shoulders, she found herself wondering what the difference was too. Why did she feel inspired, motivated even, to work obsessively on the book with Maverick's help when sitting and writing with Ethan had almost become a chore? Why did kissing

Maverick make her stomach bottom out and her blood heat while Ethan's touch couldn't even do it in the dark of their bedroom? She shook herself before the thoughts cleared her head.

"It's nothing."

"What happened while you were out there?" He shook her hands off and paced around her to get a bottle of water from the fridge.

Roxanne bit her tongue. "Nothing," she said finally, sure that the lie would do him more good than harm. "Nothing happened between us. And I'm finally back home here with you. Can't we just put this behind us now? It's over."

"I thought we were at least friends, Roxanne."

"What are you talking about?" Her lips turned up in a soft smile, even as the guilt passed through her slowly. "Did you hit your head at the gym this morning?"

"I knew that you going out there was going to be…hard on us. And we both know that you being back hasn't made that any easier."

He had the kind of look on his face that screamed *I knew it* and *I can't believe it* at the same time. Roxanne wasn't sure what to do other than stand helplessly and let him get the words out.

"But I thought that we were friends. If nothing else, I thought that the two of us were at least friends," he whispered.

"I don't understand."

"You couldn't finish this thing here. You spent hours staring at a blank page and trying to figure out your ass from your hands for months. You got out there for like six weeks, and it's finished? How does that work?" He pounded his hands onto the countertop. "What happened while you were out there?"

"Don't you think that you're overreacting just a little bit? Did it ever occur to you that I just had more time on my hands while I was out there?"

She crossed the kitchen to put her hands on his shoulders. Ethan didn't usually yell or aggressively pace the floor. He wasn't the kind of person who got worked up over every little thing. Roxanne had never seen him this worked up before. A rush of dark colors were brewing in his eyes. If things had been different, if it had been only a handful of months before, she would have been concerned or intimated or invigorated. She wasn't sure by the glean in his eyes.

Roxanne was just tired. Tired of treading on unavoidable eggshells, tired of feeling displaced by being back in the place she had called home for years. They were similar feelings to when she'd been back in Pennsylvania, but they had nothing to do with the man she was looking at.

"Maverick kissed me. The day before I left. He kissed me." Roxanne forced her hands through her hair. "That's it. As soon as it happened, I practically got out of there as fast as I could."

Ethan didn't say anything for a long time. The muscles in his neck and his face hardly moved.

Roxanne tried to keep her voice from breaking. "He didn't mean it, and it didn't mean anything. He was just super confused. He'd only been out of the hospital for a couple of weeks."

"You went out there. You finished your book. Your ex kissed you. And you lied to me about it." Ethan made each statement hurt like a knife in her gut. "Can you just explain to me why you just let it happen?"

"Things were intense, Ethan! I spent weeks in that hospital watching my—"

"You're what? What the hell is he to you, Roxanne?"

When Ethan whirled around, he was a hurricane, unstoppable in his force. He smacked the towel off of the cabinet under the sink's door and threw it on the ground in frustration.

"I've spent two years trying to figure out what he is to you. I watched you run after him at Silas and Nancy's wedding. I listened to you and your girlfriends' chat circles around the fact that they didn't like you living with me when we moved in. I dealt with your parents comparing me to the prodigal boy who, by the way, thanks for telling me sooner, works at the law office your father used to own. And I have tried to tell myself that it's in my head. That being with me wasn't some consolation prize. Then you go jetting out there to be by his side, and you don't come home for months. Months, Roxanne, months. And when you do come back, you're…you're…"

"I'm me. I've always been the person I was before we met. I'm, apparently, the person I was always destined to be. I am me."

Her shell cracked. Tears ran down her face, the flood separating them even as they stood so close together, and she shook, hands trembling, body quaking.

"Oh, don't even, Roxanne. You lied to me about what happened between the two of you. Looked me in the eye and lied. You're not the woman I fell in love with." Ethan was levelheaded as he leaned against the counter.

"I was trying not to hurt you," she said through tears, pushing them and her own discomfort down.

"It's about three months too late for that, Roxanne." Ethan pushed off the counter. "I'm going to go grab dinner. Are you hungry?"

Just like that the fight was over. Just like the fights were always over. Without Roxanne getting a word in edge wise because Ethan felt like he had justified the end. Roxanne shook her head, both in response to him and the question. She felt raw, like she'd been played, and so confused, wondering how she could have ended up with someone who could so evenly just leave her out of a discussion that had to do with both of them, some sharp words, and a jerk of his mood.

He pushed past her, out of the kitchen, and headed for the door. "I'll bring you back something anyway," he said before closing the door between them.

Chapter Thirty-Three
October 2016

The end.

Roxanne stared at her laptop screen and jammed her fingers down onto the backspace key. Hard. Until the two solitary words disappeared from the mostly white page in front of her. It stared back at her mockingly until she keyed in the six letters again, sans period.

Backspace. Three letters.

Fin

Finished.

Her lips quirked, and she back peddled once more before slamming the laptop shut.

Its definitive click resounded through the quiet apartment, breaking the uncomfortable silence in the air. Ethan was asleep. He'd taken to going to bed before nine just to avoid the space between them, not that it would have been much help if he were awake.

It'd been a week since Roxanne had told him about Maverick's kiss. In that time, things had gone back to their quasi-normal, post-Pennsylvania, pre-kiss state. Only Roxanne slept on the couch every night, despite promises to join Ethan in the bedroom when she was done at the keyboard. They'd been tense but amicable, and Ethan had even kissed her goodbye that morning before going to work. Thinking about it caused Roxanne to wonder if he'd felt anything at all when their lips had touched because she hadn't.

She pulled at the collar of her t-shirt and scooped up her phone in need of a distraction.

She could call her cousin and listen to a nonsensical baby prattle around three in the morning or catch up with Cheyenne and listen to her grandfather's latest escapades. Her mother was asleep and even if she weren't, Roxanne probably wouldn't have called her. That phone conversation would only end in her being hounded about her plans for Thanksgiving. Silas had been freezing her out since she'd left, but he wasn't great at writing advice anyway, and Wesley was still too close to his semi-permanent roommate in Pennsylvania.

Her fingers stopped their casual stroll through her contacts, stopping at the 'S' section. She saw Maverick's name in its foreign serif print, still feeling odd that he had taken up residence in her contacts when she call without thinking about it. Once the phone had started to ring, she couldn't bring herself to stop it.

Maverick answered with a tired, and confused, "Hello."

"Hey," she said softly, smoothing down her long curls subconsciously. "Did I wake you?"

Maverick coughed on the other end of the line. "Yeah, but it's fine. Is everything okay?"

"Yeah. Yeah. Everything is fine. Sorry for waking you up."

They both sat in silence. They could hear each other breathe while each of them contemplated whether or not they would make their next move in the conversation. Maverick chapped his lips while staring at the ceiling, and Roxanne opened up her laptop and logged into her email server. She could hear him puttering around on the other end, wrinkling his sheets as he struggled to sit up with sore muscles. He bit back a groan as he stood up. He would be the last person on the face of the planet to let her know that he was still in pain.

While he woke up, Roxanne sent an email to Professor Kahn about their impending lunch date and then returned to her Word document. The sixty-one thousand word second draft of her novel mocked her, its lingering last 'alone' imprinting itself on her eyelids.

"Okay," Maverick yawned. "I'm conscious. Are you still there?"

"I'm here. Just stuck."

He didn't say anything for a long minute. "Ethan's no help?"

She couldn't help but hear the slight in his voice, the twinge that begged for attention while trying its hardest to remain undetected.

Roxanne sighed, her thoughts lingering on their tumultuous kitchen argument. Things were still tense between them, Ethan's bitter words lingering in the air, untouched.

"He's asleep."

Another long silence filled the line. Roxanne peaked up at the closed bedroom door, wishing more than anything that she'd feel guilt staring at its shadowed surface. Maverick clicked his tongue eventually and drew her attention back to the open document and the conversation.

"Is it too pretentious to end with 'the end'?" she asked and turned down the brightness on her laptop as her head was starting to hurt.

Maverick let out a surprised chuckle on the other end. "I mean, yes, but how many people have made their fortunes off of that singular air of pretention and whit?"

Roxanne gave a snort.

On the other end of the conversation Maverick stretched his left leg slowly, wincing at the taunt muscles. "Fitzgerald, Sparks, Eliot, I could go on."

"Yeah, but do I really wanna be compared to them?" She smiled lightly.

"Read me the last chapter, and then we'll see if it warrants that amount of arrogance."

Maverick's offer mirrored her own small joy. Roxanne listened to him settling back into bed. He exhaled sharply, as if he'd hit his left knee on something, and she jerked with him. Her mind flashed back to him in the hospital bed, to all of the nights they had fallen asleep in an awkwardly content silence with their heads on the same pillow. The nights in his apartment when they'd fallen asleep in front of the television where she'd felt normal. It all rushed back to her.

She coughed and fanned the heat flushing her cheeks.

"Ready?" she prepared him.

"Aye, captain," he yawned once more.

"Incendiary," Roxanne started, running her fingers over the mouse pad to move the document along.

"You have chapter names?" His soft chuckle warmed the edges of her chest, threatening to spill into the silence of her night. "What kind of—"

She rolled her eyes and cut him off. "Do you want to hear this or not?"

He was still laughing to himself when he urged her to continue. She read, and he made little quips, offering up stark advice when he could and making notes of things he would remember from that moment long after it was over. Maverick could remember the last time they had spent this kind of time together, back when the world made sense and he knew that he'd be home at the end of the day with her in the bed beside him. Her soft voice, the way she didn't laugh at her own jokes, even the breaths she took in between words combined to soothe him.

For the first time since she'd left, he felt at peace, like he could sleep through the night.

Roxanne listened to his even breathing—her heartbeat matched each inhale, exhale, pause, repeat. When she finished reading, the companionable silence that met her painted the room around her in beautiful shades of pink.

For the first time in weeks Roxanne felt at home.

The bedroom door creaked open, and Ethan looked out at her. His eyes screamed accusations, spoke questions, and acknowledged the elephant that neither of them wanted to be in the room. When she smiled at him, a guilt-ridden glimpse, he shook his head and gestured for her to join him in the bedroom. Roxanne closed her laptop and stood, shaking the sleep out of her limbs. She could have ignored the request but knew she was going to give in to it in the slim hopes of fixing her relationship.

He left the door open as he faded back into the bedroom. Roxanne rubbed at her left temple, returning to reality. "You still awake?" she asked softly into the phone.

"Yeah. I'm still here."

Maverick sensed the change in her voice and sat himself back up in bed. She was grateful that he didn't acknowledge it, instead, carrying on the conversation as if nothing had changed.

"I think I have an answer for you."

"Hit me."

"Alone should be the last word. Like…you're trying to emphasize that we all have this feeling, ya know? So, leave that be the end."

"Maybe."

He chuckled. "You should probably go to bed, Rox. It's one in the morning there."

"You're one to talk. It's after four."

"Wes'll be up soon. I should pretend I slept."

"'Night, Rick."

"'Night, Rox."

222

Before Ethan left for work in the morning, he asked her, implored her to leave Maverick out of the equation and commit to taking the time to try and put their relationship back together with him. Unable to hurt him anymore, Roxanne had agreed.

Chapter Thirty-Four
October 2016

"I bought a house."

Maverick had found Wesley in the bathroom, sitting in his bathtub with his camera pressed to his eye and his shins and shoulders pressed into opposite ends of the ceramic. A thin stream of cold water leaked out of the showerhead toward him. His long frame was so severely folded into the tub that the knees of his dark jeans were straining, and his back curled inward in a sideways 'c'. His friend didn't look up when Maverick spoke. Instead, he held his right index finger up to ask for silence.

Since Silas had left, Maverick's mood had improved. He could attest it to finally telling someone about the ring, about that winter, and to the fact that he wasn't going home to an empty apartment. Wesley, ever the agreeable houseguest, had used the empty apartment to catch up on his contract and do some fun shots. They spent their evenings in a harmonious silence for the most part, Maverick still brooding and continuously checking his phone for a peep out of Roxanne and Wesley living in his own brain.

Despite having lived together before and despite the quiet rhythm they had built together, he would never understand his friend's compulsive need to fully immerse himself in his lens.

Maverick rolled his eyes but waited for Wesley to get in a half dozen more shots before he dragged the conversation back to him.

"It's a nice house."

"You're funny." The tall man sat up, his knees still bent toward the ceiling, and propped his chin on his palm. "And where is this imaginary house?"

"In Penn Ridge. Remember the old Catchum house?"

Maverick didn't blink. He'd known the announcement was going to be met with disbelief. He himself honestly couldn't believe that he'd put a bid in on the house and heard back so fast. It had been a brainchild based off the early October conversation he'd had with Roxanne. If Ethan wasn't a good help, couldn't provide feedback for her to work out her dreams, then Maverick still had a shot. And that shot couldn't be capsized by the fact that he still lived in a small apartment in a small, noisy city.

"I was driving past it a few days ago with Nate—we have a case out that way, and we had to go assess some damage—and I called Misty Noble. Did you know she and her husband own their own real-estate company? Anyway. I called her and told her I wanted to make a bid. And they picked it up."

Wesley chuckled as he climbed out of the tub. "You really did your research for this didn't you?"

Maverick dug the email out of his phone's inbox and showed it to his friend. The taller man stopped laughing as he squinted to read the fine print.

"You're buying a house." He exhaled softly, a quiet whistle at the price Maverick had agreed to and the house he had chosen.

Wesley remembered the Catchum house, it had been the favorite neighborhood 'haunt' when they were kids.

It stood on a small grassy knoll on Court Street and had been abandoned since both men could remember. When they were in their early teens, Maverick had dared Roxanne and Silas to break into the house and return with a souvenir to prove it. The aftermath had been Silas' first black eye and a scar on Roxanne's back. Wesley still didn't know where the doorknob they'd wrestled free ended up.

"That's...huge." Wesley blinked at the phone, at his friend, and shook his head. "Congratulations, man."

Maverick himself wasn't exactly sure what kind of response he'd been anticipating, but Wesley's confused mug didn't sway him too far. He was conflicted with himself and the decision, knowing that, in buying the house, he was putting himself in a weird position. If he managed to tell Roxanne about the three-story purchase, he wasn't sure how she'd react. Would she be happy that he bought the house? Or would she call him insane and tell him he'd crossed a line he might have tiptoed near while she was in the East? Maverick rubbed his lower lip with the pad of his thumb while Wesley dried off the lens of his camera.

"I know you said you found a place in Maryland, but the house needs a lot of work, and I could really use the help," Maverick said finally. "If you aren't desperately needed back home."

"Yeah...no. I mean, if you need the help." Wesley fished his phone out of his pocket and tapped out a quick message to

Silas about the house. "Maybe Si and Nance can come back up and give us a hand?"

While Silas hadn't told him why Maverick had been so pissed upon his arrival or the reason why Maverick blamed him for the breakup, things had calmed down between the two men in the days that Silas had stayed there. It had been nice for Wesley to be back home, to be with the closest thing to family he had aside from his father and brother.

"Whataya think?"

"Sure, sure. I mean, I still have a ton of paperwork to sign and stuff to work through but if they wanna come up for a weekend, I wouldn't complain." It was the nicest Maverick had been toward Silas' existence since the man had left. "I'm going to go out there after work tomorrow and take another walk around the property. Do you want to come with?"

"Sure." Wesley packed the camera away and grinned at his friend. "Food?"

On the other side of the country, Roxanne was having her own moment trying to digest some news. She was sitting in a little café off of Sunset, watching the professor thumb through the printed copy of her manuscript, his face unchanging. He'd paused only to take a look at the menu when she sat down, and he poked his nose through the binding of the document once more. It was covered in his small handwriting and Post-It notes, and she couldn't stop staring at the open page, trying to read what he'd said.

Kahn paused again to smile at her and take a sip of iced tea.

"I'm thinking the Rueben," he stated and set the menu down. "You?"

Roxanne smiled tensely and picked up her iced tea glass. "Maybe a BLT? I'm not really hungry."

Kahn watched her glance at the manuscript and then forced her attention back to him.

"You need to eat." His fatherly tone, soft gaze, and nudge of the packet of paper toward her made her sigh and scoop the menu back up.

He waited until after they had ordered to lean forward and give her a wink. "It's crap."

Roxanne stopped, her glass hovering just before her lips. "It is?"

"It's a second draft. It's not going to be much better than the first." He'd silenced her with a deft hand raise. "The story itself is entertaining, and you're trying to create a tortured character. Your voice definitely reflects that, but a first draft is never good."

Kahn opened to a random page in the first half and ran his finger over the first full sentence. "The person who wrote this"— he turned to the end and ripped off a heavily used Post-It note— "is not this woman. This narrator."

"I don't think I follow."

"Were you in Pennsylvania when you started this?" His wrinkled smile made her feel uncomfortable in her seat.

228

"No." She set her glass down and rubbed at her temples. "I had been in Nevada for two months when I started this."

"But you were in Pennsylvania when you finished it?"

"The airport in North Carolina."

Kahn nodded. "Russel started off as an angry man, an angry man with a stunted voice. By chapter nine he stops being so angry and by chapter fourteen you were back in Pennsylvania."

"How did you...?"

"The first nine chapters take forever to read through. Chapters ten through fourteen are a little better; I'm assuming you were on the plane for at least two of them. And suddenly Rupert meets Jane, out of nowhere."

Kahn flipped to the start of the second to last chapter, where he had circled a handful of sentences on the first page itself. "And right here, you were in the airport."

"Hm?"

"Rupert leaves to find Jane."

"I guess it does coincide with all that." Roxanne slid her finger around the glass's rim. "What do you suggest I do to make it less 'crap'?"

Kahn started to say something and then swallowed back his words. "Work on it. Figure out what makes it so easy to read the Pennsylvania chapters and so hard to read the Nevada chapters. Why did Rupert have to chase after Jane just when they were falling in love?"

Roxanne rubbed the back of her neck as the two sat awkwardly, as if they were trying to come up with an answer that would hurt less than the obvious truth. When their meals arrived, they ate in silence, both of them sifting through the ocean of emotions that sat steeped on the table between them.

Kahn shifted in his seat and set his sandwich down. "I like Russel. He's honest, if a little confused."

"Thank you for not lecturing me like an English professor." Roxanne smiled, her nose wrinkling at the poor grammar just as he chuckled at it. "I'm sure your notes are very thorough, but I don't know if I could hear them now."

Kahn chuckled and took a drink. "The mark of a good writer is the ability to take in a reader's feedback and let them make their own interpretations of the piece. I'm sure my notes will be helpful and mortifying but just know that I do enjoy Russel. Regardless of your intent."

Roxanne shook her head, stunned. She concentrated on making sure none of her iced tea dribbled while she came up with a witty response—it was easier than acknowledging the problem he had posed in front of her.

"Authorial intent is a hoax." Her weak response was met with a comforting, if patronizing, smirk from the other man.

Kahn switched the tone of the conversation away from the stack of marked up papers between the two of them and into a full-blown lecture on the validity of authorial intent and author-based criticism. Roxanne let her mind wander while his soft lecture filled the space that the manuscript had so carefully created.

With the end of the lunch came a promise for revisions, to which the man had offered his wife as a less harsh critic, in a few weeks' time. The two wandered out of the little café, into the harsh Nevada afternoon heat, still chatting casually about literary criticism. Roxanne clutched the packet of papers to her chest, guarding it from the world while she offered her own stance on the new wave feminism that had plagued her classrooms back in college. Kahn laughed, stopping on the sidewalk that separated them from her car.

"I think you'll be just fine," he chuckled and opened the passenger door for her to deposit her bag and papers in. "Just remember that there really can't be a line that separates you from Russel, or from you and any character really. My wife...well, I've been talking about you a lot, and she's in complete agreement there. She says she can always tell when a writer is really into or is really separated from what they're working on."

"Does Anya read a lot?" Roxanne propped herself against the car, her back stretching out against the curve of her car.

"You'll have to meet her sometime." That was all he said before he stepped out on the one lane road and opened her driver side door.

"I'll see you next week." He gave her a paternal squeeze. "And don't stress too much. The things at home will clear up eventually."

"I'll have to take your word for it." She couldn't help the doubt that filled her chest. Things had been tense between her and Ethan since he had caught her on the phone with Maverick. He seemed to have taken it as a larger offense than the shared kiss in his office. She'd gone from attempting to sleep in their bed to having given up entirely and crashing on the couch. And it was only getting worse. While it provided her plenty of time to write, it was slowly whittling away at her constitution.

She was sure that the professor had seen it on her face because when he got in his car, he gave her a friendly wave and a sympathetic smile. It made her miss her parents in its paternal concentration.

Chapter Thirty-Five
October 2016

Roxanne called her mother on the way back to the apartment in an effort to speak what was on her mind. She had an issue, and her mother would surely know a way to fix it. Her eyes roamed over the manuscript as she stopped at a light on her empty street. She tried not to make out the annotations from the corner of her eye. Rather, she focused on the ring blaring through her speakers. She hoped, as she often did when she called her parents, that her mother would answer with some sterling advice.

"Roxy? Is everything all right?" Her mother's sugary voice floated through the speakers. "Your father is here, too."

"Hi Mom, Dad." She flicked on her turn signal while she fought the smile that hit her face. Talking to her parents, while she did it probably all too often, always seemed to improve her mood. She was lucky to have parents that were young and capable of providing her with advice—and that she liked to talk to them.

"Everything is okay. I just wanted to call and say hi."

"Oh, good. Good." Rhea Wortham's voice relaxed, and Roxanne could visibly see her mother's tiny, bony shoulders relax. "Do you know how Rick is doing?" Her mother's one-track mind, like so many of her other thoughts, were in the one place where she had been unable to come back from.

"He's alive. I guess…Wesley told me that he's moving back to Penn's Ridge." Roxanne couldn't believe it when Wes had let it slip that the other man was moving back to the town of their childhood. It had been something she had never thought possible. He'd been more eager to leave the Ridge behind than she was.

Her own disbelief was mirrored in her father's laugh on the other end of the line. She could have sworn she heard her mother say that Maverick moving back home was the first sign of the apocalypse, spurring her father to laugh harder and causing her face to become inflamed.

She deftly guided the conversation away from Rhea and Ralph's favorite topic of conversation as she pulled into her numbered parking spot. "How are you guys doing tonight?"

"We're good, very good." Her mother's attention, while diverted, still held the tone of a woman looking to talk about her favorite child some more. "Your father joined a new golf game with some of his friends at the club. And I joined a new book club."

Retirement was habitual for Rhea and Ralph. They had settled down in the Carolinas after Roxanne had graduated college, living on the substantial nest egg they had put together from years of law consultancy. Ralph still worked part time as a consultant for finance lawyers in the area, while Rhea enjoyed the full benefits of being a retired lawyer's wife. They had a healthy relationship of thirty-two years that withstood more than its fair share of bad karma over the years, still coming out on top, even after the death of Roxanne's older brother and their daughter's miniature mental breakdown.

"Rebels." Roxanne laughed as she dropped the manuscript between her and the steering wheel and started to leaf through it.

Kahn's messy scribble was hard to decipher, the scathing comments she could make out causing a tension to build in her shoulders. *Remember—the part of you that started this novel isn't the part of you that finished it, which made it great.* The professor's final note on the blank space of the very last page was the one thing that kept Roxanne from chucking the bound papers out the car's window.

"Roxy?" Her mother's voice brought her back from the carefully composed scribbles and caused her to press her fingertips to her eyebrows. "Do you know what your plans are for Thanksgiving yet?"

The deadline was approaching. The holidays were looming over the horizon, and there was absolutely no stopping it. She had forgotten, gotten distracted by her time in Pennsylvania, by her time at home. How had two and a half months flown, from the first time her mother brought up her lack of plans to the moment now as she sat at the wheel of her car, watching the Nevada sun start to lower over a dust kissed earth?

"I don't know. I'll probably just spend it with you guys." She sighed, pinching the bridge of her nose.

"And Ethan?" Her parents had always tried their hardest to make Ethan feel welcome for holidays, vacations, and family get together, even though he wasn't a part of the equation. He wasn't, as she knew, where they thought she should end up. But Ralph's earnest question, the inquiry into whether or not her supposed other half was coming with her for the next holiday, caused tears to fill Roxanne's eyes.

"I don't…know." She sniffled and reached for the car's keys, still sitting in the ignition. The vehicle shuddered to a stop as she killed the engine, sighing in release. Her parents were silent on the other end of the phone, as silent as the air that filled the cab of the car.

"Ralph, why don't you go start the grill?" Her mother's calm voice, the collective capacity of Rhea's patented 'fix it' tone, only caused her heart to crack a fraction more.

While Roxanne wished her father a good night and obviously trying to hide the emotion clogging her throat, Rhea filled her water glass. She made sure Ralph was outside, the door firmly closed between them before she turned her full attention back to the pain in her only daughter's voice.

"What's wrong, sweetheart?"

"How do you know when a relationship is over?"

The girl, she was little more than a girl in Rhea's eyes despite the collected way she had dealt with losing Maverick and starting over somewhere new to preserve her sense of personhood, asked around a hard swallow.

Rhea's heart gave a little, trying to see her daughter—her only living child—as something more than the stoic sixteen-year-old girl who had to identify her brother's body because her parents had been too emotional to do their jobs. She could still see her, the pigtailed girl in the ripped *Rocky Horror Picture Show* t-shirt talking to a police officer three times her age calmly. It had shattered her mother's heart.

"What do you mean?" Rhea asked the child—the woman.

"I mean...I didn't know that Maverick and I were over. We just...were. So how do you know when a relationship is over? Like...actually know?"

Roxanne could write about falling in love, and she knew the prescribed formula the books and the movies pushed for when two people's eyes met in a crowded room, or a quiet space, and they realized they were it. She could even remember the trauma in Maverick's eyes the day they first met, when she took him out at recess. Had she known he would forever define her as a person in that second? No. Probably not. But she also hadn't known when he'd looked at her and decided that she was no longer enough. Or when she had looked at Ethan and decided he was probably no longer enough.

Rhea took a while to answer, weighing the ways she could respond. As a mother of a twenty six year old woman, she counted her blessings that she'd never had to have this conversation before—that when it had boiled down to it, Roxanne had known, regardless of what her parents thought, how to move on from her situation when she and Maverick had ended. Even then, her daughter hadn't sounded lost when she had called them to say that the relationship was over. Angry? Sure. Annoyed? More than Rhea would have thought possible. But she had saved the confusion, the purposelessness, for a relationship that she hadn't belonged in, to a person she didn't know how to connect with.

"Do you think that it's over?" Rhea asked eventually.

"I don't know if it ever truly was," Roxanne responded evenly, the momentary tears having passed. "At least. Not the way I had thought. And lately…nothing feels the same, Momma. Like…like I came back a different person." Or she came back the same person she'd been before, the person she'd liked and admired, her momentary lapse into someone else having gotten lost.

"Do you…do you want it to be over?"

Roxanne didn't know what to say. She looked down at the manuscript, at the working title splashed across the page, and thought of Russel and how he fell in love—without wanting to, without trying to. Just like a seven-year-old could fall in love without even knowing it.

"I don't think I ever wanted it to be," Roxanne said finally.

It was like the white apartment walls. It had bothered for years, but she'd been too comfortable to address or to even change the way it made her feel.

She'd been able to hide the whiteness from her subconscious for years, finding solace in Ethan's stability and everything about him that made him…not Maverick. But she'd fallen into the relationship at a turning point in her life and had depended upon it more than she should have. Roxanne rubbed her face, looking through the glass at the hot, sterile world around her.

"Mom…I don't know what I'm doing here." Her voice shattered on the words. Had she ever known what she was doing with him?

Rhea was silent for a moment. Roxanne's heavy breathing, the onslaught of emotion she tried to squash under the surface, was enough noise to fill their connection. "Why don't you come out this weekend," Rhea reasoned quietly. "Instead of flying out next Wednesday just…come out now. We still have that converted apartment space above the garage."

"My job—"

"They let you work remotely for two months. They can give you another week or two," Rhea insisted calmly. "And if not, I know for sure Noelle is looking for a legal stenographer.

"I…okay. Okay. I'll see what I can do."

"Roxanne," Rhea's careful voice filled the space between Roxanne's ear and the phone as she slid out of the car and hefted the manuscript into the cradle her arms. "Just…just when you do it, if you do end up deciding to come, remember to give him a reason."

Her mother's unspoken words hung between them as Roxanne ended the call and stared up at their building, her lips trembling. She had to remember all the reasons she'd fallen in love with Ethan—all of the reasons she'd been able to hide the white from herself and find a way to express the feelings in her gut. Ethan deserved a reason, A reason for their relationship imploding, a reason for her turning away as sharply as she'd turned into him. He deserved a reason, and she needed to find one. For both of them.

Chapter Thirty-Six
November 2016

"Irate. Deposition was derailed by plaintiff threatening his legal counsel."

Maverick's pen balanced on the tip of his index finger while he listened to his partner read. His gaze was focused on the window, tracing small flakes of snow flurrying outside the thickly paned glass. The blanket of white that was accumulating on the eaves of the stone edifices of the opposite building threatened to spill onto unsuspecting passersby below. Maverick's eyes tightened as he struggled against a chuckle.

"Christ," Nate griped, drawing Maverick's attention back to the deposition. "This psycho threw a chair at his lawyer."

"I'd throw a chair at Beechum if I could," Maverick offered with a dry smirk.

Nate rolled his eyes and put the manila folder down with a thud. "You're not helping."

"It's your case." The pen hit the desk when Maverick sat up straight.

"Yeah—which makes you an objective third party." Nate raked his hands through his curly flop of hair. "I need help. There is something going on here, something fishy. I just can't figure it out."

Maverick sighed and eased out of his chair, his leg protesting as he put weight on it. Sudden pressure still caused the bones to eek and ache, especially when he spent more than a half hour sitting down still.

"You're right." He limped to the white board across the room from his desk and uncapped a marker. "Something doesn't feel quite right. Start giving me the numbers."

Nate read off the cost of the property damage, the legal fees, and the additional money that the plaintiff was asking for. When Maverick was done, he capped the marker and limped back to lean on the desk next to the other.

"How do you cause over fifty thousand dollars' worth of property damage to a house in Hawley?" Maverick scratched his nose with the marker, frowning between his friend and the board.

"He drove his car through the house. And when I mean completely through the house, I mean completely through it. Moved the couch through the kitchen and into the pool in the backyard and rearranged the cabinets."

"How?"

"Hit the gas on impact. They found a couple of flowerpots in the undercarriage of the truck."

"Brand new truck, right? A Ram?"

"The ink was sill dry on the lease when it happened."

Maverick eased back into his chair and rubbed at the tender spot below his left knee where they had to pin his bones back together.

"And the defendant is calling it an accident?" Maverick questioned.

"Yep. Which is what feels weird, ya know? As far as I can tell there is *no reason* for this man to have driven his brand-new truck through this other man's house, right? But you don't just hit the gas when your car collides with the front of a freaking house."

"And you can't find any connection? Or any reason why the number the plaintiff is asking for is so low?"

"None."

Maverick took the file from his friend and rubbed at his eyelids before flipping through the pages.

"He's newly divorced," he said after a moment.

"The plaintiff?"

"The defendant." Maverick showed him the alimony costs that had been factored into the man's monthly earnings. His fingers hovered over the man's financials, amazed at the dip in earnings he'd taken since the divorce popped up in his records.

There was no reason that someone would have forcibly just driven through a house. If the man was suicidal, he could have gone another two miles and gone off the edge of a cliff. If he had been distracted while driving, he would not have hit the gas once his car collided with the house. Looking at his financial statements only furthered Maverick's confusion.

"Is the plaintiff married?" Maverick passed the folder back to Nate.

"Filed his taxes last year single. Clyde's been looking at his finances so we can adjust negotiations. He's demanding too little and won't listen to me when I try to tell him he can go for more."

"Screw negotiations." Maverick shot to his feet as best he could and rounded the desk. "This is going to end up in court."

"That is way more than Brace wants," Nate protested as he followed the limping man out of the office. "He just wants his property damage covered."

"He should be suing for more. Cost of damages, legal fees, and about three years' worth of his girlfriend's salary." Maverick called over his shoulder as he turned the corner, cursing healthily at the pop and shift in his left knee.

"'Girlfriend?' He's made no mention of a girlfriend."

"Exactly." Maverick shrugged. "I would bet a month's salary that the driver's ex-wife is Brace's girlfriend. He's not going after him because it would fuck her over."

Nate caught up with Maverick at the threshold of Clyde's office, his eyes muddled in confusion. "I don't understand."

"There is only one person on the face of this planet whose house I'd drive a fucking car through." Maverick hitched a lip up at him. "And he's sleeping with my ex."

Clyde agreed that the case was sketchy and had issued the two junior partners an order to dig up as much as possible on the two. Nate, slightly shell shocked at the commotion, had asked

Maverick to take on co-counsel of the case—his first real case since the accident. And he spent the rest of the day reveling in the fact that he had a case, had real work to do. Despite the pain in his knee from all the walking he'd done that afternoon, he left the office in the highest spirits he'd felt since Roxanne had left.

Maverick was thankful for the silence of the drive from Scranton to Penn Ridge and sat with the radio on softly in the background. His mind wandered as he took the roads slowly, driving three miles under the speed limit while thinking about the case. He thought about the issues they had discovered when it became clear that the plaintiff was definitely divorced from the defendant's girlfriend, and he couldn't erase the image of the crushed glass and shattered wooden frame.

He turned onto his street still thinking about the hub of the wooden frame that was once the center of the house and the couch floating in the frozen-over pool. How much could the driver have felt he had been wronged to destroy his brand-new truck? Maverick pulled in behind Wesley's rental car, still thinking about the prospect of driving his new car through a house. If only Ethan owned a house.

His car sat low to the snow-covered ground of his first driveway. Maverick patted its hood affectionately as he walked slowly through the dusting of snow. Each step was halting as he still favored his left leg.

Wesley met him at the door and offered him a smirk.

"Need help?" He leaned against the open-door frame, wearing a paisley apron with yellow strings.

244

"You need to stop shopping online," Maverick grunted and shoved past his friend.

"If you still lived in Scranton, you wouldn't have to hobble through snow to the door."

Wesley laughed and followed Maverick through the living room. They had been in the house for two weeks already, thanks to a little extra money Maverick had been willing to put forward to speed up the process. Wesley still thought Maverick was crazy for buying the house, but he'd been a good trooper, helping to unpack and arrange the little bit of furniture that Maverick had. They had spent the past weekend putting up sheetrock and ripping out flooring on the third level. The top-down approach meant that the first floor, where both Maverick and Wesley did most of their living, was a hazardous waste zone of unpacked boxes, men's clothes, and half-built furniture.

"The city is too crowded."

"It's Scranton, Pennsylvania."

"Too many people."

Wesley shook his head and moved around the stack of moving boxes in the living room.

"You need more silverware and drinking glasses," he told the other man as they walked through the dining room to the kitchen.

"It's just me." He found a stool an eased on to it. "It should be just me anyways." Maverick grinned at Wesley. Both men knew, although neither would admit it, that he was grateful for the company.

Maverick maneuvered around a stack of packing boxes filled with books on his way into the kitchen.

"What are you making?" Maverick opened his briefcase on the breath of a puff of cumin.

"Chili." Wesley dumped a handful of chopped onions into his simmering pot. "What happened?" He nodded toward the image that Maverick had unearthed—the car sitting in the front of the house.

"Guilted ex-husband attacks new lover's house."

"Yikes."

"Oh yeah. And then they lied about the situation. It's a riot." Maverick uncapped a highlighter and looked up at Wesley. "Have you...heard from her...?"

His friend's eyes narrowed at the corners. "Yeah."

Maverick waited, trying to look as patient as possible at his file folder.

Wesley sighed. "She's doing good...working on her manuscript. Work's good."

The executive order from Ethan for the two ex-lovers being on a contact embargo had put a sour taste in everyone's mouth. They had done a pretty good job of keeping them separate, but Maverick checked in once and a while.

The police report was out next. When Wesley tried to crane his neck to see more of what was on the red and white pages, Maverick tucked it under a picture of the debris filled backyard.

"Oh. Good."

Maverick cleared off the police report, letting Wesley's snooping eyes wander for half a second before the file was slipped away.

Maverick continued, "Maybe that will encourage her to finally get the damn thing in print."

Neither man spoke again until they sat down to eat. The quiet pleasantries that were exchanged over the meal were quiet, proof that the two could operate on their own in peace and silence.

Chapter Thirty-Seven
November 2016

"I quit my job."

Cheyenne hadn't been awake very long when the sure sound of her best friend's voice had her begging for a fresh pot of coffee. She rolled over to check the time on her nightstand clock and stretched from head to toe.

"You did what?"

"I. Quit. My. Job." Roxanne breathed out slowly. "And uh, I am breaking up with Ethan."

Cheyenne slid out of bed, snatched a pair of partially worn jeans off the floor, and swayed into the bathroom.

"You…" She stuffed her toothbrush into her mouth and twisted her hair up off the back of her neck. "You quit your job?"

"Mom invited me to spend the next couple of weeks with them for Thanksgiving. So, I walked into the office, all set to ask for remote time off again, just so I could clear my head, right? But then it suddenly hit me. Ethan and I aren't talking to each other, and we aren't sleeping in the same bed. He won't look me in the eye, and it sucks, but I just don't know if it's hurting me the way it should. And he can feel it, and I can feel it, and the whole damn world can see it. I mean you guys saw it, and you weren't even here."

Cheyenne stopped brushing at the quiver in her best friend's voice.

"Anyway." Roxanne took a deep breath and squeezed the bridge of her nose. "Anyway. So, I walk in. And I go to my boss's office. And I quit. Just tell her I'm…done."

"Okay." Cheyenne spit out a mouthful of foam. "So, you quit your job."

"I quit my job. And now I'm home. Waiting for Ethan to come home from work." Roxanne was breathless, anxious, lost in her own head.

Cheyenne knew the sound of it—knew the look of it. Roxanne had run on nervous energy from the day they met in pre-school, a ball of a person with her own brain and her own sensitivities. She heard Roxanne drop something, a suitcase she assumed, while she swiped on deodorant and forced a green sweatshirt over her head.

"I just woke up." Cheyenne steered the conversation back to herself. "It's my day off. And I just woke up. And you're rambling about quitting your job."

She peaked in the mirror, after avoiding her reflection for as long as possible, to swipe on some mascara and lip-gloss. Her green eyes had large bags under them and her freckled skin looked about six years older than it should have. Owning her own business was aging her more than she could have expected.

"Rox?"

"I'm here," her friend reaffirmed, still lost in her own brain.

"Why are you breaking up with Ethan?" Cheyenne forced herself down the rabbit hole as she gathered her shoes and deposit book.

Roxanne exhaled. "I think I need to. No. I know I need to. I've been pretending for far too long."

Cheyenne rolled her eyes and resisted the urge to say something mean. The woman, who peaked at her through the screen of her TV, was rolling her eyes, thinking about the conversation she'd had when she'd seen the inevitable end of Ethan and Roxanne. She had told her that getting immediately involved after she and Maverick broke up was going to be a decision that Roxanne would come to regret. She hated that she was right.

"You quit your job," Cheyenne said again to her reflection before she slipped out of the apartment.

"Yes."

"And you have to figure your life out?"

"Yes."

"Okay."

Cheyenne turned the corner, away from her apartment building and a block from her bakery. The cold breeze trembled through the streets of Albany, blowing around in the early morning's dusting of snow. She kicked a clump of snow into the street while waiting for the signal to shift.

"Well, you know that we'll all support you no matter what. Unless, of course, this decision has to do with a certain someone."

"Chey." Roxanne's warning, surrounded by the sound of clothes falling over, made Cheyenne's lips quirk. "Can you just…not tell the guys?"

Cheyenne rolled her eyes hard before she made her way across the street to stop in front of her mint green storefront. "I won't say a word."

The door to Little Taste of Celeste shot refractory light onto the sidewalk, inviting and warm. She knocked snow off the street sign out front, boasting of her weekly cupcake flavor and the new type of bread she'd started selling fresh out of the oven.

"Just. Not until I have a plan." Roxanne's voice was knocked a peg, unsteady and almost confused. "Please."

"Mum's the word. But I've gotta get going. My half-day has officially begun." Cheyenne waved at her cashier as she propped the door open to the bakery and grabbed a coffee cup from the little bar in the front corner. "I'll talk to you more tonight?"

"Huh? Yeah. Yeah. Thank you for listening."

"Anytime. Ciao."

Cheyenne waited until the call had disconnected before she sent an "S.O.S" text to Wes, Silas, and Connor. As she slipped her phone into her pocket, she caught another glance at her reflection in the store's window. She was tired and worn around the edges but had a smile on her face as she bid hello to the baker and the college student who ran the front of shop four mornings a week. As she closed the office door between them and the back office, she could hear Jonathan start dishing on Ella's romantic life.

"Seems to be a lot of that going around," she mused to herself and to the bakery's safe as she heard Jonathan shout about a recent break-up he'd witnessed.

Chapter Thirty-Eight
November 2016

Maverick hadn't blinked in ten minutes. He watched the time tick down on the screen of his computer while he balanced a pen on the tip of her index finger. His corneas were dry, his neck ached from the concentration, and if he read one more page of the plaintiff's testimony, he might actually throw the computer clear across the room. He switched from the electronic document to the open, unanswered email that occupied the other screen.

Ralph Wortham had written to him that morning, an essay of conversation—checking in on the practice, on Mavericks' health, on the house he'd heard the young man was renting. Maverick had started to write a reply, his focus looming on the invitation for Thanksgiving dinner that had closed out the seventh paragraph.

Maverick didn't blink until Nate walked into the office, a bag of fast food dangling from one hand and a fast grin on his face. "I come bearing gifts."

He blinked a handful of times and closed out of the testimony. The email remained on the screen for Nate to read while he set up their lunch on the desk Nate them.

"Gifts...plural?"

"Grilled chicken sandwich, real French fries, and..." Nate dug a can of regular Coca Cola out of his jacket pocket and pushed it over to his friend. "Now, I know Roxanne asked us to make sure you were taking care of yourself, but you looked like you could use some pure sugar."

"You are a gift from above." Maverick grinned as he snatched the can from his friend.

Nate unwrapped his burger and nodded at the screen. "Anything good?"

"Roxanne's dad invited me to Thanksgiving."

"I wish my in-laws liked me as much as your exes' parents like you." Nate grinned at him around a mouthful of beef, cheese, and bun.

Ralph and Rhea had done more than just 'like' Maverick. They had taken care of him and Sid when they moved to Penn Ridge. Ralph had kept Maverick on as an intern every summer in high school and college to help pay his way into law school—and he had hired him full time at the practice before he sold it. He'd spent holidays with the Wortham's, had thought he'd spend the rest of his life splitting Christmas with them and the memory of his parents and his grandmother. Even after the breakup, they'd harbored no hard feelings. Ralph had come to see the firm, to see

Maverick once and a while when he and Rhea came back to the area.

But Maverick hadn't been invited to a holiday celebration since the breakup.

"They're good people," Maverick said quietly. "Much better than I deserve."

When Maverick had ended things, he let his fears get the absolute best of him. He'd been afraid that he'd lose Rhea and Ralph. He hadn't...but he also hadn't done much in the last few years to hold on to them either.

"You gonna go?"

"I don't know. I think Rox's parents like me better than she does, so I think showing up to Thanksgiving dinner might be a little awkward."

Nate shrugged. "Did you finish the testimony?"

He could see the mood in Maverick's eyes and knew better than to push.

"This guy is a nut job." Maverick reopened the file and scrolled to the second page. "I might hate the man that Roxanne is seeing, but I don't think I'd ever go through this much effort to make his life miserable."

"I mean, if some guy was sleeping with my woman after she and I split, I'd kill 'em."

Nate crammed a handful of fries into his mouth.

"Your fiancé is a totally different story. Once kids, or, I guess, in your case, *dogs* are involved, it gets kind of nuts."

Maverick picked at a few fries himself and winked at his partner.

"How is the lil' guy?"

"Strong. Hopefully sane." Nate cracked a grin back. "We should probably go over the testimony one more time."

Wesley was cooking when Maverick got home. The smell of Indian spices and broiled chicken met his nose before he moved through the front entry. He hung his jacket, swallowed some fresh air before shutting the door, and moved into the living room.

"Honey, I'm home," Maverick called out as he moved back by the couch. "Whatcha making?"

"Curry. I cannot wait until this contract is almost up." The photographer grinned at the lawyer over the steam rising out of the pot. "I hate cooking."

"You're a damned good housewife." Maverick dipped a spoon in the curry and blew until it was cool enough to taste. "This is damned good, Wes."

"How much snow has accumulated out there?" Wesley ladled curry into two different yellow bowls, one a golden color and the other pale.

"Quarter of an inch. Is that mine?" Maverick reached for a bowl, his stomach rumbling under the layers of his suit.

Wesley smacked his hand with a plastic spoon. "Not yet. You can help me take these outside. Grab some of that bread over there?"

"I don't know if these two go together." Maverick picked up a plate of a sliced-up sesame loaf.

"It's not for the camera. It's for you, you oaf. C'mon."

Maverick watched Wesley set up the bowls outside, pushed together in a mound of snow at the base of the yard's only tree. Wesley moved around, crouching, stretching, laying in the fluffy white matter, anything he could do to make use of the flitting November light. Neither man spoke while he worked. Maverick caught up in the process of his friend's body contorting with the use of his camera.

"I've got some news for ya," Wesley said casually as he let the camera dangle around his neck, his shots done. "But you can't tell anyone what I'm about to tell you."

Maverick followed him inside, holding both bowls. "All right. I'm game."

Wesley waited until they were sitting down to eat, curry mixed with white rice and the slices of fresh bread. He watched Maverick wolf down his food, guzzling water like he was dying. Ever since Wesley had gotten there, he'd been eating like food was going out of style and spending as much time as possible out and about. "Roxanne broke up with Ethan. And moved in with her parents."

Maverick stopped eating. He coughed down the food he'd been chewing and set his fork by his plate.

"Excuse me?"

"Rox. She…she left him. She packed up her things and left Vegas. She moved back in with Rhea and Ralph."

Wesley kept eating. His phone screen had lit up twice beside him, and he couldn't force himself to look at it. He also couldn't look at his friend's face while he spoke. "This affects all of us…so you can't do anything stupid."

"Stupid?" Maverick's mouth had run dry. "What do you…what could I possibly do?"

All the thoughts that were going through his head, all the things she wanted to say, wanted to understand, were lost around the idea that she'd left the man she was living with. He'd stood up without realizing it and was standing away from the table.

"She left him?"

"She did." Wesley had stopped eating too. He sat, watching Maverick as calmly as he could.

When Maverick stalked all the way up the stairs, locking himself in the bedroom, Wesley's response was to send his own "S.O.S" text.

Chapter Thirty-Nine
November 2016

Ethan had known she was leaving before she said goodbye— before he had even walked into the apartment. He'd steeled himself for the knowledge and the fond thought that they had really had something for a while there. Even when their worlds didn't entirely connect, they'd had something real. And she'd fallen in love with him the same way he'd fallen for her: hard, fast, and with very little consideration for the future. And that'd been their downfall.

When he met her in the living room, her bags piled around her and her keys sitting neatly on the coffee table, he hadn't yelled, hadn't sighed, hadn't even blinked. He'd dropped his keys on the kitchen counter and loosened his tie, trying to drown out the sounds coming from her spot on the couch. She was crying, silent tears that hurt them both for different reasons.

She put her head in her hands as she eased onto the couch and waited until he sat beside her. "I'm sorry."

Ethan hadn't touched her when he sat down. He used the couch cushions to separate them and spoke violent words that made them both uncomfortable. "I knew it was over the minute you told me that you were going to help him."

"This has nothing to do with him." Roxanne had felt her own defenses rise when he said it. "Nothing to do with him at all."

"It has everything to do with him, Roxanne. It's always been him." The way his eyes had flickered to her face made her retreat for a moment. "From the moment we met, it has always been him. And I couldn't compete. I could never compete."

"Ethan, I—"

"Someone else has always been in our relationship, Roxanne." His throat felt raw. "I…I couldn't compete with a ghost or the outline of a ghost, but I tried my hardest."

"I loved you," Roxanne said quietly, swiping at her eyes.

Ethan rubbed at his eyebrows. "Just not enough."

She nodded her agreement. She could have lied to him, told him that the decision had nothing to do with the fact that she couldn't get Maverick off of her mind, that she loved him but that they were too different. Roxanne could have hugged him. She could have comforted him. Instead, she fought irrational tears.

"Ethan. I'm…I'm sorry."

"I could have married you," he said calmly, the words filling the air between them as uncomfortably as possible. Ethan had never talked about marriage with her, about wanting something more. But when it sat there, between them, something that could have never happened and that neither of them had thought of, it made them both shirk away. Ethan couldn't have married her, just like Roxanne couldn't have loved him the way he needed her to— had wanted her to. Not forever.

Ethan had taken her to the airport. Their goodbye had been amicable if a little cold but had the satisfactory snap of a drawn out chapter finally coming to a close. He stood in front of the McCarran airport about as far away from her as he could while still being heard in the sea of tourists. He promised to mail her the rest of her belongings to her parents, and she, in turn, gave him the keys to her car and a promise that he could have whatever he got out of the sale.

He was hurt, even if he squared his shoulders and locked his jaw and stood as straight as he possibly could.

"I could apologize, again," she said softly, hoping he wouldn't hear but grateful when he turned his gaze to her.

"It wouldn't do any good." He didn't smile at her, just raked his hands through his unruly red curls. "None of this has done either of us any good, Roxanne."

He forced himself to swallow and crossed the space between them to give her a halfhearted hug. "You'll be okay. Better than me." Ethan's word against her hair made her arms tense around him. "Just…do me a favor."

"Anything," she promised against the fabric of his shirt, against the sea of emotions crushing into her, against the space that separated between them. "Anything."

"If you get back with him." Ethan stopped, let her go, and took a step back. When his eyes met hers, they were angry, almost empty. "If you get back with him. Don't…don't invite me to the wedding."

"Ethan." Roxanne licked her lips and was jostled by a woman trying to catch up with her kids as they exploded into the airport.

He didn't let her finish. His hands came up to cup her face to press his lips to the soft pucker of hers lightly. "We can be friends. We can…talk if that's what friends who used to live together do. Just don't invite me to the wedding because I'm liable to kill him."

"There will be no wedding." *There will be no me and Maverick,* she thought as she dried her eyes. He gave that up a long time ago. "But I would like to be friends."

Chapter Forty
November 2016

"You can't just go to North Carolina."

"I'm not *just going*, Ralph invited me to Thanksgiving dinner."

Wesley stood between Maverick and the door of his bedroom, his hands locked onto the frame to keep himself from being swayed as the shorter man glared up at him. They'd been locked in the same argument for the past hour and had gone through similar renditions of the argument every few minutes, alternating between abject irritation with each other and sincere moments of why Maverick had to go. He wouldn't tell Wesley the real reason. He just kept circling the drain to dinner and Thanksgiving and how he used to spend the holidays bouncing between families.

Maverick saw the cycle in his friend's eyes and sighed, dropping his hands to his sides. "I need to go, Wes. I've put this off for too long. I've messed it up too many times."

"Messed what up, Rick?"

Maverick pushed past his friend while his guard was down and grabbed the black velvet box out of his nightstand.

"Do...do you know how expensive these things are?" Maverick asked after a long second of staring at the black box, his fingers clutching its velvet casing. "And...and how much thought goes into buying one? A third of your salary, half your salary, and no more than five figures, no less than four. Everyone will tell you something different and at the end of the day, it's your decision."

"Rick is that...?" Wesley took the box from his friend and held the box out to catch the light.

Maverick eased himself onto the bed, his leg smarting.

"I was going to...four years ago. And I talked myself out of it." He shook his head. "It was the biggest mistake I ever made, Wes."

Wesley nodded in agreement. "So what? You're gonna go hunt her down at her parents' house? And what? Ask her to marry you?"

Maverick shook his head hard, his eyes tearing a little with the effort. "I don't know what I'm going to do. I just know that I need to do something while there's still a chance."

"Rick..."

"Wes, she broke up with him. She wouldn't have done that if...if the kiss and coming here didn't mean anything."

Maverick massaged his knee, wincing. "She wouldn't have come here in the first place if there wasn't still something here."

Wesley sat down next to his friend. "And if she says no?"

"Then I am four years too late, and I deserve to spend the rest of my life wondering if she would have said yes the first time." Maverick held his hand out for the ring. "And I spend the rest of my life pining after her."

"Well you've got practice on that already." Wesley grinned and dropped the box back into his hand. "Don't ask her to marry you."

Maverick stashed the box back in its drawer and shoved himself to his feet.

"Not yet." Soon…but he had to show her that he was absolutely in it, in their world, before he did. Or else he'd be right back where they were now.

Roxanne sat in the back of her parent's car, listening to the two of them bicker about what to make for dinner with a placated smile on her face. Being back with them had been a nice little breather, a momentary lapse from the crazy position she'd put herself in. Quitting her job, leaving Ethan, and basically moving back home had all been hits to her self-esteem, her sense of her own life. Watching Rhea and Ralph interact was a sense of being home that she hadn't realized she'd needed until her mom was fawning over her at meals and her father was giving her a hard time about figuring out her next step. It was like being home again.

"Honey, can you go around back and see if the gardener is still there?" Rhea's soft voice pulled Roxanne's attention away from the window and her own thoughts about the meaning of being home with her mom and dad. "I need your father's help bringing in the groceries."

That had been a trip. She'd forgotten how intense her mother got in the grocery store and how much of a child her father acted like when they went up and down the aisles. Her father sent her mother a roll of his eyes before winking back at her in the rearview mirror. "What she's really saying is that we need some one-on-one time, if you know what I mean."

Roxanne all but scrambled out of the car while her mother giggled and smacked her father's arm. She laughed, shook her head, and made her way around the house to the back garden where her mother had invested so much time and energy since the couple had moved to North Carolina.

In the rays of setting sun, the terrace over the back porch, and the water, she could see through the fence slats what looked like fairy lights. She could appreciate the beautiful house, the quiet North Carolinian air even if she couldn't see herself living there. Roxanne sighed, pressed her face into the top of the gate, and closed her eyes. The gardener was rustling around. Bushes were moving under his weight, and he was humming to himself. It was a soft song, a song that Roxanne felt was very familiar. She paused to push the gate closed behind her, hoping that the click would catch the man's attention.

He stood from his low crouch on the other side of the patio and turned so that they were face to face. As he moved, hundreds of little Christmas lights, on green wires that raced across the top of the patio gazebo, flickered to life. Roxanne stopped short, eyes filling her face as they illuminated Maverick's grinning face.

It had been well over a month since she had seen him last and in that time, he hadn't gotten a haircut or shaved his face it seemed. He stood before her, under the lights in a long sleeve shirt and dark jeans, his hair curling under his ears and the beard he sported nearly glistening in the dark. She tried not to laugh, despite her initial shock at the curls of black hair that had gathered around his ears.

He was smiling against the bags under his eyes and the awkward right tilt to his gaze.

"Hey," he said when all she could do was stare at him.

"What are you doing here?"

"Good to see you, too."

Roxanne just blinked.

"We need to talk."

"Why are you here?"

"We need to talk," he repeated himself, the smile spreading.

Without waiting for her acknowledgement, he pulled out a lawn chair and gestured for her to sit down.

"I'm here because we need to talk. Can you please sit down?"

"I think I'm good here. What's going on, Rick?"

Maverick bit his lip. She took a step back, moving closer to the garden gate before the sight of her parents staring at them through the sliding glass door made heat rise up under her collar.

"What's going on?" she asked again, this time less patient.

"I bought a house."

When she didn't respond he pushed forward.

266

"That old blue one on Court Street? With the French front doors and the wrap around porch? It's been on the market for a year, and I was driving through for work, and I saw the 'For Sale' sign, and I bought it."

The words came out fast, nervous. The fairy lights made the air warm, and the sound of her mother's garden fountain gave him a soothing soundtrack to lose his mind to. She would have been amused by how picturesque it was if Maverick didn't look like he was about to keel over.

"You bought a house?" Roxanne's soft question seemed to ground him.

He nodded and pushed his hair back out of his eyes.

"I bought a house...and a dog. And the house needs work but I figure that's fine because it'll feel like home when y—Okay. Okay. I'm doing this wrong. Back up." Roxanne physically took a step back. Maverick shook his head. "No, you come here. I need to back up."

She hesitated but crossed the patio, the smell of daisies catching her nose and she fondly stepped around the basket of them that Maverick had been tinkering with when she arrived. He took her hand and squeezed it affectionately.

"I know I've made a thousand mistakes, Rox. A million. And we still have a lot of issues we need to work out. But that's okay because therapy's not all that expensive in the long run, and I have good insurance."

She giggled a little, but he shushed her from speaking, obviously pleased that his one-liner had evoked such a reaction out of her.

"We've got a lot of work to do to get back to where we were, but I want to do the work. I want us to get past where we were. Being without you for the last few years has been...more than I can ever bear to do again. I won't do it again. Which is probably why I just made the biggest financial decision of my life in like twenty minutes. But it's fine."

He squeezed her hands, gazing into her eyes.

"I have made more mistakes than I ever thought possible. I have let you down in so many ways. And I have let you get away twice now. And I'll be damned if I do it a third. So, I'm here, Rox. To ask you to forgive my mistakes, to look past the idiocy, and understand that I'm in this. Forever. For you. And do me the honor, the greatest honor, of giving me another chance. Just one more try to get things right. Because I was right. I can be all you hold on to—I want to be all you hold on to—from now until the end of your life."

Roxanne stared down at the man who was struggling to stay up on his right knee. *His opposite leg must have been killing him,* she thought. His eyes stared wide up at her. A thousand words raced through her mind, a million questions on how they were going to make it work or what had brought it on. There was the knowledge that they were still new to each other—entirely different people than they had been when they had lived together, loved together, in what felt like an entirely different life time.

268

There was going to be a lot of work. It was going to take some time. But she knew, before she even opened her mouth or threw her arm around his neck, that she was willing to put in the work if he was. She kissed him, hoping the touch would communicate more than her lips were able to express on their own.

When they broke apart, Maverick held her back just enough that he could look her in the eye, and she smiled at him through a haze of tears.

"You get one more shot." She hiccupped and pressed her face into the side of his neck. "You mess it up this time Maverick and I swear…"

"I won't, Roxy. I won't." Maverick kissed the top of her head and squeezed her tightly. "Not this time."

Epilogue
January 2017

Roxanne hit send on the email she had been drafting and closed the laptop lid. The professor had been amazed at how fast she'd churned around the third draft, and he sent her first four chapters along to his publisher. In response, she had been asked to write a traditional query, the email she had just sent, and include the next chapter. With the manuscript finished and her correspondence caught up for the day, she could take a breather.

She leaned back in the plush desk chair and smiled in satisfaction at the storyboard in front of her. Another handful of Post-Its could come down and join the hundreds that sat in the shredder. Roxanne reached for the silver coffee mug that sat in front of his computer monitor and heaved herself out of the chair. Mug in hand, she wandered down the stairs from his small second floor office to the open concept kitchen.

He had made her a pot of coffee, and she had rationed it out enough to salvage one last mug-full. She smiled as she stirred in a spoonful of sugar and a splash of milk, watching the color lighten in the green ceramic. From the open basement door, she could hear grunting and loud profanities—the sound of what she had hoped was a desk being built.

She poked her head around the corner at the base of the stairs to see Maverick and Nate puzzling over the engagement present her parents had sent. The white painted wood was strewn across the new beige carpet, and the box was in shreds at her feet. Nate was holding the instructions manual close to his face and squinting while Maverick crouched over the pile of wood and huffed. His hair, still growing out toward his shoulders, curled with the perspiration his afternoon of furniture building had drummed up. When he stood, the fitted gray t-shirt hugged his torso and strained over the muscles that were still filling out again after the accident.

Roxanne bit her lip and stepped over a stray screwdriver. "Problems, boys?"

"Nope. None at all." Maverick threw his screwdriver on the carpet and walked away from the pile. "Are you sure you want the desk put together?"

He shot her a wink and reached for her mug. "You can just keep using mine," he offered.

"We finished the basement and hooked it up so I could have my own television and everything down here for *my* office, Rick." Roxanne giggled and handed him the mug. "Nate, would you like a drink?"

"Nah, I gotta head out. Last regular day before the wedding madness takes over?" Nate grinned. "I'll see you guys tonight?"

"We'll be there at seven." Roxanne hugged Nate. "Tell Sarah we'll bring the good wine." The two women had formed a friendship based off of wedding magazines and dress fittings.

Much to Maverick's relief, the additional friendship had kept Roxanne busy while he put in the time finishing small adjustments to the dream house.

After Nate had left, the pair settled down on the gray love seat that had taken center stage on Roxanne's office space. While Maverick worked on the coffee, Roxanne surveyed the destruction the furniture had caused.

"Desk that much of a pain?" she asked hesitantly.

"Neither of us are hand tool inclined." Maverick handed her the coffee cup back. "And he has worse wedding fever than his wife-to-be does. We talked about flowers for a half hour."

"He's excited." Roxanne laughed and rested her head on his shoulder. "Are you saying you won't be that excited when that's us?"

"I've been waiting for this for years. Of course, I'll be excited."

She was still giggling when he put the mug down and captured her face in his hands.

"I still can't believe it." Roxanne looked up into Maverick's gaze, feeling herself swell at the love she saw there. "I can't believe it."

"Can't believe what?" he asked good naturedly before he pressed a soft kiss to her lips.

"That we're here. That this"—she gestured around them at the chaos that would soon be her own corner of the house—"is all real."

"Well believe it, babe." He let her snuggle against him and dropped his arms around her shoulders. "Because, between you and me, seven-year-old Maverick hasn't stopped gloating for two months, and he's getting really annoying." Maverick's teasing voice made her laugh.

"And what can I do about this intense mental turmoil?" Roxanne giggled into his arm.

"You can accept it," Maverick groaned and gave her a squeeze.

Roxanne looked up at his profile while he chuckled to himself and felt her lips turn into a huge grin. Secretly, she knew that her own seven-year-old self was also gloating from the recesses of her memory over the fact that, in a little under a year, she would, in fact, be marrying Maverick. While it still didn't seem real, it felt like she was always meant to be there. Holding onto him, no matter what else life threw at them.

Thank you for reading *All You Hold on To.*

Please consider posting a rating or review to sites like
Goodreads and Amazon.

Reviews are the lifeblood of authors and help more readers
like you find their new favorite books!

About the Author

K.T. Egan is the author of the *Anderson Creek* series and several short stories and poems published in journals out of Northeast Pennsylvania. When not writing, she works with students and their families at a tutoring firm in Bethesda, Maryland, helping them prepare for secondary education and beyond.

She holds a bachelor's degree in English and History, with a minor in Women's and Gender Studies, focusing on Writing and Anthropology from Wilkes University, and is a graduating member of the university's chapter of Sigma Tau Delta, where she served as both the VP and later President. During her time in college, she also ran and edited a departmental magazine and a literary arts journal.

Her writing focuses primarily on contemporary women and small-town themes, stemming from her childhood in the woods of NEPA. She has a strong passion for powerful imagery and believes that everyone has a soulmate out there – no matter the form.

K.T. currently lives in Maryland with her partner in crime, Alec, their seven-pound fur-tyrant, Winnie, and their goofy puppy, Baxter. Outside of writing and education, her passions are baking, knitting, Netflix binges, and the occasional video game marathon.

For more information on the Anderson Creek kids, you can check out her social media pages.

Facebook: @KTEganAuthor
Instagram: kteganauthor

Made in United States
North Haven, CT
29 November 2021